the Vanishing Throne

Also by Elizabeth May from Gollancz:

The Falconer

the Vanishing throne

ELIZABETH MAY

GOLLANCZ
LONDON

The right of Elizabeth May to be identified as the author
of this work has been asserted by her in accordance with the
Copyright, Designs and Patents Act 1988.

First published in Great Britain in 2015 by Gollancz
An imprint of the Orion Publishing Group
Carmelite House, 50 Victoria Embankment, London EC4Y 0DZ
An Hachette UK Company

A CIP catalogue record for this book
is available from the British Library

ISBN 978 0 575 13046 3

1 3 5 7 9 10 8 6 4 2

Typeset by Deltatype Ltd, Birkenhead, Merseyside

Printed in Great Britain by Clays Ltd, St Ives plc

The Orion Publishing Group's policy is to use papers that
are natural, renewable and recyclable products and made from
wood grown in sustainable forests. The logging and manufacturing
processes are expected to conform to the environmental
regulations of the country of origin.

*For my dear friend Tess Sharpe, who taught me to embrace
my dark stories and tell them to the world.*

Chapter 1

I remember how it felt like the air around me burned with ash and cinder. How his blade broke the skin at my throat, a stream of blood warm down my neck. How the war around me seemed to go quiet and slow as if time had stopped.

It was just Lonnrach and me, my life determined by the tip of his sword. One small *push* —

Darkness.

My eyelids are heavy, weighted down and burning. Images flash in my mind of the battle, of those precious moments I had to solve the puzzle of a Falconer device to trap the fae under ground again before it was too late. The shield of light around me began to weaken, disintegrating from the force of fae attacks.

A laugh startles me from my memories. Other voices join in between images. *Where am I?* Lilting accents like Kiaran's echo around me, dulcet murmurings in words I don't recognise or understand.

Open your eyes, I command myself. *Open your eyes.* Panic forces me awake, a minuscule flash of light visible before I'm shoved down again with a hand at my throat, a searing pain at my temple.

'I didn't say you could move.' The words come out in a hiss, spoken through rows of sharp teeth at my neck.

I go numb. I'm immobile, even as someone scratches the

length of my arm, nails sharp enough to draw blood. A laugh, deep and purring. A whisper in my ear, breath hot at my throat.

You lose. Now you're mine.

Then I'm dreaming again – memories of my life before, of my almost-deaths. A series of near-fatal experiences, each one strung from the other. The first time, when Kiaran saved my life from the water-horse. The many ever since; hundreds of nameless faeries I slaughtered, who each left their mark on me in different ways. The first one who scarred me. The first one I killed with Kiaran, when his expression showed something akin to pride.

We're going to kill them all, he'd told me, a ghost of a smile on his face.

The memory fades like smoke. Suddenly I'm back on the battlefield; my armour is so heavy that every movement is agony. Kiaran's unmoving body is at my side, bone shining through the burn along his cheek. Dead?

No, not dead. He can't be dead. I scream at him, striking him with my fists. *Wake up. Wake up! Wake —*

My eyes snap open, closing just as quickly against the light. I draw in a breath, wincing at the pounding pain that lances through my skull. I press the heel of my palm to my temple.

Wet.

I draw my hand back and blink against my blurring vision until it clears. My fingers are coated with blood, sticky remnants of my injury.

I didn't say you could move.

My armour is gone. I find dried blood spattered across my chest, leading down to three distinct claw-marks stark against my upper arm. The skin is barely broken, as if it were a threat. A warning.

You lose. Now you're mine.

Dread unfurls within me, but I shake my head against it. *Focus. Find your bearings.* The thought comes out in Kiaran's voice, one of his no-nonsense lessons. Just the thought of him almost holds me back – a quick succession of *where is he is he dead is everyone I love dead* – but his practical advice stops me again. *Assess your surroundings.*

I tamp down my emotions, suppressing the hot rising panic in favour of cold rationality. I'm wearing a shift like Sorcha's, form-fitting and exquisite. I brush my hand across the silken fabric – except it's not like any silk I know. It's smoother, shinier, and warm. As if raven's feathers and flowers were somehow woven together to form the garment. The sleeves are loose around my wrists; the fabric slips back when I lift my arms. Slippers adorn my feet, delicate things made of dark orchids and metal beads stitched together.

After a quick evaluation of my injuries, I look up to see where I am. *Oh god.* Alarm breaks through the detached, analytical calm I'd achieved. *This can't be real.* Can it?

I'm on a slab of black rock that gleams like obsidian, broken off and floating above a valley of dark crags, a crevasse extending beyond my sight. It's as if the land has split right down the middle into separate halves, with scattered platforms like mine gliding down the empty space like leaves carried by a stream.

The other hovering slabs are topped with buildings – one of them a castle set atop a rugged piece; the rock broken off at the bottom is as sharp as blades. The castle itself is magnificent, more beautiful than any structure I've ever beheld. It looks as though it is made of pure, gleaming metal – only with a sheen that betrays its otherworldly origins. Even from this distance it has the multicoloured luster of opal. Shardlike towers flank the sides of the castle, surrounding a dome of red and blue and yellow metal resembling trapped clusters of stars.

Other buildings float on their own platforms below the soaring castle, suspended in the vast space between the towering cliffs. Some have domed ceilings constructed of metal, and others of glistening rock, as if cut from the purest sapphires.

In contrast, the cliffs on either side of me are monochrome, with not a single hint of colour to break up the uniformity. Even the trees seem made of glass, with thin spiky branches that appear sharp enough to kill. Flowers glow beneath the trees along the cliff face, with delicate buds of iridescent frost.

When I breathe in, the icy scent of winter makes my chest ache. It smells like the beach after a snowfall. Like salt and frost on the wind, with a hint of something like myrrh.

I'm dreaming. This has to be a dream. I press my palm to the cold rock at my feet, tracing my fingers across the glossy surface. Along the outer edges of the platform, small shards bite into my skin and leave red, aching welts.

Not a dream. *Not a dream.* A panicked rush of breath bursts from my lungs. I jerk my hand back and push to my feet, stopping just before the platform ends.

I make the mistake of looking over the edge.

My stomach clenches. Below me is nothing but darkness, an escarpment that descends to nothingness. No light penetrates the blackness below and there's nothing to grab onto if I need to escape. No other platforms nearby, or rocks to jump onto, and the floating buildings are too far into the distance.

This is a prison, with the only escape a lethal drop. *Where the bloody hell is this place?*

'Good. You're awake.'

I whirl to find Lonnrach on his own platform, smaller than my own. In my distraction, I hadn't even noticed the taste of his powers, the lingering touch of flower petals against my tongue and the sweet taste of nature and honey. Gone is his gleaming fae armour. Instead he's dressed like a human, in smoke-grey trousers and a white lawn shirt. His salt-white hair is pulled back and gathered at the nape of his neck.

His eyes are on my head injury. 'I'd hoped that didn't cause any permanent damage.'

Why? I almost ask, but just the sight of him still alive fills me with rage. My gaze strays to the mark on his cheek, the one left by my sword. I had the chance to kill him and I didn't take it. I won't make that mistake again.

'Where are we?' I ask. My voice is rough, my throat raw. *Calm. Stay calm.*

'The *Sith-bhrùth*, in what was once the Unseelie Kingdom.' As Lonnrach's gaze lingers on the crags to either side of us, his expression hardens. 'What's left of it.'

Were we in a ballroom, and I didn't know Lonnrach as something other than human, I would have described him as achingly beautiful. Magnetic. But that's all part of his physical allure, his ability to entice human victims with such ease – a skill that all *daoine sith* possess. I was tempted by that power back on the battlefield, but now he's just the bastard who injured me, made me bleed, captured me, and —

'If you've done anything to my home ... ' My voice dips low, dangerous. 'I'll kill you.'

I'll kill you regardless. I'll just take my time.

Lonnrach tilts his head slightly. There's an amused, slow lift to his lips, as if we're at an assembly and he's participating in light flirtation. His smile is unnerving. An arrogant hint of *I know something you don't* and whatever the *something* is almost breaks my hard-won control.

'Will you?' he asks.

I bite my tongue to stop myself from asking about Kiaran, about everyone I love. I can't let him know my worry that they're all dead; I have to pretend that I don't feel a thing.

Instead, I brush my fingers against my *seilgflùr* necklace, plaited together in a single strand. The soft thistle is deadly to Lonnrach's kind, effective enough to burn through his flesh. 'I could wrap this around your throat if I wanted. It's not a quick way to die. I've seen it.'

Lonnrach stuffs his hands in his trouser pockets, and I'm certain if his platform had something to lean on, he would be standing against it. Cold, casual, obviously not the least bit concerned.

Perhaps he has a talent for lying, too. Just like me.

'You're not in any position to make threats,' he says lightly, glancing down into the crevasse at its deepest and darkest point.

I try to resist looking, too. I fail. Even if I managed to kill Lonnrach, I'd be trapped. Pushing him over the edge isn't exactly an option – he'd likely survive the fall, damn his indestructible fae body.

I let my expression settle and appear cold, detached. It takes every skill in deception I've learned since I first discovered the fae were real and one of them had murdered my mother. With the fae, everything is a game. Even grief. If given the chance, Lonnrach would use it against me, torment me with it. I have to play the game, too.

One breath, two, to steady myself. 'How do I know it's not a trick?' My voice is almost playful, chastising; it is as calm as a mountain stream. I am a masterful liar. I learned from the best, after all. 'This place?'

Lonnrach's expression doesn't change. 'It's not.'

I think of his fleeting smile and the possibility that everyone and everything I care about is gone. Then I really do have nothing to lose by being reckless.

But Lonnrach does. There's still one thing he needs: Me. If he didn't, I'd be dead.

Time to test that. I approach the edge of my small platform on the side closest to him. 'So if I do *this*' – I balance on one foot, on the tips of my toes, so close to the ledge – 'and fall, it'll kill—'

Before I can even blink, Lonnrach is off his platform. His body slams into my own, knocking me off my feet so hard I fear we'll go over the other side and he'll kill me anyway.

We don't. In the end, he hauls me up, his hand painfully gripping my upper arm. His silver eyes glow bright with anger. I'm surprised by the display of emotion; the fae always seem so in control, every feeling perfectly reined in.

'You are a *foolish* girl,' he says.

Now I know. Lonnrach forgot the foremost rule of our little game: Never let your enemy know how desperately you require something. He *needs* me alive, not just as a prisoner of war. That's why he cared about my head injury causing lasting damage.

But I can't focus on that. I can't. I find that the question I truly desire to ask – if he's killed everyone I love – sticks in my throat. So I try another. 'Where is Kiaran?'

I don't miss how Lonnrach's eyes avert briefly from mine, as if he's trying to smooth his expression first. 'His sister killed my men to rescue him.' His smirk is brutal; it cuts right through my heart. 'They obviously didn't think you were worth saving.'

Another memory of Kiaran flashes in my mind from the battlefield. Of his motionless body and his scorched face. *Wake up. Wake up!* I couldn't get him to move. Not even his lashes fluttered.

Lonnrach said Kiaran was alive, but if that were true, Kiaran would never have left me behind. He couldn't have.

'You feel for him.' Lonnrach's fingers grasp my chin, forcing me to look at him. 'He made you think he cared about you.' He looks almost sorry for me, but I know it must be a trick. 'Kadamach doesn't give a damn about anyone, least of all you.'

Pretend his words don't affect you. I try, but then Kiaran's words from that night whisper in my mind. *Have I ever told you the vow a sìthiche makes when he pledges himself to another?* A featherlight kiss, then two words against my lips that I felt down to my very soul. *Aoram dhuit.*

I will worship thee.

Lonnrach's next cruel words cut short my memory: 'You're not the first human pet he's discarded.'

Before I can stop myself, I wrench out of Lonnrach's grip and smash my fist into his face. He staggers back. I bury my knee in his gut and punch him again. And again. I wind back to keep at him, but he grabs my wrist and twists my arm behind me at a painful angle. He's at my back, breath tickling my neck.

'You need me alive.' I swallow hard to keep the pain out of my voice. I wiggle to extricate myself from his grip, but he holds firm; any movement on my part is excruciating. 'Why?' When he doesn't answer, I press further. 'Why?'

'You can unlock an object I seek. That is your sole purpose.' I understand the subtext: *And when I get what I want, I'll kill you.*

I snap my head back and slam it into his nose. The satisfying crack of cartilage and his startled fae curse only makes me smile. I round on him, but he's too fast. He locks me into a hold, fingers digging into the wrist of my blade hand. Any sudden movement from me and he'll break it. I may heal faster than the average human, but I'd rather not learn how long it takes for my bones to mend.

As if in subtle warning, his grip tightens. I grit my teeth against the pain. 'If I knew what you were looking for, I'd destroy it before I let you have it.'

I feel his body shudder, as if in anger. 'You really don't understand, do you? You think this is just about war. Your kind against mine.'

I'm surprised by that. 'Isn't it?'

'Look around you, Falconer.' He motions with his free hand, sweeps it across the landscape. 'Do you think it's always been like this? The *Sìth-bhruth* was once full of a thousand different colours your human eyes have never beheld. The land was whole and now it's cracked right down the middle. It's all falling apart.'

He draws me in closer, releasing some of the pressure at my wrist. 'I brought you here to show you this chasm. It's a reminder that one day soon everything here will crumble to dust. The kingdoms are dying and the throne here is vanishing. It's already begun.'

I can't help but look to the cliffs on either side of us, studying how the landscape only exists in shades of grey and deep black. How the buildings floating in the middle are the final remnants of the place Lonnrach describes. 'I don't see what that has to do with me.'

'What I seek could save the *Sìth-bhrùth*. You're the key to finding it.'

At that I pause. Not that I care the slightest bit about the *Sìth-bhrùth*, but Kiaran might. He spoke very little about the fae realm, of course. He once told me it was beautiful and brutal, that he both hated and loved it. I wonder if he would consider saving this place.

But I have to know one thing first. I ask the question I've been avoiding all along: 'Why save your home instead of mine?'

Lonnrach's silence is deafening; it stretches vast, eternal. He wouldn't be like this, unless ... unless ...

I have no home to save.

I swallow back the lump in my throat. 'Show me.' When he hesitates, I snap. 'Now.'

Lonnrach releases my wrist. Before I can even move, his fingers are in my hair, pressing against the wound at my temple.

Then I blink ... and I'm in hell.

It's too much to take in at once; I can barely focus. Ash rains from the sky, fluttering to the ground like snow. All around me are destroyed buildings, as if something had rammed through them with tremendous force. The cobbles lie broken up, the streets naught but barely visible rubble through the thick layer of ash. I can barely see beyond the buildings in front of me; the smoke is too thick. I inhale the scent of scorched wood, metal and stone and my lungs constrict.

The swirling dust and soot clears just enough for me to recognise where I am. Princes Street. What's left of it. Barely any of the shops that lined one side of the street are left standing. The Scott Monument – that beautiful, pointed ivory-coloured monument that had just been finished in the months before the battle – lies

9

toppled on its side. Scott's own statue is ground to dust.

I caused this. *I caused this it's my fault they're dead and it's all my fault.* 'Stop.' The word is a strangled breath, barely audible. 'I said *stop!*'

Suddenly I'm back in the faery realm. I'm on my knees in the sharp, obsidian-stone dirt. Hot tears blur my vision as I draw in ragged breaths.

How could all that have happened in such a short time? I press my fingers to the injury just above my ear. It's still wet. Desperately, I feel for the small cut Lonnrach left when he pressed his blade to my throat back on the battlefield. Inflamed, still stinging. No healing has begun.

'This is a trick,' I say. It has to be. The fae couldn't have destroyed Edinburgh that quickly. 'My injuries are still fresh.'

Lonnrach doesn't move, not even to kneel next to me. 'You're in the *Sìth-bhrùth*,' he says simply.

I shut my eyes. *Oh god.* I forgot the simplest rule of all: Time passes more quickly in the human realm. I could have spent mere hours in the fae realm and weeks would have gone by there. Days here could amount to months.

'How long have I been here?' I whisper, hating the horror in my voice. Hating how I've shown Lonnrach that small bit of weakness. 'On the outside. How long?'

'I don't understand your human time.' He sounds so nonchalant, uncaring. 'Days. Weeks. Months. Years. They mean little to me. All I care about is finding the object hidden in your realm. And you're going to help me with it, willingly or no.'

I can't get the images of destruction out of my head. I created that. I helped. What would Derrick and Gavin have thought of me in the end? Catherine? They must have thought I'd died or abandoned them. That I stopped fighting.

Fresh tears sear my cheeks as I look up at Lonnrach. 'So you destroyed everything in your search. You sacrificed my realm to save yours.'

Lonnrach's expression doesn't change. 'You say that as if I had a choice. You would have slaughtered us all to save *them*. Your humans.' Now he kneels. His face so close to mine. 'You would kill to protect your own. We both would. We're the same, you and I.'

Kiaran's whisper resounds from deep in my mind. *I made you the same as me.*

A night creature. A devil. A monster who deals in death and destruction. *We're the same, you and I.*

Then so be it. My gaze locks with Lonnrachs and I see a flash of vulnerability there – fear. Good. He *should* be afraid of me. 'I hope your kingdom rots. I'll burn it to the ground myself.'

Lonnrach's face goes hard, angry. 'More threats. I could leave you right here, for as long as I wanted. Maybe I'll shove you in a watertight box and throw you into the sea below until I need you. A thousand years could pass on the outside and you'll still be as youthful as the day I took you. You're at *my* mercy.'

The sea below. So that's what's down there at the bottom of the cliffs. That's why it sounds like it breathes; it's the waves hitting rock, scraping stone against the base of the escarpment.

Before I can reply, Lonnrach is already back on his own platform, a leap that's at least twenty feet – one I could never hope to attempt. He looks back at me. 'You have no choice, Falconer. If this place burns, you'll die with us.'

Chapter 2

I think of a thousand potential ways of escaping. I try to use my own weight to push the platform closer to the cliffs. I leap up and my feet hit the onyx soil so hard that it sends a jolt through my body, but the platform never so much as budges.

Instead it floats steadily through the ravine as if it were a flowing river instead of empty space. The castle and the other buildings are the same distance they were before; never closer or farther.

Minutes or hours pass, but I can never tell which. Now I know why Lonnrach dismisses the concept of time; it doesn't exist here. The light always stays the same: a grey, foggy haze to the atmosphere much like what I'm used to back home. The heavy rain clouds never move, even as the platform flows down the empty space and the landscape changes.

I never see another faery; not even a shadow of a figure in one of the majestic buildings floating in the fissure. This place is barren, empty. If I screamed, no one would hear me.

This must be Lonnrach's strategy: Isolate me, make me defenceless, use me, and then kill me.

As my platform keeps moving, I search for some means of escape – anything. But the ravine is a ceaseless thing, constantly shifting and yet never ending. I pass an ever-evolving scenery of mountains and forests, all in the same bleak monochrome. I float through fields of glass flowers and forests of black metal trees that are so dark and thick I can see no light beyond them.

It's as if the landscape were a charcoal drawing. The cliffs on either side of me are etched in dark, aggressive strokes, the rock jutting out roughly on either side.

The land was whole, and now it's cracked right down the middle.

As time passes, I notice that every so often stone breaks off the jagged crags and tumbles down into the ravine below. This place is breaking apart bit by bit and falling to dust.

Just like Edinburgh. All those buildings reduced to rubble on the street. Gone. Just like —

I close my eyes hard and pull my knees into my chest, sitting down on the biting rocks. I try to block it all out, the images. My memories. My feelings.

Far below my platform, the sea breathes. I listen to the calm *inhale exhale inhale exhale* of water against earth and pretend I'm somewhere back *there*. Scotland. The human realm. I pretend that there's still a place worth saving. That the people I love survived.

I pretend I'm not the only one left.

When I wake, the breath of distant ocean waves is gone and everything is quiet The cold winter breeze has stilled.

I open my eyes and realise I'm no longer outside in the ravine. No longer lying against the rough rocks of the platform, but a smooth, cold floor instead. The only reminder of that place is the red, pockmarked texture of my arms where the obsidian pressed to my skin and left imprints, soon to fade. Temporary reminders.

I roll onto my back, flinching at a sudden thought. It's like the darting tongue of a snake, that thought. *It doesn't matter where you are. You're all alone now because you let everyone die. You didn't save them. You —*

My fingernails bite into my palm. The pain redirects my

focus, something I learned to quiet the guilt after my mother's murder. All it takes is a pinch, a near draw of blood, and the *your fault your fault your fault* is pushed down inside my chest where I wear it always, an aching scar inside. It's bearable, at least for a little while.

When the thoughts pass, I open my eyes. *Where am I now?*

High above me arches a dome made of mirrors that are all focused on the centre of the room where I lie. The floor beneath me is mapped with vivid green vines, pressed flat against the ground as if they've grown that way. It's the first sign of colour in nature I've seen in the fae realm; the only thing that isn't glass or black stone or metal. It's grown the entire length of the floor and snaked up the walls between the mirrors.

I'm in the middle of the foliage, the copper curls of my hair stark against the greenery. Even from the ceiling I can see the freckles on my cheeks and the tops of my shoulders where the black shift leaves my skin bare.

The blood is gone, wiped away as if my injuries never existed. I press a hand to my temple, my neck. Both are healed over, needle-thin scars where the blade bit into my flesh.

I shudder in disgust at the thought of *them* touching me, healing me, and cleaning me up as I slept. I know it wasn't done out of kindness.

You can unlock an object I seek. That is your sole purpose.

I have to get out of here. I may not have a home to return to, but Kiaran is still out there. Maybe Gavin and Derrick survived by escaping in my ornithopter.

Maybe maybe maybe. Maybe they're dead, too.

I tamp down the thoughts and push to my feet. What I thought at first was a room is actually a hall as vast as a palace ballroom, covered wall to ceiling in mirrors. I turn around and around, seeking a door – some means of escape – but only my reflections stare back.

Each reflection is different. One with a subtle, mocking

expression. One overcome with mourning. One with blood-splattered skin and eyes as vivid green and violent as a devil's. That Aileana terrifies me the most; her gaze is heavy, sharp as pricks of a blade-tip all over my body.

Like she'd cut out my heart and love it.

I step back, but the mirror only seems to draw closer. Violent Aileana's gaze holds mine. A chill spreads down my arms, the blade jabs growing more acute.

And then she smiles.

I run. As fast as I possibly can in those damn delicate slippers. It feels like I pass a thousand mirrors, a thousand different versions of myself, and never reach the end of the room. Though the side walls press closer, the hall stretches longer. That last mirror grows farther and farther away.

Violent Aileana is close, her reflection overtaking all the others. Her presence feels like fingernails drawing blood down my back as I run, unrelenting and sharp. Her image lingers in my mind as if I were still looking into the mirror, her eyes a glittering peridot like Sorcha's, the faery who murdered my mother. She is inhuman, monstrous. She is death.

She is all the times I've killed and enjoyed it. *Crimson suits you best.*

Something breaks inside me, unleashing a torrent of memories I can't control. My mother, the night of my debut, embracing me so hard that my ribs ached. My mother lying in the street, dead. Me, screaming her name and no one even hears.

I hit a wall of mirrors, my fingers scratching desperately at the surface. I slam the sides of my fist to the nearest mirror to break it, only to discover it isn't glass.

It's rock.

Damn damn damn. Shaking, I back away. Hands seize my shoulders, turning me roughly.

Lonnrach.

My first instinct is to fight – drive my heel into his kneecap

– but my feet become tangled in the vines along the floor. The plants rise up, wrapping around my legs as I struggle. I try to kick – to do *something* – but I can't even move. I tug with my hands, but the vines close around my wrists.

'The more you fight, the faster it grows.'

Lonnrach's half-smile is mocking. He's changed clothes. This time he wears all black, from his trousers to his shirt. Even his long, tailored coat doesn't have a hint of colour in it.

I go still, and sure enough, the vines stall their ascent to my hips. 'Is this my new prison, then?' I try to match his acerbic tone. I lean forward with my own mocking smile – sheer bravado, but from the way his jaw clenches, it's quite effective. 'I suppose it was different once, too. More beautiful or colourful. Just another example of how your kingdom is falling to ruin.'

I hope this place burns. I hope I get to light the bloody match.

Lonnrach's face hardens. His finger is on my cheek, tracing downward. I recoil, and the movement only incites the vines to grow farther up my arms. 'I can't wait to see what memory you were running from.'

A memory. Violent Aileana was the symbol of a memory. Though she's gone from the mirrors, I still sense her in the back of my mind. The knife-pricks haven't disappeared completely. I can picture her fierce smile.

'What do you mean?' I try to keep my voice calm, even as the whisper of *crimson suits you best* brushes across my mind like the quick swipe of a blade.

'We found that information could be extracted from the memories of our enemies.' Lonnrach steps away. Now he's slowly removing his coat, folding it. 'This hall amplifies the images and allows them to take form. Since Kadamach slipped out of my grasp before I could do this, I'll have to settle for you.'

God. The first fragment of fear makes me shiver. Sorcha had used my memories against me before, forced me to relive things I'd rather forget.

'Whatever you're looking for, I don't know where it is.'

Lonnrach places the coat on the floor. Then he's rolling up a sleeve, baring the smooth, shining skin of his forearm. Like he's about to get messy.

'It's fascinating the way human minds work,' he says casually. 'My kind can recall flawlessly, our memories perfectly intact. Humans remember in pieces. Everything is given an order of importance and the rest is repressed.' Now the next sleeve, ever so slowly. 'Of course, that means slower extraction, more time-consuming. Your mind would break too easily.'

Slower extraction. Your mind would break too easily. He'd fracture it anyway, bit by bit, to find what he wants. I may be a Falconer, but I'm still human.

'If I knew of an object that aided the fae, I would have remembered it,' I say quickly, trying to defuse the situation. *And I would have found it and destroyed it.*

Lonnrach's eyes meet mine. 'You spent a year training under my enemy and that rogue pixie. I assume they often spoke about things you didn't understand.'

I press my lips together before I utter an oath. Kiaran and Derrick were fond of riddle-like sentences, hinting about things in their past they both refused to discuss. Sometimes they used another language entirely, either in *Gàidhlig* or a fae language that resembled it, knowing damn well I couldn't understand them.

'Even what you did understand would be useful,' he continues. 'Their weaknesses. *Your* weaknesses.' Before I can say anything, Lonnrach is suddenly right in front of me, reaching for my wrist. 'I want to know everything,' he whispers, his steel-grey eyes glinting. 'I'll take every memory you have, if that's what it takes. I just need to use your blood to see.'

Your blood.

A sudden memory of my mother strikes me. Her in Sorcha's embrace, Sorcha's teeth dripping with blood. My mother's.

No. No no no. The vines tighten in my struggle, only slacking on my arm to allow him to pull it up – toward his lips.

Lonnrach opens his mouth and over his perfectly white, straight teeth, two rows of razor-sharp fangs descend.

Just like Sorcha's.

I go numb, dead inside. I couldn't move even if I tried. He's a *baobhan sith*, too. A vampirelike faery who resembles something out of a nightmare.

Lonnrach utters six words over my wrist, spoken with a hint of a smile, the words coming out in a hiss: 'This is *really* going to hurt.'

Then he bites down.

Chapter 3

*L*onnrach's bite is like venom moving through my body, burning within my veins and down my spine. It's pain so explosive that I feel nothing and everything all at once: my skin stretched over bone, my blood rushing and pounding through my limbs, my muscles seizing.

Lonnrach lifts his head, only for a moment. His mouth is smeared with my blood. His eyes are closed. Just before I feel the bite of his fangs again, he whispers, 'You taste like death.'

Memories explode through my mind, images passing by so quickly that I can't even hold onto them. At first they're all inconsequential thoughts, repetitions of the time when my mother was alive. Back when my days were all etiquette, tea, and practising dances, with evenings spent building inventions with her.

I can feel Lonnrach tossing them aside, deeming them unimportant.

My mother's laugh startles me from my outrage. I almost shout at him to stop, but all he allows is a split-second image of her wide smile, as clear as if she were in the room with me. As if she were *right there*. The scent of her heather perfume fills my senses, then is gone just as quickly.

I'm whisked away. Images flood harder with no order to them at all. The nights before the battle when Kiaran and I hunted together, when we ran through the city like vigilantes. The images are a torrent of hunt, stalk, kill, and depart.

I can feel Lonnrach trying to redirect everything into a cohesive stream, to slow down the memories so he can inspect them more closely. He's going back to the beginning, to the night before I met Kiaran.

Don't!

Before I can stop him, I'm suddenly standing in the back garden of the Assembly Rooms. I'm wearing my white silk dress with its lace and floral trimmings. My beautiful slippers peek out at the bottom, the painstakingly embroidered pink rosebuds visible in the bright moonlight. Mulled wine is warm in my belly and my vision is swaying and unsteady from drink.

Don't make me remember this, I think to Lonnrach. *There's nothing here that will help you.* But my protests only encourage him to hold onto the memory more firmly. It plays on.

I know exactly what's coming. I've relived this in my nightmares night after night. First it's the low intake of breath from the other end of the garden that startles me. I nearly turn to go inside when I hear something else – a strangled scream, caught in a gasp.

No no no. I watch myself cross the garden to where the gate overlooks the street. No matter how many times I remember this I always hope for a different outcome. I hope that I'll run for help. I hope that I'll pull out a blade and fight. I hope that someone will come. I hope I hope I hope.

But it's exactly the same. It always is.

I sense Lonnrach watching, too. We see his sister with her face pressed to my mother's throat. Sorcha raises her head to reveal teeth glinting in the moonlight, dripping with my mother's blood. We hear Sorcha's laugh, a deep, throaty purr that makes my stomach clench. In a single, swift motion, we watch her tear out my mother's heart.

Next to me, Lonnrach's body goes still when he sees how the

memory blurs from panic. How I can barely get enough breath into my lungs, how my thoughts are racing as Sorcha escapes into the night. How my memory of the event seems to speed up and black out until the moment I find myself next to my mother's body, pressing my hands to her chest.

We watch as I scream her name until I lose my voice.

Without warning, I'm standing back in the hall of mirrors. Lonnrach is still holding my wrist, his mouth hovering above where his teeth left their marks in my flesh. His lips are wet with my blood; it drips down his throat. Just like in my memory of *her*.

Sorcha.

I can't stop the sound that escapes my throat. When Lonnrach's gaze meets mine, his breathing is ragged and I'm startled by the glimpse of emotion there.

Before I can think to analyze it, he turns away sharply. He raises his arm to wipe his mouth, smudges my blood across his wrist like a brand. 'That's enough for now.'

Lonnrach grabs his coat from the floor and strides through the nearest mirror, disappearing into it as if it were water. It undulates, spreading ripples across all of the mirrors before they finally settle into my reflection.

I'm alone once more. The vines retract into the floor and I'm surrounded by the different versions of myself again.

Only then do I realise my cheeks are wet with tears.

Lonnrach doesn't speak when he comes to visit me after that. He makes every effort not to meet my gaze, keeping his expression carefully composed. Guarded.

I resist at first. I become desperate enough to attack him – to loop the *seilgflùr* around his neck – but the vines wrap around my limbs so fast that I'm forced to give in. In the days that follow, the physical weakness from blood loss and venom takes its toll and I stop fighting entirely.

I begin to view my time with Lonnrach as a nightmare I can't escape. When he sinks his teeth into me, I shut my eyes and almost manage to convince myself that I'm dreaming and it isn't real. That *he* isn't real.

After a while, I become so used to the pain of his bites that it barely affects me. Now it's just a quick prick of teeth through flesh and the sting of venom through blood.

Lonnrach watches my memories and leaves like a thief with his bounty. Every image with Derrick and Kiaran is carefully examined, played slowly and deliberately.

Through his explorations, I relive the last year of my life. I hate the way I've come to view his bite as a respite from the loneliness of my mirrored selves. Violent Aileana hasn't attacked again, but I still sense her behind all the others. Waiting, watching. I see her as a quick flash of a monster's smile, a reminder that Sorcha still lurks in my memory – and then she's gone.

At first I would use the reprieve from her to press my palms against the reflective rock. I tried for the longest time to pass through like Lonnrach does, but the surface is always solid, hard. I count the mirrors – one thousand four hundred and sixty-seven – and all of them are inescapable. On particularly bad days, I hit the mirrors until my hands bleed. Until I'm left with bruises on my fists.

The longer Lonnrach drains my blood, the weaker I become. I barely improve when I finally take the food he leaves: servings of bread, cheese, and fruit. Kiaran always taught me never to accept food or drink from the fae, that it allows them greater control over a human. Accepting it is my tacit compliance to stay in the *Sìth-bhrùth* until Lonnrach decides to release me.

He'll kill me first.

I've memorised the shape of his teeth imprinted into my skin. My fingers trace the marks they've left as I recall each memory he conjured and examined.

Thirty-six human teeth. Forty-six thin fangs, tapered like a snake's. Together they form two crescents, grooves worn into each arm and each side of my neck, over and over and over.

Twenty-seven times.

Some are flecked with dried blood. Others have scarred from the rapid healing of *baobhan sith* venom. I used to call my scars badges, each one earned from a fae I killed. But these … these aren't badges. They aren't marks of victory.

They're reminders of how I lost everything.

Today, Lonnrach sifts through the longer streams of my memory. He lingers on those before my mother's death, those he should find unimportant. I wonder if he realises that I've noticed the way he slows down the hours I spent building with her, or the days I took tea with my friend Catherine. Inconsequential memories of simple pleasures before I had ever felt the mark of grief.

As if embarrassed, Lonnrach pulls forward in time. I watch a stream of images go by before he settles on the memory of Kiaran and me in the Queen's Park. Though it was the night of the battle, it seems so long ago now. Kiaran had resolved to take his sister's place if we managed to trap the fae once more. I thought I would never see him again.

At one time I would have resisted Lonnrach's intrusion on these memories, but now I eagerly go along with it. I am desperate to feel again, for the spectrum of emotions my memories bring. They remind me of who I was, and that I'm still human.

Just for a little while, I think. *So I have something to hold onto.*

I sense Lonnrach's surprise when Kiaran and I kiss, when Kiaran grabs my coat to pull me closer. This is one of my few memories that remains whole, complete. That kiss is imprinted in my mind: the press of Kiaran's lips, his fingers against my skin. I know that kiss by heart.

In my memory, I pull away. '*Leave.*' I can hear the desperation in my voice. '*You still have time. Save yourself—*'

Another kiss, as if Kiaran's telling me this is goodbye. As

if he's memorizing my lips, too. 'Have I ever told you the vow a sìthiche *makes when he pledges himself to another? Aoram dhuit. I will worship thee.'*

Lonnrach pulls out of the memory so quickly that I sway on my feet. We're back in the hall of mirrors and he's already wiping his lips with the white kerchief he brought. Always a different one. My blood stains them all.

My legs won't hold me. I sink to the ivy floor as Lonnrach turns away, wordlessly striding toward the nearest mirror.

'Wait.' I'm surprised by my voice. It seems like an eternity since I've spoken. I sound raspy, my throat dry from disuse.

Lonnrach stops. He doesn't even turn. 'Is there something you need?'

It's been so long since I've heard his voice, too. He has no need to taunt me anymore, to break me with his words. I've accepted his food and drink. He has taken my blood. He's stolen my memories. What else is there to say?

And yet ... that memory made me feel longing again. Passion. Grief. Once I'm alone, that will all go away and I'll go back to pressing my fingers against his bloody teeth marks, hoping to conjure it all up again.

'I only want to talk.' I swallow once. *Good god, I can't believe I'm doing this. I'd kill him if I could.* 'That's all.'

This time, Lonnrach turns and looks at me. The weight of his gaze is heavy, assessing. 'Why?'

Because I don't want to be alone anymore. Because I don't know how long it's been since I've been here. Because I don't have anyone left. Because we've shared more than a year of my memories. Because you've left two thousand two hundred and fourteen individual teeth marks on my skin that will never, ever let me forget that everything I've lost is my fault.

I bite my tongue so none of those words spill out. Maybe one day I'll become hopeless and desperate enough to utter them.

Maybe. But not yet. 'Because you've seen my memories and yet you've said little about yourself at all.'

'Your memories serve a purpose.' He takes another step, raises his hand to the mirror. 'Mine don't.'

I try again. I don't mention how he extracts the inconsequential memories of my life before I saw my first faery, ones that serve no purpose at all. 'Why do you hate Kiaran?'

Lonnrach's hand curls into a fist. I persist, possibly against my best judgement. 'You told me I would regret not killing him. I want to know why.'

Lonnrach slowly turns around. His eyes are sharp and slate grey; his gaze falls upon the teeth marks he left on my wrist.

I immediately pull my knees into my chest like a shield.

Just when I think he might do something to make me regret my words, he finally speaks. 'Your *Kiaran* is the worst sort of traitor, and his sister is no different. Now it's up to me to fix their mistakes.' The way he regards me, his message is clear: *Which includes you.*

Me. He considers me a mistake. Because Kiaran made me the same as him.

'And save your realm?' I try to say it lightly, but I can't stop the bitterness that tinges my words. *You sacrificed my realm to save yours.* 'Is your monarch dead?'

Lonnrach seems to go still, as if startled by my question. 'Perhaps.' He considers his words carefully. 'No one has seen the Cailleach for thousands of years. The heirs she left behind to rule were … unworthy. Without a monarch, the *Sìth-bhrùth* will wither. Someone must take her place.'

'And you think you're worthy.' It sounds like an accusation, but I'm trying to understand why he has spent so much time painstakingly exploring my memories.

He casts me a meaningful glance, as if he can read my thoughts. 'No. But I will be.'

I call his name when he turns to leave. I see the tightness in his shoulders, as if he dreads my next query. 'What was it like when you were trapped below the city?'

Was it like in here? Did you stop fighting, too?

Lonnrach speaks deliberately, devoid of emotion. 'The first hundred years we spent trying to escape until our nails wore grooves into the underground rock. Energy we stole from the occasional humans we managed to compel through the prison's shield were barely enough to keep us all sated. That place became like a tomb.'

In his profile, I notice how tight his jaw is, as if he's controlling his anger. 'I won't ever forget that it was your kin who put us there. That your precious *Kiaran* and his sister helped.' He looks over at my mirrors, to my hundreds of different reflections. My cage. 'Now you know precisely how it feels to be that helpless.'

Chapter 4

I'm beginning to forget my life more easily now. It's been *daysweeksmonthsyears* – I don't know precisely – since I've seen anyone but Lonnrach. I can't recall the things he's stolen on my own any more.

To remember, I have to press my fingers a little harder into his teeth marks each time, until I leave half-moon marks of my own over the scars of his bites on my skin. I have to shut my eyes so hard that I see stars beneath my lids.

It's a rush of relief each time I manage to relive precious moments with all the people I care about. I can't help how often Kiaran lingers in my thoughts, even though the sting of Lonnrach's words is still there. It hasn't even faded.

He let you think he cared about you. You're not the first human pet he's discarded.

I flinch and try to redirect my focus away from Kiaran. I need to forget about him. He left me behind. I've been in the *Sith-bhrùth* through dozens of Lonnrach's little sessions. Through hours and days or maybe weeks spent alone with my reflections. Through counting mirrors and leaves of ivy. I'm discarded. I'm —

'Kam.' Kiaran's whisper of my nickname invades my thoughts. I almost shiver at how he says it. Like he loves the sound of it. Like it's an intimate word, a promise.

I try again. Desperately, I pull up another image of my mother. Her smile, her laugh, the way she could always —

'*Kam.*' Kiaran's voice, louder this time. More insistent.

'Go away,' I hiss. I press my fingers harder into the bites beneath the sleeve of my shift. My nails dig in. *Focus. Remember.*

His impatient Highland brogue tears through my concentration. 'Goddamn it, open your eyes and look at me.'

What the ... ? My eyes fly open. *Oh, lord.* My imagination doesn't do Kiaran justice. He's standing over me, inky black hair long enough to rest at the collar of his pale wool shirt. My memories never could quite capture the way light gives his skin a tawny glow, or the way his eyes are as bright and vivid as a lilac in bloom.

I can't help it; my gaze lingers on his cheek, where the light shield had burned him so badly that I could see the bone beneath. All of his injuries have healed over with smooth, unblemished skin.

He can't be real. I'm only imagining him. Not real. 'You said you couldn't enter the *Sìth-bhrùth*,' I say, certain now. Lonnrach must have created him just to torture me. He's changing tactics. 'Not without dying.'

With an impatient look, Kiaran holds out his hand. When I reach for him – entirely without thinking – my fingers pass through his skin. They *pass through*. As if he was a bloody specter.

I snatch my hand back. 'So Lonnrach did conjure you up. Well, it won't work.'

He mutters a curse, so very Kiaran-like. Lonnrach is good at this.

'I can project myself here without dying,' Kiaran says, sounding somewhat irritated. 'If I feel inclined to use an exhausting amount of power.'

I'm still suspicious. 'Then why have you never visited before?'

'Lonnrach put wards up that made it difficult to track you, and they take time to dismantle. My sister is still working through the one that leads to this room.' He gestures to himself. 'She was able to lift it just enough for this form to pass through while she finishes. Satisfied?'

If I allow myself to believe him … no. I can't. Lonnrach has been in my mind. I've taken his food. He can make me see whatever he wants. 'No. I don't believe you.'

'Your stubbornness is commendable, truly,' Kiaran says drily. 'I'm grateful you still have it.'

'See? That's how I know you're Lonnrach's creation.' I wag my finger at him. 'Kiaran always hated my stubbornness.'

'Honestly, at the moment I'm having a hard time not mistaking it for stupidity.'

I glare at him. 'As a figment of my imagination, I demand you stop insulting me.' I press my fingernails into the grooves of the bite-marks again and shut my eyes. 'And go away.'

He's quiet for so long, I swear he must have gone. I refuse to open my eyes to find out.

'Kam.' This time when Kiaran says my name, I hear the hint of emotion there barely contained.

When I open my eyes, he's staring down at me – no, not at me. At where my fingernails are embedded. The sleeve of my shift has slipped back to reveal the length of my forearm. I watch as he takes in my new scars, my scabbing marks, up to my neck where a dozen more are puckered and healed over. The latest one, just above my collarbone, is still bleeding.

I don't think I've ever seen his expression so cold and brutal. Not like this. Lonnrach could never have pulled that from my memories. This is really Kiaran. *Kiaran.* He didn't abandon me. He's here *for* me.

Kiaran kneels by my side. This time when he reaches for me, his touch is solid. I'm startled by it. It's been *daysweeksmonthsyears* since I've been touched by someone other than Lonnrach and I almost forgot how gentleness felt. I don't pull away. Not even when he wraps his fingers around my wrist to draw my arm closer.

I'm embarrassed by the marks. Now he knows I stopped fighting. That I didn't resist any more. 'He wanted … he—'

'I know what he wanted.' Kiaran's voice is rough, tinged with anger. He traces my scars with his thumb, as if memorizing the pattern of them. 'I'll kill him for giving you these.'

'No,' I say, a bit forcefully. Kiaran looks at me, surprised. 'It'll be me. It has to be me.'

I will him to understand. Lonnrach could have broken me. He practically did. All I had left were my memories, my feelings, and once I lost those – I would have been his. *It has to be me.*

'Very well,' Kiaran says simply.

That's not good enough. 'Promise.'

Kiaran strokes my wrist with his thumb – once, twice, three times. Stopping when he reaches the part where several marks overlap. 'On one condition.' He holds my gaze. 'You let me be the one who supplies the blade.'

'Aye,' I whisper.

He understands. We've hunted together. We've lost a battle together. That's a bond that lasts a lifetime.

Kiaran nods. 'Let's get you out of here.'

I'd imagined those words a thousand times, picturing myself strong and capable again. In my imagination, I stand without difficulty. The truth is, when Kiaran helps me to my feet, my vision sways from the blood loss and lingering venom of Lonnrach's bite. My knees almost immediately buckle.

Kiaran grasps my shoulders – or tries to. His hands go right through me and I just barely manage to catch myself.

'Listen to me.' His voice muffles slightly, as though he's speaking across a great distance. 'This mirror' – he indicates the nearest one – 'will lead you to my sister. The ward that was preventing you from leaving should be down by now.'

'You're not coming?' I try to keep the emotion out of my voice. I just got Kiaran back. I can't lose him again.

'I can't keep this form for long.' He's already fading, his body blurring around the edges.

'Wait! Don't—'

With his last bit of strength, Kiaran cups my cheek. His fingers are warm, so warm. 'I'll be waiting for you on the other side.'

Chapter 5

Once through the mirror, I blink hard against the sudden on-slaught of natural light. My vision clears and I'm surprised to find myself on the edge of a platform that looks across the *Sith-bhrùth*'s crevasse. The other floating platforms are familiar, and I realise they're the ones I saw when Lonnrach first brought me here. That seems like so long ago now, from another life entirely.

I peer up at the building on the platform with me. Its mirrored dome rises high toward the thick rain clouds, glinting in the rays of light that shine through. I recognise the glimmering, star-patterned dome and the opulent structure as the magnificent palace I noticed when I arrived. So it wasn't a royal residence at all – but a prison.

I take a moment to close my eyes, to breathe in deep. My lungs fill with winter air, fresh and crisp.

Later, I tell myself. *Once I'm safe.*

I scan the lip of the platform; there's little space between the wall of the palace and the rim of the rock that descends to the darkness below. Kiaran's sister is nowhere to be seen.

Damnation. I edge closer and look over. My stomach drops and I sway on my feet. Instinctively, I crouch closer to the ground, placing my palms to the dirt. No, there's nothing down there. Not even a platform to leap onto.

'I wouldn't,' a voice says, only a moment before I'm hit with the taste of power. Rose petals across my tongue, down my throat.

My head snaps around to see a faery crouched on her own rocky platform a good stone's throw from the castle. Even at this distance, her beauty is the type to make one feel instantly inadequate. Her long dark hair shines even in the drab landscape. It's pulled into a plait that reaches her narrow waist. Molten silver eyes meet mine, and there's a spark of interest there, as if she's sizing me up.

She wears fitted trousers and knee-high boots with brass buckles. A raploch coat hangs off her narrow shoulders, so long that it drapes around her like a long blanket.

This is Kiaran's sister? I search her face for a resemblance and she immediately says, 'You're staring. Is there something wrong with my face?'

I clear my throat. I *had* been staring rather intently. 'Quite sorry. Kiaran said—'

'Who?'

'Kiaran.' *Is she daft?* 'He said—'

'Hmm.' She considers for a moment. 'I'm afraid I don't know anyone by that name.'

I edge closer to the castle, away from her. Maybe she's a guard for Lonnrach, here to make sure I don't make it out of here alive.

I search for a platform nearby. If this faery is one of Lonnrach's soldiers, I can't risk waiting for Kiaran's sister. I'll either have to fight or flee, and in the state I'm in, this faery could tear through me like gauze.

Flee it is.

'Are you thinking about jumping?' the faery asks.

My voice hardens. 'No.' I didn't survive all that and get this far just to jump.

'Because it wouldn't be a good decision. You'd fall right to the bottom.' She smacks her hands together. '*Splat*. Emptied into the sea on the other side of the *Sìth-bhrùth*. A human, of course, would never survive such a thing.'

'Likely not,' I say drily. So Lonnrach has sent a deranged faery to guard me. He must have been *very* certain I'd never make it out.

Maybe Kiaran's sister is on the other side of the castle. I push to my feet and start walking, nearly letting out a groan when the platform the faery is on follows me. Oh, confound it.

'You have blood on your neck. Is it yours? Have you noticed?'

I freeze. My fingertips immediately feel for the bite marks there, the last ones Lonnrach left on me. Fear quickens my pace. I have to get out of here before he returns. I can't go back to that. I can't.

I try to hold myself together so I don't stumble, but my knees are trembling. *Stay calm. You're going to escape. You won't go back there.*

'So is it?'

For god's sake. I whirl on her. 'Is it *what*?'

She nods to my neck. 'Yours.'

I narrow my gaze. 'Has it escaped your notice that I'm mere seconds away from leaping over there and boxing you in the throat?'

Her hand immediately smacks against her chest. 'Oh. But I rather value my throat.'

Maybe if I ignore her, she'll go away? I continue my circuit around the castle, finally reaching the other side. I sigh. There's no one else to be found.

I begin to assess my surroundings on this side. I step toward the ledge and look down again.

'You keep looking down there.' I grit my teeth at her voice. So ignoring her doesn't work. 'If you're not thinking about jumping, is there something you need?' she asks me. 'Something you lost?'

'If you must know,' I say tightly, 'I'm trying to get off this blasted platform.'

'That's a relief,' she says. 'I was afraid what you'd lost was important and we'd have to find it at the bottom of the sea.'

Before I can blink, the faery's platform is right in front of me and she's grabbing my wrist to yank me aboard. I pitch forward with a sound of protest. By the time I right myself, our tiny island of rock has moved away from the castle and into the space of the ravine.

'What on earth do you think you're doing?'

The faery merely lifts a finger, licks it with a quick darting tongue, and raises it into the air. 'Feeling for wind. Under the right conditions, I'll be able to open a door between the worlds without Lonnrach detecting.' She gives me a slow smile. 'It's a gift.'

I narrow my gaze. 'So you *are* Kiaran's sister.' *And you're completely mental.*

'Hmm?' She's not looking at me. With her finger still in the air, her eyes have gone shadowed, their molten-silver irises swirling and swirling. 'No, you must be mistaken. I'm Kadamach's sister. This Kiaran fellow sounds like trouble.'

Confound it. 'Kiaran. *Is.* Kadamach.'

'Ah.' She wiggles her finger as she checks the wind, never breaking her look of intense concentration. 'Well. That certainly explains why you keep mentioning him,' she says absently. 'I'm Aithinne. You must be the Falconer I've had a devil of a time finding. Pleased to meet you.'

I finally notice the subtle resemblances between Aithinne and Kiaran. They have the same gleaming dark hair, the same skin – pale and shining like moonlight. And their eyes, while different in colour, share a similar intensity. She presses her brows together in concentration the same way he does.

For Kiaran's sake – and for mine – I suppose I should be pleasant. 'I'm glad you made it out of the mounds,' I blurt without thinking.

The second the words leave my mouth, I regret them. I notice how she goes still, how her concentration seems to waver and the light fades slightly from her eyes.

'Aye,' Aithinne says softly. 'I made it out.' Finally, she looks at me. Her gaze lands on my scars, on the one she noticed before that's still bleeding. 'And so shall you.'

And now you know precisely how it feels to be that helpless.

Unlike Aithinne, I didn't have a thousand faeries in the mirrored room to torture me. *I won't ever forget that it was your kin who put us there. That your precious Kiaran and his sister helped.*

She was trapped there for more than two thousand years with the enemy in a tomblike underground with no escape. I couldn't even begin to imagine what she went through.

As if realising I'm studying her, Aithinne sucks in a breath and concentrates harder. After a few quiet moments, she says, 'I can't open the door here. The wind is blowing in the wrong direction and we don't have time to wait.' She presses her palm flat against the platform. 'We'll have to find it.'

She's speaking in riddles, for all I understand. 'Find what? The wind?' Perhaps my sanity? I believe I have lost something after all.

Aithinne gestures over my shoulder and I look. *Oh, bloody hell.*

Atop the cliff is one of the deep, dark forests I had seen when I first arrived. This one is so thick that no light reaches below the canopy of branches. The shadows there are a curtain hiding everything from view. The black metal trees tower high, the area in front of them obscured by thick mist that settles at the edge of the cliff.

I'm not at full strength to defend myself, and she's suggesting we go through *there*?

'Hell,' I mutter. Louder: 'Couldn't you open a door somewhere else?'

'I could open one anywhere,' she says, not seeming the least bit concerned. 'But if we don't want Lonnrach to send an army after us in mere seconds, we must go through there. That's where the wind changes.'

I realise then that Aithinne is making our platform move out of synch with the rest of the rocks and buildings. We rise above the dark ravine, higher and higher, until we are level with the edge of the cliffs. From here, I have an even better view of the forest.

If anything, it's only more frightening close up. At least from afar the trees didn't seem capable of mortally wounding me. The branches are sharp and pointed, like spikes shooting off in all directions, and so knifelike that a mere brush against them could prove fatal. They gleam black, smooth as polished chalcedony. Despite their semireflective surface, no light escapes from between them.

The platform reaches the edge of the cliff and Aithinne waits for me to step off. My slippers touch the soil; the rocks beneath my feet glitter like smooth, perfectly cut and polished clear gemstones. Diamonds, perhaps. At any other time, I would have stopped to admire them. Instead, I stare up at the trees with dread.

'Whatever you do, don't wander off,' Aithinne says, moving to stand beside me. '*Ruaigidh dorchadas.* The shadows in there are living creatures. Do you understand?'

'Not really.' I have visions of murder by tree. It's rather gruesome.

Aithinne straightens. 'It's really very simple,' she says, looking up at the branches. 'Try not to die in there. Don't trust the darkness. Easy. How humans managed to survive from caves to tenements without knowing any of this, I'll never understand.'

I bristle, offended on behalf of my own kind – but then haven't I thought the same thing? I've marveled before that humanity – which was once hunted to near extinction by the fae – let their wisdom be whittled away to mere children's stories. Half of the stories are misleading nonsense, and the other half are outright rubbish. The folly of humans is truly astounding.

'People know about the fae from stories,' I tell her, listening to the metal tree limbs sing and whistle as the breeze rushes through the forest. 'They just don't believe in them any more.'

She studies me quietly, for the longest time. I don't miss the flicker of pity that crosses her features, quickly chased away. 'You're wrong,' she tells me. 'I'd say they believe in them now.'

I think of the scenes Lonnrach showed me what seems like so long ago. Princes Street in ruins. Ash falling from the sky. I've lived with those images in my mirrored prison. They're burned into my memory. Eventually I had to stop wondering whether Gavin, Derrick, and Catherine survived. I had to stop picturing the horrible ways they must have died. If I hadn't, Lonnrach would have found a way to use those memories against me. He would have broken me.

If anyone had survived, they'd have new nightmare stories to tell their children. About how one day an army of fae came through Scotland and destroyed everything. They'll never even know about the girl who failed them all.

'Aye,' I say softly. 'I suppose you're right.'

Together, we enter the forest.

Chapter 6

*B*eyond those first few trees, the darkness in the forest is thick. It presses against me, a solid weight. The temperature drops. Suddenly, the air is frigid enough that I shiver in my thin shift.

It smells of ash in the forest, like smoke and embers from a recently extinguished fire. The taste of power here is strong, a dryness like soot, with a lingering taste of peat. It's abrasive, as rough as pumice.

A high, thin whine sounds from somewhere nearby, like sharp nails scraping against metal. It echoes through the forest from no discernible source. My hand drops to my waist – where I would normally keep a weapon – and I get a fistful of air. Of course there's nothing there; Lonnrach made sure of it. 'What the devil was that?'

'*Mara.*' Aithinne keeps her voice low, barely above a whisper. 'I believe your kind call them demons.'

Somewhere in the dark woods, teeth click together in a hard bite, followed by a soft whine. Muttering a swear, I edge closer to Aithinne when I'm startled by a sudden burst of illumination. A ball of light at least the size of my fist appears between her cupped hands. It swirls and glows brighter until it stings my eyes to look at directly. She tosses it into the air and it explodes above us, casting flickering stars across the sky above the trees.

The shadows flee. They actually *flee*, leaping behind trees to hide from the light. Although it's not bright enough to illuminate their bodies, I can see that their fur gleams lustrous and thick. Farther into the forest, huge, shadowed bodies hunch among the sharp branches. A thousand pairs of eyes watch us from the darkness.

The shadows in there are living creatures. Do you understand?

Now I do – all too well. I never encountered another faery in all my time in the *Sìth-bhrùth*, not even a glimpse when I first arrived. At times I wondered whether it was empty except for Lonnrach and me. Whether he did that deliberately so I was more isolated.

It seems some creatures have been here all along, gathered away from the crevasse. These faeries are wild. Their stares are unsettling, intense, and ravenous. I swear I can hear them licking their teeth, jaws clicking in hunger.

I stay close to Aithinne as we hurry through the trees. Our pace is slowed by the bladelike branches pointing out in all directions, only just visible in the dim light. As the last orb fades, Aithinne readies another ball of light.

A growl to my left is close. Though I've managed through sheer force of will to overcome the dizziness left by Lonnrach's venom, I don't have a blade to defend myself from the *mara*.

'I don't suppose you have another weapon?' I say in a low voice, skirting around a long branch. I can't help it; I test the end of the branch and my skin gives as though I'd pricked it on the edge of a knife. My finger comes away with blood.

Well. That proves my theory that the trees really could kill me.

Aithinne pauses. Her grin is slow, devious. She pushes open her coat and I realise she wears two belts, one for each blade. She unbuckles one and passes it to me. 'I always come prepared.'

I'm starting to like Kiaran's sister.

She hands me a raploch pouch from her pocket. 'And this, in case of emergencies.'

Seilgflùr. All right, I *really* like Kiaran's sister.

I pick out a few heads of thistle and twist them to knot around my neck, leaving the remainder in the pouch fastened at my wrist. Not only is the thistle deadly enough to fae that it burns right through their skin, but it gives me the ability to see them at all times. Without it, if the *mara* – or even Aithinne – willed it, they could disappear from my human vision and I'd never even know they were there at all.

Once my necklace is secured, I push my tangled hair out of my face to see where the sword belt buckles, pulling the strap tightly around my hips.

Aithinne smiles. 'You know,' she says thoughtfully, 'your hair rather looks like an octopus.' Then, as if to reassure me: 'I love octopi.'

And Aithinne is obviously a bit barmy, but nobody's perfect.

She readies another ball of light for us to move forward. Though we continue quickly through the trees, I'm beginning to wonder whether this forest has an end. No light is visible from the other side, only a ceaseless number of trees.

A bray from somewhere behind us makes me jump. My fingers close around the hilt of the sword. 'I assume they see us as ... a meal?' I can't think of a way to word it more delicately. *Bloody hell, these faeries want to dine on me.*

'No, no,' Aithinne says. 'They're here to eat you, not me. I don't think I'd taste very good to them.'

'Comforting,' I say drily. 'Very comforting.'

I might have a blade, but I doubt I'd be terribly effective in a fight. It's been too long since my training; my body is slighter than it was when I battled last. But I can run. At least I can run.

'Don't worry,' Aithinne says. She casts up more light. 'They'll keep to the shadows.'

'Are they Unseelie, then?'

Human books about the fae always split them between two kingdoms: light and dark. Seelie and Unseelie. The Seelie are considered the not-so-bad faeries. They're described as seductively beautiful and are said to ride on gleaming horses. The Unseelie, on the other hand, are creatures of shadow. They're described as cold and brutal to any human unfortunate enough to meet them. They're rumoured to enslave and eventually kill anyone they steal from the outside world, while the Seelie – considering themselves better – return humans to their home realm, even centuries after they're taken.

Such is the supposed *mercy* of the immortals. Bastards, all of them.

'The *mara* were devoted to our former monarch,' Aithinne says. 'Not the courts.'

Though we continue at a brisk pace, Aithinne's feet never make a sound as she strides beside me. I am clumsy in comparison, my slippers crunching through the gemstone soil.

I remember Lonnrach's words. *No one has seen the Cailleach for thousands of years. The heirs she left behind to rule were … unworthy.*

'The Cailleach?'

Aithinne doesn't answer right away. She tosses up another light and it sizzles as it disperses. Shadows flee through the trees in trails of gleaming fur and burning eyes. There are more than there were before. They're so quick that I can barely see what they look like, but from their height, they're bigger than wolves.

Finally, her gaze flickers to me, her expression unreadable. 'Aye. When the Cailleach left, the *mara* chose not to align themselves with either kingdom,' she murmurs. 'This forest belongs to them now.'

A low growl comes from behind us, a rumbling, full-bodied sound. All the fine hairs on my body stand straight up and I shiver. Going through this forest is like wandering the Highlands at night, with wildcats lurking in the darkness, just waiting to pounce.

I know with certainty that the *mara* are watching and preparing for the moment Aithinne's light dims just enough, and I'm theirs. They wouldn't even take me back to Lonnrach. They'd devour me, flesh to bone.

Aithinne is quick to make sure that never happens. As soon as the stars twinkling above us begin to dim, she casts up more. They flicker, so abundant and beautiful, as if we were looking at the night sky through the trees instead of her own created light. As if we are at the centre of a private galaxy.

'Quickly, Falconer.'

Aithinne increases her already hurried pace. I can barely keep up with her any more. The muscles in my legs are already trembling. I haven't used them this much in a long time.

I'm breathing hard, shaking all over. Lonnrach's venom has this effect if I go too long between bites. My stomach cramps with nausea.

I try to ignore it and continue, only to stumble and lose my balance. Gasping, I realise I was mere inches away from impaling myself on one of those blasted tree branches. 'Wait,' I call, skirting around the branches with more care. 'Slow down.'

Though no emotion crosses Aithinne's features, I can sense her urgency. 'Very well.' She slows ever so slightly, just enough for me to catch up. Though we maintain haste, I match Aithinne's pace with only a little difficulty. The pain is bearable.

She sends up another light, bursting up to the tops of the trees. This one reminds me of nights in Edinburgh beneath clear skies. Moonless winter evenings spent in the garden when the stars are bright and abundant.

I can't help it. My fingers brush one of Lonnrach's marks at my wrist and I picture the Edinburgh he showed me. My home is gone and in its place is ruin, destruction. Perhaps I really am just leaving one version of perdition for another.

'Aithinne? What's it like in the human realm now?' At her hesitation, I say, 'I know what happened immediately after the battle. That Edinburgh was destroyed.'

I almost ask her how long it's been, but the question sticks in my throat. I can't. Not yet.

She seems reluctant. Her hand is cupped, a ball of light swirling in her palm. 'It's difficult out there,' she says carefully. 'But you'll be with your own kind, at least.'

My breath hitches in surprise and I stop walking. *You'll be with your own kind.* Surely she can't mean ...?

I reach out and clamp a hand around her wrist. 'There are survivors?'

Aithinne seems surprised by the force of my words. 'Well. Aye.'

I *break*. I can't help it. When she tries to move away, my grip tightens. Hope is a traitorous bastard and I'm letting it squirm its way into my heart all the same. 'Catherine. Gavin. Their surname is Stewart. One of them might have a wee pixie with them. Does that sound at all familiar?'

Something flickers in her gaze as she tries to extract herself from my grip. 'I can't say.'

I breathe a curse then, a vile one I learned from Kiaran. I don't give a damn about whether Lonnrach has discovered I'm gone, or even about the *mara* surrounding us. I need to know. Hope already has its claws sunk inside me, deep and relentless. After all that time I spent thinking I was the only one left, Aithinne has given me my single most important wish and now she won't share a thing.

Maybe Lonnrach and I are the same. Maybe I'm just as bad as he is, just as monstrous and beyond redemption. It's the only explanation I have for why I sink my fingernails into her skin until I know it hurts. For why I would have put the blade to Aithinne's throat if I had a free hand to reach for it.

For why I find satisfaction in seeing her wince. 'Tell me,' I say, the threat clear in my voice.

There's no fear in her gaze. I've never met a faery who didn't feel at least a bit threatened by me when they discovered I could make their impenetrable fae skin bleed. 'I said I can't.'

'Don't toy with me. It's a simple question. Catherine. Gavin. A pixie named Derrick. Have you heard those names?'

I sink my fingernails in deeper. I ignore my sudden memory of the Violent Aileana in the mirrors, how gleeful she'd be. How she'd smile at me now in pride. I tamp down my disgust at my actions and hold fast. 'And no faery riddles, either. I am in no mood.'

The light is dimming. Invisible paws shuffle in the dirt around us. The heavy, hungry gaze of predatory fae settles on my shoulders. They breathe together as a collective, and it's as if we're inside a living forest. The air around us heats from it, growing sticky and wet. But I can't release Aithinne now. Not yet. Not until she tells me.

'The light is going out,' she says, no emotion in her voice.

I glance up at the last vestiges of the stars. If I don't release her the *mara* will attack us, and I'm still weakened from Lonnrach's imprisonment. I swear in frustration and release her.

Aithinne swiftly creates another light and tosses it. The shadows around us disperse again, their agonized wails filling the silence. The *mara* return to watching from the darkness, their growls impatient, resentful.

Aithinne holds out her arm, blood welling from the cuts my fingernails left.

I stare at it. *We're the same, you and I.* Lonnrach's words echo through my mind, a cruel taunt. I step back and press my palm to my neck, to the last marks that bound he and I together. Still bleeding. Still sore. *We're the same.*

I marked Aithinne, too. Even as I watch her wound heal over into smooth, unblemished skin, I still would have done it. I wonder if when Lonnrach took out pieces of me, he filled up the hollow inside with fragments of himself.

'I'm sorry,' I whisper. I can't tear my eyes away. 'I'm so sorry.'

Aithinne watches me carefully for the longest time,

understanding in her features. This time, she tries her words more deliberately. 'If what I say gets back to Lonnrach, he'll hunt them down. He has spies everywhere. Kadamach won't let me share anything to protect—'

Her voice suddenly chokes, a horrifying sound, as if she almost let something slip. She doubles over, face contorting in pain. 'My vow,' she manages to gasp. 'Written on my tongue.'

If what I say gets back to Lonnrach, he'll hunt them down. He has spies everywhere. Kiaran is practical, occasionally to a fault. He knew I'd demand answers that might potentially put people in danger – especially if they're hiding from the fae army.

'He made you vow not to tell me?'

She nods. 'It was too broad. I can't reveal most things about the outside, or even speak around it—'

'I know,' I say as my initial anger calms. 'I'm aware of how faery vows work.'

No wonder she almost choked on her words. A fae vow is something never to be taken lightly, or uttered on a whim. Kiaran once made a vow never to kill humans. If he ever breaks it, he'll die slowly, painfully. For Kiaran to make Aithinne say one … the situation in the human realm must be dire.

My memory of ruined Edinburgh flashes. I can practically smell the falling ash before I shove it to the recesses of my mind and shut the door. *Don't think about it. Escape from Lonnrach first.*

I force myself to speak. 'Let's get out of here.'

Chapter 7

*A*ithinne and I keep a steady, brisk pace through the trees for the longest time – like hours, it seems.

I imitate the movement of her body to avoid the shadowed metal limbs of the trees, the razor-sharp branches. They tug the bottom of my shift, ripping the material.

I take another step and flinch as a branch slices through my leg in a long, thin cut, superficial but damned painful. Blood wells around the wound and drips down to my feet in a stream. *Damnation.*

The high wails of countless *mara* suddenly echo through the forest.

'Wait,' Aithinne says sharply. 'Don't move. The *mara* have sensitive noses. If enough of them smell your blood, they might risk getting burned by the light.'

The *mara* stalk through the shadows, between the creaking branches. I start when something moves out of the corner of my eye. *Hell. Oh hell.* They're getting closer. Even with the light above us, they're moving into the shadows between stars, edging nearer. Waiting, waiting.

Something nips near my feet with hot breath and I grasp the hilt of my sword. A growl comes from my left, and I have the blade out without thinking. My muscles tremble in response, but I ignore it. 'Run or fight?'

Aithinne's smile is a fierce thing, wild. 'Both.' She has her blade in her hand before I can blink. 'Definitely both.'

I pause. 'I'll be damned. You really are Kiaran's sister.'

A single breath later, she leads the way and we both take off running. Like before, I mimic the movements of her body to avoid the sharp branches. I'm not graceful. My limbs are clumsier from lack of use, but I urge myself through. *Keep going. You can do this. Keep going.*

The last lights over the trees are beginning to fade; one by one they burn out like candles being snuffed. The rustling in the trees grows louder, more urgent. A howl resonates from somewhere to my left. The *mara* are running with us, waiting for their chance.

Aithinne stops just at the edge of our remaining circle of light. She grasps my hand and deliberately turns me so she can press her back to mine. 'Fight as many as you can,' she says in a low voice. 'Then you run, and let me distract the rest.'

I nod once, wiping the sweat from my brow. My breathing is uneven, weak. I'm trembling, queasy from our run. I'm too close to escaping to care.

Then the last stars finally fade, and we are pitched into darkness.

I listen to the shadows, to the rustle of fur and bodies around me. Hot breath blasts against my face and I cringe at the stench of it.

Teeth snap. I strike with my blade, catching skin and fur. A high wail of pain fills the shadowed silence. Then the galloping of feet, dozens of them, right toward me. The *mara* move the way shadows descend upon a forest near nightfall – precisely that quickly.

I don't hesitate. My blade whistles through the air, cutting, slicing. I fight the way Kiaran always taught me to: by instinct. Every single one of my senses is honed, alive from the deprivation of my sight. The taste of *mara* power, of smoke and heat, burns my lips and my tongue – an indication of how close they are.

My muscles remember how to fight. My body battles as easily as breathing. Though my strikes are less refined, less smooth, I make up for it with sheer tenacity. Each kill only energizes me until I'm finally keeping up with Aithinne. Her back remains pressed to mine, her breathing in cadence with my own.

We are an impressive team.

Claws slice open my arm and I grit my teeth. My blood sends them into more of a frenzy. Just as I cut one down, another comes at me, then another.

I arc my blade and fur catches and gives beneath it. Blood splatters clear across my face. The powers of dead *mara* flow inside me, thick like the sweltering heat of summer's warmest day.

Normally, I'd revel in it. I'd cut each of them down with a bursting euphoria, but not this time. I don't feel that urge, that pleasure with a kill. Only necessity and the need to survive.

The realization slows me down for only a moment, but that's all the *mara* need. One of them latches onto my arm, teeth sinking in just above my wrist. I gasp in pain, slashing downward to sever its head in a single quick stroke. Its teeth rip across my arm as it drops to the ground.

'Get ready to run, Falconer.'

The ball of light Aithinne produces is enormous, the size of a carriage wheel at least. The *mara* surrounding us yelp, seeking shadows outside its reach.

Pulling back her arms for leverage, Aithinne launches the light up to the sky. It explodes, stars shooting all around us. They light up the forest, illuminating large creatures with dark fur and shining eyes and teeth like knives. Their screams are piercing as they flee, leaving behind the hideous stench of burning fur.

Aithinne gestures to a parting in the trees. 'That way. Don't look back.'

We're running again, pounding through the forest. I hate how weakened I am, how my entire body is aching from such a short battle. The effort it takes to avoid the sharp branches only makes it worse. Fabric along the bottom of my shift tears, the spikes scratching through. I wrench myself clear and dart after Aithinne.

The guttural roars of the *mara* echo around us. I realise then just how badly the cuts on my arms are bleeding. The scent is probably driving them mad.

The lights above us are twinkling out, fading fast. We pick up speed, our legs pumping. My muscles burn from the strain, my chest aching.

'There,' Aithinne gasps.

Just up ahead is a dim light beyond the trees. Almost there. *Almost there.* Darkness is falling around us. The heat from the pursuing *mara* is slick down my back. They are growling, panting, their heavy paws pounding through the trees behind us.

Hurry hurry hurry. The lights on either side of us are completely snuffed out, with only the glow up ahead to guide us. I map my escape. I memorize the path through the trees where the spikes are absent.

I push myself harder, ignoring the strain in my legs, the pain of it. *Almost there.*

The last stars go out. Something claws at my leg, catching skin. I don't lose course. I stay on my mental route. Just as I feel the heat of the *mara* unbearably close, I leap for the forest exit.

My body slams into the ground, and I roll through the grass. I close my eyes hard against the sudden daylight, not even opening them when I hear the yelp from a *mara* in pain behind me.

Moments later, others growl from the forest. They let out low whines and whimpers of frustration.

Don't worry. They'll keep to the shadows. That means I'm safe. Finally.

I lie on the ground, breathing deeply. The trees around me groan, the leaves fluttering in the cool breeze. I never want to move again.

At the stomp of boots on grass, I ease my eyes open. Aithinne leans down with a grin. 'You didn't die. See? I told you it was easy.' She offers me a hand and I take it, rising unsteadily to my feet.

'I've been bitten by some demonic woodland creature. My legs have been shredded by razor-sharp trees. We almost died. *Easy*? I'm getting you a damn dictionary.'

I inspect my bleeding arm. The cut bisects five of the marks Lonnrach made, and I feel inexplicably proud of that. *Good. Replace the old, bad memories with new badges. Start over.*

'A dictionary,' she repeats. 'Is that a type of dessert?'

For the love of – 'A type of book that explains the meaning of words.'

'Oh. That sounds terribly dull. I was really hoping for dessert.'

I'm hoping to end this rescue with my sanity intact.

I stare at the beautiful scenery around us. The meadow is up high on a ridge, a muted landscape with even more extreme chiaroscuro than the area around the fissure. The clouds are black and heavy with rain.

Every part of the land is rugged. Near where we stand is a waterfall that drops from the crags to the canyon below. The river at the base of the canyon is dark; it resembles descriptions I've read of dried lava, right down to the rough texture created by the rapids.

It looks like a scene painstakingly etched by an expert hand. As if the artist had delicately stroked the charcoal pencil to get the texture just right. The shade just right. Each detail etched in fine brushes. *The Sìth-bhrùth was once full of a thousand different colours your human eyes have never beheld.*

This place must have been even more magnificent before the colour faded. From the expression on Aithinne's face – the longing, mixed with sadness – she thinks so, too. Her gaze is unfocused, as if she's remembering the way it was.

'What did it look like before?' I can't help but ask. 'Was it beautiful?'

'It was always beautiful,' she says, rather mechanically. 'That was never the problem.'

'What was?'

Aithinne seems to shake herself, closing herself off the same way Kiaran does. 'Lots of things.' She looks over at me then. 'You're bleeding again.'

Without warning, Aithinne seizes my arm. Before I can ask her what she's about, she swipes a finger across my arm wound and licks the blood off with a quick dart of her tongue.

'Ahh!' I stare at her in shock. 'You licked – you just – my god, I want the last five seconds of my life back.'

Her face scrunches into a grimace. '*Baobhan sìth* venom. It's all over you; I can smell it.'

I go rigid. Lonnrach marked my body. He stole my memories. Of course it would follow that he's polluted my blood.

I want to know everything. I just need to use your blood to see.

I'm tainted. My skin isn't mine and my blood isn't mine and my mind isn't mine. There isn't any part of me that he hasn't claimed or taken by force except for my will. And he almost took that, too.

Aithinne notices my expression. 'Falconer, I didn't mean it like that. I—'

'Of course.' I can't help the urge to scrub myself clean. To get the scent of *him* off me. 'It's all right.'

Her grip on my arm loosens. "No, it's not,' she tells me. 'It's not all right. What he did to you' – she presses her fingers to my wrist, where he bit me most – 'it's not all right.'

Since meeting Aithinne I've never heard her sound more serious. Like she *knows*. Like she's been through it. Maybe she has.

I almost say *thank you*. I'm tempted to break the rule even though the fae don't like to be thanked. Because she might be of *them*, but I spent *daysweeksmonthsyears* with no kind words except those that existed in my memories.

Aithinne's eyes don't leave mine. 'I can heal you. The venom has to be purged on its own, but I can take away its effects.'

Yes. Yes yes. To get rid of trembling limbs and short breath and something to take the pain away. *Yes.*

At my nod, Aithinne places her hands over my ears. She muffles the noise until all I hear is the rushing in my ears, the wavelike sea sounds.

Next comes the searing pain. I flinch, but I've become so used to it that it barely affects me any more. My knees don't buckle like they used to. My eyes don't sting with tears. I use it as a gauge of *I'm here and I'm alive and I still feel and you can't take that away.*

I open my eyes just as the cut on my arm knits closed beneath the blood. The injuries along my legs vanish, perfectly smoothed over. The aching in my muscles fades and the helpless trembling weakness dissipates, and with it – all at once – the agony goes, too.

Now only the scars remain.

Aithinne pulls her hands away and smiles. 'Better?'

To the devil with faery conventions. I don't care. 'Thank—'

Then I hear it. The distant sound of hooves on dirt, crossing the countryside somewhere near us. Too far for me to taste their powers, but close enough to know that there are at least a dozen of them – and they're heading right for us.

Chapter 8

*A*ithinne mutters something foul. 'We'll have to use the trail.' She gestures with a nod. 'It's a passage that juts out just below the top of the crag. As long as they stay up here, they won't see us.'

I study the path she indicates and my stomach clenches. The cliff down to the river below is layered with perilous bends and twists in the rock that end in a steep drop right to the bottom. Like something out of the mountainous paths in the Cairngorms. They're majestic to look at, but there's a reason some say those blasted things are haunted, and it's because every year some explorer goes out and doesn't return.

If we fall, *she* would survive the impact. I would – in the words of Aithinne – go *splat*.

I immediately take a step back. 'Oh? We can't just—'

'No,' Aithinne says shortly, in a very Kiaran-like voice.

I bite back a curse and follow her across the meadow. We continue down to where the narrow ridge extends just below the cliff edge and out of the riders' view. The rocks there are rough as scoria, and coloured a red so deep they're almost black. They smell of ash, as if a fire had been lit recently. From here, there's nothing directly below us – it's a long drop all the way to the bottom, straight down.

Unable to stop myself, I step closer to the edge and peek over.

I wish to hell I hadn't. My head spins as if I'm whirling and nausea cramps my stomach.

I'm certainly not one to fear heights, but even I'm not mad enough to flee from the fae this high up. The trail is barely wide enough for my feet; it's only a small lip of rock that could break off and tumble to the bottom at any moment.

I scan the path for any branches to hold on to in case of a fall. None.

The pounding of hooves through the trees grows closer. They're almost to the meadow. If we don't go now, they'll see me and I'll be put back in the mirrored prison.

Lonnrach will steal my memories again. He'll punish me for escaping, and this time it might be worse. I won't go back to that. I might not have this chance again.

When Aithinne starts down the trail ahead of me, I don't hesitate. I take the first steps down the rocky path. I mentally recite my encouragement, my mantra. *Almost there. Almost there almost there.* Almost safe. Almost home. Almost free of *him.* Each step is *almost almost almost.*

When I hear the fae enter the field above our heads, I try to keep my steps as quiet as Aithinne's. The rocks are too unstable. My slippers have barely any grip on them at all.

Halfway across the path, my feet slip and I slide with a scrape over the rocks. I open my mouth to scream, but Aithinne smacks a hand over my mouth and hauls me to safety. She pushes us up against the rough crag, a finger to her lips. Then she releases me and gestures upward. The riders are on the ridge right above us.

'You said you tracked them this way?' I hear Lonnrach say.

My pulse quickens. I picture him in the mirrored room, teeth at my wrist. *This is really going to hurt.* It hurt every time.

Almost there. I return to my desperate chant, a reassurance that Kiaran will be there once I escape. *I'll be waiting for you on the other side.*

Almost there.

I'm so distracted by my own thoughts that when I finally look over at Aithinne, I'm startled to find that she's gone entirely still. Her eyes are wide and panicked. When I move to touch her fingers, they're ice-cold.

'They went through the forest,' another voice says, one I don't recognise. 'There are two energy trails here. She had help.'

One horse is so close to the edge that a hoof knocks off small bits of dirt and rock to rain on our feet. Aithinne doesn't appear to notice. Her breathing grows more unsteady, gasping. Loud.

Above us, the horse shuffles closer to the edge. The fae are silent – too hushed and still. Dawning horror makes me grow cold. They're *listening* for us. Aithinne's breathing has turned heavy, a roar in the quiet.

I press my palm to her lips to quiet her down, and she doesn't react. Her gaze is unseeing, distant now. She's lost in a memory.

'It's Aithinne,' Lonnrach says, his voice tight. 'She's with the Falconer.'

Aithinne gasps against my palm, her eyes squeezing shut.

'It can't be,' the other faery says. 'She couldn't have come through without our sensing—'

'Oh, she could,' Lonnrach says. 'But with limited power, she'd need the right conditions. She'll be looking for a way to escape.'

Aithinne is wheezing against my palm, her lips moving. I edge closer. I can hear what she's saying through my fingers, her lips forming words against my skin. Three of them. Three words like icy fingertips down my spine. 'It doesn't hurt.'

'Shh.' I try to make my breath sound like the air. I don't know how to comfort her or to get her back, not without speaking. If I touch her further, she might respond badly.

'Go through the forest,' Lonnrach says. 'Try to pick up their trail there. We'll double back and see if we missed anything.'

The riders disperse, their steps heavy on the ridge above us. I listen until it's quiet around us again, and I lower my hand from

Aithinne's mouth. She still has her eyes shut, her chest rising and falling quickly as she repeats her three words: *It doesn't hurt.*

'Aithinne,' I whisper. 'They're gone. It's all right.'

It's not all right. What he did to you, it's not all right.

She stops mouthing her chant, but it takes so much longer for her breathing to slow.

I made it out. And so shall you.

It was Lonnrach. It had to be. Aithinne became like this the second she heard his voice. She spent two thousand years trapped in the mounds with him. Two thousand years for him to do to her what he did to me.

'Did he—' I can't say the words. So I touch her fingers to my marks. *Did he try to mark you, too? Even though he'd never succeed, did he try? Did he steal your mind like he did mine?* 'Did he do this? Like mine?'

Aithinne's eyes open. They're not silvery any more, not molten. Now they're as unyielding as steel, not emotionless, but cold and numb. 'Worse,' she says, her hard voice slicing through me. 'He did worse.'

Now you know precisely how it feels to be that helpless.

I don't ask. I don't want to picture how much worse it could have been for someone who doesn't scar and who can't die.

Aithinne pushes to her feet, her emotions shuttered again. Her movements are stiff as she brushes the dirt from her coat. 'We have to hurry.' She's brusque, cool and detached. As if nothing happened. 'Before the wind changes.'

Before I can say anything, she starts down the path. I follow behind. Though I can't see her face, the set of her shoulders remains tense. Her fingers are clenched into fists. I consider saying something – pointless chatter to fill the silence – but I don't.

I prefer the quiet, too. It gives me time to observe the landscape, how the sun is beginning to set across the loch on the other side of the bend, where the river empties. Stars fill the space between clouds and the landscape has darkened since we first arrived. I can hear the wind blowing through the trees above us, rattling the leaves and branches.

Aithinne maintains a quick pace and I try to keep up. I stay focused on the path, never daring to let my eyes stray over the edge of the cliff. If I do, the dizziness comes back – so it's one foot in front of the other, over and over again.

Unlike me, Aithinne seems perfectly content on the trail. Her steps never waver. She still doesn't speak, not even to ask infuriating questions. She keeps herself shuttered, a perfect study of indifference.

Suddenly, she snaps her head up at the same time I taste Lonnrach's power heavy on my tongue. *Oh, hell.*

As one, Aithinne and I turn. Lonnrach is on the very far side of the trail, mounted on a metal horse with a dozen fae at his back.

He sees us. I can feel his eyes on me. He's in my mind, probing, pushing, gaining entrance – all because I accepted his food and drink. He whispers a single word: *Falconer.*

It's a command, that word. A simple command. *Come back to me.*

Damned if I don't take a step forward, as if I have no control over my body. No control over my mind. *Aye,* he says. *That's it. That's it.*

Now you know precisely how it feels to be that helpless.

I jerk back at the memory of Lonnrach's words, breaking his influence. 'No,' I snarl.

I whirl so I'm no longer facing him. Beside me, Aithinne has frozen at the sight of him. I don't have the time to soothe her, to say comforting words to bring her back. So I grab her coat and yank her down the path with me, my fist white-knuckled around the fabric.

But Aithinne is still too distracted, and that's all it takes. Her feet slip. She slides forward and nearly goes over the edge, but I grasp her arm. I dig my heels into the dirt and pull, straining hard, using my weight to wrench her back.

Aithinne manages to recover just enough to gain her bearings and then we're running again. We sprint down the treacherous path with the fae at our backs. They've dismounted their horses to pursue us on the narrow path.

Around us, the ridge begins to quake. Rock cracks around us, as loud as cannons and gunfire. The taste of faery power is slick down my throat, aching, burning. *They're* doing this. They're causing the ground to tremble beneath us.

A fissure forms beneath our feet, the soil breaking, parting. I lose my footing. Aithinne grasps my arm, pulling me painfully hard to safety.

'Hold your powers!' Lonnrach's shout echoes across the canyon. 'I need the Falconer *alive*.'

The tremors stop just as we reach the end of the trail. Aithinne and I, breathing hard, climb over the rocks to the top of the crags. All I can hear are the rapid footfalls behind us, determined and quick. It won't take them long to reach us. If we don't do something, they'll be here in minutes.

At the top of the rocks, Aithinne stops short – so fast that I nearly careen into her. At the sudden, unexpected taste of iron heavy in my mouth, I go cold. It's like a thick stream of blood, concentrated enough that I nearly heave.

I recognise that taste. *Sorcha.*

I shift around Aithinne and Sorcha smiles. 'Falconer,' she greets me. 'And *Aithinne*. My, my, this is quite a reunion.'

She's dressed in a shift like mine, only the black fabric of hers glitters like the night sky. The *baobhan sith's* beauty is uncanny, terrifying. I watch as fangs lower over her teeth and elongate enough to press into her full lips. She smiles wider, a nightmarish grin of pointed teeth.

Normally I'd picture my mother the night of her murder. I'd see Sorcha standing over my mother's corpse, licking the blood off her lips as if she'd just had a satisfying meal.

Now I can't help but compare her teeth to Lonnrach's. Her

eighty-two teeth resemble the ones that have left marks all over me. The truth is, Lonnrach and his sister have both claimed parts of me. Lonnrach claimed me body and mind, and Sorcha – she took part of my humanity. Ripped it away until I was left with that violent girl from the mirrors.

I grip the hilt of my sword so hard that my hand aches. I press down the memories just enough for me to speak. 'You're lucky Kiaran made that vow to you,' I tell Sorcha. 'If his life weren't entwined with yours, I'd put this blade through your chest and cut out your heart.'

Just like you did to my mother. I'll make sure you know exactly how it felt for her at the end. You should die the same way.

'Tit for tat, as they say?' Sorcha flashes her fangs in a hiss. 'I'd dearly love to see you try.'

'That's *enough*.' Aithinne lashes out with her powers, quick and strong as lightning. I watch as a single cut opens across Sorcha's flawless face.

Blood drips down Sorcha's alabaster skin. '*Striopach*,' she snarls. I may not be familiar with the word, but I'm certain it's *not* a nice thing to call someone. 'I'm here to help you, and this is how you repay me?' Her lip curls. 'I wish they could have killed you in the mounds.'

Aithinne stiffens. Out of the corner of my eye, I see her hand curl into a fist. 'You *don't* help,' she says coldly. 'Never have.'

Sorcha, here to help? She can't honestly think we're daft enough to believe her. More than likely she's distracting us, preventing us from fleeing. I can hear Lonnrach and his soldiers drawing nearer. They'd be halfway down the path by now, moving faster.

'You want to help me?' I say. 'Get out of the way.'

Sorcha looks amused. 'Oh, believe me. There's nothing I'd love more than to see Lonnrach snap *your* pretty little neck.' She looks at Aithinne. 'You need to open the portal here. It's not going to close fast enough and he will just follow you right through. I'm here to make sure that doesn't happen.'

Aithinne narrows her eyes. 'And why should I trust you?'

'Well,' Sorcha says lightly. 'You have two choices: Trust me, or take your chances with my brother.' Her smile is cruel, cutting. 'The word is you're both *very* familiar with his ... *unique* methods of interrogation.'

I want to know everything. I just need to use your blood to see.

I can't help it. I step forward, pulling out my blade —

Aithinne puts a restraining hand on my shoulder. 'One day,' she breathes, too low for Sorcha to hear. Then a nod at Sorcha. 'Fine.' At Sorcha's smug look, she adds, 'But if you betray us, I will string you up by your intestines and make Prometheus's eternal punishment look like a stroll through the woods.'

For the first time, I see fear flicker in Sorcha's features. She's afraid of Aithinne. Sorcha glances at me and, as if sensing I've noticed, hardens her expression. 'I'll hold Lonnrach off with my powers for as long as I can without him seeing me.' At Aithinne's sharp look, Sorcha grins, fangs flashing. 'Wouldn't want to make an enemy of my brother.'

Aithinne shakes her head and pushes past the other faery to continue across the rocks.

'Oh, Aithinne?' Sorcha calls after us. Aithinne stops to listen. 'Just so you know, this changes nothing between us. My loyalty is to him. It always has been.'

Aithinne's jaw sets and I frown at her response. Before I can analyze Sorcha's words, Aithinne is already striding away and I'm forced to follow. We can't stay to see how she distracts Lonnrach and the other fae; we don't have time.

Aithinne leads the way to the other side of the ridge.

We're over the loch now, above the shimmering waters. The waves lap against the hard crags. She stops at the edge and looks over. 'Here. I have to open it here.'

My heart leaps. Surely she can't mean to jump. The drop to

the bottom must be more than four hundred feet – high enough that a fall would leave me dashed against the rocks.

'Right where we're standing, aye?' I say warily, dreading her answer. *Please say aye. Please say aye.*

Aithinne shakes her head and my hope wilts. 'About halfway down.' At my small sound of protest, she flashes a quick smile. 'The rules are simple again. Don't let go of me. Don't let yourself fall to the bottom. You'll likely die. See? Simple.'

I glare at her. 'We really need to review your definition of this word. I don't think it means what—'

Before I can blink, Aithinne grabs hold of me and I'm airborne. I let out an undignified yelp and grip her coat so hard that my hands ache. The air rushes around us, a deafening surge in my ears. We plummet down and down until I feel weightless, until it's as if we're flying and mist envelops us, thick and blinding white.

When I finally land, it's so much softer than I expect, just a light jolt. I roll down a gentle grassy slope and open my eyes to a cloudy grey sky.

A frigid wind blasts through the delicate material of my shift. It's still winter, then. It seems like I was gone so much longer. It smells of rain; the drops stick like ice to my skin.

Home. It smells like home. I made it. *I made it.*

I open my eyes with a smile – until I see the flat slope behind Aithinne. I frown. The ruins of St Anthony's Chapel used to be there. *Didn't they?* I rise slowly and ignore the dizziness as the blood rushes to my head.

'That's not right,' I whisper, unease slicing through me. 'It doesn't look right.'

It doesn't look like home.

The Queen's Park has changed since the battle. The landscape is altered – there are slopes in the hills where there shouldn't be, pockmarks across the land. The dirt path through the park is gone, and grass has grown tall over it, with patches of scorched, ink-black earth where the grass hasn't grown back; remnants of the battle fought here. Jagged rocks have risen up from the once flat meadow below Arthur's Seat.

I knew it would be different. I had been braced for it; I had told myself that if I ever escaped, I would have to be prepared to see the Edinburgh Lonnrach had only let me glimpse.

I'm not. I'm not ready, and I doubt I ever will be. But I *have* to see the rest.

'Falconer, I—'

Aithinne's words choke around her vow and I don't wait for her to try again. I take off running. I sprint up the slope for the view of the city.

The entire way, I replay the vision Lonnrach showed me. I prepare for the feelings that will lance through me – because what he showed me was a mere suggestion of the destruction. My thoughts are a litany of reassurances. I tell myself that I've seen it. That I've prepared. That I'll be all right.

I stumble and fall. Sharp rocks slice into my bare legs, but I haul myself up and keep going. Making it to the top of the crags is all I care about. I don't focus on the cold, or how my slippers can barely grip in the wet dirt. I slide down and keep going. I use my fingernails, sinking them into the mud to climb. When my slippers stick in the wet sludge, I leave them there and make my way up barefoot. My preparations are spoken aloud in harsh breaths. *It'll be all right. It'll be all right. It'll be all right because you're safe now and —*

I reach the top and drop to the ground on my knees. My chant sticks in my throat. None of it makes a difference, because no matter how much I thought I'd prepared, I'm not ready for what I see.

Below me, the city of Edinburgh lies in ruin.

Chapter 9

I can do nothing but stare at the sight below.

Whole buildings have been smashed; some are entirely gone and others left only partially standing. The once towering tenements of Old Town and Holyrood have been flattened, leaving nothing but piles of rubble.

Edinburgh's castle – a stronghold that survived siege after siege in this country's history – was once an imposing presence atop its own cliff at the centre of the city. Now it's been left in a pathetic state, with only the half-moon battery at the front still standing.

Below that, the damage in the newer parts of the city where I once lived is even more sporadic, some buildings left whole and others in various states of decay.

The battle is long over. So long, that nature has begun to claim the city. Weeds and grass and moss have grown throughout, a sign of the time that has passed. The disaster here – the Wild Hunt – was not recent. The city has been abandoned, grown over and left to crumble. The *daysweeksmonthsyears* I spent with Lonnrach in the *Sith-bhrùth* were slowed down in comparison to the time that has passed here. I dare not wonder how long it truly was.

I wasn't prepared for this. The vision of Edinburgh Lonnrach showed me was an immediate aftermath; the shower of ash from the sky and the thick smoke from the burning buildings was proof of that. It was a mere hint of the chaos.

The truth is, this is hell. Hell is seeing my home destroyed. It's knowing I tried so hard to prevent this destruction – and I couldn't.

The loneliness is back, an ache stretched vast inside me. I'm in the mirrored room with my various selves. My fingers press into my marks, playing each memory left behind by eighty-two teeth. Because that's all I have left of this place the way it was before I failed all my friends.

Tears scorch my eyes and sear paths down my cheeks. I avert my gaze from the sight before me and squeeze my eyes shut.

Aithinne moves to stand beside me. 'I couldn't warn you.'

'I told you; I already knew. He showed me,' I say, swallowing when my voice threatens to break.

'Knowing isn't the same as seeing,' Aithinne says softly. She rests a hand on my shoulder. 'You don't have to look. We can—'

I pull out of her grasp. 'No. No, I need to.'

All sense lost, I run toward the city. My feet pound through the dirt and grass as I make my way down the crags. Aithinne calls after me. Her voice is carried by the wind, her power trailing behind me in a soft, lingering caress across the back of my neck. I grimace at that brief inhuman touch, a reminder that she is one of *them*, and they destroyed everything.

I've never hated them more.

I splash through puddles along the slope of the crags. The skies have opened in a sudden downpour that slicks my skin and makes running all the more difficult.

When I finally reach the streets that once surrounded the Queen's Park and Holyroodhouse, my shift is soaking wet. My legs sting from various cuts and bruises but I hardly notice as I race along the thoroughfare now overgrown with weeds.

The palace itself has been decimated, the once beautiful towers destroyed. All that remains are scorched black bricks and a few pieces of wall from the quadrangle still left standing. Fragments from the nave of the beautiful abbey that had once graced the property lie in pieces on the ground, covered in moss and grass.

I sprint past it all, up to what was once the centre of the city. My feet pound across dirt and rock, but I don't stop – not even to look at the destruction any more. If I pause for even a moment, I'll have to remember that I failed. Kiaran and I tried to prevent this, and we didn't succeed – I didn't succeed. And Lonnrach's army destroyed it all.

You sacrificed my realm to save yours.

Now nothing remains but the surrounding rubble; a city that has been entirely demolished and left to ruin. The earth has come to reclaim it in vines and moss that now cover everything.

Home. I have to go home. The North Bridge is still only half-standing – the result of my fight with the redcap. The city workers never had time to rebuild it.

Don't think about it. Keep going.

I take the long route up what used to be the High Street, past the collapsed stone buildings of Old Town, and make my way to the underside of the castle crags. My feet are sore and wet with blood, slapping against stone with every step.

It isn't until I reach New Town – where Charlotte Square once stood – that I even pause. The square is deathly silent, no birds or animals rustling amid the rubble. There is only me, my body trembling, the sound of my panting from running so hard.

My house ... god, my home – it's still standing, but it's hollow, empty. The foundations groan as I approach, as if the structure could cave in at any moment.

It's far too dangerous to enter, but I approach the white-columned abode anyway. I slip through the overgrown grass that peeks between the cobblestones. The front door is propped ajar. Dust falls and the door creaks on its hinges, resisting as I push my way inside.

Destroyed. It's entirely destroyed, as if something came

through here with immense force. Splintered wood litters the beautiful Persian rug that once graced the antechamber, now ruined by dust and soot and dirt. My mother's paintings – her beautiful Scottish seaside views – are in pieces on the floor, stained and barely visible beneath the mold.

It doesn't smell like home. My father's scent doesn't linger at all, not even the aroma of pipe smoke that always remained in the hallway no matter how long he'd been gone. My home smells empty, as though no one has lived here for a number of years. As though no one has even *been* here for years.

I sense Aithinne behind me without hearing her approach. I choke back the sudden taste of her faery power. She's so silent, the way Kiaran is. I don't even hear her breathe.

I'm ready to ask. I have to. 'How long was I in the *Sìth-bhrùth*?' I try to keep my voice steady and barely succeed.

The *daysweeksmonthsyears* stretched on so long that, like Lonnrach, I had no concept of time. There was nothing to measure it, no clocks to give me a sense of its length. Even if I spent a short while with Lonnrach – no matter how long it felt – the days would have gone by more rapidly here.

Aithinne sighs. 'It would have only been weeks for you there. Seven or eight at the most.'

'Don't do that,' I say sharply. 'Don't pretend to misunderstand me. How much time passed out *here*, Aithinne?'

'You know I can't say.'

'Then find a way to tell me. The plant growth out there couldn't have happened in a short amount of time, I know that much.'

'*Daoine sìth* are more connected to the earth than most *sìthichean*,' she says. 'When the others escaped the mounds, they would have influenced nature without meaning to—'

'Aithinne.' My hands curl into fists. Violent Aileana is in my mind, smiling, encouraging my anger. I try to tamp it down, to put her back where she belongs. 'I said find a way to tell me.'

'Months,' she whispers. Even with that, her voice trembles around the vow.

The trees here couldn't have grown in mere months even with the fae affecting growth. The vines couldn't have overtaken whole buildings. They could only have done that in the span of years – and years consist of *months*. The fae are experts at deceptive language.

'No tricks.' I don't bother to keep the sharpness out of my tone. I'm finished with faery vows and riddles and secrets. 'No half-lies. *How long?*'

I turn to her, then. I let my rage show, the Violent Aileana Lonnrach saw inside me. *We're the same, you and I.* I'm past reason, past all sense. I am the inhuman thing he saw who mirrors his own. Now I know that grief has carved parts of me hollow. It let in the darkness, and now it's marked in my bones. A sleeping beast.

I issue a single command: 'Count. Count how many years.'

Aithinne's silence seems to last forever, her expression uncertain. Finally, she begins. 'One.' Her voice trembles, her breath catching. 'Two.' The word seizes in her throat and I almost tell her to stop. 'Three.' The last word. A simple word that leaves her doubled over, coughing until blood splatters across her trousers.

'Three years,' I whisper. I should have helped her, checked to see if she was all right. I can't. Violent Aileana recedes and I'm left in shock. *Three years. Three. Years.*

'Falconer,' she gasps. 'Wait.'

I barely hear her. My vision is tunneled as I climb the creaky stairs. The hook that once held our family portrait is still there at the top of the stairs, stark against the dusty, torn wallpaper.

I step over the destroyed portraits of my ancestors, reaching the door of my bedroom. It looks as though it's been ransacked. Glass fragments from the overhead lamps litter the ground amid the dirt and dust. The roof itself has caved in partially just above the frame of my bed. It's left the space open to the elements, and everything smells musty. Not even pigeons would deign to live in such a horrid place.

In the corner, the helm from an old schooner that once hung on the far wall is lying on the floor in pieces. The furniture is broken and discarded, the colour blackened with mold.

'Lonnrach will be looking for you,' Aithinne says, her voice hoarse. She comes up beside me and wipes the blood from her lips. 'We have to leave. It isn't safe here.'

I hear her but the words barely register through my shock. As if she's speaking to me across a vast valley.

I approach my closet, where the tattered remains of my silk dresses are thrown about, the fabric brittle and torn. It smells putrid from the layers upon layers of dust and old fabric. Beneath it all, I spot the corner of my locked trunk.

I shove all that old, disgusting fabric aside – it almost disintegrates in my hands – and unlatch the trunk. *Please still be in here. Please still be in here.*

Tears burn my eyes when I pull open the lid and see my mother's tartan sash. It's still there, unchanged and protected by the airtight casing. I draw it out and the scent of coarse wool remains the same, unpolluted by dust.

A hint of my father's lingering pipe smoke fills my senses and I come undone. I sink to my knees and fight against the tears. *Don't cry*, I tell myself like always. *Don't cry.*

I wrap my hands around the tartan and press it to my face. I try to remember. I try so hard, but the images of my former life don't come. It isn't until I scrape my fingernails across Lonnrach's marks on my arms that the images of my mother return. This mark is her smile. This mark is her laugh. This mark is a thousand little moments and words and deeds that said *I love you* and *You are precious* and *You matter.*

And I can't recall a single one of them on my own.

'I can't remember,' I say to Aithinne, knowing she's still lingering there. 'Not on my own any more.'

Wordlessly, Aithinne kneels beside me and peeks in the trunk. 'Oh, good. Sensible clothes.' She reaches to draw out the trousers, shirt, coat, and boots I kept inside. My old faery hunting garments. 'Put these on. We have to go. Kadamach will be wondering why we never came out of the portal where we should have.'

This house is all I have of my mother and my former life. If my memories are fading, there will be nothing to remind me. I've already lost everyone I love and the mementos in this house are the only physical remnants left. Once I leave ...

'Not yet,' I say. 'Just a few more minutes.'

Aithinne glances at me impatiently, looking very much like her brother. 'We don't have time for this.'

She reaches for me then, but I jerk away. 'Don't,' I say sharply. 'Don't touch me.'

Lonnrach used to reach for me like that, grasp my shoulder hard if I didn't move fast enough.

I don't miss the hurt that flashes in her gaze, as if she can read my mind. 'I need to heal you,' she says carefully, her hands up as if she were approaching a feral animal. 'Your feet are bleeding, I can smell the venom on you again, and we have to run.'

I'm always running. It never stops. Lonnrach has imprinted himself on my life the same way his sister has. She might have taken my mother, but he's the monster in the darkness. He's stealing my soul piece by piece, scraping the parts of my life away until there's nothing left.

Now you know precisely how it feels to be that helpless.

'Why can't I remember?' I ask Aithinne, not moving when she presses her hands to my temples. Her touch is gentle, deliberate, the way one might treat an injured bird.

'You can,' she tells me. Her eyes are steady, calm. 'But he's left his imprint on your mind. Each memory has faded with his influence. If you want, I can help.'

'Help?'

The prickling pain of her healing starts. At first I flinch, but then I let it wash over me, a calming influence. *Still here. Still alive. This is mine. I still have this.* I can form new memories over the old ones.

Once my injuries are healed and the sting of venom has receded, Aithinne pulls away. She is breathing hard, a thin line of blood trailing down her chin from her earlier coughing spell.

'Aileana.'

She says my name. Just my name. It's been so long since I heard it, I had almost forgotten I had a name at all. Lonnrach always called me *Falconer*. Until that word was the only thing I had left that belonged to me. *Falconer*, an insult. *Falconer*, a thing. *Falconer*, a duty. And I'm a girl. I'm just a girl. Aileana Kameron. Kam.

Aithinne tells me, 'I can help you forget.' At my unasked question, she says, 'What Lonnrach did to you. The place he kept you.' She glances down at my marks. 'I can make it so you believe you got these in the battle.'

God help me, I'm tempted. I don't shake my head or say no. Not even when she places her hands on either side of my face again – her fingers twisting in my hair – and shuts her eyes.

Her power warms beneath my skin, soothing, comforting. My memories of that place begin to fade around the edges, blurring like fog-covered glass. She's taking them into herself, stealing them from me – just like Lonnrach.

I want to know everything. I'll take every memory you have, if that's what it takes.

'Stop.' I tear out of her grasp and suddenly I'm back here in the ruins of my home. 'They're my memories to bear,' I tell her. 'Not yours.'

Aithinne wipes the blood from her lips again, pressing her sleeve there. Disbelief is evident in her features. 'You think you deserve what happened, don't you?'

I grip the tartan in my mud-caked hands, remembering why I left it in the trunk before the battle. I felt my mother wouldn't like the person I had become. A part of me hoped I would save the city and finally – *finally* – be worthy to wear it.

I felt guilt for the longest time after failing that night of the Wild Hunt. A part of me still does.

Before I can respond, Aithinne says, 'There is nothing you went through that I haven't already endured. Lonnrach had two thousand years to break me and he never could.'

She tries reaching for me again. Even when I shrink away, she keeps her hand out, palm up. An offering. An absolution. 'You were captured while performing a task that was never meant for you alone. You aren't responsible for what Kadamach and I started. That's why I'm offering to carry them for you.'

I almost ask her what she means, but the words don't come out. I stare at her outstretched palm and nearly take it.

Now you know precisely how it feels to be that helpless.

That's why I should never allow myself to forget. I'll never be that helpless again. 'No.' I swallow back the lump in my throat. 'I won't do that to you.'

Did he do this? Like mine?

Worse. He did worse.

'You,' she tells me, her gaze never leaving mine, 'are extra-ordinary.'

I smile wryly, forced. 'For a human?'

She returns my smile. 'It's just that now I see why Kadamach wanted me to move heaven and earth to find you.' She passes me the clothes and boots. 'Now get dressed. We need to hurry.'

She leaves the closet, shutting the broken remains of the door and offering me some semblance of privacy.

Now I see why Kadamach wanted me to move heaven and earth to find you.

No, I can't think about what that means right now. My relationship with Kiaran is another complication I can't even begin to fathom.

Quickly, I remove my torn shift, its light material like a

whisper across my bare skin. Despite all it's been through, the fae material is still soft as ever, perfect for bandages if I need. I fold it up and stuff it in my coat pocket.

The cotton shirt I pull over my head is so rough in comparison, and the raploch trousers and coat are even worse. But I would still rather wear my own clothes – as rough and worn as they are – than the delicate material that reminds me so much of Sorcha. After a moment's hesitation, I tuck my mother's tartan into my coat pocket, too. I can't leave it here.

I sit on the damp floorboards to pull on the boots. I lace them, then grab the only weapon in the trunk – my self-loading blunderbuss, still snug in the holster that fits across my back. It was one of the first weapons I made to kill the fae, perfect for an untrained lady. As long as I was close enough to my target, the ammunition sprayed wide and I never missed, even when my hands shook.

I empty the remains of *seilgflùr* from the blunderbuss's hold. The thistle inside would never be effective after three years.

Three years three years *three years* —

Focus. I pull the fabric-wrapped *seilgflùr* Aithinne brought me from the pouch at my wrist and deftly tear up the petals to deposit into a compartment in the altered blunderbuss. Then I click the hold shut and stuff the weapon in its holster, adjusting it so the strap is firm across my chest.

Boom. I'm startled by a noise in the distance, like a cannon going off. I press my fingers to the floor, surprised to find a slight tremor there. The puddle of water near the door is unsettled into ripples.

'Aithinne?'

Just as I call for her, the distant, heavy rumbles start to grow louder and closer with each second. The room begins to shake, the structure groaning. *Boom. Boom. Boom boom boom.* The old dresses shudder on their hooks. From the other side of the door, something falls to the ground and shatters.

Aithinne bursts in, nearly ripping the door from its hinges. Her eyes glow bright as she ushers me through. 'They're here. We have to go *now*.'

BOOM. BOOM. The entire house is quaking now. Dust falls all around us from the weakened rafters. At the back of the room, a piece of the wall falls to the floor and breaks apart.

'What *is* that?' I ask as I follow her from the room. The explosions are so loud that I can barely hear myself speak. I grab the balustrade for balance and it wobbles beneath my hand as we descend the stairs.

An awful crashing drowns out Aithinne's response. Rock and wood splinter above us, and then the roof caves in.

Chapter 10

$\mathcal{A}$ ithinne's body crashes hard into mine. She rolls us to the ground, fallen detritus digging into my back. Debris drops all around us. A stone slab smashes into Aithinne so hard that the bones in her body would have shattered had she been human.

We're pressed against the building, buried under rubble. A curved slab of the collapsed staircase blocked the fallen ceiling from crushing my limbs. I see nothing but a few spots of daylight between the remains.

There's a moment's silence, stark and heavy. No more distant rumbles, no falling rock.

'Aithinne,' I whisper. 'Are you—'

Then I hear it – what sounds like a mechanical whirring – and something crashes through the rubble to pick Aithinne right from off top of me.

'*Run!*' she screams.

I look up, my muscles braced for a fight – and freeze. *What in god's name is that?*

A mechanical creature, at least thirty feet tall, towers over the remains of Charlotte Square. It's built like a redcap, with thick limbs and long, hanging arms, but it appears made from the dark metal I saw in the *Sith-bhrùth*, all smooth and semi-reflective with ebony liquid pushing through the veins of its giant hands.

It's covered in black armour, the plates glistening as if

created from polished obsidian. Between the links of armour at the creature's core, a bright blue light pulses like a heartbeat. When it reaches its other hand toward me, I see a whirring mechanism in the centre of its palm, the pieces moving fast and glinting with blinding light.

With a sharp cry, Aithinne wrenches out of its grasp, ripping her coat right down the back. 'Run!' she screams at me again. 'It's activating its weapon!'

We shove our way out of the rubble, vaulting over a collapsed wall of the house and into the back garden. The whirring grows louder, a constant hum that rings in my ears.

The creature is right behind us, its massive treads shaking the ground beneath our feet. I look back in time to see it reach for us with its weaponless hand, and I yank Aithinne out of the way just in time, pulling her through the ruins of an empty house on the street.

The creature crashes through easily, sending brick and dust flying. Aithinne and I pick up speed, flying across the cobbles.

Aithinne tries to shout something, but the humming is deafening. We scramble through the overgrown shrubs and vault over the garden wall.

The weapon must be almost ready now – just over the hum I can hear parts clicking and locking into place.

Aithinne shouts again, this time pulling me closer to put her lips at my ear. 'We need to find shelter to block the blast. *Now!*'

Her power is rough in my mouth. It's not like the usual flower petals and honey – now it's thorns and smoke. Strong and over-powering. She's readying something of her own.

At the top of the street, I spot a stone wall left standing. *There!*

I pull Aithinne with me, gesturing to the wall. The ground beneath me quakes and I'm nearly thrown off-balance. We throw ourselves behind the wall and I tuck my knees tight into my chest, keeping my head down.

Aithinne locks her arms around my shoulders. I'm startled

by her eyes, the whirling silver glow of her irises that only grows brighter.

She mouths something and this time I don't need to hear. 'Hold on tight.'

Aithinne's power scorches my tongue and paves a path of fire down my throat. I've never felt anything like it. It intensifies just as a near-deafening blast sends dust, dirt, and debris flying all around me. I hold my breath, cradling myself tighter. The wall behind me shudders and strains. My hearing is muffled, a ringing resounding inside my ears.

Then, silence. A heavy stillness. Aithinne's power ebbs, leaving a dry coating inside my mouth. I raise my head. I'm completely covered in dirt and fine dust.

Crawling out, I peek around the wall and gasp. There's nothing there. *Nothing.* Every building in the square was obliterated by the metal creature's weapon. All that remains are smoking piles of brick and a crater of blackened dirt where my home once stood.

The fallen creature lies on its back amid the rubble, blown back by the force of the explosion.

'What did you do?' I whisper to Aithinne.

Aithinne pushes to her feet, dusting off her clothes. 'I redirected its blast away from us so it used its weapon on itself.' She scans the destruction. 'Easy.'

'Ah, yes,' I murmur, trying to quell the emotions that rush through me at seeing my childhood home destroyed. 'Simple's sibling, Easy. I don't even want to imagine the levels of chaos that would prompt visits from their cousins Straightforward and Uncomplicated.'

The creature's limbs begin to twitch, its metal bones clicking back into place. I reach for the blunderbuss on my back, but Aithinne is already ahead of me. She has her sword in her hand before I can blink.

'If you'll excuse me …'

She strides over to the creature. In a single, clean motion, she rams her sword into its neck. The creature immediately stops moving. Then she's walking back to me, muttering, 'That bloody bastard Lonnrach. I can't believe he sent a *mortair*—'

There's another distant explosion. We turn and see another *mortair* running toward us with incredible speed. It rounds the castle crags, long arms pumping by its sides. With every leap, the ruins of old buildings in its path are pulverized. Its massive body tears through brick walls like paper. It'll be upon us in seconds.

'Go!' Aithinne pulls me with her. 'Don't stop running.'

'What is that thing?' I can barely hear myself over the creature behind us.

'*Mortair*,' she gasps. 'They only have one purpose: Seek and destroy.'

We're not fast enough. Rather, *I'm* not. Aithinne is slowing down for me to catch up. My human speed can't ever match hers, or the *mortair's*. It's gaining on us, the ground shaking as it runs. The hum of its weapon quickens to an agitating trill and I glance back as it raises its hand, the metal shifting to a blinding light in its palm as it aims.

The direct blast slams into Aithinne. *BOOM*. Light surrounds us and the ground beneath us cracks and breaks with the impact. I'm thrown back by it, my body slamming into the cobblestones. I roll hard, my shoulder landing painfully on a fragment of brick. Aithinne's sword skitters across the street just out of my reach.

I look up as the light clears. Aithinne is on the ground, bruised and bloodied all over. Her eyes are glazed over with pain.

I can't stand this any more. I push to my feet, pulling the blunderbuss from my back holster before I even think. It's the simplest thing in the world. Hunt and kill, the game I've played since the night my mother died.

'Falconer, *don't*!'

Aithinne reaches for me, but I dart out of her grasp. The creature is still advancing toward us, moving breathtakingly fast.

It's reached the ruins of Charlotte Square now, racing down the street right for me.

With Aithinne injured, the *mortair* won't draw its weapon again, not if Lonnrach needs me alive. That makes it vulnerable – I can hurt it, but it can't hurt me.

I'll leave it for Lonnrach to find. A message: *I'm not yours. You don't have me any more. The next time we meet, you'll realise that I'm the one who's going to end you.*

I let the creature come to me. The ground quakes as I plant the base of the blunderbuss against my shoulder and aim for its legs. I let out a slow breath to calm myself. As the creature approaches, I have to readjust my aim: up and up and up.

There. Just before it reaches me, I pull the trigger.

The blunderbuss recoils into my shoulder hard enough to bruise. The air fills with smoke between the *mortair* and I. I watch as the *seilgflùr*-laced scrap metal sprays wide and blasts into the *mortair*'s armour.

The smoke clears and the creature is still standing. There isn't a mark on the obsidian plates that cover its chest. Christ, the blunderbuss didn't even cause a dent with the *seilgflùr*. It should have. It should have worked. The *mortair* raises the weapon in its palm at me … 'Oh, hell,' I whisper, backing away. My hand goes to the hilt of my blade and I pull it out, ready to fight. 'Hell.'

'I gave a simple instruction,' Aithinne says from behind me. '*Don't*. Which means *Don't do that; it's a bad idea*. Nothing can break its armour except my own blade.'

'What?'

The mechanism grows brighter and brighter, a blinding sun in the centre of the *mortair*'s hand.

Nothing can break its armour except my own blade. Then my only option is to disable the *mortair*'s weapon. Before it can act, I sheath my own weapon and snatch Aithinne's sword from the ground.

Then I'm on my feet, leaping at the *mortair*. I aim to slash at the *mortair's* weapon hand, but the creature turns at the last second. The blade slices through its other hand, severing it right at the wrist in a single, clean swipe. The metal piece arcs into the air and hits the ground with a mighty thump.

The *mortair* roars, a ghastly high-pitched, mechanical whine. Its jaw opens so wide that the clockwork structure of metal in its throat is visible, the jagged pieces of its teeth.

Its foot sends a massive chunk of wall flying and I narrowly avoid getting hit.

'Falconer!'

My moment of distraction is all the *mortair* needs. It takes a swing at me, but Aithinne puts herself between us. The *mortair* knocks her off her feet and she smashes through the remains of a stone building across the square. Bricks collapse on top of her.

The *mortair* advances on me, the light in its palm brightening. Soon it will release its destructive weapon and I'm trapped; there's nowhere to go. Steeling myself, I leap at the *mortair*, arcing the blade into the air to try and sever its weapon hand again.

Metal breaks beneath my sword, but I didn't curve the blade high enough to detach the limb. With a growl, the *mortair* knocks into me. I roll to the ground, using the momentum to land cleanly on my feet. I spin out of the *mortair's* reach, slashing with the sword again, and I catch its armoured finger at the knuckle. The screech of breaking metal echoes across the square, and the finger lands in the overgrown grass.

Before the creature can recover, I launch myself at it, climbing up its plated armour. The *mortair* thrashes and tries to throw me off, but it's too damaged to make a grab for me. It growls deep within its clockwork throat, the sound vibrating through its body.

The blade almost slides from my grip, but I recover, taking advantage of the swinging motion of its body to lever myself up.

Aithinne shouts, 'You have to slit its throat!'

The *mortair* aims for a building and scrapes its large body through the rubble to crush me. I swing down at the last second and grab an armoured plate on the underside of its arm as the *mortair* smashes through. Its armour takes the brunt of the impact, destroying the side wall of the building.

While it's occupied, I grasp the scale-like armour, pulling myself up plate by plate. My muscles burn with the effort, my limbs trembling to keep hold. The plates are warm beneath my palms, textured like rough rock instead of smooth metal.

The creature bucks to throw me off, but I leap up to its left pectoral. The whirring mechanisms inside its body are deafening, a hum of clockwork beneath my palms. The blue light between the strong plates is hot and blinding as I climb past the cracks in its armour.

Finally, I reach the *mortair's* shoulder. I hang on with one hand and aim for its neck. My blade slashes and bites through what feels like skin between the armoured plates.

I don't stop. I hack and hack until the metal insides give way, and even then I don't let up. The creature sways beneath me. I pause only when it falls, maintaining my hold as it slams into the grass and dirt in the square below. I continue my assault. I slice through more metal. I slash until I'm out of breath, until I'm covered in its thick ebony blood. Until tears sear my cheeks and my muscles ache.

Until the *mortair's* head lies in a heap of scrap, severed and destroyed.

Then I reach to draw the fae fabric out of my coat pocket, and slice off a long piece. I slide a strip beneath one of the plates of the *mortair's* armour so the fabric drapes across its face like a shroud.

So it's the first thing Lonnrach sees when he comes looking.

This is my message. I picture him finding the fallen, mutilated *mortair. I don't belong to you and I never will. I spent* daysweeks- monthsyears *picturing this, and now I'll wait for it. I'll wait for you. I'll savour the moment when we meet again.*

Because this is how I long to kill you.

Chapter 11

*a*ithinne comes to stand silently beside me. Black blood drips from my fingertips, splattered like ink across my clothes. It smells so strongly of iron and scorched metal, as if her sword had seared its way through.

The *mortair*'s head is at my feet. The clockwork pieces are still gleaming, the fae metal more polished and bright than even the smoothest metal I've seen. The rest of its body is naught but a pile of obsidian armour. I would have admired the craftsmanship once. I would have wished for the talent to build something like this.

Now, I don't care about the skill that went into creating the *mortair*. I don't care about the kill, not even a little. I don't give a damn.

All I can do is assess the *mortair*'s interior parts, its pinions and gears and rivets. It's familiar. It's the same beautiful metal as the seal Aithinne had built. 'You made them, didn't you?' I say flatly. 'The *mortair*.'

Aithinne is so still, as if she isn't breathing at all. 'Aye.' She sounds casual, as if we had just taken a walk through the park.

'Lonnrach just sent one of your inventions to attack us,' I say, 'and you don't sound the least troubled by it.'

'He knows the *mortair* are unparalleled at seeking.' She looks fondly at it. 'I didn't build them to be terribly intelligent, but they're quite useful. I had them slaughter more than a dozen soldiers in mere seconds once. They're such loyal companions.'

I stare at her in shock. 'Remind me never to anger you.'

Aithinne smiles serenely. 'I was a very formidable' – she stops speaking abruptly, as if she was about to say something she shouldn't; then – 'inventor.'

What the devil had she been about to say?

As if sensing my unasked question, Aithinne starts down the road, her movements slow from her injuries. 'We need to keep moving. Lonnrach won't be far behind and we have to meet Kadamach outside the city.'

Kadamach. I think of kissing Kiaran, the desperate hard crush of his lips against my own. The heat rises to my cheeks just remembering it. I follow her, my boots silent on the moss-covered cobblestones. 'I thought Lonnrach needed me alive. Why would he send an assassin?'

'It was here to incapacitate me and find *you*,' Aithinne corrects. 'You interfered with its second mission when you protected me.' She glances back at the remains of her invention, at the ink-black blood splattered across the rubble. 'Sending my own weapon was a message. A declaration to me.'

'How very sentimental,' I say as we make our way down the battered thoroughfare to the west end of the city. 'I particularly enjoyed the part where it smacked you off your arse and clear across the square through a building.'

'Arse.' Aithinne's face breaks into a smile. 'Your language is very expressive, especially the swear words. I'm quite fond of fu—'

'Good god!' I glance at her. 'What on earth has Kiaran been teaching you?'

'That one,' Aithinne says proudly, 'I learned in the mounds. Part of it was below an inn where they played fiddles and sang vulgar songs with *that* word. You can put the sword away now.'

I hadn't realised I was still holding it. The blade drips black blood onto the street as we descend the long hill to Dean Village and the Water of Leith. The destruction is less apparent in this part of the city; it was already overgrown with trees and vines before the Wild Hunt.

I hold out the weapon to Aithinne, hilt first, but she shakes her head. 'You keep it,' she says. 'I should have given it to you before.'

'Why?' It's a powerful weapon to give away so lightly.

Before I can blink, she has my wrist in a vicelike grip, pulling me to a halt. Gone is her smile, and with it our easygoing conversation – which had helped me forget, just for a moment, that we are surrounded by the ruins of my city.

Her eyes are so intense now, the way Kiaran's get just before a battle. Despite her human-like body, she's still fae, and a faery's temper can come as quick and fierce as a storm. When I'm with Kiaran, I forget that about him sometimes; now I've done the same with his sister.

I should never forget. For my own protection, I can't make that mistake.

I try to pull away, to ignore the way my heart begins to race. She has me by the wrist. *By the wrist.* I can't stop the sudden flash of Lonnrach opening his mouth to bare his teeth, his grip hard, fingers over my pulse.

This is really going to hurt.

As if sensing my memory, Aithinne's hold loosens. She tugs open my fingers until my palm is visible. My blood is smeared across my skin, mixed with the ink-black of the *mortair*.

'*Fuil nan aiteam chathach,*' she tells me firmly, her eyes never wavering from my own. As if willing me to understand. 'This is the blood of your lineage. I made blades for all the Falconers, and now it's the only one of its kind left – just like you.' She presses the hilt into my hand and closes my fingers around it. 'Consider it an apology.'

'For what?'

'For everything,' she says softly.

With that, she releases me and walks away, a slight limp to her stride. I follow her, my injuries beginning to ache now.

I have questions for her – so many that I don't know where to begin or what, really, to ask. *Later,* I decide. When we are out of immediate danger and I have time to think.

If such a time ever comes.

I stay silent as we travel through the village of Dean, where the grass between the cobbles reaches our knees and thick vines cover the destroyed buildings around us. Nature has claimed the once picturesque village, as if humans left this place centuries ago. Without anyone here to tame the ivy and foliage, the plants and trees have blossomed freely.

The few buildings left standing are overtaken, marble and stone cracking and breaking under the onslaught of vines and roots. After all the trouble Edinburgh went through to make the city clean and immaculate, now it's a ruin.

I'm exhausted by the time Aithinne and I reach the Water of Leith. This place used to be surrounded by quaint stone cottages, raised up along the banks and nestled in the valley the river runs through. Now the buildings have gone, and only thick trees and the occasional traces of old walls remain.

This is where I met Kiaran. I so naively went on my first hunt – and found my intended victim, an *each-uisge.* I attacked the water-horse with an iron blade, the metal I discovered to be useless against fae. The creature nearly drowned me. Without Kiaran's intervention I would have died that night and the Falconer lineage would have gone extinct with me.

Right there. I'm surprised by the memory, one less faded by Lonnrach's influence. Water rushes over my boots, but I pay it no mind. *That's where it happened.*

I haven't been here since that night, but I recognise the rock formations, how they jut out of the water near one of the falls. The water-horse attacked me there. I can still taste the river water at the back of my throat, the grit of dirt on my tongue as I fought back.

'Falconer?'

I ignore Aithinne and slowly make my way along the bank until I reach the spot where the water-horse tried to pull me under. I disregard my aching muscles to crouch next to the rock and rest my fingertips on the jagged top. Four years have passed here since that night and the ridges are still so sharp. I vividly remember how the *each-uisge* dragged me into the river, the skin at my back sliced open on the vicious edge.

I swear I can see the stain of my blood on the rock, now rust-coloured and faded to become part of the stone. My injury from that night took forever for the mechanical stitchers to close.

I still bear the scar, spanning from my neck to lower back. My badge of survival. My first one. There was no going back to my old life after that. It's my brand now, a claim on my soul. *Falconer.*

'I tried to kill my first faery here, just after Sorcha murdered my mother,' I tell Aithinne. 'I nearly died.'

Aithinne crouches in the water next to me, so at ease despite the cold. It's as if she doesn't even notice how the water runs over her boots and dampens her trousers. Her gaze is like Kiaran's, so startling and intense.

This close, I notice a scar on her forehead just beneath her hairline. Long and thin, the mark is so faded it's barely notice-able. I wonder what might have caused it.

'Where I come from,' Aithinne says, resting her hand on the rock just over the bloodstain, 'the first hunt is considered a trial. We call it *là na cruaidh-chuis*, the day of hardship. Before we come into our powers, every *daoine sìth* must go into the forest and kill a stag without a weapon, without our strength and speed, our mind connected to the animal.'

I'm beginning to realise how much Kiaran never told me about the fae. 'I never knew that.'

Aithinne's smile is quick, fleeting. 'No human does,' she says. 'During my own hunt, I saw through the stag's eyes. A quickly turning world, limited in colour but bursting with life. We ran together. We drank from a stream. For that day, I was a wild creature, untamed. But there came the moment I had to take its life.'

She closes her eyes, remembering. 'I had my hands around its neck and felt everything it did – the press of my fingers, its struggle to breathe. I'll never forget when it sank its teeth into my shoulder, somehow managing to break the skin. I had never seen my own blood before.'

Aithinne stops and I wonder if she'll continue. I'm holding my breath. 'What happened?'

'I understood the true purpose of the trial, my first hunt.' She raises her eyes to mine. 'It teaches us what it means to be hunter and prey. To make the choice to kill or be killed.' With a firm grip on her shirt, Aithinne pulls the fabric down to bare her shoulder – the scar there, teeth marks pressed into her flawless skin. 'Now we both carry that lesson with us, don't we, Falconer?'

She pushes to her feet and I follow her down the river a way. 'Do some fae fail the trial?'

Aithinne walks with her hands in her pockets. Now that her injuries from the *mortair* have healed, she moves across the rocks with graceful speed and agility. 'Aye. Others pass and only come out worse.' She glances at me. 'Many *sithichean* fear death, and yet they consider mortality to be a weakness. One that ought to be reserved for humans and the creatures of this realm alone. They learn the wrong lesson.'

'What's the right lesson, then?' I ask, curious now.

'In the end, we are all the stag,' she says simply.

We continue downstream. My injuries slow me down, but Aithinne is patient. Both of us are quiet for the longest time. It seems like hours go by. The winter sun is low on the horizon, shining its last vestiges of light through the skeletal branches.

We still don't speak. Our journey is filled with the roar of water falling over rocks, the soft rain pattering against stone and bare trees. Kiaran and I used to walk like this, lost in our thoughts, content with the silence.

Aithinne's presence is so different from his, less intense. Her eyes rove over the landscape as if she's memorizing every rock and tree and branch, as if she hungers to see more.

I've never seen anyone so entranced. Her step has a lightness that Kiaran's never did. Sometimes a small smile plays on her lips as if something has delighted her. Her fingertips brush the branches as we stride by, lingering on the trunks of the trees.

After all that time Aithinne spent in the mounds surrounded by dirt, it must be wonderful for her to walk above ground again. I'm surprised that being trapped with enemy fae hasn't affected her the way it has me. That she could offer to take my memories as if the burden of them meant nothing at all.

There is nothing you went through that I haven't already endured. Lonnrach had two thousand years to break me and he never could.

'How do you bear what Lonnrach did to you?' I whisper. It takes me a second to realise I've spoken aloud and I wince.

Aithinne heard me. She falters in the middle of a jump and loses her footing on a rock, splashing into the cold river water. In the last lingering bit of sunlight, I see her stricken expression, the way she curls her hands into fists at her sides so tightly that her knuckles are white.

'Aithinne?' When she doesn't answer, I try to apologize. What's *wrong* with me? 'I'm sorry. I should never have—'

'Don't,' she snaps. Her shuddered breath slices through the air between us. I watch her struggle with the memory, not knowing what to do. *Wishing* I knew what to do. 'Don't come near me.'

Drip. Drip. Oh god, blood from her closed fists hits the rocks by her feet. *Drip. Drip.*

I grasp her arms. The blood drips onto the rocks so fast now, streaming through her hands. '*Aithinne.*'

Aithinne stares at me. 'I'm fine.' Her expression has gone cold, emotionless, and shut off. 'It doesn't hurt,' she says mechanically, as if she's repeated it every day of her life. *It doesn't hurt*, I remember her whispering on the trail. Her mantra.

I stare at her dumbly for a moment, then take her hands and pry her fingers open. I can't help flinching at the sight. Her palm is marred with half-moon marks, dug so deep that the flesh is peeling away. Blood pools there, so dark against her pale skin.

As I watch, the skin begins to heal, leaving nothing but blood behind. 'It always heals,' she tells me in that awful dead voice. 'See? It always heals.'

I don't say anything. I can't. I know from experience the lies we tell to comfort ourselves, to comfort others, so others never realise how broken we really are.

My scars are all on the outside; what I went through is bared for the world to see. Aithinne's scars are so well hidden that she fooled me.

The truth is, memories weigh a great deal. Each one bends your bones a little more until the heft of them wears you down. Now I know that some scars go so deep that they never fade.

Chapter 12

L ong after nightfall, we are far beyond the limits of the city. We walk through overgrown grass in fields that were once prosperous farmland. In winter, the land outside Edinburgh would always be bare, ready to be tilled before the growing season.

I remember how ravens would gather in the soil, all black flapping wings and sharp laughter. Now the rapeseed and weeds are so unkempt that they reach my hips. No animals rustle through the fields; it's quiet around us but for the soft patter of rain.

I follow Aithinne's steps carefully. The only light in the field is from the moon peeking through the thick rain clouds overhead. Its halo burns through the clouds, tinged a rust red. I try not to think of how seeing it like that reminds me so much of the battle, of saying my goodbyes to those I loved.

I never thought I would be responsible for … *this*. All of this. Before the battle I tried not to think too much about what the human realm would be like if I lost. I always assumed I would never live to see a world taken over by the fae. That I would die before I let that happen.

You sacrificed my realm to save yours.

My chest tightens. *Stop thinking about it,* I tell myself. *Keep going. One foot forward. Now the other.* That's how I hold it all back, every ounce of regret. One step and then another, over and over again.

Aithinne pauses for a moment, brushing her fingers along the tops of the weeds. She's been so quiet since the river. She washed the blood off her hands and hasn't spoken to me since. Now she has her head tilted as if she's listening for something. It's so dark I can't make out her expression. She breathes deeply once, twice.

Her voice startles me. 'Just up ahead.'

Before I can ask her anything, she's starting forward again, her steps quick. I follow her, wading through the tall grass. There's nothing in front of us but fog, so thick around us that the moisture presses against my skin, my face, dripping down my eyelashes. I can barely see more than a few steps in front of us.

Something is silhouetted in the fog, three figures in the dark – animals. Horses? Once I notice the light that emanates from them, I stop abruptly.

The faery horses are as beautiful now as they were the night the fae army rode into Edinburgh. They are alight from within, the metal that holds them together so soft and delicate it's slightly transparent. Beneath it, glowing golden blood races through thick veins around mechanical pieces that *tick tick tick* gently inside. Ensconced within is a real horse's heart that beats in a steady rhythm. The horses breathe together, thick smoke streaming from their nostrils and across the dark grass.

The night of the battle, my first instinct had been to pet one of these horses. To run my fingertips over the smooth surface and savor the metal so soft that it resembled fur. I wanted to make something so exquisite.

Now I just keep picturing Lonnrach astride his horse in the canyon, his eyes meeting mine.

Come back to me.

I want to shoot *seilgflùr*-laced scrap metal through the fae horses so Lonnrach finds them dead. I want to leave a trail of fae in my wake, each one a message for him. This one is: *I will kill you all.* The second one is: *Come find me.* The one after that: *I dare you.*

I start forward, grasping the blunderbuss to draw it from its holster at my back. I'll be quick. I'll be merciful. Not like *them.*

'*Falconer.*' Aithinne speaks so sharply that I stop dead in my tracks.

'Aye?' I try to keep my anger subdued, hidden deep again. I can't think clearly through it. It's what got me here in this desolate place to begin with.

'Take your hand off the weapon,' she says softly.

I'm about to do as she says – she's earned that at least, if not my trust – when I see another figure in the fog. My mouth is suddenly assaulted with faery power and I act without thinking. The blunderbuss is in my hands, the stock pressed to my shoulder.

'*Wait,*' Aithinne says.

I've already pulled the trigger. The blunderbuss slams into my shoulder and the blast echoes across the field. Smoke curls in the air between us.

A familiar voice shouts, 'Goddamn it!'

I lower the blunderbuss. 'Kiaran?'

He strides through the smoke and fog until I can finally see him clearly – and my breath catches. His gaze is so intense that I can't help but think of our kiss. Without my meaning to, my thumb brushes over the marks of that memory on the inside of my wrist. It's a brief, vivid flash of *his lips his hands his kiss* and *yes more.*

My cheeks are hot when he stalks right up to me, eyes narrowed. Pinched between his bloody fingers is a piece of scrap metal laced with *seilgflùr* from the blunderbuss – a shot that would have killed any other faery.

'*Really?*' he says.

'You were traipsing around in a low-visibility field while enemy fae are afoot,' I say defensively, hoping he can't tell I'm blushing. 'What is *wrong* with you?'

Aithinne snickers and Kiaran casts her a sharp glance. 'It's not funny.'

His sister tries to hold back a laugh, but doesn't quite succeed. 'I'm sorry,' she says. 'But you just ... I've never seen you look like such a *complete* mess.'

Kiaran studies her with a narrowed gaze. 'And both of you look like you've gone three rounds with a roving band of feral cats. I'd say we're even.'

'Even? Oh, *please*.' Aithinne ticks off each finger. 'Thus far the Falconer and I escaped through a forest of spiked trees, fought off the *mara*, fled from Lonnrach's soldiers, and defeated two *mortair*. You were shot by accident with some weapon composed of a wooden stick with a barrel on the end—'

'A blunderbuss,' I correct helpfully. Kiaran gives me a pointed look that says, *Whose side are you on*?

'—so I'd say I win this round.' She finishes with the sort of arrogant grin that makes it very clear that this must be an on-going competition.

Sibling rivalry, it seems, is not just for humans.

If Kiaran's glare is any indication, he's contemplating about fifty different ways of killing his own sister. 'Just remember,' I whisper to him, 'murder is frowned upon in most societies.'

'Not mine,' Kiaran says shortly. 'She's lucky I love her.' He snatches the blunderbuss from me and inspects it. Then he un-locks the hold and dumps its contents into the grass.

'*Damnation*!' I make a grab for the weapon but he expertly evades me. 'You're wasting perfectly good ammunition—'

'I'm sparing the next bastard you shoot, who could very well be one of your human friends.' He thrusts the blunderbuss back at me. 'The next time you want to kill someone, wait until you can actually see them.'

'It's no less than you deserve for—' Then his words sink in. 'I beg your pardon, did you say *human friends*?'

Aithinne had said there were survivors, but could she have meant ...? *No, don't hope. Do. Not. Hope.*

'That unbearably smug Seer, his mildly tolerable sister, and their group of humans,' he says, 'none of whom – I'm fairly certain – would survive being shot by that bloody thing you're wielding.'

I press a palm to my mouth. 'They're *alive?*'

'Aye,' he says drily. 'It was a surprise to me, too. The pixie led them up to Skye to stay in the remains of his old kingdom. That's where we're headed.'

I'm so close to crying, I don't think I can stop myself. They're alive. They're *alive* and nothing else matters. Tears are already starting to burn my eyes, clouding my vision.

Kiaran looks at me with an expression I've never seen on him. It takes me a moment to realise it's dawning horror. 'Kam. Kam, don't do that. Don't cry. Don't—'

Then I'm crying and he puts his arms around me in quite possibly the most awkward, stiff embrace I've ever had in my life. And I adore every second of it.

Aithinne speaks from behind us. 'I admit to being somewhat unclear on the function of human tears,' she says. 'So we're sad about this? Should I menace someone?'

In lieu of a response, the only thing I can manage is something of a half-laugh, half-sob, because *they're alive* and I haven't felt like this in so long.

'For god's sake, Aithinne,' Kiaran says, his voice rumbling through his chest, 'put the blade away. You're not going to stab Kam's idiot friends.' Then, after a moment: 'On second thought, the Seer really serves no purpose ...'

'Oh, shush.' I look up at him, whisking the tears off my cheeks. 'Don't ruin this. It helps if you don't speak.' Then I press my face back into his chest. 'And if you stop responding to my hug like I'm torturing you.'

Kiaran makes some attempt to relax, but he could use lessons in hugging. He ends up with one hand shoved up in my hair and the other giving my back a *there there* pat, but it's the thought that counts.

'Oh, don't give me that look,' he says to his sister. 'Aithinne. Stop it.'

When I open my eyes, Aithinne is staring at us with her head tilted, a silly smile on her face. 'Don't mind me,' she says, putting her hands up. 'It's not every day I see my brooding, sullen brother comforting anyone. I think it's splendid. Please continue.'

Now I see why Kadamach wanted me to move heaven and earth to find you.

Oh lord, my cheeks are burning again. If the earth opened up and swallowed me whole, I don't think I'd object.

Kiaran speaks to her through clenched teeth. 'Any time, Aithinne. You're welcome to shut up any damn time.'

That reminds me – Aithinne still has the fae vow written on her tongue. I pull back and Kiaran untangles his fingers from my hair. Is he reluctant? I can't tell. 'Release Aithinne from her vow,' I say. 'Now. It's already hurt her enough.'

A flicker of regret flashes in his gaze and I'm startled by it. I'll be damned. He never regrets anything. He looks over at his sister. 'I release you from your promise.'

Her smile is gone. Aithinne doubles over, her tongue darting out of her mouth. A gasp of pain escapes her lips, her breath shuddering. Her delicate shoulders hunch forward.

I've never seen a vow rescinded. If it hurts that much, I can't imagine what it would look like if a faery ever broke it.

Kiaran watches Aithinne intently, as if checking to make certain she's all right. When her body seems to relax, he turns back to me. The carefully controlled mask he's always worn – that keeps his emotions so composed – has slipped. He's preparing to tell me something, and this time it's not good news.

I almost tell him to wait. I want to keep the happy cocoon of joy. I want him to put his arms around me for a few minutes more before it's bad news all over again. But putting it off doesn't make it go away, nor does it become any easier when the time finally comes.

You thought all of your friends were dead. You dealt with your home being destroyed. Whatever this is, you can bear it.

I steel myself for this revelation. 'What is it?'

'There's one last thing you should know.' *Wait*, I almost say. *Wait. Don't say it.* But he does. 'We couldn't find your father, Kam.'

I wasn't expecting that to hurt so much, for me to *feel* so much. I turn sharply away from Kiaran, so he won't see that my eyes are getting wet again. Because this time I couldn't bear an embrace.

'Oh,' I say softly, unable to form even another word.

My father and I were never close. We were never affectionate, not even after my mother died. He spent so much time away in the country and even when he did return, we lingered in our Edinburgh home like ghosts haunting our familiar rooms. When he spoke to me, it was always briskly, bordering on irritated, and I always assumed he treated me that way because I wasn't the son he so desperately wanted.

After my mother died, Father's indifference toward me only grew worse. He was stuck with a daughter and had no chance for a son unless he remarried. According to Scottish law, I was his heir.

I can't forget the night I said goodbye to him. When he told me, *You look so much like her.* Like *her*, my mother. Before she died, I was a reminder of all the years they tried for a son. After, I was a constant reminder that he had lost her and she wasn't coming back. That I was a poor substitute. I was never as kind or as patient or as selfless. I was always the daughter he didn't want.

Yet I hoped – always hoped – my father would come to love me. I still did, even after I went into battle. Now I am a true orphan, both parents lost to the fae.

'He could still be alive,' Aithinne suggests softly.

Out of the corner of my eye, I see Kiaran sharply shake his head at her. He knows as well as I that it can't be true. More than likely, my father is dead. He was probably killed the night I sent him away from the city; when the fae rode in, he wouldn't even have seen them coming.

I block out the images from my mind – of my father dying, being murdered by *them*. 'We should go,' I say, no emotion left in my voice. 'I'm sure we've lingered here too long already.'

Chapter 13

W e ride through the countryside on the faery horses Kiaran brought. The only time I ever rode one was during the battle, and then briefly. I don't remember it being this fast; the creature – Kiaran named it Ossaig – cuts through the landscape like a blade through skin.

We don't stop for the longest time. When the horses reach water, they leap through the air, graceful as ever. Their hooves are a blur across the water, so featherlight that they sprint across the surface. It's as if we're flying. Their hooves strum against the ground like hummingbird wings, like a song on the breeze.

But the air around us is still, as if we're moving so quickly that all time has stopped. As if we're frozen in a single moment – except we aren't. Though it feels as though mere minutes have gone by, nightfall turns to deep dark starry night, which turns to morning as the sun rises over the mountains. The entire countryside is illuminated, the rain clouds tinged golden from the blazing light.

The scenery around me is startling. I've never seen the landscape so vibrant, so *alive*. Just as in Edinburgh, the faeries' freedom has caused the flora to grow over, far more rapidly than it would have naturally. The horses race through forests that weren't there before, and hills that have risen in my absence. The countryside of Scotland has been reshaped, re-created through battle. The land south of the Highlands, once flat farmland, has been made uneven by craters and valleys and rivers.

We cut across a field and down a hill, where we're met with the sight of another city in ruins. My heart slams against my chest. *Glasgow.*

I haven't seen our rival city in years, not since my father took my mother and me there to oversee another one of his properties. The city is now nothing more than smashed buildings and piled rocks and overgrown shrubbery; the damage is far more extensive than in Edinburgh.

We pass between ruined tenements, fallen stones piled high. I try to close my eyes and block it all out, but I can't take it any more. 'Stop.'

My horse comes to a halt and I slide off her back to stand among the ruins, so bright in the setting afternoon light. As in Edinburgh, there are sporadic domiciles still standing, but the fae have shattered all the beautiful modern buildings on Queen Street. And the rest … there are craters amid the destruction, new valleys between the streets. As though the fae were playing a game while they destroyed it all.

My fists clench as I stand in the thick grass and deep muddy soil. Something sticks out of the dirt. I nudge it with my foot. When it doesn't dislodge, I lean down to pull it out of the mud.

A boot. A child's boot.

I drop it and back away, sensing Kiaran and Aithinne have stopped behind me. 'It's like this all over Scotland, isn't it?' I can barely say it. My throat almost closes.

Suddenly Kiaran is next to me. He's standing so near that his arm brushes mine. 'Not just Scotland,' he says quietly.

I can't breathe. As if sensing my response, Kiaran curls an arm around my shoulders and pulls me against him. I'm startled by it. Kiaran isn't affectionate. Before our first kiss, he always kept his distance. He only ever touched me in combat.

His words ring in my head, and each one slices through my gut. *Not just Scotland not just Scotland not just —*

I pull away from Kiaran. I can't handle his touch, not now. Not when I wish my vengeance would rise. The Violent Aileana from the mirrors would have gone out for a kill. She would have torn out their hearts and loved doing it.

But she's been buried by something even more dangerous: guilt. Because I was supposed to save them. That was my task. I failed them all, and now they've paid the price.

'I didn't think there could be anywhere worse than the place Lonnrach kept me,' I say numbly. 'I was wrong.'

I know a thing or two about prisons, and this one may not be a locked, cramped room of mirrors, but it's no different. It's still a cage. This one is built with the bones of the dead.

A single, harsh thought directed at Kiaran flickers across my mind before I can stop it: *You saved me from one prison without realising you were putting me right into another.*

Kiaran stares down at me and I swear he reads my mind. He abruptly steps away. 'We'll stop here. I'll find us a place to rest for the night.' He turns on his heel and stalks off, as if he can't get away from me fast enough.

Now I see why Kadamach wanted me to move heaven and earth to find you.

I almost call him back, but the words die on my lips. I watch him walk away as guilt settles heavy inside of me.

After a while, Kiaran returns and leads us to a building with a roof left partially intact.

Inside, the second-floor ceiling has collapsed onto the old, dusty stone floors. The carpets on the ground level are covered in mud and dirt. Clothes are strewn about, moth-eaten and dirty.

I find a spot to lie down. I press my cheek against my arm, pulling my coat tight around me.

I've never stayed in such meagre conditions. At the end of a hunt, I always returned to a warm bed in an immaculate house. There were always clean sheets, a fire, and my inventions to stave off my nightmares. I washed the blood off my clothes and went right back to the comfort of my ladylike life – as easy as changing coats. They were soothing, those rituals. My home was always safe. My room was always safe. After all that happened, I counted on that. I depended on it. I took for granted that it would always be there.

Now there is no safe space. There are simply safe hours spent in the ravaged shelters where the dead once lived.

I watch Kiaran lead the horses inside, their hooves clicking against the stone as they move to stand opposite me.

Kiaran's gaze meets mine, but I shut my eyes and turn my back. I pretend to be asleep, even as his words fill my mind. *Not just Scotland.*

I press my fingers to my scars, my new nightly ritual. And I remember. I remember safety. I remember warmth. I wrap those memories around me like an old blanket and bask in the comfort of them. They're all I have left.

I wake later to the warmth of fire and the scent of burning wood. I'm surprised I managed to fall asleep, but I was exhausted after all the fleeing and fighting with Aithinne.

I open my eyes to find Kiaran sitting next to me, feeding more wood into the flames. He has put together a makeshift pit with stone from the surrounding buildings. A small stack of firewood is piled next to it.

'Where's Aithinne?' I ask.

'Out scouting the area.' Kiaran glances at me. 'We heard *sluagh* a few hours ago.'

Sluagh. I'll never forget the time one of those creatures went through me, a ghostly presence invading my body and sheathing my insides with ice. Kiaran told me that when the Seelie and Unseelie kingdoms were still standing, *sluagh* were the perfect aerial spies – quick, efficient, and brutally destructive if they needed to be.

'Why didn't you wake me?'

'Because' – Kiaran nudges the fire with a stick, sending cinders up into the air – 'you never rest, even when you should. When was the last time you slept?'

I don't remember. I didn't sleep in the mirrored room so much as … lie there. In a constant state between sleep and awake and dreaming.

When I don't answer, Kiaran says, 'I thought so.'

I sit up to smooth my hair, wrestling back the rebellious copper curls with a scrap of twine left discarded on the ground. After some success, I shift closer to the fire, stopping only when I realise my thigh is now touching Kiaran's. *Damn.*

Instinctively, my thumb presses against one of the marks at my wrist. I remember precisely how his lips feel. I counted the seconds of our kiss. I memorized the pressure.

Aoram dhuit. His whispered words flutter like moth wings across my mind. *I will worship thee.*

Our second kiss was even more desperate, right in the middle of the battle. My fingers trail up to just above my collarbone where the puckered scar from Lonnrach's teeth is uneven; it was deeper than the others. The memory there flickers through my mind, quick as a pulse. It was a kiss that said, *You carved out a part of me and filled it with a part of you and now you plan to leave me forever.*

You have to let me go, he'd said.

I only wanted to hold him closer.

Kiaran stokes the fire again and I pull out of the memory fast. Do I shift away? Would he notice? My cheeks burn, and thank god he can't tell it's from embarrassment.

'I never thanked you,' I finally say. 'For not giving up when you searched for me.' I want to take his hand, but I don't. My fingers curl against my palm. 'And for finding me.'

Despite my earlier thoughts, I'd rather be here than in the mirrored room. At least I stand a chance of surviving. At least I can fight Lonnrach on my own terms instead of bound by ivy and weakened by his venom.

Kiaran stares into the flames, his skin glowing in the light. I've never seen him look more beautiful. 'If it had been me, you would have done the same.'

'Aye,' I reply quietly. The heat of the fire is warm through my coat – too warm. I unbutton the heavy raploch garment.

I don't miss how Kiaran's gaze strays to the marks at my neck, the only ones not covered by my coat. Or how he grimaces and turns back to the fire, his jaw tight.

'You should button back up,' he says, rather stiffly. 'Before you catch a chill.'

I can't help the sting of hurt at that. He hates my scars. They're not badges. I didn't earn them fighting. I earned them the way an animal in a snare gets its throat slit: restrained and unable to fight back. A prey animal; not a predator.

Now you know precisely how it feels to be that helpless.

Something in me snaps. I'm on my feet and yanking off my coat to toss it to the floor. I shove up my sleeves to bare my arms. I pull the neck of my shirt open until the fabric strains. Kiaran hadn't seen the extent of my scars. My shift had hidden the worst of them. I want him to see.

'Look at me,' I tell him.

He doesn't. I notice he sets his jaw. 'Stop it, Kam.'

'No. Look at me.'

Kiaran is on his feet with my coat in his grasp. I see that light in his eyes that I remember from the mirrored room. The cold, hard rage that I'd never seen from him.

He shoves the coat into my hands. 'You've made your point,' he says. 'Now I've seen them.'

When he backs off, the Violent Aileana from the mirrors rises in my mind. One minute, I'm standing by the fire. The next, I have him pinned to the wall, my arm pressed to his throat. The coat is discarded on the floor.

'Do you think I'm not ashamed? You trained me to resist, and I *tried*,' I say, hissing the words. 'Until one day I was too tired to fight him anymore and I *let* him.' My voice is rough with anger. 'I let him, and I have to live with that. You don't get to judge me for it.'

The moment I release Kiaran and step away, he grasps me by the arms – then he has me pressed against the wall in his place.

He doesn't speak, not even as his fingers trace the marks on my inner forearms, then back up again along my neck. His touch is featherlight, slow. As if he's committing each scar to memory, one by one.

When his gaze meets mine, it's intense. Like he's staring into my soul and pulling up every secret and emotion I've worked so hard to bury.

'You're wrong,' he finally says.

'Am I?' I think of his grimace, how much it hurt.

'You think I can't bear to look at them, that I believe these mean you're weak.' Kiaran's fingers are at my pulse now, thumb sliding down to my collarbone. 'That couldn't be farther from the truth.'

Kiaran leans in and his lips brush the scar at the top of my shoulder. He doesn't know that's the memory of our second kiss. Right. There. 'When I see these I'm tempted to break my promise and kill him for what he did. I want it to be me, not you.'

'Why didn't you just tell me?'

He continues his exploration to my other shoulder. Where we met, when we were first bound together. I close my eyes when he pauses. *Don't stop*, I almost tell him. *It's been too long. Don't stop.*

'Because I'm still learning,' he says quietly.

'Learning what?'

'How to feel.' Kiaran glides his fingers down my arm and I shiver. 'How to empathize.' He looks up at me. 'How not to behave when you're upset. None of it comes easily to me.'

I can't resist any more. I touch him, tracing the veins at the back of his hand and wishing I could say the right thing. I used to assume the fae were simple creatures, unfeeling and dangerous. I'm learning, too. Just like him.

'Why is Aithinne so different from you?' I ask. His sister might not understand tears, but Aithinne's more open about her emotions than he is. She doesn't bury them.

'My sister and I were raised separately, in different kingdoms.'

I draw my hand up his wrist. The skin there is smooth, so smooth. 'Which kingdom were you raised in?'

He's quiet. As if he's preparing himself for my response. 'Unseelie,' he says.

Unseelie. The shadow fae who slaughtered indiscriminately. Who used humans like playthings.

You're not the first pet Kadamach has discarded.

I flinch and almost draw my hand away, but something about Kiaran's touch stops me. *Not Kadamach,* I tell myself, pressing my palm to his. *He's not Kadamach any more.*

'In the Seelie Kingdom,' he continues, 'Aithinne wasn't taught to suppress all emotion. She wasn't taught that emotions are a weakness.'

'What about me?' I ask. I can't help it. 'Do you think me weak because I feel?'

Because I stopped fighting?

'No. Never.' Kiaran cups my cheek. 'That's what makes you Kam.'

My breath catches. His lips are so close. 'MacKay,' I whisper. 'I—'

Kiaran steps back abruptly, putting cold distance between us. Mere seconds later, Aithinne's footsteps echo as she returns. '*Mortair,*' she whispers urgently. 'Just over the hills.'

As if on cue, thunder rolls in the distance, startling me. Fat raindrops suddenly beat against the roof in a constant rhythm, almost as loud as the thunder. I hear a screech from the outside, high-pitched and wailing. I remember that call from the battle in Queen's Park. *Sluagh.*

'Damnation,' Kiaran says. He reaches for the fire. The flames snuff out in an instant and the smoke is pulled into his palm. The scent of burning strengthens for a moment before it dissipates completely.

Aithinne crouches to press a palm to the stone floor. Her power is suddenly stark on my tongue. '*Mortair* can sense heat, too, Kadamach.'

'Shh,' he says.

I try to quiet myself, not daring to move at all. What I had thought was thunder is another *mortair*, its steps growing louder, ever closer. The walls shake. Dirt falls from the rafters and the entire structure groans and trembles. Rain drums hard and fast on the floor. At the far side of the room, the horses are still; they don't even blink.

Another *sluagh* screeches, closer this time. They're looking for us in the ruins. My hand automatically goes for the hilt of the blade, prepared to pull it out and fight.

Kiaran is suddenly right next to me with his back pressed to the wall. 'Don't.' I ignore the shiver that goes through me at how close he is. 'If they find us, they'll alert the others. Don't move, Kam.'

Others?

The *mortair's* footfalls shake the structure. I press my lips together to muffle my surprised gasp.

It's here. The *mortair* is here. Directly on the other side of the wall. The whirling mechanism of its clockwork interior hums as it powers up the weapon. The purr of the weapon grows faster, louder, louder.

I shut my eyes, my heart slamming painfully hard.

'Your heart,' Aithinne breathes.

With a soft curse, Kiaran immediately shifts closer. 'May I?' he asks.

He's asking permission? I'm so surprised, I nod.

His hand presses to my chest – *oh, that's why* – and I feel a gentle burst of his power, calming, soothing. My breath quiets. My heartbeat slows. He takes the energy – the rush of danger – from me until I'm left shaking. His power washes over me, a hint of flower petals at the back of my throat.

It's joined by the subtle taste of Aithinne's. I glance over at her, and I'm startled. Her bright silver irises cloud over to create a swirl of molten metal, deep and vast. The air thickens around us so hot, it's hard to breathe through.

The *sluagh* screeches again and the *mortair* takes off running. The ground quakes under its heavy treads and my hand tightens around the hilt of the blade as I prepare for the worst – but it's moving away from us, footfalls growing quieter and quieter. Until all is still around us, silent. Even the rain has slowed.

Aithinne releases a long, slow exhale. 'I sent a stream of power off in another direction,' she says, 'but it won't take long for them to realise it's fake.'

Kiaran doesn't respond. His hand is still pressed over my heart, his lips to my ear. This time his breathing is ragged, as if he's trying to get himself under control.

Suddenly, before I can blink, he's halfway across the room. The warmth from his body is gone and his expression is carefully composed, even cold. *She wasn't taught that emotions are a weakness.*

'I'll get the horses ready,' he says, his voice hollow. 'We should move quickly.'

Chapter 14

*O*nce we ride out of Glasgow, I realise that I've never been this far west of Edinburgh.

People always spoke of the Highlands reverently, as if they were a magical place, otherworldly. Now I know why. I have never seen mountains so majestic, so textured with steep, rugged rocks. Clouds settle at their peaks, capping the ranges in white mist. The snow dips lower, extending to touch the base of the mountains in a sprawl like spider webs across the rocks.

Below the mountains are meadows where grass and shrubs have turned brown and green and gold and red, a kaleidoscope of winter colours stretched vast. The scent of rain and wood invades my senses. We pass waterfalls that start between the sharp, jutting rocks of the crags and spill down and through the meadows.

The fog lingers around us, spraying my skin with the cold and damp. It is a magnificent thing, Highland fog. It feels electric.

I never thought of winter as beautiful, with everything so barren and cold and dark. But I've also never seen scenery so magnificent that it made me ache from the sight of its beauty.

Now I understand why this place changes people. Why those I met from the Highlands said Edinburgh would never compare. Why they said magic isn't dead here. I can feel it in my lungs with every breath, through my veins and in my blood. I think magic was born here.

I'm so enraptured that I don't even notice Aithinne has stopped until Kiaran rounds his horse close enough to tap my arm. I slow. 'What is it?'

Aithinne shakes her head once. 'I sense something.'

'I don't,' Kiaran says.

His sister glances at him. 'Of course you don't, you silly thing. You wouldn't if it were right up your arse.'

I snicker, and at Kiaran's glare, I say, 'You're the one who taught her to swear, not me.'

He opens his mouth to respond, but turns sharply toward the fog. He senses something, too. Then a familiar sensation settles on my tongue: gingerbread and spices, all the things that remind me of home.

I break into a smile as Derrick flies through the fog. He shouts in delight, 'You're alive!'

In an instant, I'm off my horse and sprinting through the tall meadow grass. Derrick barrels toward me in a streaming golden light. He flings himself into my shoulder, wings flicking hard. I hug him – as much as it's possible to hug such a wee creature – with my fingers curled tight around his tiny body.

Derrick's trapped wings pulse against my palm. 'Aileana.' He coughs. 'Those are my ribs. You're crushing my ribs.'

I release him, but I continue to stroke the silkiness of his wings. It feels like it's been so long since I'd last seen him in Charlotte Square, just before I went off for battle. I never thought I'd see him again. I never thought we'd survive. Derrick clings to my shoulder, reaching into my hair to run his fingers through it. He inhales, wings twitching.

'You damn pixie,' I say softly. 'How did you know to find me?'

'I was scouting and I sensed a Falconer,' Derrick babbles, his wings so fast that they're but a blur of light. 'It had to be you and I raced to see if it was really you because we all thought that after this long you were probably *dead*—'

'I thought you were dead, too,' I say softly.

Derrick twists my hair. 'You never thought you'd see me again. You *loooove* me and you *miiiiissed* me. You – Holy hell,' he says in amazement, his wings fanning. 'Are those tears? Are you *crying?*'

'I just have something in my eye,' I say, blinking hard. *Damnation.*

Derrick blinks at me, his eyes wet, too. 'You're right,' he says, dabbing his cheeks. 'No tears here, either. Definitely the rain. It's really wet out here. I—'

At the same time, we both remember we have an audience. Kiaran looks rather repelled by the whole exchange, and Aithinne has her head slightly tilted in unabashed interest.

Aithinne says to Kiaran, 'That's lovely. Isn't that lovely? You didn't greet me like that when I saved you.'

'I was unconscious,' Kiaran reminds her.

'Oh. That's right.'

'*You!*' Derrick flies from me, hovering in the fog just over the grass. The other two faeries look up. 'Not *you,*' he snaps at Kiaran. 'I'll get to you later. The one who said *I'll be right back with the Falconer* and returns *three bloody years later.* What the hell happened?'

Aithinne seems to consider that for a moment. 'No, no, I most certainly said I *shall return shortly.* I only spent about two months on the other side—'

'Or the equivalent of three years in human time, you ridiculous ninny. Don't pretend you didn't know.'

'*Derrick,*' I say sharply.

'What?' Derrick zips around me. 'She let me believe you were dead. I haven't seen her for *years* and she couldn't even send word that you were alive—'

'It's not *idiotic,*' Kiaran says in a low voice, 'to misjudge how long it takes to dismantle the wards Lonnrach set up in the *Sith-bhrùth* without being detected. You couldn't have done it.' He steps forward. 'Aithinne brought Kam back. Now stop complaining.'

'Make me,' Derrick snarls. 'I'll slice your insides to ribbons before you grow it all back.'

'Kam,' Kiaran says, his eyes never leaving Derrick. 'Control your pixie.'

'*Control me?*' A wee blade is suddenly in Derrick's hand. 'I'm going to gut you, you sonofa—'

'I don't think so,' I say, grabbing Derrick's wings. He yelps in surprise when I manage to pinch them together. It took me the longest time to learn that trick and I only had to use it when he tried to hunt cats in the back garden.

He hangs there helplessly, his arms crossed, a murderous glare on his face. 'I'm not apologizing,' he says sullenly.

'I won't ask you to apologize,' I tell him. 'Just put the blade away.' When he looks like he isn't going to, I say firmly, 'Derrick. The blade.'

Derrick thrusts the blade into its sheath at his waist with a hiss. 'There. Are you *pleased* now?'

I place him on my shoulder and press my cheek to his wings. The physical contact always calms him down, even when he's at his angriest. 'Thank you.'

'Don't do that,' he says sternly, leaning away, but I persist. 'Stop it. You'll never soften me. You're not winning. You're not – damn it.' He crosses his arms again. '*Fine.* I'm sorry, Aithinne,' he mutters. Then he looks at Kiaran. 'Sorry not sorry to you, bastard.'

'Well,' Aithinne says. 'It's nice to see some things don't change.' She leans in toward me. 'They've been fighting like this for *thousands* of years.'

'Don't you dare say it like that,' Derrick snaps, suddenly angry again. 'Like this is some petty rivalry. You know better than that and so does *he*.'

Aithinne goes still. 'Aye,' she whispers. 'I do.'

What on earth just happened? Everyone is silent after that. Kiaran stares at Derrick with that unfathomable gaze, like he wants to say something – but he won't. Whatever it is, his regret isn't enough.

'Kiaran—'

'Don't, Kam,' he says stiffly, and steps toward his horse to grab the reins. 'To prevent any future reunions like this one, I'm going to ride ahead and let the others know you're not dead.' He speaks to me without his eyes meeting mine, because it's a damn faery half-lie and he knows it. 'Aithinne will bring you the rest of the way.'

Aithinne steps aside as he swings his lithe body up on the horse, settling neatly in the saddle. 'Kadamach, you don't have to—'

'I do,' Kiaran says shortly. 'The pixie and I have never kept good company, and he can block you from being detected by Lonnrach better than I can.' His eyes flicker toward me and I wish he would show his emotions again. 'I'll see you soon.'

Nudging the horse, he rides off – so fast that when I blink, he's gone through the fog as if he were a ghost. The rest of us are quiet, only the hum of Derrick's wings between us.

'Would someone mind telling me what the bloody hell that was about?'

'I don't want to talk about it,' Derrick says shortly. 'But I'm glad he's gone. If he gave you that calf-eyed stare one more time, I was going to vomit up all my honey.'

Calf-eyed stare? Surely not.

Aithinne is gazing sadly in the direction her brother went. Despite everything I've gone through, I still feel as if I'm piecing together the long past of the fae, their relationships, their enemies. It's such a vast, extensive history, so convoluted.

'I think we should rest here,' Aithinne says softly. 'I find I'm not in the mood to continue our journey just yet.'

Before I can reply, she strides off into the fog.

*

After listening to Derrick tell me about the abandoned pixie kingdom, my eyelids begin to grow heavy. I eat the wild rabbit he caught and cooked for me, and settle next to the horses in the empty meadow. Derrick rests on my stomach, his wings fanning softly with the even movement of his breath.

It's a myth that faeries don't sleep. Every so often, Derrick would fall asleep like this, with his body curled up just below my ribs. He looks so peaceful with his wings twitching, a soft smile playing on his face. I often wonder what he dreams about.

Aithinne has been gone for hours. Derrick suggested we wait and use the opportunity to rest before riding the full day tomorrow.

I pass the time by watching the sky overhead. I lie on the bundle of my coat, Derrick's warmth around me like a fire, soft and soothing. I watch the stars peek through the thick clouds, brighter and more numerous than I have ever seen them. With no city lights here to dull their shine, they stretch vast, the sky reflecting the dimmed colours lingering from the sunset.

I scratch my fingernails over a mark at my forearm and let the memory of my mother's voice wash over me. For the first time in so long, I can hear her vividly, without immediately thinking of her death. *Can you name them, Aileana? Here now, repeat after me. Polaris. Gamma Cassiopeia. The Plough.*

I remember her face. How delighted she was when I identified each constellation correctly. I picture the memory so vividly as I close my eyes. How she used to say, *Aye, and this one?* until I finished my recitations perfectly.

A shout echoes in the distance and I start, listening hard. There it is again – not a shout: a cry of pain. Derrick remains fast asleep on my stomach; when the fae sleep, they sleep heavily. Hardly anything wakes them.

I pick up Derrick carefully and set him down closer to the horses, grabbing my coat as I leave to find the source. The field is illuminated only by starlight. The high peaks of the mountains in the distance are dark, clouded, and foreboding. The mist makes it difficult to see much as I make my way through the clearing in the direction of the sound.

I grip the hilt of the blade at my hip. If a faery comes at me quickly through the fog, I need to be ready.

The meadow is silent now, still but for the light breeze on the air. I hear another gasp, this one closer. I clutch the hilt tighter as I cross a stream, careful to keep my footsteps light, quiet. The element of surprise could be what saves my life.

But then I see a figure lying in the grass, the familiar dark hair and gleaming pale skin. I release my weapon and sigh in relief. It's only Aithinne.

Just as I start to relax, I hear her groan as if she were in pain.

'Aithinne?' I step closer, coming to a halt just before I reach her.

'Don't,' she says in a whisper that cuts me deep. 'Don't come near me.'

A memory strikes me before I can resist. Aithinne and me on the banks of the Water of Leith, her hands clenched into fists. Her blood dripping rapidly onto the rocks below. *Drip drip drip drip.*

Don't. Don't come near me.

Another ragged gasp from Aithinne snaps me from my memories. I reach for her. 'Aithinne.' I shake her shoulder.

She grabs my wrist and flips me. Suddenly, I'm on my back in the wet grass, the wind knocked out of me, and Aithinne is leaning over me. Her eyes are wide and unfocused.

'*Aithinne!*' I shout her name, but she seizes me by the throat.

Her hand tightens, squeezing hard. My sight is covered in bursts of stars as I struggle to draw in air. Desperately, I use what coordination I have to grasp my *seilgflùr* necklace and press it to the skin of her wrist.

The hiss of her burning flesh lasts only for a moment before

Aithinne releases me with a startled yelp. 'Falconer?' Her face twists into a grimace. 'You smell like *him*.'

I roll in the grass to put some distance between us, pressing my cheek to the cold, wet earth. My vision is still clouded over and it hurts to swallow.

You smell like him.

I'll never get the scent of Lonnrach off me, his venom out of me. It wasn't enough that he marked me. Now he's in my blood, too. It doesn't matter that I escaped, that I ran. I'm still not free of him.

At my stricken expression, Aithinne reaches for me. 'Here, let me—'

'No,' I tell her. My voice comes out in a croak. 'No healing.' I couldn't handle it, not the pain. Not right now.

Aithinne pulls back, but I don't miss the hurt that crosses her features. 'I'm sorry.' She opens her mouth, and I swear she's going to say something else. Instead, she whispers again, 'I'm sorry.'

I draw myself into a sitting position next to her. 'Bad dream, I take it?' I say, my voice raspy.

'They're all bad,' she whispers.

We are silent again as I contemplate my thousands of questions. The first few drops of rain splash on my nose and I pull the coat tighter around me. The mist has cleared, making the cold more penetrating. The meadow stretches vast before us, framed by silhouetted mountains on either side. It truly feels as though Aithinne and I are the only two people in the entire world.

'What do you dream about?' I ask softly. She curls her fists and I grasp her hand tightly in mine. 'I'm not asking what happened to you in the mounds,' I tell her, trying to keep my voice calm. 'I'm asking you what you dream about.'

She glances at me, the white of her breath visible against the dark night sky. I hope I'm giving her a way to tell me what happened while thinking of it as a dream rather than a memory.

'He kills me,' she whispers. 'In my dream. A thousand different ways. More. First just to see if I'll stay dead' – she's tugging at loose threads of her trousers and they begin to fray at her knee – 'then to make me scream.' She tugs harder, the fabric splitting. 'Then to break me, make me beg—'

Did he do this? Like mine?

Worse. He did worse.

I press my hand to hers. 'It's a dream,' I say. When emotion almost cracks my voice, I swallow. 'Only a dream. He's not here.'

I recall the strike of Lonnrach's teeth, the precise amount of pressure it took to get eighty-two perfect impressions into my skin. How he'd bury his fangs a little deeper each time so it was more painful.

After it was over, he'd look over my mark with pride. The more it bled, the wider he smiled.

I shut my eyes. Aithinne and I are quiet for what seems like hours. We both fight against our memories. I put mine away in a little compartment in my heart; I shove it in and lock it up tight. Even so, I can still hear the echoes from deep down.

That's what prisons do to you. That's what it means when someone else carves away a piece of your soul until the shape of him fits inside. You can bury it, but it's always there. *He's* always there.

Aithinne suddenly speaks. 'It's a different death every day,' she continues. 'Some worse than others, but all of them are agonizing. They—'

Her hand grasps mine so hard that I swear the bones almost break, but I don't cry out. I won't. 'You don't have to tell me anything you don't want to.' I keep my voice calm, so she never knows how much she's hurting me.

It's not all right. What he did to you is not all right.

'Then without specifics,' she says numbly, 'they all participated, but he did it most.'

I fight against my emotions. I try to control my reaction so

116

she won't see it. But the rage within me rises, heats, and burns through my veins.

She was trapped with almost a thousand enemy fae in those mounds. *A thousand.* I can't help the ache that spreads through my chest, the memories of Lonnrach that rise despite how tightly I locked them away. *He did it most.*

I hate him. I don't think I've ever hated anyone more.

'After,' she continues, 'he waits for me to heal. It always heals. Sometimes I wish it didn't.'

It always heals. Her injuries, her deaths. No wonder she utterly froze on the path in the *Sith-bhrùth* when I asked her how she bore her memories. I swallow, trying to calm my thoughts.

I've pictured Lonnrach's death a thousand different ways. The last thing I'll say to him. The last thing he'll say. At my cruelest, I'd always hoped he'd beg for death at the end.

'Did they bring you back deliberately?'

'No,' she says. 'Only Kadamach and you can kill me.' I glance at her sharply. I'm about to ask her to explain, but she turns to me. 'Why didn't you take my offer?'

My offer.

I can help you forget. What Lonnrach did to you. The place he kept you.

My murderous thoughts dissolve. Violent Aileana fades to the background again and I can finally think clearly. I remember the *daysweeksmonthsyears* of the mirrored room, how they spanned together until they had no beginning and no end. How Lonnrach became my one constant. How I measured time by when he showed up, and by how long it took me to heal after he left. That despite everything, I became so broken that I asked him to *stay.*

'I never want to forget what he did,' I say. I can't hold back the emotion in my voice. 'I'll never let anyone make me that helpless again.'

Aithinne stares at me for the longest time. 'I feel the same,' she tells me.

I release my breath and say nothing. I don't tell her how much I'm struggling with my anger over what Lonnrach did to me. I don't tell her that letting go is the hardest thing I've ever had to do, because I've spent hours upon hours envisioning the precise way I'd watch him die.

I want it to be me. It has to be me.

I squeeze my eyes shut. Lonnrach isn't my kill; he never was. He's Aithinne's.

'We'll make him pay,' I promise her. 'I'm going to help you.'

She presses her hand to mine and I understand. *Together.*

Chapter 15

We travel the next day until the sun is low on the horizon. Deeper into the Highlands, the ground is entirely covered in snow. It glitters from a fresh fall, clinging to branches. It crackles under Ossaig's hooves as we pass through the trees. The air is so crisp that it singes my cheeks.

Derrick rides between Ossaig's ears, his wee hands clinging to the thin metal fur to keep himself steady. She runs so fast that I don't know how he manages not to slip off at all.

'Just there,' Aithinne says, gesturing.

Up ahead is the curving bay where the mainland ends. Skye lies just across the shimmering waters. The mountains there are shrouded in mist, rolling and white from the snowfall. I had always heard excessive deforestation had cleared away much of the woodlands on Skye, but the island across from us is covered in thick snowcapped trees with dark trunks.

It wouldn't be possible for a forest to rise up that quickly, not without the fae affecting growth there, too. Like the jagged rocks that emerged in the Queen's Park in Edinburgh, the fae must have altered the landscape and brought back the ancient forests. Before their imprisonment, the entire Isle of Skye would have been covered in dense woodland.

'Can the horses make it to the island?' I ask.

The stories used to say that the fae on the mainland couldn't cross water. It was one of the ways Scots were advised to escape them if they ever encountered a hunt. Fae couldn't follow or their powers became weakened. Ossaig has already crossed rivers and streams, but perhaps deeper bodies of water are different.

Aithinne smiles at me. 'Of course they can. But we have other means.'

Of course they can. 'Those stories humans made up about the fae really are absolute nonsense,' I mutter.

Derrick is snickering. 'I'd love to know who spread those silly rumours. Humans are so gullible.' His eyes widen. 'D'you think if I told them that honey repelled faeries they'd put some out for me?'

'You're horrid,' I tell him.

'No, no, no,' he says with a serene smile. 'I'm *brilliant*. I like my plan. It's a good plan.'

I give him a pointed glare. 'So what are these other means?'

Aithinne pulls the horse to a halt and dismounts. I do the same, waiting as Derrick lifts himself from between Ossaig's ears to my shoulder. Absently, I reach up to touch his wings, a gesture that's now become a habit.

'There's a portal from here to Skye that can't be sensed by other *sithichean*,' Derrick says. '*Sluagh* have been watching the island from above, and Lonnrach's soldiers have been scouting the forests, so the horses can't cross without them detecting.'

I go cold. 'Have they?' Lonnrach learned that from me; he heard Derrick mention Skye in my memories, and stole that information to try to find my friends.

You spent a year training under my enemy and that rogue pixie. I assume they often spoke things you didn't understand.

My hand shaking, I reach beneath my coat to press my thumb to a mark on my forearm. The memory is shortly after I met Derrick, when he decided to live in my closet. A seemingly unimportant memory I would never have thought to consider vital.

'Nice closet,' he'd said. 'This is a good size. Not as big as what I had at home in Skye, but it'll do.'

'It'll do?'

'As my new home. It's perfect. I like it. It's mine.'

Once Lonnrach saw that memory, he knew where Derrick would likely take the others. Where I'd most likely run to after escaping from the mirrored room. I had given away their location without even meaning to.

'Aileana?' Derrick tears me from my thoughts. When he sees my expression, he misinterprets it. 'Don't you worry,' he says, patting my hand. 'They haven't managed to find us yet, daft bastards. We built it to stay hidden.'

'Derrick—'

'And you'll like it. We have good food.'

Tamping down my guilt, I watch as Aithinne steps up to the edge of the crag. 'Then why did you abandon your kingdom?' I ask him distractedly. 'You told me the pixies fled to Cornwall.'

His wings go still. 'It was discovered once, a long time ago.' I don't like his tone, the hurt there. 'But I rebuilt the wards two years back. They're holding.'

The way he says it prevents any further questions. A very clear *I don't want to talk about who found it, under what circumstances, or why we fled.* Well, it seems nothing has changed in my absence. The fae remain as secretive as ever.

Aithinne places a palm flat against the grass at the edge of the crag, her eyes wide and unblinking. Her power is suddenly thick in my mouth, the strong taste of flower petals and dirt on my tongue.

I'm about to ask what she's doing when she slams her fist into the ground. The soil around me cracks and shakes. I step back, praying like hell that she didn't just break off this part of the crag. The fall to the water is a long one.

Then I look on in amazement as roots begin to rise from the cracks in the earth. I've seen this before when Kiaran opened up a portal to the *Sìth-bhrùth*, the way it manipulated the flora to become a doorway. The roots grow and wind and twist, lifting and surrounding us, thickening like an untended briar patch. They bend and weave around each other, becoming a tree that rises up toward the sky with thick pointed branches made of dark material that glistens like glass. It looks too much like those in the *Sìth-bhrùth* forest for my comfort.

'Aithinne,' I say uncertainly as the branches start to curl around my feet.

She doesn't look at me. Her eyes are still wide, irises swirling and turning like molten silver. 'Let it take you,' she says.

Take me? The roots are closing around me, thicker and darker. The air becomes oppressive. As if sensing the tension in my body, Derrick tugs on my ear and tries saying something to me, but I can't hear him over the roots that close in.

Suddenly my throat closes up. I grasp the glassy tree root and push hard against it, but it doesn't even budge. I twist to find another way to escape, diving for a hole between the overgrown root, but it closes before me.

It's enclosed. It's too enclosed and I'm trapped. The smooth material is semireflective – just like the mirrors.

Now you know precisely how it feels to be that helpless.

Any rational thought fails me. My shoulder smacks into the hard material, a bruising impact. I'm heaving, but I can't get enough air. The roots close in overhead and my heart leaps painfully fast in my chest. Panic rises until I can hear my pulse slam through my ears. *I can't breathe.*

'Aileana!' Derrick is calling me, his wee fingernails digging into the skin at my neck. I can't hear him over my panic. I can't think anything else except *I can't breathe*. I claw at the roots until my fingernails bleed.

But they keep closing, tightening, until it's dark around me. Black as pitch.

I close my eyes. Just when I'm certain the tree will crush me, the crackling of growing roots stops. I gasp, falling to my knees. When I open my eyes, it's bright, so bright. Amid my dizzying vision, all I manage to see are looming rocks towering over me, the dark entrance to a cave, and – and …

'Gavin.'

I don't even think. One moment I'm kneeling on the snow-covered ground, and the next, I'm on my feet, wrapping my arms tightly around him. I take in the scent of him: whisky and smoke and strong soap. It calms my racing pulse, the ragged, quick pace of my breath. Suddenly I feel safe, warm.

He's alive. He's really alive.

'Aileana,' Gavin murmurs, his body uncharacteristically stiff in my embrace. The way he says my name is cautious, as if he's testing the weight of it on his tongue. 'Aileana,' he says again, as if uncertain.

I don't think to analyze his response. I bury my face in his warm neck. He smells like safety. He smells like home. He smells like a thousand wishes in the mirrored room, that I'd see him again and hug him just like this.

'Well, hell,' I hear Derrick mutter, squirming out from between us. His wings flutter against my skin as he flies off. 'This is embarrassing. Oy! Aithinne! Stop staring like a shameless freak and go find your brother.' A pause. Then: 'All right, well. I'll just be in this tree. Over here. Call me when you're done.'

Derrick's wings flutter and Aithinne's footsteps disappear into the cavern. I hold tightly to Gavin for a moment longer, noting that even though he's relaxed a bit, his shoulders are still tense.

How different this is from the last time I saw him. Before the battle, he had hugged me like he knew he had to let me go and he wasn't ready. Like he would never see me again.

Like he thought I was going to die.

I pull away to ask him what's wrong … and I flinch. 'Christ,' I whisper.

There are scars around his right eye, what look like claw-marks across his skin. Another long, jagged mark runs from his lips over his cheekbone, stopping right beneath his eyelashes.

The scars don't detract from his features. It's Gavin's eyes that gives me pause. His vivid blue eyes – always so bright and familiar – are battle-weary. He's looking at me as if we've never met before. As if we hadn't grown up together or fought fae together or were nearly forced to marry after a misunderstanding.

I reach up to touch the scars. He flinches, but doesn't pull back. I draw my fingers over the grooves they've left in his skin. 'How did it happen?' My voice catches without my meaning it to.

I slide my finger down the longest one and Gavin captures my hand in his. 'The night you left, they tried to take my eyes.' His voice is hollow. 'Your pixie saved me.'

I swallow hard. *I was supposed to save him. Not Derrick.* 'I'm so sorry.'

Gavin steps back and regards me for the longest time. 'I thought you were dead. We all did. After three years I assumed Aithinne was gone, too.'

'They took me to the *Sith-bhrùth*,' I say. 'Didn't Kiaran tell you?'

Gavin has always been easy for me to understand. I've known him so long that every part of him is so familiar: his face, his expressions, his feelings. I know his likes and dislikes. I know that when he lost his father, he buried his emotions deep, just like I did when I lost my mother.

This Gavin ... three years later he's almost unrecognizable. The way he holds himself is different, his body taut, as if he's prepared for an attack at any moment. I don't miss the way his eyes flicker in a careful assessment of our surroundings.

'Aye, he told me.'

The trees around us rustle and Gavin's gaze slides to my left, my right. The forest towers high above the cavern, leaving shadows on the snowy ground. The woodland is thick and dark, nothing visible except for the entrance to the cavern. I can sense the power around it, the press of it against my tongue, just like the portal Kiaran took me to once. This place must be hidden from Lonnrach's soldiers.

The trees shudder again and a breeze rustles my hair. Gavin's body tenses – as if he's listening for something. After a moment, he speaks. 'You were gone a long time, even in the fae realm. You don't look any different.' Now his gaze shifts to behind me. To see whether I was followed? 'You don't even have a mark on you.'

I step back. 'What's that meant to mean?'

Lonnrach's marks are hidden beneath my clothes, but he never touched my face, never left an imprint there. And unlike Gavin, I haven't aged. I was eighteen when Lonnrach took me to the *Sith-bhrùth* ... and I'm still eighteen.

Gavin is twenty-four by now. He's grown into his shoulders. His body is leaner, more muscular. I notice the small, puckered scars along his neck, just above the collar of his coat.

'I've seen people taken by *them* to the *Sith-bhrùth*,' he says tightly. 'They don't come back the same. They pretend to be who they were, but their allegiance is to the fae. They've betrayed us before.'

I almost tell him that I'm not the same. That a part of me came back broken, too. That there's a Lonnrach-shaped hole inside of me that I don't know if I'll ever be able to fill with the parts of me I lost.

My fingers itch to pull up my sleeve. To show him my scars. *I'm not unmarked. I'm not whole. I'm still trying to put the pieces of myself together again.*

But I don't. I place my trembling palm against his cheek to force him to look at me. 'You think I'm like that?' When he doesn't answer, I say, 'I would never betray you.'

He sets his jaw. 'I don't know that.'

I have to convince him. Gavin is a product of this world I

left behind when I was captured. Lonnrach showed me a mere glimpse of the ruined Edinburgh just after it happened and it's burned into my memory. Gavin was there. He saw everything.

'Aye, you do,' I tell him. 'You wanted me to make you a promise before the battle. Do you remember?' He shakes his head. 'You wanted me to promise you that I wouldn't die.'

Gavin jerks from my touch. 'And you never said the words. I remember.'

I couldn't say the words. I don't make promises that I can't keep, and a part of me believed I wouldn't live to see the following morning. If I did, it would be because I had saved them all. If I died, it would be because I had failed. There was no in-between, no other possibility.

I know better now.

Before I can respond, Gavin says, 'Prove it to me. That you're still Aileana.' The way he says it gives me pause. He speaks softly, calculating.

'*Prove* it?' I step toward him but he backs away. 'Gavin, I'm standing right here. I'm alive. What more proof do you need?'

'They can control humans easily. Why should I believe you?'

I'm beginning to understand that whatever he's been through has made it so he doesn't trust anyone. Not even me. 'Because I'm a Falconer,' I say simply.

Gavin's expression doesn't waver. 'That *baobhan sìth* has got into your head before. Being a Falconer didn't stop her then.'

My lips close and my fingers curl into fists. *Being a Falconer didn't stop her then.*

He's not wrong. It didn't stop Lonnrach, either. Not from getting in my head and stealing my memories as if it weren't difficult at all. Kiaran once told me I hadn't come into my full abilities as a Falconer; even though I could fight the fae and move just as fast, I couldn't see them without *sieglflur*, and I still struggle to resist their mental influence.

The only difference between me and any other human who

returned from the *Sith-bhrùth* is that my Falconer abilities have given me the power to withstand more physical damage. That meant Lonnrach could torture me longer and his bites would be nearly healed before his next visit.

It always heals. See? It always heals.

I push down the memories that threaten to rise. 'How can I reassure you?'

Gavin calls for Derrick, who flies from his perch in the nearby trees, leaving a trail of gold across the air. 'Is the hugging done, because I can't – wuh. Did someone kick a kitten? What happened?'

'I'm taking her to the underneath,' Gavin says tightly. 'Go get Daniel.'

'No,' Derrick says sharply, his halo suddenly tinged in red. 'I don't believe I will.'

'It needs to be done,' Gavin replies. 'You *know* why.'

At that moment, I swear the forest goes silent. The trees are entirely still around us. And even the breeze has paused.

Derrick stares at Gavin for the longest time, as if considering what he'll say. 'She's not like the others. She's—'

'A Falconer,' Gavin replies, his gaze rising to meet mine. 'I know.'

Oh, for god's sake, enough of this. '*She* is right here,' I snap, 'and *she* would like an explanation.'

'It's a test,' Derrick says. He flies over to my shoulder as if in solidarity against Gavin. His wings tap my cheek. 'An unpleasant one to prove you're not under *sithichean* control. You're not doing it.'

Gavin glares at him. 'Aileana is still a human. She's been influenced by the fae before, and there are no exceptions. *You're* the one who made that rule. Remember?'

Derrick's wings flick my skin painfully fast. 'We're making one *this time*, you—'

'*I'll do it.*' I almost shout the words. Thank goodness, they both immediately cease their bickering. Derrick's wings stop tapping my cheek. 'I'll do it,' I say again more calmly. 'I have nothing to hide.'

After a moment's silence, Derrick whispers in my ear. 'You don't want to do this. You don't have to.'

The way he states it can only mean one thing: *This will hurt*. I shut my eyes briefly before saying, 'If this is what it takes to earn his trust again, then I do.'

Derrick sighs. 'They won't let me in there with you, but I'll have Daniel come get me when it's over. All right?' He flies off my shoulder and hovers in front of Gavin. 'Aileana's test won't be like the others.'

'I beg your pardon?'

'Her being a Falconer will make it worse. I'm not leaving until you promise me.' Derrick crosses his arms. 'Once. No more.'

'Fine,' Gavin says tightly.

Derrick nods. 'And I want you to know that I loathe you right now,' he says. He flies off before Gavin says anything. His halo illuminates the entrance of the cavern for only a moment before he disappears into the darkness.

'I take it I'm not going to like this,' I say, trying to keep my voice calm. 'What, exactly, does it entail?'

You went through daysweeksmonthsyears *with Lonnrach. You can endure this, too.*

Gavin waits until the flutter of Derrick's wings fades before he speaks, his features softening slightly. 'One of *them* will need to test your blood.'

I try to control my instinctive response, my urge to back away. My blood. My tainted, faery-venom-filled blood. What if that affects the outcome? A sudden flash of Lonnrach's face crosses my mind. His whispered words, a promise of pain. *I just need to use your blood to see.*

I have to take the risk. If I don't, Lonnrach will find me again. I'm not ready to fight him off, not yet.

As if he senses my thoughts, Gavin says, 'If you really are the girl I grew up with, then I'm sorry for this.'

Chapter 16

I'm blindfolded with Gavin's kerchief. He quietly leads me through a long hallway, then down so many steps that eventually I lose count. His hold on my hand is gentle and patient. I descend slowly so I don't trip, trying to listen for some indication of where we're going.

The only sound other than our footsteps is the steady patter of dripping water. The temperature grows colder as we go further underground; the musty scent of the rock is overwhelming.

When we reach our destination, Gavin has me sit on one of the damp rocks. 'Give me your hands,' he murmurs.

I do as he asks and before I can respond, he clicks heavy shackles over my wrist. A sense of dread fills me. 'What are you doing?'

'I told you that you wouldn't like this,' he says. He touches my shoulder; a tender touch, as if he regrets what's about to happen. That's the Gavin I know.

'Wait—'

He walks away, his footsteps disappearing back up the stairs. When no one else comes, my body begins to shake with cold and fear. I can't see anything through the blindfold, and having my hands bound threatens to bring back too many memories.

It's one test. Only one. You can get through it.

'Gavin?' I call. I wait. Somewhere behind me water drips to

the ground with a sharp *thwop* – other than that, I don't hear a damn thing.

It remains quiet for the longest time and I can't take it any more. I shake my head hard to loosen the blindfold. It inches down my face. I try again, again – throwing back my head – until the blindfold slips to my mouth. Then I use my teeth to tug it the rest of the way and the material slips free.

I'm in a cavern, musty with dirt and humidity. I'm propped against rocks that look like none I've ever seen. A shaft of moonlight shines from an opening at the top, illuminating the sparkling inclusions in the walls. They glisten like stars trapped in clusters, bright and shining. I'm able to lower my palm to my side to feel how smooth it is, like volcanic rock shaped, buffed, and smoothed to perfection.

'I see you've slipped the blindfold,' a voice says.

I look over, straining my eyes to see. I didn't even hear him come in – unless he was there the whole time, watching me. He's standing just beyond the moonlight, where it's too dark to see anything but his outline.

His tall form is leaned against the boulders on the far side of the room. After a moment, he steps into the circle of moonlight and I'm able to see his face.

The man has ruggedly handsome features – a nose that's been broken before – and he's even more muscular than Gavin. He's seen battle, that much is obvious. One of his eyes is covered with a patch.

'I take it Gavin won't be returning,' I say.

'Correct. He'll be drinking himself to oblivion, I imagine,' the man says, his eye shrewdly assessing me. 'It's a bit of a tradition whenever we have to do this.'

His rolling accent is distinctive; I recognise it from the time I accidentally wandered from my parents' side and into one of the more impoverished areas of Glasgow. Father spent an entire afternoon berating me for that.

His cadence and pronunciation is different from the accent spoken by my affluent peers in Edinburgh and Glasgow. Our speech lessons from childhood were deliberately intended to curtail the Scottish brogue so we sound more like those in English society; it is meant to be a mark of our wealth and status. Unlike mine, each word of his is spoken with a thick burr.

'You must be Daniel,' I say, trying to sound cordial. 'Is there a formal name I may call you?'

'Nothing formal,' he says gruffly. 'Not here. You're going to want to be able to curse my Christian name.'

I feel a twinge of fear. The shackles are already biting into my skin, dredging up unwanted memories.

I try to calm myself. 'If it's all the same to you,' I say, 'I'd prefer a surname. If you please.'

Being concerned about etiquette when I'm shackled to a wall in a dark cave might be a bit silly, but at least one thing I can control about this situation is what to call him.

'Mr. Reid, then,' Daniel says with an exaggerated bow. '*My lady*.'

I ignore his sarcasm and lift the thick chain that secures me to the rock. 'Is there a reason I'm shackled to this wall like a prisoner?' My voice is steady, calmer than I feel. 'I'm here willingly. I won't run.'

Instinctively, I give the shackles a slight tug to see how well attached they are. If I could pull them out just a little – if I had even that small level of control – it might quiet the thoughts. Already my pulse is uneven, panic rising.

'The shackles aren't to keep you here against your will,' Daniel says, a catch in his voice that I don't understand. 'They're so you don't hurt yourself.'

I'm about to ask what he means when he whistles once between his teeth, a shrill sound that reverberates through the cave. I go entirely still, holding my breath, waiting, dreading. My pulse is stuttering; heat rises in my cheeks.

Something rustles at the back of the cave. It sounds distinctly like a flutter of wings. A taste settles on my tongue, soft and sweet as honeysuckle. Then a light, even brighter than Derrick, flies to Daniel. It stops to hover in front of him. Those tiny wings on its back snap and flutter as it says something in its language, its voice as lyrical and flowing as chimes.

The faery's halo is too brilliant to reveal its features, but it's smaller than a pixie, no taller than one of my fingers. *Teine sionnachain*, a will-o'-the-wisp. The wee creature is exactly how Kiaran described them. They're rural dwellers with an inherent dislike for city lights and noise. I've never seen one before. They've always stayed on the outskirts of the city, hidden in trees or caves.

Daniel nods in my direction and addresses the faery. 'You know what to do,' he says.

So my companion is a Seer. That explains the missing eye; a faery must have taken it.

Whatever he's told that wisp to do ... I begin to struggle then, tugging hard at the chains. They groan with my efforts. I pull again, but there's no give in the rock, not even a grinding to indicate I've loosened it.

I can't be at the mercy of any faery, not like this. Not ever again.

'Wait,' I say. I can't form a coherent sentence. I can't *think*. '*Wait*, don't—'

The faery flies to me and I yank at my shackles, straining away from the creature. *Damnation*. 'Be still,' the wisp says in that voice like chimes.

It lands on my thigh, its light fading to reveal a wee humanoid creature with pointed ears and wide black eyes. Its skin is dark and smooth as onyx, glistening with what looks like flecks of mica. Golden-veined wings like a dragonfly's fan behind its body.

The creature looks harmless. I know better. Even the smallest fae are capable of killing a human or causing plenty of damage.

If you really are the girl I grew up with, then I'm sorry for this.

The wisp lays its hands on my thigh, and its power flows over me like warm rays of sunshine. 'I like this one, *taibhsdear*,' it sings to Daniel, petting my wrist. 'She smells like fire. Can I keep her?'

'We have a truce,' Daniel says. 'Your kind doesn't get to keep humans.'

The faery pouts. 'I could offer you something for this one. A wish, *ma thogras tu*. Whatever you desire.'

'No,' he replies sharply.

The faery lowers its lashes, but not before I see the flash of anger cross its features. It doesn't like being commanded by a human. What kind of place is this, that a faery would do anything for a Seer? That they would have such an agreement?

'Gavin said there were no exceptions to this test. Why?' I say. My voice shakes. I hate that it shakes.

'We made the mistake of indiscriminately allowing human survivors into our last location,' Daniel says, watching the wisp in displeasure as it moves to stroke my arm. 'We won't make it again here.'

I start as the wisp turns over my palm and licks my hand, wrist to fingertip. 'Tastes like ashes,' it murmurs. 'Like burning.'

I freeze. All I can think of is Lonnrach's lips against my skin, his mouth smeared with my blood. *You taste like death.*

I squeeze my eyes shut, only for a moment. *You're not there. You're not there. You're not his.*

'I'm not under control of the *sìthichean*,' I tell him. 'I swear I'm not.'

'Gavin said you were in the *Sìth-bhrùth*. Three years, our time.' I'm so unaccustomed to Daniel's rolling accent that it takes me a moment to understand him.

'Aithinne rescued me—'

'They could have let you escape. The fae take humans and break into their minds. Then they send them to find us, hoping that we'll betray our location by offering shelter. But there's one way to test fae influence,' he murmurs, watching me. 'They leave an imprint in your blood. It makes a human feel only pleasure from a faery, never pain.'

I go cold inside. I recall Lonnrach's hand on my wrist, his finger trailing down my cheek. *I want to know everything. I just need to use your blood to see.*

No, I can't be under his control. I can't be, I —

The fae take humans and break into their minds.

My body goes still. I accepted his food. I accepted his drink. He's been in my head, he's had my blood, he's taken my memories, he's left his mark on me.

You lose. Now you're mine.

'That didn't happen,' I whisper.

Or did it? I swear Lonnrach almost had me under his control on the path out of the *Sìth-bhrùth*. I took that step forward against my will. For a single second, my body wasn't mine to control any more. It was his.

'I can't take that risk.' Daniel moves back to lean against the rock again, away from the light. All I can see is his silhouette, the massive breadth of his shoulders and how they lift in a shrug. 'But if you haven't been faestruck,' he says simply, 'then I'm sorry. This is going to hurt.'

I've heard that before.

The will-o'-the-wisp smiles wide and whoops with glee, baring long pointed teeth that shouldn't fit into a mouth that wee. Before I can blink, it sinks those razor-sharp teeth into my palm.

No no no. Not again.

The bite burns. I'm suddenly hyper-aware of the pain, how the wisp tears through my skin until the blood spreads a path across the lines of my palm.

I don't scream. I don't. The *daysweeksmonthsyears* are stretched vast and long behind me. I didn't scream then. I didn't give Lonnrach the satisfaction. It was the one thing I had. *Don't scream don't scream don't scream.*

'Stop,' I say. I beg Daniel with my gaze. The faery suddenly bites harder, its teeth digging in, tearing. '*Stop!*'

'Make sure she isn't pretending,' Daniel tells the wisp calmly.

Just then, the faery pulls back and lifts up my sleeve. 'She's been bitten before,' it says to Daniel in that sweet voice. It gives me a small, secret smile, its next words just for me: 'Many, many times. The first bite tasted like him.' Then it sinks its teeth into me again, latching onto a vein.

I watch in horror as the creature draws back, its mouth dripping with my blood, and looks up at me with dark and cavernous eyes. It breathes a single chilling word. '*Seabhagair.*'

Seabhagair, Kiaran whispered to me that day in the park that feels like ages ago. *Falconer*. Now it knows what I am.

The will-o'-the-wisp lets out a high-pitched, startling cry. Its mouth opens wide, jaw dropping almost to its feet, to project a screaming call that echoes through the cave. I hear wings flap in response. Hundreds of them. Their cries echo in unison and soon the entire cave is filled with their piercing shrieks. The taste of honeysuckle forces itself down my throat, thick on my tongue.

Daniel stumbles forward. 'What the bloody hell?' he murmurs, staring behind me toward the back of the cave.

My heart slams against my chest. I jerk my chains, straining with the effort to pull them out of the rock. 'They know I'm a Falconer,' I tell Daniel. 'Unshackle me. *Now!*'

He lunges for me, reaching for the shackles, but it's too late. The will-o'-the-wisps are upon us. They circle in a massive group, hundreds upon hundreds of bright moving stars. As one, they dive for me, knocking Daniel out of the way with their supernatural strength.

I don't even have time to brace myself. To go back into that numb place I went during Lonnrach's visits, just so I could endure the pain. This is worse than his bite. This is worse than the mirrored room. It's not one mouth, one bite, one faery, eighty-two teeth – it's hundreds.

I can't stop myself. I *scream*.

The wisps tear at my clothes, biting, slicing into my skin. Their teeth burn, their nails scrape and draw blood. They latch onto my veins and suckle there. Blood drips from my skin, my fingernails, down to the rock in a steady *drip drip drip drip*. The wisps keep biting over and over again, and just when I think I'll faint from the blood loss – that the pain will numb – agony blossoms anew.

Through the flutter of wings, I hear Daniel shouting for someone. He mutters a stream of curses as he tries to rip the fae from my arms, my clothes, but their teeth only clamp down harder. My voice is hoarse, my throat aching from my screams.

Just when I think I can't stand the pain any more, I taste power, strong and familiar. *Kiaran.*

All the wisps are suddenly torn from me, their shining bodies slamming into the cave walls all around. Now they scream, wings flapping, and flee to the back of the cave with their calls echoing like ghosts.

Chapter 17

I can't raise my head. I've slumped forward in my chains, doubled over from the wisp venom burning through my veins. Suddenly Kiaran is there next to me, his warm fingers lifting my chin.

God, those eyes. Kiaran's beautiful eyes flicker over my face and down my neck where the wisps latched onto the artery – and with each passing moment his expression grows colder. Not with rage, not with any emotion. Just calculating determination.

As if he's preparing for a slaughter.

I try to lean into him, but the shackles stop me, clanging against the rock.

Kiaran sees them, and I didn't think it was possible for his gaze to grow more brutal. He wraps his hands around the metal at my wrists. I feel his powers surge, and the metal disintegrates to ash.

With nothing to hold me, I pitch forward. Kiaran catches me and I hiss in pain, my vision blurring.

'Can you move?' he murmurs. He sounds gentle, but there's a violent undercurrent that makes me hesitate.

I flex my fingers and test my limbs, flinching at how much they ache. 'I think so.' It hurts to speak.

My arms are entirely covered in small, bleeding bites, some deeper than others. My shirt, trousers, and coat are all torn. The fabric hangs off me in flaps.

'So she's *yours*,' says a voice behind us. Daniel. 'I thought there had to be a reason you would go through that much effort to rescue a human.' He doesn't bother to hide his disgust. 'She's your pet.'

Kiaran's eyes are on me, but I don't miss the way his body goes still at Daniel's words. Cinders burn in his irises and I taste his power on my tongue.

I lean closer. 'Don't. Whatever you're thinking, don't.'

'You're testing the limits of my patience.' Kiaran's voice cuts across the air, as cold as winter wind. 'I'm not making you a promise, Kam. Not this time.'

I can read him clearly for once. I know his thoughts. He'll slaughter the wisps, and though his vow prevents him from killing Daniel, he'll hurt him. Badly.

The temperature suddenly drops to below freezing. My breath is visible in the air and gooseflesh rises painfully along my skin. It's so cold that it burns.

Kiaran studies my bites again, each one, as if he's counting how many he'll have to kill.

'MacKay,' I say. My lungs ache from the cold; I can barely gasp in air enough to form words. 'Stop.'

Kiaran is on his feet, reaching for the blade at his waist.

I do the first thing I can think of. I grasp his wrist and have just enough strength to yank him down to me. I kiss him.

At first it was just to distract him, but then … god. The temperature goes back to normal, and I can't think any more. It's just Kiaran's lips on mine, the shape I had perfectly memorized. It's the pressure of his kiss, exactly right. It's the way he makes a sound in his throat, a low growl that makes me shiver.

Then I'm in his arms and he's tugging at my coat like he wants it *off*. He's pulling at the buttons and his hands are underneath and —

I gasp in pain against his mouth. He touched one of my wounds.

Kiaran pulls back, as if he suddenly realised why I kissed him. 'Nice diversion,' he says, voice brittle. 'I don't recall teaching you that one.'

'I improvised. I had to get your attention.' I can barely speak above a strained whisper. 'No violence. I did this willingly.'

His gaze narrows. 'You allowed yourself to be feasted upon by wisps?'

I don't answer him; he wouldn't take it well. 'Don't hurt Daniel.'

Kiaran pulls me to my feet. He slides an arm around my waist, sensing I'm too hurt to hold myself up. 'You mistake me for a human again, Kam.' This time when he speaks, his lips are at my neck, his words whispered kisses there. 'Where I come from, we don't practice compassion. If it weren't for my vow, I'd kill him without a second thought for what he did to you.'

Before I can respond, he looks over at Daniel. 'Kam passed your test,' he says with deadly calm. 'Now you'll find a place for her to sleep and heal.'

Daniel meets Kiaran's gaze, not masking his hostility. 'I don't let humans into my city who are intimate with fae.'

'Your city?' Kiaran's smile is mocking. 'I'll be certain to tell that to the pixie.' He gestures to me. 'Right after I inform him that his human companion isn't welcome.'

Daniel's hands form fists at his sides, as if he's ready for a fight. 'I don't care who she is; she looks to me like another faery's whor—'

Before I can blink, Kiaran pulls out his blade and slices it through the air. It rips through Daniel's shirt and into the rock behind him with a thud – just missing a killing blow in his torso. 'Finish that sentence,' Kiaran says, 'and the next one goes right through your throat.'

'I heard a rumour that you can't kill humans,' Daniel says, pulling the knife from the rock with a swift jerk. 'Is that true?'

'I don't have to kill you,' Kiaran says, in that terrifying fae voice. 'It's incredible what the human body can endure without dying.'

Daniel snarls and throws the dagger. Kiaran releases me to catch it easily without even blinking. 'The first throw was a courtesy, Seer. Next time, I won't miss.'

'Gentlemen, please,' I say faintly. 'That's quite enough.' Stars dot my vision and I sag against Kiaran with a groan. My head is swimming, light, filled with air. It's as if I'm floating.

'Damnation, Kam.' Kiaran jerks me back up when I start to fall forward. I'm not sure I can walk. 'You're bleeding all over the place.'

My voice comes out in a croak. 'I'm not happy about it either.'

Kiaran guides me at a slow, steady pace toward a passage that leads to the back of the cavern. Daniel's voice cuts through the dark. 'I told you I wouldn't allow her into the city, faery. Take her right back out the way you came.'

Kiaran stops and turns slowly. 'I assume you value that remaining eye, Seer. One more word, and I'll blind you.'

'Daniel, are you in here?' A familiar voice calls from the passage at the back of the cave. 'Gavin said—'

Catherine freezes when she sees me and Kiaran. At twenty, my best friend's features are mature, even more beautiful. Her hair is pulled back into a single plait that falls to her waist. Instead of the dresses she usually wears – always in the latest style – she's dressed practically in dark trousers and a raploch shirt.

She mouths my name, as if she can't believe it's me. 'You're *alive.*'

Then she's striding forward and her arms are around me and she's crushing me against her. I make a sound of pain and she releases me, as if she hadn't even realised that I was bleeding.

'Oh god.' Her eyes meet mine. 'They tested you?'

'Your husband did,' Kiaran says sharply, 'and your idiot sibling helped. I'm surprised you didn't know.'

Husband? She married *Daniel?* Good god, this is like a never-ending nightmare.

I try to step away, but I sway from the blood loss. Not wasting any more time, Kiaran swings me up into his arms. He's much better at it now than the last time he held me, when I was ill. He shifts me in his grip with care as my blood continues to drip from my hundreds of bites.

I open my eyes. Catherine sharply assesses my wounds, the blood around Kiaran's feet. 'No one told me you were alive. *No one.*' She looks away then, at her husband. 'Daniel, I believe I need a word.'

'Cat—'

'To the study. Tell Gavin to meet me there, too. *Now.*' She waits until his footsteps disappear down the passage before addressing me more gently. 'Some of your wounds look deep.' She presses a hand to one of the scars on my arm and I bite my tongue. 'I would have been here with Daniel to help you if I had known. I would have greeted you.'

He is her husband? Really?

Catherine looks so upset that I can't help but say, 'It's all right.'

'No, it's not,' she and Kiaran say at the exact same time.

She glances up at Kiaran and I don't miss how she goes rigid, or how her voice shakes slightly when she speaks. 'Where do you intend to take her?'

My vision clouds and my head starts to pound. I don't hear Kiaran's response. He says something about a door. *What door?* I open my mouth to ask, but just before I can, the lightheadedness becomes too overwhelming. The last thing I remember is Kiaran cradling me gently against him.

Chapter 18

I slip in and out of consciousness. I could have been lying here for hours, or days. For the longest time, it's as though my limbs are weighted, too heavy to move. My entire body feels like it's burning from the inside.

During the haze, I manage to open my eyes. I stare down at my arms to find hundreds of bites healed over into scars. My skin is overly reddened – as if I spent too much time in the sun – and damp with fever. Even the brush of my fingertips is painful.

Sometimes there are people in the room, voices I recognise. I try to open my eyes, but they are so heavy. Always heavy. My lips move to ask for Aithinne, for her painful healing, but I can't speak.

Everything hurts except for when he's near. *Kiaran.* The taste of his power lingers on my tongue, the breath of his name on my lips. I could swear I hear him whisper to me in that fae language that sounds as soft and lyrical as a haunting lullaby. I want him to say the words again, the ones he said to me before the battle.

Aoram dhuit. I will worship thee.

He never says them. I almost ask him to as I wake, my eyes opening painful fractions at a time. Then I realise it isn't Kiaran sitting next to me whispering soft unintelligible words. It's Catherine.

'Hullo,' I say. The word is barely more than a croak.

Catherine raises her head, her eyes weary, as if she's been awake for hours. 'Hullo,' she returns.

I take in my surroundings, trying to ignore how hot my eyes feel, how I can barely keep my eyelids open. I'm in a room. *My room.*

Everything is just as I remember it. The walls made of teak, with hundreds of tiny bulb lights placed between the wooden panels. A ship's wheel I salvaged from an old schooner that hangs on the far wall, next to a map of the Outer Hebrides. Clicking gears along the edges of the ceiling that connect to the electricity tower in the heart of New Town.

Home. Am I dreaming? *Was* I dreaming? My head is pounding, my vision starting to blur and blacken around the edges again.

'Home?' I ask, my lips barely moving.

I see her hesitation. Catherine takes my hand. 'Shh. Go back to sleep. I'll be here when you wake up.'

I dream about home. Not my old life – tea parties and dancing and balls – just the place. In my dream I'm with my mother and we're sitting on the grass in the Princes Street gardens.

It's summer, and the flowers are in full bloom. My favourite was always the lobelia; the delicate flower covers the ground in vivid purple buds. During this time of year, the perennials are spread across the green space in beautiful splashes of colour. They blanket the hillside below the castle in yellows, reds, purples, and pinks, and the grass has never been more lush.

The sun is warm on my face. My hat is tipped back so I can feel the heat of the rays. I wear a day dress of light blue, its muslin thin enough that I can feel the heavenly summer breeze.

'It's beautiful, isn't it?' my mother says. She closes her eyes, her skin glowing gold in the afternoon sun. 'I miss this.'

'I do, too,' I say.

'We ought to visit the shore later. Just you and me.'

'I'd love that,' I say, a catch in my voice. *I don't belong here with you.*

Mother glances over at me. 'Is there something wrong?'

'I just … I wish I could stay.' I rip the petals off the lobelia. One at a time.

'Why wouldn't you?'

How do I explain this to her gently? 'There's someplace I have to be. People I'm responsible for.'

Mother's laugh sends a shiver down my back like a stroke of cold, wet fingertips. 'What a silly thing to say,' she says. When she tips her hat further back, her red hair and green eyes are a little too bright. Were they always that bright? 'Of course you're not responsible for anyone.'

The way she says it stirs something inside me. She sounds dismissive. Mother never sounded dismissive. 'But—'

'We ought to build something new, lass. Whatever you desire. Wouldn't you like that?'

Whatever you desire. Wouldn't you like that?

'No,' I say. Something isn't right.

Sharp cawing laughter draws my attention. Ravens gather in the grass around us, hundreds of them. They weren't there before. Now their inky, flapping wings cover the ground, their beaks sharp and bright red and dripping. Blood?

Mother grasps my hand so tightly that I gasp. 'I'll find you.' When my gaze meets hers, I go cold. Her eyes are black as pitch, like a starless night. I could drown in them. 'Wherever you go, I'll find you.'

'Minnie?' I whisper, calling her by the nickname I gave her so long ago. *Not her. It's not her.*

As I look on, her face begins to fade away, skin peeling off until her skull is visible. With a sharp cry, I try to tear my hand from her grasp, but she holds firm.

Before I realise, the sun is gone. The sky has darkened quickly until there is nothing left but black clouds. The flowers around us wilt and die. They turn to dust. The ravens laugh with sharp squawks and flapping wings.

'Let go of me.' I'm pulling so hard that it hurts. Her grasp is so tight that her fingers dig into my skin, a bruising pressure.

'After this, you're on borrowed time, Falconer,' she tells me. Her voice drops until it's unrecognizable. She pulls me close, whispers in my ear. 'I'll see you again soon.'

I wake with a start, groaning at the pain. It feels like my entire body is on fire. I claw at the blankets, at my skin. It *hurts*.

'*Aileana.*' Hands gently push at my shoulders. 'It's all right. You're all right.' Catherine.

I open my eyes to find her leaning over me. She looks even more exhausted than she had the last time I awoke; I wonder how long she's been here now.

'Too hot,' I rasp.

Catherine frowns, pressing her palm to my cheek. 'You're still running a fever. Give me a moment.' She reaches for something. I hear water splash before she holds up a wet cloth. She folds it over and places it on my forehead.

The cold water breaks through the heat and I sigh with relief. 'Thank you.'

She takes my hand again. 'Better?' My response dies on my lips when I notice where I am. So that part wasn't a dream. I'm in my bedroom. *Home.*

My head falls back against the pillows and I stare up at the gears along the ceiling, the lights above me. I'd seen that part of the wall caved in with a hole in it. The furniture rotting. This place doesn't exist any more, not as it once did. It's a heap of rubble, destroyed by the fae. And what remained of the room I adored so much – that I lovingly designed with my mother – was completely levelled by the *mortair*. But here it looks so … perfect, surely I can't be imagining this.

I touch my fingers to the counterpane, so much like my old

one, the silk flattening beneath my palm. 'Is this real?' I whisper. *Am I still dreaming?*

I'm not. My arms are still covered in healed-over fae bites, the skin red and angry.

'That depends on what you consider real,' Catherine tells me. She presses my hand to the wooden frame of my bed. 'Does this feel real to you?'

The grooves under my fingertips do. So do the designs carved into the headboard. I raise my head just enough to see the way my fingers press to the wood; I feel the texture of it, even as a pounding headache forms at my temples.

Finally it hurts so much that I have to lie back again. I shut my eyes against the pain. 'Where am I?'

'You're still in the pixie kingdom. I'll tell you everything when you're better,' she says. 'Aithinne will be back soon to heal you again.'

My lips feel so dry. 'What's wrong with me?'

'She said the old venom in your blood is reacting badly to the new.' I feel Catherine's fingertips on the scars at my wrist. 'From these?' she asks.

She asks the question lightly, but I note how it sounds like she's holding back emotion. 'Aye,' I say, moments from sleep again. 'From when I was in the *Sìth-bhrùth*.'

'I'm sorry I wasn't there for you,' she whispers.

I tighten my hand in hers. I can't tell if she's talking about what happened with Lonnrach or the wisps. I can only manage three words: 'I'm sorry, too.' *I'm sorry this is the world I left you with.*

The next time I wake I feel sharper, more alert. When I look over to see if Catherine's still there, I'm surprised to find Gavin is sitting in a chair beside the bed, reading a book. He looks up when I stir. 'You look better.' He closes his book and sets it aside.

Someone has changed my clothes. I'm wearing a clean white

raploch shirt that's about twice my size and trousers that fit only slightly better. My injuries are all healed from Aithinne's work. The lighter bites hardly left any outline at all; the deeper ones are still small, barely more than circular marks between Lonnrach's bites.

Unfamiliar scars wrap around my wrists. From the shackles, I realise. When the wisps attacked, I had strained against them so much that they cut into my skin. I hadn't even noticed.

I set my jaw. 'Where's Catherine?'

'She's been with you for days now,' Gavin says. 'It was my turn.'

'What if I don't want you to have a turn?'

Gavin looks away. 'I know you're angry.'

'You really don't know how I'm feeling.' I stare down at the scars again. I managed never to resist against the ivy in the mirrored room. I never had a reminder of that. Now I do.

Gavinwinces when he notices the scars. 'I should have told you about—'

'You didn't tell me about the wisps, either,' I say sharply. 'If you had, I would have told you they can tell from my blood that I'm a Falconer. My energy is just as intoxicating to them as a Seer's, Gavin.'

Guilt flashes in his gaze. 'I didn't know about that.'

'Because you didn't *ask!*' He opens his mouth to speak, but I'm too fast. 'Derrick told you I was different and that being a Falconer would make it worse. You lied to him about going easy on me, didn't you? You tried to kill me.'

Gavin steps back. 'No. No, I didn't. I swear I didn't.' He looks like he's about to reach for me, but his hands drop to his side. 'Because you're a Falconer I wasn't certain if you could handle the pain of their bite better than a human. For god's sake, Aileana, I've seen you fight before with injuries that would have killed anyone else.'

I shove the blanket off my legs. 'I'm not particularly in the

148

mood to hear your excuses.' When I move to stand, Gavin grasps my wrist. 'You're not well.'

I jerk away from him. 'Don't touch me.'

He puts his hands up. 'Aithinne might have healed the wisp bites, but you're still recovering from the energy they took.'

'And how, exactly, do you intend to keep me here?' I ask coldly. 'Will you shackle me again?'

Gavin flinches, but he doesn't back down. 'You're not well,' he repeats more firmly.

'I'm well enough to break that pretty nose if you come near me again.'

When he steps away, I take the opportunity to scramble out of the bed to put some distance between us. 'Get out. Tell Catherine or Aithinne to come back, or get Kiaran if you can find him. If I must have someone here to watch over me, I'd rather it be anyone but *you*.'

Gavin doesn't move. We stare at each other, a silent battle of wills. His gaze drops first, but he doesn't leave. 'I deserve that,' he says. I notice his eyes flicker to my scars again. 'And for what I said to you earlier. I shouldn't have assumed—'

'That they didn't torture me? That I wasn't *marked*?' I say tightly. I look down at my arms. 'How does this change your little narrative now?'

'It only makes me hate them more,' he says sharply. 'I hate them, Aileana. I *hate* them.'

I don't miss the way his expression is pleading, begging me to understand, but I can't. Not right now.

I make my way to the window. Charlotte Square is entirely intact, pristine. My flying machine is parked in the central garden, just as always. Seeing it there makes my chest ache, because none of this exists anymore. The greenery flourishes as it does in the throes of springtime, and the sun shines through the clouds in beams of light that settle on the grass. The weather is too beautiful, too inviting.

As my mood darkens, the sun disappears completely. The light is gone. The grass shrivels to winter brown as the storm clouds gather. I watch as snow falls onto the cobbles, settling there until the street is completely covered.

'Please go away,' I tell Gavin when he comes to stand beside me.

'Let me explain,' he says softly. 'If you want me to leave after that, I will.'

I shut my eyes briefly. 'Tell me about this place first.' I slouch against the window seat, sliding down until I'm on the cold hard wood. 'It's not real, is it?'

Now that I study the room more closely, I see that there's not one bit of *me* in it. It's just a replica, a re-creation of all the things I love in this world, the room my mother and I had designed together.

There's none of *her* here, either. There isn't a single thing I could point to as being different, but there's an emptiness to it. A neatness, as if it has never been lived in. My mother and I didn't create this place together.

I reach for my coat that Catherine left out on the window seat and dig into the pocket for my mother's tartan. I clench it so hard that my hand aches. As if I could bring everything back. As if I could bring *her* back.

'It's an illusion,' Gavin says, sitting next to me, resting his arms on his knees. 'Your pixie calls the effect *cruthaidheachd*, the creation. His kind used it to build their own worlds. Now we use it to create our old homes from our memories.'

This is like a torment, then. An empty place that has no meaning except for the parts we remember. 'Could I create anything?'

'You could. But we surround ourselves with the things we wish to see. Whatever place is foremost in our minds.' A bitter smile plays on his lips. 'I suppose this was your room?'

'Aye,' I say.

I miss it like an ache. This place doesn't smell the same,

it doesn't feel the same. 'It's an imitation,' I say. 'It has all the pieces, but they're not right. They mean nothing.'

'I disagree.' His voice is so quiet. 'Our memories mean everything, don't you think?'

I lean back and close my burning eyes again. 'What if the thing I want most isn't my room, but a city?' I swallow. 'A loved one?'

'We can't bring back the dead,' he says. 'Not even here. Believe me, more than a few of us have tried.'

I look at Gavin then. *Really* look, not like when I first saw him and was simply glad he was still alive. I see him for the man he's become, so unlike the boy I grew up with. His features are so familiar, not at all different except for the scars. But I notice other things, too.

His hair is slightly longer than I remember, just past his ears. He hasn't shaved in at least a few days – so very unlike the Gavin I knew. The shirt he wears is rough wool, open at the neck – like my hunting wardrobe. There's a scar at the base of his throat, thin and faded, as if a blade had caught him with a quick swipe.

'When we were outside you looked at me like I was a stranger,' I said. 'Like you didn't even know me. Why?'

'Is that what you assumed?'

'What else was I supposed to think?' I press my head to the wall and sigh softly. 'You were so cold. I've never seen you like that. You lied to Derrick. You sent me—'

You sent me to be tortured.

'It's been three years, Aileana,' Gavin says. 'I'm different. I had to adapt to survive. And you ... ' He searches my face. 'You weren't here for any of it. Not the hunt or the fall of the cities. You don't know what we went through.'

Why save your home instead of mine?

Show me. Now.

I only saw the smoke and the buildings. The destruction and the ash as the buildings burned. I wasn't here to see all those people massacred by the fae army. I wasn't here while the survivors picked up the pieces.

'No, I don't,' I say. Gavin looks around my room. He never saw it before it was destroyed. I changed it after he had left for university. One time I snuck him up to my old room, my —

I can create it for him, I realise. I project the memory onto the room; it's as easy as simply picturing it in my head and willing it into existence. The old gold-and-crimson-urn-patterned wallpaper, the delicate, cream-coloured curtains pulled back from the windows. A matching Persian carpet over the hardwood floor.

The furniture was all framed in teak, the cushions ivory and gold. Those were my favourite colours. When I snuck Gavin in the first time, I hid my dolls; I was so embarrassed by my blasted dolls. I didn't want Gavin to see them. But there they are on the mantel where they used to sit before my father told me it was time to give up childish things and he gave them away.

Gavin takes in my old room, his expression flickering from wonder back to shuttered and cold. 'Change it back.'

I raise an eyebrow, ignoring his tone. I've dealt with Kiaran for the longest time. Gavin is no match for me, even at his most hostile. 'Memories mean everything,' I say, quoting him, 'don't you think?'

'What is it you want me to recall?' he asks, in that dead voice I don't recognise. 'The last time I was in this room, you kissed me. Or have you forgotten?'

In an instant, the room changes back to the one I designed. The paneled teak drops over smooth patterned wallpaper, and the carpet fades into wooden boards. The furniture disappears, except for the settee, stained by my greasy, oiled fingertips touching it as I rested after metalworking.

'That was a long time ago,' I say. 'I just thought you'd be more comfortable.'

'It wasn't that much time for you.'

'Long enough, Galloway,' I say softly. He starts, staring at me in surprise. 'What? Did I say something wrong?'

Gavin shakes his head, leaning back against the window seat. 'You called me Galloway. No one's called me that in a long time.' At my confused expression, he explains, 'I don't have a title any more, Aileana. I don't have lands. After everything that happened, it just seemed like a silly formality.'

'You said you'd tell me everything,' I say. 'What happened while I was in the *Sìth-bhrùth*?'

He stares up at the clicking gears that keep the electricity going, now connected to nothing. It takes so long for him to speak, minutes. 'After *they* came – we lived in the abandoned ruins of villages first. Rounded up whoever survived. The fae found people and influenced them to betray our whereabouts.' His voice shakes, and he swallows. 'Every time we moved, they came into our villages at night to slaughter people. Those without the Sight never saw it coming.'

I watch his hands, how they toy with the fabric of his shirt as he speaks.

'So you made the test.' I try to keep the emotion out of my voice. I might understand *why*, but I don't forgive him yet. Not for that. 'With the wisps.'

He nods. 'Humans are easily influenced by the fae. Another raid would leave our population decimated.'

I study the scars on his face, how they look as though one of the fae had made a grab for his eye and sliced through the flesh around it. The scars are faded now, so pale against his skin.

'Hideous, aren't they?' His voice startles me, and I realise I must have been quiet for a while. I notice how his jaw tightens.

I shake my head. 'Not to me.' I can't stop myself from reaching up, sliding my fingers down the four jagged scars above his brow. Finally, the single one that mars his cheek. 'Your scars aren't flaws, Galloway. They're not imperfections. They're stories written on your skin.'

'*Stories?*' It sounds like he thinks the idea is silly.

'Aye,' I say. 'They tell the tale of how you survived. There's no shame in that.'

He looks at me then. 'And what stories do yours tell?' he asks me. 'Survival, too?'

I jerk away. Behind him, I notice my map, the one of Scotland on the far wall. The red ribbons tied around pins that signified Sorcha's kills. I burned that map once, scattered the pins on the floor. Now here it is again, complete and whole.

One time, I would have told Gavin that my scars told the tale of how I killed each fae. How I did it to train for the faery I most wanted dead. I would have pointed them out with pride; they were badges of victory. My scars told the tale of a girl who had stripped away the parts of her old self until nothing was left but the vengeful huntress from the mirrors.

The things that ended up mattering most in my prison had nothing to do with vengeance, or slaughtering the fae, or being a Falconer. They were dances. Laughter. Grief and friendship. Crushing embraces and hard goodbyes. Stolen kisses beneath a blood moon.

'No,' I say softly. 'These tell how I became human again.'

Chapter 19

I sleep another day. Though my limbs are still shaking when I pull myself out of bed, I'm able to walk steadily to my closet. I press my ear to the door and listen, smiling when I hear Derrick inside singing a bawdy jig. His voice is drowned out by the occasional rustle of fabric.

I knock twice before opening the door. And there he is, sprawled on a mountain of multicoloured silks, his needle and thread in hand. '*Aileanaaaa,*' he sings, wings fanning behind him. 'You're better! You're awake! You look like you were run over by a carriage and tossed into the river.'

Leaning against the door frame, I say, 'Had to add that last bit, did you?' I flex my limbs; they still ache. 'In any case, I swear this is worse. Wisps are vicious.'

Derrick's golden halo turns red at the reminder. 'I should have known that Seer was lying. If he weren't your friend, I would have flayed him alive and taken his skin as a trophy.' He pulls over one of the silks, a deep royal blue. 'But since you seem to value his life, I bit the bastard on the arm. Tit for tat. He tastes like misery.'

'And I see you came right back to my closet afterward.'

Derrick threads a needle that's almost half the size of his entire body. 'I was so happy you created it for me! I've been sleeping in my own version of your closet for the last three years and it never smelled the same. Just of wood. I hate the smell of wood.' He looks up at me. 'You've made it smell like roses in here again. And lovely waterfalls.' He smiles lazily. 'And ladies.'

I almost tell him that I didn't create the closet for *him* specifically, but he looks so pleased that saying so would make me feel like a right killjoy. So I sigh inwardly and nudge one of the silks with my toe. 'What's all this?'

'I'm sewing dresses. When I came in here, the closet looked like hell.'

'Empty, I assume?'

Derrick blinks at me as if I've suddenly turned daft. 'Of course, you silly human. What use is an empty closet? As it is, you're walking around in those hideous clothes lent out by your friend, wisp spit all over your skin.' *Wisp spit?* Good heavens. He begins stitching again, moving so quickly that all I see are streams of light. 'I even made you silk. So much better than your human silk, not that you ever asked me for it before.'

I look at him suspiciously. Pixies normally move quickly, but he's got the same twitchy movements that he gets when he's – 'Did someone give you honey?'

'Aithinne gave me just a wee dram.' He holds out his thumb and forefinger, a mere fraction apart. 'A thimbleful. I *love* her. I should make her a dress.'

Oh, for goodness' sake. Honey does make Derrick productive to a fault. Sewing, cleaning, polishing. He could build a season's wardrobe after a bowlful. 'We don't require dresses. There aren't any balls or assemblies. Remember?'

He pauses and looks up at me. 'So just because the world ends you can't dress fancy any more?'

I sigh. This must be a trick. Is there a right answer to this question? 'Well, no, but—'

'Good! Anyway, I made these for you, too.' Derrick tosses clothes at me, and I'm still too damn slow from the wisp bites to catch them. They drop to my feet in a heap. 'Hunting clothes.

Now kindly remove those hideous, ill-fitting ones, clean the foul-smelling wisp slobber off you, and put these on.'

'Brilliant,' I say drily. 'I'll do that.' I look down at the clothes Catherine dressed me in. They don't seem to be her own – they're about two sizes too big and I'm drowning in the shirt. I probably look ridiculous.

'It's all right if you smell bad,' Derrick says serenely. 'You're still my favourite.'

He goes right back to singing the bawdy jig he was in the middle of when I came in, a hint for me to close the door and leave him in peace. I respect his wishes and bend to pick up the bundle at my feet.

I lay the clothes out on my bed. The wool is flawlessly woven; I didn't think it was possible for raploch to be this soft. The stitching is, of course, perfect. The pixie could never do anything less than impeccable work.

Slowly I remove my borrowed clothes, wincing at how my muscles ache. As I do, I notice the new injuries along my arms and legs. The wee bites from the wisps are now scarred over.

The oval mirror in the corner of the room shows me the angles of my body. Even before I became a hunter, I never fit the ideal of beauty expected for a woman in society; my skin was considered so freckled that my governess once advised me to slather myself with cream to achieve smooth ivory skin. Now my peers would have considered me too muscled, the pockmarks and grooves from my healed injuries unfeminine and, in their minds, undesirable.

But after everything I've been through, I'm proud to have a body that's strong, that bears the marks of how much it has endured. No matter how painful those memories might be.

I quickly clean myself up in the basin and pull on my new clothes over my new scars. Just as I'm tucking the shirt into the trousers, the bedroom door opens.

'*Oh!*' Catherine says, stopping short. She has a tray in her hands. 'I'm terribly sorry, I expected you to still be in bed.' She frowns, shutting the door behind her. 'You *should* be in bed.'

'I've been awake five minutes and you're already mothering me?' I say, raising my eyebrow. I take a closer look at the steaming dish she carries. 'Is that food?'

She rolls her eyes and passes me the tray and I set it down. A steak of some kind with a white sauce that looks utterly unfamiliar. Not at all what I'm used to eating in the morning.

'What is this?' I'm so hungry, I hardly care. I dig in, stuffing the lean meat in my mouth. It could be as bland as scones and it would still taste like the best meal I've ever had.

'Venison. The fae here hunt and bring back the meat for us.'

I almost drop my fork. 'The *fae?*'

Catherine regards me patiently. 'I like it even less than you do, but we have a truce, and we honor it – as long as they don't kill a human.'

So this truce extends beyond letting the fae torture people in a cave as a test to prove they haven't been faestruck. I suppose I shouldn't be surprised. This is a pixie city, after all. It was made by fae, never meant to be a human space. It only makes sense that we would be forced to share it with them.

Derrick belts out a note from inside the closet that sounds like a *very* inappropriate word for a certain part of the male anatomy. Catherine stares at the door. 'My god, what's he doing?'

'Sewing,' I say, shoveling another forkful of meat into my mouth in a decidedly unladylike manner. Then I realise what just happened and I gape at her. 'Wait – you could *hear* him?'

Catherine lifts the sleeve of her shirt. There, wrapped around her wrist, is a thin strand of *seilgflùr*, the rare thistle that allows humans to see the fae. 'Everyone in the city has to wear it.'

'Where did you find it?' I've never known where Kiaran grew the thistle. He always provided my stock, part of which I used for my weapons. Without it, I would never be able to fight the fae. I wouldn't even be able to see them.

'It was a gesture of goodwill. Aithinne told me how to cultivate it before she went to find you,' Catherine says. 'So those of
us without the Sight would stand some chance of surviving.'

I should have realised it would be Aithinne. Kiaran would
never reveal such a thing to a human. 'So she taught you all how
to grow it?'

'No,' Catherine says distractedly, still listening to Derrick's
singing. 'Only a single human. I just happened to be the one she
chose.' Her eyes linger on the closet door for a moment. 'So you
just ... lived with one of them like this?'

I try not to be offended by her tone. Derrick brings out the
protectiveness in me, I suppose. He was the first faery I came to
care for, the one who taught me that not all the fae had to die.

'He's my friend,' I say shortly.

Catherine lowers her lashes, a flush creeping up her cheeks.
'I'm sorry. I didn't mean for it to sound like that. He saved us
all by letting us stay here.' She sighs. 'I just – I have difficulty
trusting them.'

She lets her voice trail off as she looks around the room. She
takes in the teak panels along the walls and the worktable beside
her – I notice now that it's empty of the metal pieces I used to
make my inventions. Another reminder of how false this place
is.

'I'm glad to see your room again,' she says softly. 'It makes me
feel ...'

'As if we're back there,' I finish for her. 'Just finishing up
elevenhours?'

'I do miss tea and shortbread.' A small smile lights her face.
'Discussing silly dances and our suitors.'

'Speaking of suitors ... you married.' I say it lightly, taking
another tiny bite of the steak.

She nods. 'Daniel. He saved my life, do you know? Mother
and I were just outside of Glasgow when the fae took the city.'

I go still. 'That must have been terrifying.' I can't even imagine.

Not being able to see them, watching people die around them. I should have prepared her better. Damnation, I just sent her away—

'We could hear the screams.' She traces her fingertips along the edge of my worktable. 'We weren't close, but even from the road we could ...'

I set the fork down with a sharp clang. Lonnrach's words from that night are still so clear in my mind.

Destroy everything.

And the fae did just as he had bid them. They reduced Scotland to nothing more than rubble and ash and Catherine was right in the middle of it. I wasn't there to protect her.

'The fae surrounded the coach,' Catherine continues. 'We couldn't see them, but their claws scraped right through the doors. Daniel fought his way inside and made us run.' She flashes a ghost of a smile, small and sad. 'He made sure they couldn't find us.'

'Lady Cassilis,' I say. 'Is she—'

'She passed last year,' Catherine interrupts, somewhat stiffly. 'Couldn't resist the fae when they called.'

I almost tell her that I'm sorry. Despite what Aithinne told me, I can't help but blame myself. In my mind I replay those last moments with the seal, and each second becomes a *should have*. I *should have* figured out the device sooner. I *should have* been stronger when Sorcha invaded my mind. I *should have* pressed that last symbol into place instead of looking to Kiaran for one last goodbye because I wanted so badly to save him.

In the end, I didn't save anyone.

'I miss it here,' Catherine says, moving closer to the window. 'No matter how much time has passed, sometimes I still think this is a dream. That it's not real.'

'I used to think that after what happened to my mother,' I say, finishing my food. I settle next to her. 'That I would wake up one day and she'd be alive and my life would be tea parties and assemblies again. But then I wonder if I was ever really meant for that world at all.'

'How silly of me.' Her cheeks darken, as if she's embarrassed. 'You knew what was out there while I spoke of suitors and dances. I must have looked like such a fool.'

'Never,' I tell her. 'Not to me.'

Somewhere a door slams shut and I hear a shout in heavy accented Scots. Catherine looks annoyed. 'That would be my husband winning at whist,' she mutters. 'It would seem I need to have another talk with him about his abhorrent behavior. I can't apologize enough for what happened.'

'It's not your fault,' I say tightly. And it might be terribly inappropriate to box my dearest friend's husband in the face for what he did, to say nothing of what he almost called me.

'Bollocks.' I gape at Catherine; I've never heard her use that word before. 'They played with your life. You could have died, and I said as much to my fool brother. He should have known a Falconer wouldn't need to be tested. You would be able to resist fae influence just like a Seer.'

I freeze. I had confided in Catherine about slaying faeries, but I had never revealed anything about being a Falconer. 'You *know*?'

'Of course I know,' she says with a wave of her hand. 'If you thought that was a secret Gavin could keep for three years ... the man can't even hide where he keeps his best whisky from me. He gives a decent bluff to anyone else, but I find him to be an *awful* liar.'

More laughter erupts from down the hall and I stare at the door that leads to the pixie city. When I imagine Derrick's kingdom, I assume it would accommodate his small size, with buildings that wouldn't fit humans at all. 'What does it look like?'

Catherine follows my gaze. 'Oh, the city?'

I put a hand up to interrupt her. 'Before you say anything else, *please* don't tell me we're in some pocket pixie realm on Skye.

All of us shrunk down to the size of bugs, or something.' At Catherine's baffled look, I say, 'This is my absurd way of bracing myself.'

'No, no. Nothing like that,' she assures me. 'We're still in the human realm. The pixies built the city underwater between the mainland and Skye. They erected tunnels that lead all around the island—' She halts, flashing a devious smile, the same one she's had since we were children. 'It seems I'll just have to show you, won't I?'

Chapter 20

When Gavin and the others referred to the pixie kingdom as a city, I thought perhaps that was what they simply called it when they came here to live, a familiar word for an unfamiliar place. In fact, it *is* a city. A real city. One so massive I can scarcely believe it has been hidden underwater all this time.

My room is on the fourth deck of a towering beehive-shaped structure beneath the sea. Tall, arching columns form the supporting framework, which is set within the bedrock of the undersea cave system. Those columns appear made of quartz. Upon closer inspection, I notice a glimmer to the rock, a fernlike pattern of inclusions along the surface. It juts out to form rows and rows of balconies with their own arched entrances, each one leading to individual doors – hundreds of them. They make up a structure that curves up toward the surface of the water between the Isle of Skye and the mainland.

Above us, some lights twinkle like stars while others zip back and forth between the uppermost balconies. It takes me a moment to realise they aren't stars; they're fae. More will-o'-the-wisps. My hand immediately touches the deepest bites on my neck, now healed over in a thick scar.

The startling sound of chatter draws my attention back to the ground. It looks so much like the streets of a Scottish city: the cobbled roads are lined with lamps that make them shine.

The buildings are tall, towering, and thin as tenements. Between them are houses of flawless white marble. Others are built from the cave stone that resembles sparkling black obsidian.

And there are people – hundreds of people – walking about and smiling and laughing and chatting. They wander the streets through something like a market, with so much produce and food.

From here I can see signs for things I've never seen or tasted before: Egyptian oranges, coconuts from the West Indies ... The fae can grow or retrieve anything a human desired. They could create food from nothing, if they wanted. Is this part of their truce with humans?

Catherine steps up beside me. 'Extraordinary, isn't it?'

I glance back at the wisps again, watching them weave around each other like hundreds of fireflies. I remember the pressure of their bites, the blinding pain. My hand itches for a weapon for protection, even though the wisps don't seem to notice I'm here. 'Aye. Extraordinary.'

Catherine must have heard the catch in my voice, because she immediately looks over in concern. 'Are you all right?' She notices the focus of my attention, still on the wisps. 'They won't hurt you here without breaking the truce, but if you need to go inside, I understand.'

I can't help my unease. I killed the fae for a year before Lonnrach put me in that prison. My relationship with the fae is marked by violence; I don't trust them, even with the truce.

Lonnrach's voice is unrelenting in my memories. A cruel taunt to the powerless girl in his prison. *Now you know precisely how it feels to be that helpless.*

'No,' I say, more sharply than I intended. 'I'm fine.'

'Aileana—'

'You were going to tell me about the city. Please continue.'

Catherine sighs and leans against the balustrade. 'We rebuilt most of it. When we arrived, the buildings had been almost completely destroyed.' She half smiles. 'And, of course, the remaining ones couldn't fit a human. We kept the structure itself, but the rest is ours.'

There is pride in her voice as she looks out at the buildings. I hate being unable to share that with her. I lied about being fine.

Focus, I tell myself. *Calm*. My hands slip to my pockets, where I usually keep wee inventions to tinker with, only to find none. So I grip the hem of my coat. 'You built all of this in only a few years?' My voice sounds strained and I hope she doesn't notice.

She does. I notice in the way she shifts closer, as if to comfort me. Or, perhaps, to prepare me for what she says next. 'The fae helped,' she says tightly. 'As part of the truce. We would never have been able to finish it so quickly – and they have increased powers here, of course. The city is built over a *neimhead*.'

'*Neimhead*?' I'm not familiar with the word, not even from Kiaran's lessons.

'A sacred place of power. For *them*.' She nods to the fae sparkling above us. 'They say this is the most ancient one of all.'

I stare at the wisps again – the vile creatures dancing without a care in the world. 'Can we go down there?' I say, control breaking. I can't handle it. Any longer up here, near to the fae, and I might end up killing them. I'd rather not start a war when I've only just arrived.

Catherine's expression is one of understanding. 'Of course we can.'

She pulls the lever next to her and the balcony begins to lower. I lean over my stone balcony to study it better. A mechanism along the bottom allows it to lift and lower to the other floors, pausing at each one, until it finally sets down on the cobblestone road. Catherine pushes the lever back into place, unlatching a portion of the balcony – an iron gate – and leads me to the street.

The city reminds me of Edinburgh at night before they installed electricity, the way the street lamps were lit, fire flickering in their glass orbs. The pools of light make the cobblestones – cut from the same cave rock as the outer walls of the city – shine in the firelight. It doesn't seem constricting down here, not at all moist or dripping as if we were in a normal cave. The air is different, as crisp as an autumn day; the scent of fire and rain mixes with the taste of startlingly sweet fae power, from honeysuckle to ginger and then to stronger tastes like black powder and ash.

A crackling above us startles me. I look up to see clouds gathering along the top of the structure, lightning flickering from within them. Rain begins to fall onto the buildings and the streets. I watch as people pause their routine and tip their heads toward the sky to feel the rain on their faces.

'What are they doing?' I ask. This is Scotland, after all. Pausing to pay attention to a rainfall would be like stopping every time a tree branch shakes.

Catherine puts out her palm to catch the raindrops. 'Most people here haven't been outside in years. It's easy to miss things we once took for granted.'

I try to hide my shock. No matter how beautiful the city is, I can't imagine being trapped in here for that long. This weather is like the rooms, a perfect, overly sanitized replica. It's missing something – that something I can't name that makes you feel *alive* whenever you walk outside. That makes you breathe deep and savor the air in your lungs.

'And if they went outside?' I ask. 'What would happen?'

Catherine thrusts her hands into her trouser pockets. 'They might not come back.'

So the fae would take them. They'd die or, worse, be taken to the *Sith-bhrùth* and kept until their captors finally tired of them and disposed of them.

As Catherine and I walk down the busy street, we draw more than a few curious stares. The road smells of fruits and flour and rain and mist, a combination that reminds of me of Edinburgh on market day when the streets bustled like this.

Aside from the splendour of the city lights and how clean

the streets are, the people here are different than in Edinburgh. They dress in the softest wool, dyed in earth tones, their trousers and coats so well made – perhaps by the fae – that there's no outward distinction of class. There's nothing to tell a commoner from those who grew up in the aristocracy, like me or Catherine. Some here have darker skin – a range of different shades from different places – and I catch whispers of languages I don't recognise.

As if sensing my thoughts, Catherine leans in to murmur, 'We don't know much about what's happened elsewhere, but the fae took people from all over. Derrick was able to save some before they became faestruck.'

Not just Scotland.

Lonnrach may have ripped Scotland apart in his quest to find the object that can save the *Sìth-bhrùth* – but destroying everywhere else is for another purpose entirely: to rebuild the splendour of the fae empire once he has saved his home. His soldiers are out conquering nations.

What was it Kiaran once told me? *We did not gain dominion over every continent by being polite.*

They did it by nearly wiping out every human in existence.

We pass another a stall with the most heavenly smelling bread and a few of the patrons stop chatting to stare as I pass.

'Don't let it intimidate you,' Catherine tells me, flashing them a disarming smile. She always was better at socializing and making friends than I. 'They're just curious. We haven't had an outsider here in a long time.'

'I'm used to people staring at me,' I say. 'Remember?'

Every ball we attended the winter after my mother's death was a disaster. I had been found sitting next to her body the night of her murder, and many of our peers believed I had something to do with it – or that I was directly responsible. Catherine spent so much time defending me against the gossip and suspicion.

'Gavin told me what really happened to your mother,' she

says, edging around a group of chatting youths who stop to smile at me tentatively. 'Aileana, I'm so sorry.'

'Don't,' I say, not wanting to speak of it further. 'You remained steadfast even when everyone else didn't. In any case, how could you have known?'

We stop next to a beautiful marble building, and I slide my palm down the column near the front door. No, it's not marble. It's smooth as glass, with colours in the rock that change depending on the way the light flickers from the gas lamp behind me. From ivory to pink to lavender ... then back again.

Catherine doesn't look away from me. She doesn't seem notice how the people around us greet her with wide smiles and me with apprehension. As if they aren't sure why I'm here after so long on the outside, or if I'm really safe. I wonder how many others came in and proved they weren't faestruck. Not many, I'd imagine – at least, not after three years. Humans nearby would never have survived this long without being killed or taken by the fae.

Finally, Catherine speaks. 'I should have listened to the part of me that always knew you weren't telling me the whole truth.'

I look at her in surprise. Her voice is clipped, more stern than I've ever heard her. I'm beginning to realise that in my absence Catherine has grown into the quiet strength she always had. Even the way she stands is no longer the hands-clasped, demure stance we were taught in etiquette lessons. She has the confident stride of a leader, a woman who has fought to survive.

'That obvious, was I?'

I never thought I played the part of debutante to perfection. I'm sure there were always inconsistencies in my performance, cracks in the mask I donned to attend parties and balls. Flickers of the monster inside me that could only be sated with a kill.

Catherine lifts her fingers to tick things off. 'You mean aside from the headaches, the disappearing during balls, the constant oil on your fingertips, the mysterious illnesses, the—'

'Thank you,' I say drily. 'Point well made indeed.'

'Face it, I know you too well. You're even worse at lying to me than Gavin is.' Catherine grins and threads an arm through mine. 'Now come along. Let me show you the rest.'

Rain beats against the cobblestones in a steady rhythm now. I follow Catherine to the outskirts of the city, where the vast cave wall looms before us. It is dotted with tunnels, some lit and others so dark that I can't see past the entrance.

Catherine chooses a narrow passage. Lamps are affixed to the walls on either side of us, firelight flickering within. The flecks within the rock catch in the light, glittering as we pass.

I shudder beneath my new coat. Not even Derrick's wool can keep out the cold, damp conditions within the cave as we descend deeper into the earth, down and down the rocky, uneven steps.

We reach a point where there are no lamps at all. The cave glistens with its own internal glow, like light beneath water, with shadows flickering along the walls. I feel my way down the steps carefully.

Catherine's movements are far steadier than mine; she must come down here often. Once we reach the bottom of the passage, the rock glitters around us as though we are dashed out in space, surrounded by millions and millions of stars.

Before us lies a vast field, lit only by the cave's own internal light. A stone pathway cuts across the meadow between rows and rows of plants. The vivid blue tips of the flowers stand out immediately and I stare in awe. '*Seilgflùr*,' I whisper.

The thistle is grown high, the stocks so very still. It's silent around us; not even drops of water reach this part of the cave. There isn't a whisper of creatures living among the plants. Everything is entirely quiet and peaceful.

I edge forward among the stocks, brushing my fingers against the thistle that is as soft as feathers. The scent from the field is strong, like fire and ash and rock – volcanic. The soil beneath my boots is cushioned and moist.

Even the air is different. As I breathe it in, I recognise hints of sandalwood, witch hazel, and iron, even flowers and sweetness. As if every bit of fae power I've ever tasted has been combined into a single scent.

'I like to come down here and think sometimes,' Catherine says, walking beside me. 'It's quiet. Safe.'

I can understand why such a place would be a sanctuary. 'I've never been able to cultivate *seilgflùr*,' I tell her. 'I tried for months.'

Not even a single clipping could grow under my care. In water, it withered and died. Even a plant pressed between sheets of airtight glass quicky lost its luster and power. The plant's gift of Sight and as a weapon always proved ineffective after only a couple of weeks.

'It's quite a finicky thing, isn't it?' Catherine says, touching one of the stocks lightly.

I smile slightly. 'I suppose you can't tell me how you grow it, can you?'

Catherine pauses. 'I can. The thistle was meant to be tended to by Falconers.' She plucks off a flower and twirls it. 'Aithinne only entrusted these fields to me until your return.'

Oh, lord. I was never terribly good with growing things to begin with. 'I'd probably kill them all. Remember, I thought the weeds were flowers and the flowers—'

'Were weeds.' She laughs. 'I remember.'

'But I'm still curious.'

'*Seilgflur* can only be grown in darkness over a *neimhead* to take advantage of its power. And it has to be fertilized with the blood of the fae.'

I look at her in surprise. 'I *beg* your pardon?'

A ghost of a smile plays on her lips. 'Ah. I see you never knew that.'

Of course not. That must have been why Kiaran kept it a secret, why he refused to give me my own plant to cultivate.

He must have assumed the worst about me: that I would have found a *neimhead* to grow a field just like this one and fertilized it with the blood of my victims.

I would have killed more just to keep the stocks tended, the plants fresh. All while oblivious to the fact that my kills alerted Sorcha to my whereabouts. It would have made me more of a monster than I already am.

'Where do you get the blood?' I ask her, my voice hoarse.

'It's part of the truce,' she says softly. 'They pay their end of the bargain in blood and service.'

What do you promise them in return?

Just then, a low light from the other end of the field draws my attention and the question dies on my lips. There's a door there that's illuminated around its frame. It towers about ten feet high, constructed of heavy, scorched wood. Symbols are carved into the panels that remind me of those I had seen on Aithinne's seal. My gaze roves over the inticate etchings. As I draw closer, I notice the door is slightly ajar, the light behind it flickering as if coming from a fire. Laughter echoes from inside, then heavy drumming starts slow. A bagpipe joins the steady beat; the high drone from the pipes echoes off the walls. The song is beautiful, with the most immaculate piping I've ever heard, each note formed together in a seamless lullaby.

I close my eyes and try to place the song. There it is, like a memory long lost. I recall a night spent in the country as a child. The bonfires burned before Hogmanay, when people carried torches throughout the village. They played the pipes and sang as I watched from a window of the estate.

I edge closer, the taste of fae powers stirring together so strongly that I can't distinguish any single type. When I finally reach the threshold, I press my palms to the thick door. The energy in the symbols is so strong that I shiver.

'*Aileana!*'

Catherine is there, grasping my arm firmly. I start. The music is suddenly gone, as if it had never been there to begin with. The door before me is tightly shut, without so much as a light burning through the slits in the wood.

'What the bloody hell was that?' My tongue is heavy, burning with power.

Catherine pulls me away. 'We don't go in there.' Her grip on me tightens. '*Never* go in there. They vowed not to harm us when they come to our side, but we have no protection if we visit theirs.' She shakes me, lashing out in her concern. 'Do you understand?'

I almost tell her that I don't understand a damn thing, but the power is still so overwhelming that it's difficult to speak, or to concentrate on anything else. I glance up at the door and the taste returns again, this time in a lingering brush of flower petals along the roof of my mouth, less potent. I swear the etchings in the door pulse and glow.

I touch the wood again and the power beats more strongly there. 'I can sense them. For god's sake, how many live in there?'

'Hundreds, maybe thousands. You heard the music?' At my nod, Catherine tugs on my arm again and I let her pull me away from the door to the comparative safety of the path. 'It's different for every person. It stirs up a pleasant memory so you can't resist.'

I suddenly recall the stories when people were convinced they could hear music in the hills or within crags. There is no music; it's simply one of the many ways the fae manipulate humans. Sorcha once made me think I heard my mother singing.

'Aye,' I say bitterly. 'A faery has used it against me before.'

'That's how they took people when we lived in the ruins,' Catherine tells me. 'We heard the music almost every night. Some people could resist – the Seers are almost entirely unaffected – but most couldn't.' She sighs and releases me. 'My mother couldn't.'

Perhaps Daniel and Gavin were right not to trust me. Being

unable to access my full Falconer abilities had left me open to Sorcha's influence, and just now the fae could have manipulated me into walking through their door. Lonnrach used the same weakness against me twice before, and I just barely broke our connection.

'How do you handle it?' I ask Catherine. She was so easily faestruck by Kiaran back in Edinburgh; I can't imagine how she managed to protect herself without any natural resistance. 'How have you withstood this long?'

Catherine sets her jaw. Without a word, she lifts the long sleeve of her thick wool shirt to bare the pale underside of her forearm. There, marked into the skin, are fingernail scratches, some long and jagged, others half-moon marks pressed hard into her arm. Some are faded, scars that look years old. Others are scabbed over and dotted with dried blood, as recent as a few days.

'Christ,' I breathe.

She lowers her sleeve and I don't miss how her fingers shake. 'I won't let them control me,' she says firmly. 'If pain keeps their influence at bay, then I'll do whatever I need to survive. I won't end up like my mother.'

I won't end up like my mother. I've lost count of how many times I made the same vow. I promised myself that I would never be murdered as my mother had, in the street, torn up and bloodied. My heart a trophy to whatever faery managed to slay me.

How can I tell Catherine to stop doing the very thing that has kept her alive? After all, I'm a less than sterling example for her to look up to. Seeing what happened to my mother made *me* into a killer.

I stare at the door again and ask, 'Why would you allow them to stay? They're not safe.'

Catherine lets out a frustrated breath. 'Because we need them. Their blood keeps the thistle alive. They hunt for us and grow food and help us build. They even keep the fae on the outside from sensing that we're here. It's not an alliance we ever wanted, but we can't survive out there.'

'But they always want something in return,' I snap. 'It's not in their nature to help without payment.'

'Aileana—'

'Don't. I think I understand.' The effect of the fae power is still so strong that it churns my stomach. 'Why there's no protection for humans who enter their door. Why the truce doesn't extend to their luring music.' I can barely say it. 'If people do hear it and can't control themselves from coming down here, you let them, don't you? You all look the other way in exchange for what they're willing to give you.' At Catherine's silence, I step away. 'That's – I can't *believe* you.'

Catherine's mouth snaps shut. 'Don't look at me like that. Do you think I haven't lost sleep over it?' She looks away. 'I deliberately put this field here to keep them safe. As long as they stay in the city, the thistle makes it impossible to hear the music.'

'Then what else do you give them?' I laugh bitterly. 'Because you can't tell me the fae are content to wait for their occasional human victim.'

'Shelter,' Catherine says sharply. 'Protection.'

I make a sound of disgust. 'They don't need protection from anything. For god's sake, *they're* the ones who kill humans. They're probably in there plotting our demise, figuring out a way to get around their truce. They can't be trusted.'

'You really don't know, do you?' she says with sudden understanding. 'They were hunted, too.'

I start in surprise. 'Excuse me?'

'It's a pledge we make before the Wild Hunt.' Kiaran's voice rings out from behind us.

I turn. Kiaran is on the stone path between the stocks of *seilgflùr*, a risky place to be. If he so much as touches the plant, the thistle will burn his skin. He's dressed in black trousers and a crisp white shirt open at the collar.

Kiaran's eyes lock with mine. It's such an intimate thing, that look. '*Marbhaidh mi dhuibh uile,*' he says softly. 'I shall kill them all.'

As if he knows. As if he's said it before.

Beside me, Catherine stiffens. I watch her hand slip just beneath her sleeve to sink her fingernails there. I flinch.

'Forgive my rudeness,' she says. 'I believe I'm needed elsewhere.' Before I can protest, Catherine strides away. As she passes Kiaran, she steps between the stocks of thistle, deliberately putting as much distance between them as possible. She disappears down the passage we came in through.

'What did you do to Catherine?' I ask. A thought occurs to me. 'Don't tell me she remembers when you accidentally faestruck her in the park.'

His lips twitch. Kiaran's almost-smile; just seeing it makes my heart leap. 'That remains our secret.'

'Then why was she looking at you like she wishes she had the means and opportunity to murder you?'

'My kind slaughtered almost everyone she knew,' he says. 'She doesn't trust me.'

'Well, you did just threaten to maim her husband.'

I know I shouldn't trust Kiaran either. Not after everything he's done. But the truth is, I can't remember the single defining moment when I decided to trust Kiaran. It just … happened. Like the way I came to care so much for him just happened. Somewhere between our hunts and our kills and our kisses, he left his mark on my bones.

Now I see why Kadamach moved heaven and earth to find you.

I don't tell Kiaran that it was the memories of us I treasured most in Lonnrach's prison. That I would spend hours trying to remember every detail of his kiss, every feeling, every word, for proof that I wasn't just some discarded pet. That it all meant nothing.

I turn away. It's safer not to look at him. I'm already feeling too many things I wish I didn't. 'You said it was a pledge *we* make. Does that mean you did, too?'

Suddenly, he's close. I can feel the heat of his body, how his muscles are tensed like a predator ready to spring. His breath is at my neck, lips close enough to brush the skin there. 'I was the one who made the pledge first.'

I don't dare move. It's too much when he gets like this, equal parts seductive and dangerous.

In an instinctive move, my hand inches to my belt, where I keep my blade. *Damn.* I left it in my room. 'When?'

'When the first Wild Hunt pillaged the land and we killed everything in our path.' I'm about to pull away, but Kiaran stops me, his fingers grasping mine. 'Who do you think brought the pixie city to ruin?' His lips are by my ear, a kiss pressed to the tender curve of my neck. I shudder. 'I did.'

I jerk away from him. Damn it all, I forgot again.

Kiaran was once Kadamach, a ruthless killer who had been among the worst of the fae. It was his love for another Falconer that changed him, made him side with humans. But that doesn't mean he's good or harmless. After all, everyone thinks badgers are harmless right before they bite you.

'You killed Derrick's family,' I say flatly.

'His family, his friends.' Kiaran's eyes glow in the dim light from the field, so startlingly vivid and uncanny. 'Almost everyone he loved.'

Good god. He speaks about slaughter so nonchalantly, as if he's telling me how to use a new weapon. How little he seems to care sparks the anger in me.

'Why?'

'*Why?*' Kiaran sets his jaw. 'Why do you sleep, or feel, or do any of the things humans do without thinking twice? I killed them because to me it was like breathing.' He tries to step closer as if to touch me, but I back the hell away. His hand falls to his side. 'It's what I was made for.'

I can imagine him like that so easily. It's the way he gets when we hunt together, as if there's nothing else in the world he loves more than a battle. It's an exhale of a sword thrust, an inhale of a blade through sinew and bone – the rhythm of a kill.

I made you the same as me. I hunted because it was how I existed, one kill to the next. As monsters do.

'Do you ever regret it?' I whisper. 'Everything you've done?'

His gaze is empty. No guilt or even a hint of remorse there. 'I have little purpose in my life for regrets.'

'That doesn't answer my question.'

Kiaran smiles, that beautiful false smile that makes my heart ache. His face is a mask, flawless and immaculate, no hint of passion or emotion. Even statues have more life.

'Do you still seek the good in me, Kam?' He grasps the flower of a thistle between his fingers, as if to remind me what it does. I wince at how his skin blisters and burns almost immediately. He doesn't release it, doesn't show any sign of pain at all. 'Do you still wish I were honorable?'

I reach out and grasp his wrist firmly. 'MacKay, *stop it.*'

Kiaran releases the thistle, the false smile now gone. 'How much do you need to learn about my past before you understand that there isn't a single part of me that's human?'

'You're not Kadamach,' I snap. 'Not any more. You haven't been for thousands of years.'

There's a flicker of an emotion in his gaze, gone so quickly. 'You speak that name as if you know what it means.' He gestures behind me. 'The *sithichean* behind that door have long memories. So does your pixie. To them, I will always be Kadamach.'

'And yet when you fought by my side to protect them all, your past didn't matter.' My eyes hold his, and my voice lowers to a whisper. 'When you kissed me, it didn't matter.'

There it is, an emotion behind that normally cool, detached gaze. Not wanting to lose it, I inch closer, just as he did. I listen to his breath hitch – only slightly, but still noticeable. How his hand tightens in mine and something akin to desire and longing crosses his features.

I press my fingers to the pulse at his wrist and relish how it quickens. 'You'll always be Kiaran to me.'

He makes a sound deep in his throat and grasps my shirt. His lips are on mine, soft, insistent. Aching. *More*, I want more. I deepen our kiss —

Then a high mechanical wail resounds all around us, startling me out of his arms.

'What the hell *is* that?'

'The early warning system.' Kiaran is breathing hard. 'It means *sithichean* are in the territory.'

Chapter 21

$\mathcal{K}$iaran leads me through the city streets. I watch as people hurry for the tenements around us, for their balcony rooms in the beehive structure.

Shutters and doors slam around me. I'm amazed by the silence, the lack of panic. If anyone speaks, it's in hushed whispers, encouragements to *be quick*. The people of the city move at an efficient, hurried pace, as if they've done this many times before. They must have, when they lived in the ruins Gavin described.

I wonder if they even realise that these walls won't protect them if the fae breach the city. Whatever wards Derrick put up would only hold for so long. They would be dead in an instant.

'Is this place under siege often?' I ask as a couple rushes past us to their dwelling.

'No.' Kiaran leads me down a close that's so narrow that the light from the street lamps doesn't reach it. 'They haven't found the city. It's usually a few stray soldiers sweeping the forests nearby.' *These alarms are for something as little as that?* He catches my surprised expression. 'We're overly cautious for a reason.'

I'm reminded of Gavin's words. *Another raid would leave our population decimated.*

Just before we step out from the buildings, the light cuts from the city and the alarm suddenly goes quiet. One by one the street lamps extinguish and we're left in darkness. I look up. Even the will-o'-the-wisps have ceased to dance above. In a stream of light, they head for a passage at the back of the cave, their lights twinkling out as they flee. The clouds are gone. There is nothing but the effervescent glitter of rocks, the steady sounds of our breathing.

'Keep up, Kam,' Kiaran says over his shoulder.

'I see your patience hasn't improved,' I mutter, catching up with him. This reminds me of our hunts, how I always had to match his hurried pace through the streets of Edinburgh. 'So where are we going?'

Kiaran grasps my hand, pressing his palm to mine as we head through another dark close. 'When the warning system is triggered, the Seers meet to assess the threat.' He leads me down a set of old stone steps. 'You ought to be there.'

The air around us grows colder, as if even the heating system within the city has shut down. 'Seers? You mean there are others aside from Gavin and Catherine's husband?'

'Two other feather-brained fools. Together, they have all the sense of a chair leg.'

My lips curve into a smile. 'Am I really the only human you can stand?'

'You have a certain charm. It's grown on me.'

I can't help laughing. 'Please, don't strain yourself with flattery.'

He's quiet a moment. I can't tell if he's smiling any more. His touch startles me, fingers threading through mine. 'Kam,' he says, voice barely above a breath. '*Bha mi gad ionndrainn.*'

He says it so seriously that I can't help but pause. 'What does that mean?'

He leans forward and kisses me once, softly. 'I missed you.'

I flush, my cheeks burning. He missed me? *He missed me.* I don't even know what to make of that.

Kiaran releases me and turns away. I hear the click of a latch before he opens a door I hadn't even realised was there. Golden light streams into the dark close.

He beckons me to enter and I follow him into a massive room so lush that it takes my breath away. Polished mahogany lines the walls, glowing in the light from the chandelier overhead. The walls are covered in tapestries, intricate in their detail, sewn with threads that shine like the inside of a seashell.

The tapestries detail epic battles between the fae and all of them show pixies as victors. Some depict the trophies the pixies took: the fallen heads of their enemies. The battles take place in front of a castle of pointed glass, a monstrous thing that towers into the sky.

I notice a familiar face in the threads. Derrick, sword in hand. Derrick, covered in blood. Derrick, standing victoriously over a pile of faery bodies. Derrick —

'What the hell are they doing here?'

I look over at where Daniel stands with his hands clenched at his sides, eye glaring at me in stark anger. Catherine and Gavin stand behind him, and the other two must be the Seers Kiaran just mentioned. The blasted pixie in question zips around Daniel in a trail of gold.

Seeing me, Derrick launches himself at my shoulder and sits there. 'Good, now you're here and we can get started finding out who's roaming around outside. Just ignore the angry Cyclops.'

Daniel stalks over, his boots heavy on the spun-gold carpet. I hear Catherine's muttered curse as she follows him. 'Daniel, don't.'

He doesn't listen to her. Now that we're in full light, I study his features better. Daniel isn't handsome in any conventional fashion – two days' worth of stubble covers his chin, and his remaining eye has the sharp glare of a hawk.

Daniel does hold himself with a confidence that is undeniably charismatic. Though I must admit: I'm a wee bit surprised at Catherine's attraction to him. She always seemed to prefer men who were the very definition of a *gentleman*: well groomed, well dressed, well mannered, and – dare I say it – men who didn't submit ladies to the torture of faeries.

Still, I suppose I ought to make *some* effort to be nice, since he is her husband.

Daniel stops in front of me. 'Get out,' he says. His eye flickers to Kiaran. 'And take that *thing* with you.'

Well, never mind being nice then.

'*Daniel*,' Catherine snaps.

'Oy, lout!' Derrick's wings flick my ear in anger. 'That's my companion you're being rude to. Say another word and—'

'If this turns out to be something more serious than a scouting soldier,' Daniel interrupts, never looking away from me, 'how do we know *she*'s not responsible for it? She could have led them right to us.'

Derrick bares his teeth. 'We don't know that. Now *calm down*.'

But Daniel isn't listening. He steps closer to Kiaran. 'And this bastard would probably just let them kill us all.'

Kiaran's eyes flash with that uncanny light. 'Now that's tempting.'

I almost intervene, but Catherine gets there before I do. She puts a hand to Daniel's chest. 'Back off.'

'Stay out of this,' he growls.

If Catherine was angry before, now she looks downright murderous. 'I said. *Back. Off.*' When he doesn't move, Catherine grips his arm hard. 'I believe I need to speak with you. Right now.' She looks at me. 'We'll be back in a minute.'

She leaves with Daniel, shutting the door behind her with a slam that echoes through the room. After that, everyone is quiet. Then I remember we still have the company of three other men who are unabashedly gawking; Gavin and two others I haven't met.

Gavin finally clears his throat to fill the awkward silence. 'Tavish, Lorne. Will you permit me to introduce—'

The large man – Lorne – laughs and it's a deep rumble in his chest. '*Permit me*. Well, la-di-da, Lord I-Have-an-Earldom.'

'Don't be an arsehole, Lorne,' Tavish says. 'There's a lady

present, for god's sake, man.' Then he looks at me. 'I'm Tavish – uh, Mr. Gray.' He smacks his companion in the stomach, who lets out a hearty *oof*. 'And this impolite son of a bitch is Mr. Candish.'

'If you call me Mr. Candish,' Lorne says, 'I won't bother responding.'

'*Well*,' Gavin says, 'after that unseemly introduction ...' He gestures to me. 'This is Lady Aileana Kameron.' He turns to Kiaran, rather reluctantly. 'And you've already seen Kiaran, who is—'

'Leaving,' Kiaran interrupts briskly. 'My threshold for human tolerance is now exceeded. Send the pixie for me in the event I get to stab something.'

With that, Kiaran turns on his heel and strides out of the room. *Damn him.*

'The fae are a crabbit lot, aren't they?' Lorne says thoughtfully. Then he glances at Derrick. 'No offense.'

Out of the corner of my eye, I see Derrick smile sweetly. 'At least we're not oafish simpletons. *No offense.*'

'Gentlemen. ' Catherine's voice cuts across the room. Daniel comes in behind her looking rather ... well, rather like a man who just received a verbal lashing. 'As much as I adore listening to you all squabble like children, we've a situation to address.' She nods to Tavish. 'Are you ready?'

Tavish sits in his chair. He moves his head from side to side and wiggles his fingers as if to relax. With one long, drawn-in breath, he settles into his seat.

I glance at my shoulder to see Derrick staring at Tavish intently. 'What's he doing?' I whisper.

Derrick's wings brush my ear as he leans in closer. 'Seers have different abilities,' he says in a low voice. 'Many, like Gavin, can see into the future. Tavish can project himself outside of his own body to view things at a distance.'

I watch Tavish with renewed interest. His entire body goes

still, fingers clenching and unclenching on the armrests. His breathing is even deeper, deeper still, until his chest expands far outward with every breath. 'Almost there,' he breathes, 'almost there.'

The entire room is silent; no one speaks or moves I watch as Tavish's breathing quickens, faster and faster as if he's running.

Suddenly, his eyes open wide. They are stark white, smooth like marble. He exhales slow, and then it's as if he isn't breathing at all. 'They're at the west boundary,' he says. His voice is calm, mechanical, barely human. 'Fifty, at least. Spreading out through the trees.'

'Should we get ready to fight them?' I can't help but ask, dreading the answer.

Lonnrach might be out there looking for me, and I'm not ready to battle him yet. I need more time.

Daniel raises an eyebrow. '*We?*'

Gavin moves to stand right beside me. He leans in, so the others can't hear. 'Don't even think about it,' he says. 'We wait until there's an immediate threat before we draw attention to ourselves and risk more lives.'

Before I can respond, he addresses Tavish. 'Are they just passing through?' He says it lightly, but there's an edge to his voice. I wonder if they've lost people before when the fae *just passed through.*

'It seems so,' Tavish says. The tension leaves his body. 'Looks like a normal sweep. They should be out of the territory in a few minutes.'

A sudden movement from Derrick draws my attention. He appears to be in deep concentration, wings fluttering as fast as a dragonfly's. His fingers press a little too hard into my skin and his halo grows brighter, the taste of his powers increasing on my tongue.

'And the wards are still up,' he says. 'Good, now I can get back to—'

'Christ,' Tavish breathes, spine going rigid as he sits upright. 'They're starting to dig.'

Daniel shrewdly assesses me. I know what he's thinking: *They're looking for me. Lonnrach is looking for me.*

All I care about is finding the object hidden in your realm. And you're going to help me with it, willingly or no.

I swallow back the curse that almost escapes my lips, my body tensing.

'Is their location above any tunnels to the city?' Daniel asks.

'Aye. They're just above the long passage to the centre of the island. If they keep digging, they'll find it.'

Daniel shuts his eye briefly. 'Then we'll have to lead them elsewhere.' He looks at Catherine, his face softening for the first time since I've met him. 'You know what to do if they breach the wards. Lead everyone through the tunnels, and don't wait for me.'

I watch them embrace, and I have a sudden sense that I shouldn't be here as they say their good-byes. It's too intimate. Too final.

Derrick tugs on my ear. 'Don't just stare. *Do* something.'

I step forward to grasp Daniel's arm. He turns to me in surprise. 'You can't go out there,' I tell him.

'It's nothing to worry about,' he says, somewhat gruffly, possibly because I'm showing any concern for him at all. 'We've done this dozens of times before.'

'For god's sake, Cyclops,' Derrick says from my shoulder. His wings flick my ear. 'Listen to her.'

Daniel glares at Derrick; Derrick glares back. Even though Daniel *knows* the fae are coming for me, he's still going to risk his life to lead them away. I can't let that happen. I may not be ready to fight Lonnrach, but I'll be damned if I allow someone else to die for me.

'Then I'm coming with you,' I say.

I recognise the look Daniel gives me then – it's the same

expression men gave me at tea parties and balls when I tried to talk to them about science or engineering. The same gentle, patronizing look of a man who wants to thank me for contributing but ultimately doesn't believe I know what the bloody hell I'm doing.

Derrick's wings are humming so fast they hurt my ear. 'Aye, and I'm going, too,' he says. At Daniel's sharp look, Derrick says, 'What? I'm immortal and she's a Falconer. We stand a better chance at holding them off than the rest of you. I've seen you with a sword. You're shite.'

Daniel is unmoved. 'I recall her yelling something about a Falconer in the underneath, and it doesn't mean a damn thing to me.'

'And it makes no difference. She's not coming.' Gavin joins us, his expression harsh. 'Aileana stays with Catherine. Tavish will remain here and watch from afar; he'll alert you if anything happens.'

What on earth is he doing?

Daniel, Gavin, and Lorne turn and stride to the exit. Catherine glares at her brother's back. 'Don't listen to him. You should be out there, too.'

I nod. 'Derrick, give me a minute.'

'No,' Derrick says. 'I don't want you alone with him after what he did to you.'

I still don't trust Gavin either. I can't help the hurt of betrayal every time I look at him, even after he explained why he didn't tell me about the wisps.

With a quick stroke down Derrick's wings, I say, 'I'll be in your view the whole time. I promise.'

He grudgingly flies off my shoulder and I hurry after the men. I pull Gavin back by the fabric of his shirt before he can escape.

'Let me pass,' he says.

'No. Have you gone daft? You *know* what I am.'

Gavin crosses his arms. 'And that's why you're staying.'

'I beg your pardon?'

'If you go out there with us, they'll stop at nothing until they have you. They'll call reinforcements and we might not make it out alive.' He keeps his voice low so Catherine doesn't overhear. 'We're trying to lead them away, not incite a battle.'

'I wouldn't fight them,' I say. 'Just let me be there in case something happens.'

'I said *no*.' Gavin speaks so sharply that I almost back away. 'I can't take your word that you won't start slaughtering them out there. I've seen you kill. I've been there. What was it you told me? *You revel in it.*' He shakes his head. 'Even if you kept your promise, you'll do nothing but give them more of an incentive to find us.'

My chest aches at his words. I don't need to find where Lonnrach marked that memory on me. I don't need to see it to recall the satisfaction I once got from a kill, the hunger to kill again. It was what I lived for; it was my purpose. I basked in the hunt as if I needed it like air.

'You don't trust me,' I say, already knowing his answer.

The truth is I don't blame him. *I made you the same as me,* Kiaran once said. *The same.* Now I wonder if he meant himself as Kiaran, or if he meant Kadamach.

Gavin's features soften, as if he reads my thoughts. 'That's not it. When the day comes that we need to fight, you're the one I want by my side.' He takes me by the shoulders. 'I do trust you. I do. Just not with this.'

This time when he leaves, I let him go.

Gavin doesn't know about the mirrored room. He doesn't know that it carved the insatiable need to kill right out of me, the need that made me go out every night with a constant whispering voice that said *hunt kill maim.*

He doesn't know that I saw that part of me in a mirror, and it scared the hell out of me, too.

I sense Catherine come up behind me. 'What did he say to

you?' I hear the anger in her voice, the protectiveness, even now that she knows what I am.

'Nothing I didn't deserve.'

Chapter 22

Catherine suggests we wait in my room in case I need to grab my weapons and ride out quickly. She has Tavish sit on the settee while he watches Gavin and the others in his vision. He remains quiet, his marble eyes wide and glassy.

Catherine and I lean against the pillows on the window seat, watching the storm outside in the fake Edinburgh. Swirling rain and ice smack against the window with tremendous force. The street lamps are all lit along the pavement, though it's barely dusk.

I want to open the window, but I'm afraid the illusion might shatter. I'm afraid the Edinburgh of my imagination might disappear to reveal the glittering rock that makes up the vast underground city.

And yet … I'm tempted to test that. Could I explore the Edinburgh built entirely from my imagination? Just me alone in the place I helped destroy.

'You could make the sun shine,' Catherine says, resting back against the wall and watching the rain with me. 'Or make rainbows. Two or even three if you wanted.'

I know she's only asking me this so I can help take her mind off what might be happening to Daniel, Gavin, and Lorne. As if by shifting the weather's illusion into something serene, it would be a comfort, however small. I want to try – just for her. But I'm held back by the longing to keep Edinburgh exactly as I recall it, downpour and wind and all.

'What if I don't want rainbows?' I ask her, feeling the cold draught every time the wind pounds the rain against the window. It's so real I find it hard to believe that we aren't really there. 'What if I want to remember Edinburgh storms the way they were? They used to last for days, remember? Weeks, sometimes.'

I look past her to Tavish, rigidly seated on the settee, his alabaster eyes unblinking. He's still in the vision, entirely focused on the place where he's trained his Sight. I could wave a hand in front of his face or shout at him and he would never even wake. It takes touch to draw him out again.

Tavish is framed by the open doorway that leads to the pixie city, the light of a thousand other doors rising to the very top of the hive structure. They each create a thousand worlds, some pockets of our old lives. I wonder at which point the magic that formed those worlds cracks and bends and eventually reveals the truth: that none of it is real.

'Yes,' Catherine says drily. 'I never could go outside in the wind without breaking an umbrella.'

'What did you create behind your door?' I ask her, not wanting chatter about umbrellas or rainbows any more. It only serves to draw our attention away from this world we live in now, where the people we love are always in danger. 'Your bedroom, too?'

Gavin says I can't bring back the dead, that I can't live in an imagined world where my mother is still alive, but what if I opened my window and the fake Edinburgh didn't disappear back into the cave? Could I go in and decide never to come back out?

'Sometimes,' Catherine says softly. 'Or it's the garden at our estate in Ayr during springtime, when bluebells cover the ground there.' She pauses. 'Right now it's a boat in the middle of the Mediterranean, warm and calm, the waves lapping around me. It's always sunset there. I make the sky burn red.'

I smile at her description. 'You've never been to the Mediterranean.'

'No.' Her own smile is sad. 'I used to read Father's journals and imagine I was there. He wrote once about how it was always warm and it hardly ever rained. I wanted to travel there someday.' She traces the carvings on the windowsill that Derrick had scraped into the wood when he thought I wouldn't notice – back in that other room, my real room. 'Now I wonder if there's even a Cyprus left. If the fae killed everyone there, too.'

'Perhaps there is,' I say, suddenly guilty that I brought all this up for her.

Catherine asked me to summon rainbows, but I reminded her of all the things she lost. I sometimes wonder if Lonnrach stole me away to that mirrored room to steal the hope from me – however small it was to begin with – at the same time he stole my memories.

I try to hold on, just for Catherine. 'Maybe the fae wouldn't care enough for such a small island.'

'Maybe.' She says it with a flash of a forced smile for my benefit. As if she understood exactly what I was trying to do. We both know Cyprus is likely gone, just like everywhere else.

'Do you ever wish you could stay on the boat without coming out?' I can't help but ask. 'In your imagined Cyprus?'

'Humans can't survive in the worlds they build for long,' she says. 'We're able to create landscapes with our minds, but only the fae have the power to make whatever they want behind their doors. They use it to supply us with food and materials.

'For us, water turns to ash in our mouths. Food turns to rock. Even things we bring inside must be eaten quickly before they rot. Some people go into the places they create just to die there. They find it easier than—' She turns sharply to Tavish, a flush creeping along her cheeks. But he is still deep in the vision, blind eyes wide.

'What is it?'

'Tavish's wife,' she says in a low voice, barely above a whisper. 'They lost their son when the purge took Aberdeen. When she came here, she swore she could bring back the wee lad, and created a place beyond the door where they could all live. Tavish went in to pull her out, but he couldn't find her. She had created a countryside that spanned for miles.'

I swallow hard. 'If he couldn't find his wife, how do you know she's dead?'

Catherine looks out the window again. Her eyes are wet, but the tears don't fall. Perhaps, like me, she's taught herself not to cry. 'When we die, the places we imagine through our doors change back to the cave. And those inside are no longer hidden.'

Oh god. Rain suddenly batters the window. I had forgotten what my emotions can do in this place. The storm intensifies, shaking the room until the glass crackles and the frame strains.

Catherine shifts closer and puts her hand on my shoulder, the way she did when we were children. She doesn't say anything; she doesn't need to. She knows me better than anyone.

Tavish's strained gasp startles us. *'Damnation.'* He almost bolts up, then sits back down so hard that the legs of the settee groan at the force.

Beside me, Catherine's body tenses. Her breathing hitches. 'Tavish?' She stands, reaching for his arm. 'What is it?'

He doesn't hear her; he's still too deep in the vision. 'No, they're too close. You're just going to run into them there. Don't—'

Catherine grips his arm harder. *'Tavish!'* He blinks, and his eyes go back to normal, the same startling green they were when I first met him.

He stands so fast that he stumbles. He grips the arm of the settee, looking nauseated and weak. 'They're riding into a trap there. The fae are going to cut them off once they get to the cliffs.'

I'm already on my feet, grabbing the sword Aithinne gave me. I wrap the belt around my waist and buckle it closed. 'Don't worry,' I say to Catherine. 'I'll bring them home.'

Tavish looks up. 'You'll *what*?'

I stride to the closet and knock twice before opening. Derrick looks up from his pile of silks. 'Well, look at you! Sword at the hip, murderous expression. Going out for a slaughter?'

I smirk. 'Going out to *save* people.'

Derrick rises to hover in front of me. 'A change of pace for you.' He grins. 'I like it. What do you need?'

'Find Kiaran for me,' I say. 'Tell him he gets to stab something.'

Derrick wrinkles his nose. 'I was hoping for a more exciting task, but fine. *Fine*. I'll go get the bastard.'

He leaves so fast that all I see is a streak of light out the door. I follow him, snatching up my freshly filled blunderbuss on the way out of the room. As I'm slinging the holster across my back, Tavish stops me. 'You're not going out there.'

'And you're going to stop me ... how?'

Tavish raises an eyebrow. 'Look, lass, I understand wanting to help, but there's nothing you can do.'

Aithinne's laugh comes from behind us. 'He's so handsome, but not too bright,' she says fondly, as if he were a pet. 'And he still hasn't learned never to underestimate a woman with a sword and a firearm.'

I turn to see Kiaran and Aithinne striding across the balcony toward us, Derrick just behind them. Aithinne flashes Tavish her most winning smile, which looks more than a bit frightening. 'Hullo!' she says to both of us serenely. 'We're here to rescue your friends, and all their limbs.' A pause, then: 'Well, no. I can't promise *all* their limbs, but most, surely ...'

'What my sister is trying to say,' Kiaran interrupts, 'is that we'll bring them back alive. Mostly in one piece.' I love the way he looks at me then, with expectation, a hint of a smile. *God, I missed this.* 'Ready?'

Yes. 'Always.' I ignore Tavish's bewildered expression and ask, 'Where do we need to go?'

Chapter 23

We ride for the cliffs on the west end of the island. Ossaig runs at full speed, charging hard across the land. Skye in winter is icy; all of the branches and grass are framed in thin crystals that crunch beneath her hooves as we make our way up the hills.

Trees have fallen across the slopes, their branches crackling and groaning around us. I can't help but admire the way Kiaran rides beside me. There's such command, such calm in how he holds himself – the way he does everything.

I force my attention back to our route through the forest. Snow falls across the icy terrain, melting against my face. The atmosphere Ossaig creates as she runs is heated. Her coat steams, as do my clothes and my skin. I rest my hand against the warm, soft fur along her neck and whisper a single word: *Hurry*.

She speeds forward. She doesn't tire; I never even hear her breathe. But I feel the movement of her mechanical parts against my thigh, the way they pump the gold liquid through her veins in a constant beat.

Even the snowy landscape in Skye is beautiful, unearthly. The hills are dusted and capped with white, the grassy meadows coated in a fine layer of frost. We head through the line of trees into an area of woodland that's thick and difficult to see through.

It's a tangle of sharp-limbed branches, covered in snow so fresh that it hasn't been disturbed yet.

Branches tug my hair, my coat, snapping off around me. Ossaig runs silently, her hooves barely touching the forest floor. I dart a glance behind us and there aren't even prints left in the snow. It remains undisturbed, as if she floated right over it.

'Head north.'

Kiaran's voice startles me. I look over. 'What? But Tavish said—'

'He's right,' Aithinne says. 'I hear them just over the hills.' She flashes a smile at Kiaran, catching up to us with a quick urging of her mare. 'So you're not completely unobservant after all, little brother.'

He doesn't look at her. 'Being forty seconds older than me doesn't give you an excuse to call me *little*.'

I don't hear a bloody thing – only groaning, cracking branches. Not even birds or rustling animals. Still, I lightly tug Ossaig's mane and urge her to follow Kiaran and Aithinne. In our way are trees with thick branches, swaying from the breeze. Past the woods up ahead I can see a clearing. Ossaig races toward it and we explode through the trees. She stops short above a high cliff. Below, the sea batters the rocks in a violent swell. Mist sprays my face and adheres like ice to my skin.

I scan the rocky edge and spot figures in the distance – three of them – with a contingent of fae at their backs. About fifty total. *Oh, hell.*

We stop and Kiaran says to Aithinne, 'It's been an age since you've seen a battle. Do you think you can keep up?'

Aithinne looks smug. 'Of course I can keep up. I'm amazing. I always was the better fighter.'

'Better at cheating,' he mutters, watching the Seers hurtling toward us with the army at their backs.

'Oh, please. Accusing me of cheating is a sore loser's excuse for not *winning, mo bhrathair.*' She smiles at him. 'You need to improve your footwork. It's terrible.'

Kiaran doesn't seem fazed. 'I don't believe you.'

It's amazing how calm they both are. Before any battle, I feel electric. My heart slams against my chest and I can barely stay still. Energy heats my skin, melting the ice there.

It brings me to life. Not like before, not with vengeance or anger or rage, but with purpose. I want Lonnrach's soldiers to see me like *this*, not the girl whose memories he stole. When Lonnrach catches word of who killed them, I want him to know that it was Aithinne and me together. That he never broke us.

My blunderbuss is already in my hand, loaded and ready to go. Its wide spray injures groups of fae more effectively than a sword would in an initial attack. I'll save the blade for closer combat.

Over Aithinne's shoulder, Kiaran catches my eye. I see a mirror of my anticipation there. Aye, he loves this part as much as I do. The calm before a squall.

We wait until the Seers draw closer. The three men stop short, their metal fae horses protesting at their forceful halt. 'What do you think you're doing?' Daniel's face is flushed, a bloody gash across his forehead.

My anticipation calms me. This must be the way Kiaran and Aithinne feel: no emotions, just a readiness.

I want this. It's such a simple thing. There's no room for fear or panic. Only the way the weapon fits in my hand, the way my body lights up at the thought of battle. How different it is from the insatiable hunger to kill.

'We're here to save your arse,' I say. 'Get to the city and stay there. We'll hold them off so they can't follow.'

Lorne growls deep in his throat – and it isn't a pleasant sound. 'You're barking mad,' he says. He gestures to Aithinne and Kiaran. 'These two are immortal; if they want to fight their own, let them. Ladies have no place on the battlefield.'

Aithinne looks amused. 'Says the man *running* from the battle. Ye're feart, Seer?'

Lorne looks away. Aye, definitely afraid.

'Lorne's right.' Daniel holds a hand out to me. A truce; he's offering to protect me. 'You shouldn't be here. It's not safe.'

To Daniel and Lorne, a human facing an army of faeries – especially a woman – is condemning herself to death. Daniel is trying to save me, the way he did Catherine.

Before I can answer him, Gavin says quietly, 'Let her.'

Daniel turns his head in surprise. 'I beg your pardon?'

'She's not what you think she is,' Gavin says. Daniel and Lorne look at him like he's gone positively mad, but Gavin's gaze doesn't waver from mine. 'Make sure you come back this time. I doubt I'll be alive in another three years.'

Gavin turns his horse to go, and Daniel and Lorne reluctantly follow. I'm sure they've left people behind before. I had to learn that lesson myself: you can't save everyone.

Kiaran, Aithinne, and I watch the faeries make their way down the snowy hill. When they see us, they let out deafening howls that echo across the field.

A war cry. The same one Lonnrach bellowed when Aithinne and I were in the *Sith-bhrùth*.

They come for us, stronger, faster than I remember seeing them in the Queen's Park. This is the moment before our two groups meet, a space between heartbeats when we are all still and quiet and ready.

'Dismount,' Aithinne says.

Kiaran slides off his horse and I follow. In a human battle, staying on our horses would give us the advantage of height, but against the fae ... redcaps would be able to cut through them in seconds. Aithinne's power is thick in my mouth as she sends the horses off. They flee toward the trees in a blur of hooves; I simply blink and they're gone.

'Steady,' she whispers to me this time. 'They're going to make a move for you by breaking this section of the crag. When they do, stay still.' She sounds like she knows what she's doing, like she commanded an army once.

'Well. All right.'

Her smile is fierce. 'Don't worry; I think I'm going to be great at this.'

'You *think*?' *Oh, god, I'm going to die, aren't I?*

I follow her line of sight and watch the fae come for us. They are a blur of ice and wind, horses with *daoine sìth* riders, faeries beautiful and deadly and powerful. *Cù sìth* and redcaps at the front – the brawn, as always.

'Remember,' Kiaran says to me, 'they're stronger than when they escaped the mounds.'

The redcaps collectively raise their hammers and slam them into the ground. The earth cracks and splits open.

Damn. I try to be still, even as Kiaran and Aithinne roll out of the way. The ground beneath me begins to buckle into the sea.

I don't move. Even as my legs tremble and my stomach drops. Even as the chunk of rock holding me breaks away from the edge of the cliff.

Then I'm weightless, plunging toward the violent sea below. I bite back a scream as the redcaps and a dozen other fae dive as one to capture me in the descent.

They're not fast enough. Before I can blink, Aithinne leaps beside me and pulls me painfully against her. We're spinning, twisting in the air within a gust of powerful wind. She's controlling it, preventing our fall with power so strong that I almost heave.

Then we're thrown out of the whirlwind and we hit the ground. My teeth click together and I stop myself from rolling off the newly formed cliff. I look over just in time to see the dozen fae who had leaped after me crash into the rocks below.

I have barely a moment to appreciate Aithinne's brilliance before the other fae are on us, dismounting and running. Kiaran,

Aithinne, and I race forward. I'm relaxed, honed, ready for a fight.

I stop just before the fae reach us, aim the blunderbuss at a group of *sithichean*, and fire. The weapon slams back into my shoulder. Black powder swirls in the air, the scent noxious enough to burn my nostrils. The blast throws a few fae from their horses, the scrap metal and *seilgflùr* burning into them right through their clothing. Blood blossoms all over their bodies. They don't even scream as they die.

I sense power all around me. God, the taste of *daoine sìth* power is so strong, pricking along my skin, heavy down my throat. A strong mixture of burning iron and snow and salt. I fire the blunderbuss again and hit more of them.

The scrap metal breaks more fae skin and blood splatters across my shirt. I suddenly feel transported back to Edinburgh, when I savored the elation of a kill. The way their powers press against me and flow through veins, calming. Soothing.

Lightning crackles across the sky and storm clouds gather overhead. The air is electric, heavy. The *daoine sìth* are creating this, controlling it. Their power bursts upward and the clouds open, sending down rain and ice. Hail pelts me, sharp enough to slice open my cheek. The sweet tang of blood wets my lips. Lightning bolts flash and hit the ground around us, burning through the snow, again and again. I try to dodge, but there are too many bolts – just as I recover, another strikes. Another. It feels as though the entire island shakes and trembles from the force of their combined powers.

'Kam!'

Kiaran slams into me just before another bolt hits. His body rolls on top of mine, and I look over his shoulder to see a crater formed, about ten feet deep. That could have been me.

He whispers a word that makes me smile. 'Together.'

I holster the blunderbuss and slide my sword out of its sheath. Kiaran and I fight alongside each other, a waltz of battle that is beautiful and smooth. We are masters. It's just him and me, the way we always are. He cuts through the fae, swift and graceful. When they try to counterattack, he blocks it and sends their power straight back and I move in to finish the job. My blade slashes and cuts and kills.

It's as if we're extensions of each other.

We continue our dance. I grip his hand, and he flings me through a group of fae and I strike. He whirls me, and I slaughter again. His power wraps around me like a warm breeze over autumn wind. He tastes of spring. He tastes of the ocean and something else, wild and desperate.

When the fae try to ambush us – to break us apart – I sheath my blade and hitch the blunderbuss to my shoulder again. I fire off another shot, the spray wide and forceful.

The wind and rain around us worsens into a monstrous storm of pitch-dark clouds. The temperature drops and freezing rain continues to pelt us so hard that the water is in my eyes and numbing my skin. The wind comes in gusts of such power that I'm nearly slammed back by the force of it.

Kiaran counterattacks with his own power, but it's not enough – he can't do that and fight at the same time. When fae rush him, his control over the weather drops. I'm picked up off my feet and flung through the snow toward the edge of the cliff.

Aithinne is by my side immediately, dodging and slicing and cutting. After a moment's recovery, I'm right by her side. For a moment, I feel as though I am back in the Queen's Park the night of the Wild Hunt, a graceful creature, as faelike as I was that night. I dance as if I am in a ballroom, my feet swift in the snow. My sword hand slices and swipes as I dodge.

And I feel it all. The keen sense of their powers within and around me, like smoke in my mouth, like cold air in my lungs. I would have savored it once. I would have basked in the kill, the vengeance.

Now, it's simple necessity. It's Aithinne and me screaming to the world – to Lonnrach – that we're alive. That we can still fight and kill. That we're not shattered. I battle like a declaration: *I'm not running.*

Then I see *her.* The midnight black of her hair, flowing around a face so beautiful that it's scarcely real. Those glittering green eyes meet mine and her lips curl into a smile.

Sorcha.

Time stops. It is only me and her. I feel her power, thick as blood on my tongue, forcing its way down and down.

She's in my mind, controlling me against my will. She issues a single command: *Stop.* My sword hand pauses midair, and the fae around me – except for Kiaran and Aithinne – halt too. As if we are all statues, still as stone. The battle has completely stalled in the wake of Sorcha's influence.

She leaves a tantalizing pulse across my temple, as if to say: *I have you.*

I hate her. *I hate her.* I try to push her out, but she's strong, so strong. I'm just like the others, unable to fight against her power no matter how hard I try.

When Kiaran sees her, his hand tightens on his blade. 'Sorcha.'

Aithinne stops right beside him, breathing hard. '*You.*' She exhales deeply. 'I can't recall if I mentioned it, but every time we meet, I quell an urge to punch you in the face.'

Kiaran casts a look at his sister, as if to say, *Agreed.*

Sorcha just smiles at Aithinne, revealing her sharp teeth. 'Believe me, the feeling is mutual. But is that any way to treat someone who's here to help you? Again?' She glances at the other fae. 'I only have a few minutes to cloud their memories, so don't waste my time.'

'Oh, this again. It's even less convincing than it was the first time.' Aithinne shakes her head, and finally notices I'm like the others, unable to speak.

She crooks a finger at me and her power is there, intertwining in a warm current that breaks through the icy control of Sorcha's power. Aithinne tastes of smoke, of black powder and blood and flame.

Sorcha resists her, holding on so strongly that I have to bite my tongue so I don't cry out. Aithinne's power wraps tightly around Sorcha's, overwhelming it. Burning through it.

Suddenly, I feel myself released from Sorcha's powers so fast that I nearly pitch forward.

I gasp for breath and am finally able to look around. All the other fae are frozen. Their eyes are iced over, gazes fixed and unmoving – like statues in the snow.

Kiaran still has his blade out. I notice how his hand tightens around the hilt. 'Why are you *really* here, Sorcha?'

If I hadn't been paying attention, I would have missed the way Sorcha's gaze lingers on him. 'What if I told you I was on your side, Kadamach? That I wanted you to defeat my brother?'

'I wouldn't believe a damn word you said.'

Sorcha tuts, but her eyes never leave him. 'We were friends once.' She looks at him from under her lashes. 'More than that. You trusted me.'

Friends? They were friends? Even Aithinne makes a gagging sound at that.

Kiaran's face shutters completely, that cold detached gaze dropping into place. 'Is that what you thought? Or have you simply forgotten how skilled I am at pretending?'

Lonnrach's words flash in my mind. *He made you think he cared about you. Kadamach doesn't give a damn about anyone.*

Sorcha's lip curls. She attacks with her power and I can taste it – overwhelming, nauseating. Kiaran blocks it with his hand, a thin slash of blood appearing across his palm. In the blink of an eye, it heals over.

'You can't deceive me, Kadamach,' Sorcha says bitterly. 'Not while you're bound to me.' Kiaran's jaw tightens, but he doesn't say anything. 'It's because of our bond that I'm warning you. My brother seeks to take the Seelie and Unseelie thrones.'

'*Please*. He doesn't have that kind of power,' Aithinne says. I hear the tightness in her voice, the fear not quite concealed by nonchalance. 'And he's not Seelie any more. He has no claim to—'

'When he finds a way to steal the Falconer's power' – she gives me a small, arrogant smile – 'he'll be one step of the way there.'

Mine? How could my power possibly help him do that?

'It won't be difficult, since your little human friend can't even access her power to fend him off.'

I don't even respond to her insult. My mind is reeling. What did Lonnrach tell me in the *Sìth-bhrùth*? *You can unlock an object I seek. That is your sole purpose.*

He must have meant that only my power could unlock it, just like the device Aithinne made.

Without a monarch, the Sìth-bhrùth will wither. Someone must take her place.

How would my power help him steal the thrones? As if Sorcha sees the question in my face, she smiles mockingly. 'Oh, my dear sweet lass. You still have no idea what you're capable of, do you? Such a waste.'

A pulse of old anger heats my skin. Lonnrach may not be mine to kill, but *Sorcha* is. One day I'll find a way to drive a blade through her heart and kill her without Kiaran dying in the process. Whatever it takes. She's *mine*.

Sorcha bares her teeth. *Come get me.*

I will, I promise her. *I vow it.*

It isn't until Aithinne steps closer that I realise I had my blade out and ready. 'Lonnrach can't take her power without the proper ritual, and even if he knew it, he's not strong enough to perform it.'

'Well,' Sorcha says, finally averting her gaze from mine, 'it seems he's found a way around that.'

You can unlock an object I seek. That is your sole purpose.

Your sole purpose.

The object. The object will be what takes my power. I almost say it out loud, but clamp my mouth shut when I remember Sorcha is here. I can't give away that I know anything.

Kiaran's smile is mocking. 'He didn't trust you enough to tell you, did he?'

'Don't bait me, Kadamach. I'm speaking to you at the risk of my brother's wrath.' Sorcha whispers so softly that I almost don't hear her at all. 'At the risk of *her* wrath.'

Her? But Kiaran's already speaking. 'And you still haven't said why.'

Sorcha's expression is so vulnerable, even Kiaran seems surprised by it. 'If my brother finds what he's looking for, he'll be able to kill you.' She recomposes herself, lifting her chin defiantly. 'This is self-preservation, Kadamach. I have to keep you alive to keep me alive.'

What rubbish. This is *Sorcha*. She killed my mother. She's betraying her own brother and can just as easily betray us. Why should we listen to anything she says?

'If you intend to help,' I say, working to keep my voice calm, 'then tell us what else you know.'

Sorcha looks like she's considering killing me, too. 'Whatever he requires to take your power is on this island. That's all I know.'

So Lonnrach isn't just looking for the city and for me. Derrick said his soldiers had been patrolling the island before I escaped. That means whatever he needs to steal my power and become monarch of the *Sìth-bhrùth* is here on Skye.

You spent a year training under my enemy and that rogue pixie. I assume they often spoke about things you didn't understand.

If Lonnrach got the location from my head, it can only mean one thing: He suspected Derrick or Kiaran knew where it was.

Kiaran steps forward. 'If you're lying—'

'Oh, Kadamach,' Sorcha says with her typical mocking smile. 'You know we can't tell lies. Now, I really do have to keep up my performance and make it look like I'm loyal to him.' Her green eyes glow bright. Those sharp teeth of hers flash as she grins. 'You had better run.'

I suddenly feel the heat from her, as if she were the source of a blazing fire. Her power grows in my mouth, stark and unyielding. Iron and blood on my tongue, down my throat in an endless, unstoppable stream.

Then, I hear it. The distant boom that has become a sound to dread.

The *mortair*. She's calling the *mortair*.

Chapter 24

I can barely hear anything over the ground shaking and cracking around us. Cresting the mountains just over the river are the metal fae, headed right toward us at Sorcha's command. The *mortair* tear across the landscape with their massive bodies. The ground buckles beneath them as they run, leaving giant pockmarks in the earth.

There are other creatures behind them, metal monsters of so many kinds, birdlike creations with long beaks and narrow bodies shaped like an egret's. They run on thin legs tipped with massive claws. Some are like cats with long ears and horns that spiral up toward the sky.

As they cross the river, I can see the large metal gears in their thighs revolving so quickly that it looks like their insides are aflame. They are beautiful creations of the same black obsidian as the *mortair* ... and yet they are horrifying.

Aithinne is next to me, her eyes narrowed and determined. 'The little ones attack in groups, so pick them off one at a time. Try not to let them surround you,' she says, pulling out her own sword. Then she passes me a smile. 'It's all straightforward. Uncomplicated!'

Oh, she did *not* just – 'Really, Aithinne?'

The creatures' legs eat up the ground fast. So fast. They're almost here now, just one more hill ...

My sword is out. I'm ready. *Now.* I run beneath the massive frame of a catlike *mortair*, its limbs towering over me as gracefully as a real animal. I thread myself between its limbs, slicing my blade through the metal there to bring down the beast.

It's amazing how quickly the creatures move. One minute I'm thinking through my options, the next I see dozens heading straight toward me. I sprint between them and cut through them at the ankles to send the metal creatures crashing down around us. As they hit the ground, snow flies up and adheres to my skin, but I'm moving so fast that the cold barely affects me.

The *mortair* crash to the ground, their limbs breaking the earth all around us. I teeter and try to find my footing, but the ground is uneven, buckling beneath my boots.

'Kam!'

I look up at Kiaran's call and swear loudly. Behind him are even more *mortair*, racing through the trees and hills from the west end of the island. Their limbs crash through the forests, sending branches and whole trees flying from the force of their massive bodies. It's an entire army. If Aithinne invented the *mortair* to withstand most weapons, we can't stand a chance against that many.

'We have to jump,' Kiaran tells me, grabbing for my arm.

I run with him. The fae creatures are pursuing us, pounding across the icy landscape. Aithinne leaps to cut down another with her sword.

Kiaran leads me up the icy slope of the crag toward the cliffs, our boots pounding through the snow. It's so cold that my toes are growing numb; I can barely run any more. Kiaran urges me forward as the mechanical creatures gain on us. Once we reach the edge of the crag I look down at the crashing waves. It's a long way down.

Kiaran looks at me with determination. Oh, Christ, he really *does* intend to jump. 'On the count of three,' he says, pulling me against him.

I wrap my arms tightly around him. Next to us, Aithinne says, 'See you both at the bottom!'

God help me.

Aithinne lets out a whoop of glee and jumps off the cliff in a single running leap, taking a graceful dive. I don't even see her enter the water; Kiaran's holding me too tightly. 'Whatever you do,' he says, 'don't let go of me.'

The ground is shaking from the *mortair*. They're going to be here any second. Already the tremors are dislodging pieces of loose rock along the cliff. 'Me, let go? I wouldn't dream of it.'

'Smart lass. Ready?' Kiaran presses his cheek to mine and whispers. 'One ... two ...'

On three, he throws us off. The frigid air whistles past us as we hurtle to the sea below. Beneath us, all I see is the jagged rock sticking up from the bottom of the crag. The cliffs on this part of Skye are high up, and the ocean waves so violent, the jump is anything but safe. We will be dashed against the rocks ... if the fall doesn't kill me first.

Kiaran shifts me so he can hold his hand, palm out, to the sea below. His power surrounds us in a sudden, nauseating burst that would have doubled me over had I been standing. Then I realise Kiaran is slowing *us* down, using his powers so we fall at half the speed to reach the bottom. For *me*; he's doing this for me. The rocks would crush me if we landed at full force. Kiaran would survive, but my entire body would be broken.

'Put your arms tighter around me,' he whispers, his breath warm on my cheek.

I press my palms to his back and pull him against me. We fall slower, slower still, then it's as if we're floating rather than falling. We are weightless above the raging sea, the air around us no more violent than a frigid breeze that ruffles my hair. Kiaran's warmth surrounds me, his power pulsing and sliding over my skin, as soft as silk. Cold sea mist sprays all around us, dampening through my coat, slicking my face. I shiver when Kiaran draws me closer to press his lips to my neck.

We hit the water. God, not even the Forth was this cold when I leaped into it after a fight with the *sluagh*. The current wasn't so strong, so forceful. The cold steals my breath and my insides ache as we plunge beneath the surface. Violent waves throw us back, but Kiaran's power meets it in a burst that slows us before we slam into the cliff.

He's tugging us away from the crag, shoving us through the water with a combination of power and the strong strokes of his legs and arms. A wave hits and we're dragged beneath the water. His hold on me breaks and I'm carried away by the violent force of the surge. I panic, waving my arms beneath the water to find him, but I can't see. Air, I need air. I can't *breathe*—

Kiaran seizes my arm, pulling me up. We surface and I heave the frigid air into my lungs. It's painful, as if the very atmosphere is solid. I push against him, struggling to breathe, to kick, but my limbs are numb and uncoordinated. He almost loses his hold on me again, but my nails dig into his coat, my limbs thrashing.

'Kam!' He presses his hands to my face so I'm forced to look into his eyes. Calm, he's so calm. His power is warming, soothing. 'You have to swim,' he says, drawing me against him. He strains not to lose me to another violent wave. 'All right? Just swim, Kam.'

I've never heard him sound so gentle. He presses his forehead against mine, holding me against another wave. 'I'll be right here with you,' he says.

I nod once and kick. The effort of swimming is like trying to move a boulder uphill, like each movement makes no difference at all. I'm panting with the effort. Kiaran swims with me, doing most of the work. His strokes are strong, assured, as if he isn't affected at all by the currents or the waves or the bitter cold. He keeps my arm in a strong, sure grip even as the current threatens to tear us apart. I'm certain his hand will leave finger-shaped bruises after this.

Water crashes against us and I swallow it. *Ugh.* The too-salty taste makes me choke. I cough and cough, but still I kick forward.

Our progress is slow, agonizing. Even with Kiaran's powers keeping me warm, it doesn't stop the cold from seeping through. I'm a tangle of shivers and uncoordinated movements. My trousers and coat cling to my skin, and my boots weigh me down. My body is heavy, like a rock ready to sink straight to the bottom of the sea.

I surge forward and Kiaran pulls. As soon as I see a small beach nestled beneath the towering cliffs, determination forces me to move faster, to ignore the pain in my limbs, the exhaustion, everything.

Finally, *finally*, we make it to a beach covered in perfectly round rocks. I drop onto them and lie down. Thank god I'm not in the damn water any more.

Just over on the cliffs, I hear the pounding footsteps of the *mortair* and I stiffen. I don't think I can fight just yet. I can't even *stand*.

Kiaran hears it, too, but settles next to me on the rocks, resting his arms on his knees. 'If Sorcha was telling the truth, she should be sending them back.' He scans the cliffs as if to be sure. After a while, he seems to relax. 'Aithinne must have gone to the inlet on the other side of the cliffs. We'll wait here until she finds us.'

I sit up on the hard pebbles, wincing at how much effort even that takes. 'Do you believe Sorcha?'

The fae can't lie, but I've learned they have many ways to circumvent the truth. They're masters at omission or stating *a* truth, leaving out the most vital information to trick humans into trusting them.

Kiaran considers my question. 'Truth can be told in fragments. If Lonnrach really has found a way to seize your power, she'll be seeking that knowledge for herself.' He leans back on his hands, seeming at ease despite the icy wind. 'It seems her brother doesn't entirely trust her, either.'

The waves crash around us, their force grinding rocks together over and over again. Despite the cold, Skye is peaceful. It's quiet now that the *mortair* have gone.

Kiaran's eyes are closed. Water drips from his hair onto where his shirt is open at the throat. I can't help but think of his words as he pulled me through the waves.

I'll be right here with you.

Kiaran eases an eye open. 'You're staring.' He sounds like he doesn't object.

I don't look away. 'I have to tell you something.'

'That sounds vaguely ominous.'

'Whatever Lonnrach is looking for,' I say, 'he – he knew to find it in Skye from me. From my memories.' I speak quickly before Kiaran can respond. 'Derrick told me his home was here on the island, so I thought Lonnrach was searching for the city.' I finally look away. 'I didn't realise it was something else until Sorcha told us.'

Whatever he requires to take your powers is on this island. That's all I know.

Kiaran is quiet for a long time. Then he gently clasps my wrist to pull up my sleeve. His fingers run over the grooves of my bite marks.

I almost wish I could show him the memories for each one. There are so many of the two of us. Our hunts imprinted on my skin, a story of how we went from reluctant partners to … this. Whatever this is.

Focus. 'Do you think Derrick knows what it is?' I ask him.

'No,' Kiaran says. 'Something that can steal power would be ancient. Before his life.' His fingers trail up to the next bite. 'Pixies were once protectors of certain relics. They were the only *sithichean* strong enough to defend objects, but not to use them. Few knew where the pixies lived, and it was rumoured they buried their relics all over the island.' He lifts his gaze to mine.

'What Lonnrach seeks is the very reason I came here thousands of years ago. I destroyed your pixie's home to find it.'

I jerk away from his touch. I can't help my guilt over caring for someone who has done so much to hurt someone I love. Kiaran isn't Kadamach any more. He's not. But I can't help but feel like caring for Kiaran means I'm betraying Derrick. Like I'm hurting him, too.

'What is it, then?' My tone is even, brutally so.

I don't miss how Kiaran's expression goes cold, as if he senses that I'm distancing myself. Now he's pulling away from me, too.

'Among my kind,' he says, almost mechanically, 'there are stories of the first *sithichean* kingdom, one built before a different realm existed for us. It was a place of immense power, created by old magic that doesn't exist any more except through the Cailleach.'

The Cailleach. The name makes me start as I remember what Lonnrach told me in the prison.

No one has seen the Cailleach for thousands of years.

Kiaran's speaking again before I can think further. 'Hostility between factions culminated in a war that destroyed the kingdom and led to the creation of a separate realm. They say a crystal from the palace is still here, hidden somewhere. Full of old magic.'

'You never found it?'

He shakes his head. 'But if Lonnrach discovers where it is, he'll use it to take your powers and kill the Seelie and Unseelie monarchs.'

The heirs she left behind to rule were … unworthy. Without a monarch, the Sith-bhrùth will wither. Someone must take her place.

I have to know. 'Why were you searching for the crystal?'

Kiaran doesn't respond immediately. 'I was Unseelie, Kam. What do you think?' His eyes are savage, fierce. 'I wanted it to kill the Seelie queen.'

My breath hitches. Before I can answer, I hear Aithinne. 'So, are you two going to sit there all day or are we going back to the city? Because I'm hungry.'

I turn just as Aithinne leaps from a rock that juts out under the cliff. She lands with a soft thud, looking very pleased with herself. Her clothes are sopping wet, hair dripping, every inch of her covered in sand. And she doesn't seem to mind one bit.

Aithinne makes her way across the larger beach rocks toward us, her movements graceful. 'You both look miserable.'

'I'm cold and wet,' I say. 'I feel wretched, and my blunderbuss is probably destroyed from the swim. No need to state the obvious.'

She glances at her brother. 'And I suppose your face is just stuck that way?'

Kiaran pushes to his feet and I do the same. 'What you see is the incessant, grave look of someone in possession of a sibling.'

'Ha ha.' Aithinne focuses her attention on me, tilting her head. 'You know, I had a kyloe look at me exactly like that once. His hair was a similar colour and everything.'

I glare at her. 'You did *not* just compare me to a cow.'

'No, no. I compared your *expression* to one. Cows truly are majestic creatures, aren't they?' With a flashing grin, she says, 'Don't worry, I'm going to fix you right up!'

Before I can protest, she has her hand on my shoulder. Her power is unexpected, so strong that it upsets my stomach. I double over at the overwhelming and unpleasant sweetness on my tongue. As it retreats, I realise that my clothes are dry, my hair is dry, and I'm warm – as if I had just stepped out of the sunshine on a warm summer day.

I straighten with a scowl. 'You could have asked.'

Aithinne starts walking toward a path that leads between the cliffs and Kiaran and I follow. 'You would have said no out of sheer human stubbornness, and got sick on the way back from … from – what do you call it?'

'Exhaustion,' I say, climbing up the path. 'I believe I require a nap.'

She's not listening. She snaps her fingers. 'Pneumonia! That's it. In any case, you would have got sick and died and then where would we be? You're welcome.'

Well, I see she's no different from Kiaran in her use of the fine art of *tact*. I tug on my newly dried coat and brush off the sand with a flick of my fingers. 'What about you? Are you going to dry yourself?'

Aithinne shrugs. 'I like the water. Reminds me of home.'

Out of the corner of my eye, I notice Kiaran stiffen at her words. A slight movement, only noticeable because I've become so familiar with how he stands, how he carries himself. When he speaks, his voice is as cold as the wind. 'We should get back.'

We leave through a passage in the forest. It extends beneath the sea, just one of the many tunnels around the island that leads back into the fae city. Above us, I can hear the waves crashing and lapping against the shore as we make our way through the dark, glittering rocks. The tunnel brings us out at the border between the fae and human parts of the city: the field of *seilgflùr* is a line of defense, a wordless way of reminding any wandering humans that crossing this field puts them in fae territory.

After Aithinne goes through the fae door, Kiaran lingers with me along the path through the *seilgflùr*. We haven't spoken since the beach. I wish I knew what to say to him; I wish my feelings weren't a tangle of wants and needs and attraction.

'Do you want me to go with you?' Kiaran asks when we stop at the stairway that leads to the main part of the city. 'I don't trust the Seers not to do something foolish.'

I dread the thought of facing them, but I don't tell him. 'I appreciate that, but I'm not terribly certain your being there will improve the situation.'

'No,' he says. 'But I don't like you being alone with them. Not after what they did to you.' He shakes his head. 'I wasn't there for you both times. I won't let that happen again.'

I almost tell him that I haven't forgiven Gavin either. Not yet. 'You care?' I breathe. I know he does, but I have to hear him say it. I *need* to hear him say it.

Kadamach doesn't give a damn about anyone, least of all you.

I wish I could get Lonnrach's words out of my mind. I wish I hadn't spent so long in the mirrored room convincing myself they were true. That the reason Kiaran hadn't found me was because he wasn't looking.

I close my eyes when Kiaran presses a palm to my cheek. 'Kam,' he says. 'I just saved the Seer, jumped over a cliff, and swam through freezing water with you in my arms.' Then he's cupping my face in his hands. 'What else do I need to do to show you?'

I shake my head. 'I'm afraid I require further proof.'

'Further proof?' Kiaran raises an eyebrow. 'It doesn't involve declarations or theatrics, does it? I have to draw the line somewhere.'

'No theatrics. No declarations.' I stand on my tiptoes and whisper in his ear. 'Just a kiss.'

Then his lips are on mine and it might as well be a declaration. For a moment, his past fades away and so does mine. As I let myself lean into his touch it suddenly feels like nothing else matters but this. Just him. Just us.

I soften the kiss until it's barely a brush of my lips against his. With each touch I tell him, *Thank you.* And *I care for you too.* And *god help me, but I trust you.*

When I pull away, I swear he understood what all that meant. 'I have to go,' I whisper.

I watch the struggle in his face as he steps away. 'If they try anything, send the pixie.'

I nod and start to climb the stairs. When I turn back again, he's already gone through the faery door.

Chapter 25

he streets are quiet. A few people have ventured out of their homes, but the lights are still down. The clouds are back, this time with a moon shining between them. The cobblestone streets glisten in its light, still slick from the earlier rainfall. I retrace the path Kiaran took earlier, through the dark closes that lead to the room full of tapestries of pixie victories.

I take a breath and enter, and everyone immediately quiets and turns. God, it feels as though I've done something horribly wrong. The door shuts behind me with a heavy clang. It's like a gunshot.

In the back, Lorne and Tavish look at me in blatant suspicion, perhaps a bit of fear. Gavin's expression is unreadable, with a hint of something else – regret? In contrast, Catherine seems both irate and concerned. The second she sees me she hurries across the room.

'Catherine, *don't*.' This from Daniel. Surprise, surprise.

She ignores him and takes me by the elbow. 'Come with me. Ignore the idiots in the corner.'

Ignore? I see Kiaran's concern wasn't entirely unfounded.

But Daniel is already heading toward us. 'Let me handle it,' he says to her.

Catherine scowls. 'I think not. Step aside.'

Daniel sighs. This time, he looks at me. Not with the suspicion and accusation that I'm used to seeing, but he seems tired. So tired. He hasn't even changed out of the clothes he wore when he went out riding.

'May I speak with you?' he asks me directly. Catherine opens her mouth to protest, but he puts up a hand. 'Alone, if you don't mind.'

I step back from him. 'Surely you understand why I'd rather not.'

Daniel runs a hand through his hair. 'Look, I'm not going to hurt you,' he says. 'I just want to talk.'

I glance at Catherine. She hesitates before indicating that it's all right. I suppose Daniel and I ought to have a civil conversation in any case.

Catherine releases me and rises on her tiptoes to whisper something in Daniel's ear. Daniel raises his eye heavenward as she smiles at him and presses a kiss to his cheek.

Well ... well ...

I can't control the sudden blush that creeps up my face at their very public display of affection. It feels so intimate.

Catherine gives me an encouraging nod as her husband escorts me out into the dark close. I open my mouth to speak, but Daniel interrupts. 'Not here,' he says in that deep burr. 'My wife probably has her ear pressed to the door.' At my reluctance he says, 'I promised I wouldn't hurt you. Please.'

'Very well.'

Without another word, he turns and starts down the alley and I have no choice but to follow. I can barely see where I'm going, it's still so dark. Even the light from the false moon above doesn't entirely break through the shadows cast by the tenements around us.

'What did she say to you?' I ask, keeping my movements careful lest I trip.

'She told me to behave myself.'

I smile. That couldn't have been the only thing she said. 'Or?'

'That part was meant for me only.'

He leads me to a heavy oak door surrounded in ivy. It groans on its hinges as he opens it. Nothing is visible on this side; only thick, impenetrable darkness. I don't trust him enough to go into a room I can't see. For all I know, it's another wisp ambush.

'Just what, exactly, do you intend to do that you don't want Catherine to hear?' I ask him.

Daniel's expression hardens, as if he's offended by the question. 'Just talk.'

'About what?'

'You'll see.' He motions me to go inside.

Steeling myself, I cross the threshold. The moment I'm inside, it changes. A blacksmith's workshop? Aye, it is. The kiln that heats metal is in one corner. All over the wooden tables and the floor are pieces of metal, wee pinions and spindles, and some larger, half-put-together mechanisms.

An anvil lies in the corner, a hammer and chisel beside it. It smells like coal fire in here, like the small garden cottage I used for my own metalwork back at Father's estate. When we were in the city, I had to pay someone else to do the work for me.

Just looking at these things makes me want to build again, to take mechanisms apart and put them back together to make something new. I miss the feel of oil on my fingertips and working with metal on sleepless nights. I miss the sense of pride that comes with completing something and discovering it works precisely as I intended it to.

I tentatively touch the anvil, feeling the marks in the metal where the hammer has hit. I look up at Daniel. 'Is this yours? This place?'

'Aye.' Daniel sits in the work chair, crossing his long legs at his ankles. 'Made to look like my father's.'

So he's the son of a blacksmith. Before the Wild Hunt, Catherine would never have been able to marry a man of his station. Marriage wasn't for love, but for property. It was something a lady *settled into*, something we simply accepted.

'It must be comforting for you,' I say, trying to be polite, 'to have something that reminds you of him.'

I'm not certain what place I'd create that would give me fond memories of my father. Aye, his death still aches when I think about it; I'm still guilt-ridden over what *should* have been between us. Not even when I was a child did Father embrace me or offer me kind words. His words were always clipped, abrasive, spoken simply to get me to leave. Even into adulthood I still possessed the childish hope that he would come to love me. He never did. That's something I'll always carry with me.

Daniel laughs bitterly. 'That's not it at all. My father was a mean son of a bitch.' He opens his collar to tap the scar below his collarbone, a star-shaped mark from a bullet. 'I remember *him* here. That's how I died and came back with the Sight.'

Christ, what can I even say to that? I almost tell him I'm sorry. Somehow, it doesn't seem good enough. 'Why do you create this place, then?' I ask him.

'It reminds me of what I had to do after I came back from the other side so my father wouldn't kill my mother, too.' His one eye settles hard on me. 'What I'm still willing to do to keep the people I love safe.'

'I take it you're referring to me?' I say lightly.

'You're not human,' Daniel says suddenly. Not an accusation, but a statement of fact. 'And don't pretend you don't know what I mean. Tavish watched the battle, and I know what I saw from the hills.'

You're not human. Not quite human, not quite fae. I don't fit into either world, not in Catherine's or even Kiaran's. At least before all this, I had the comfort of falsity around me. I could *pretend* I was normal, just another debutante. I could wrap myself in lies and no one knew I was living a falsehood. I don't have that cocoon of dishonesty to protect my secret any more.

'Mr. Reid—'

Daniel puts his hand up to stop me. 'No. I don't need an explanation. Just answer one question: are they looking for you?'

I raise my chin and meet his gaze directly. 'They are.'

Daniel swears softly. 'I was afraid of that.' He closes his eye. I'm surprised when he doesn't immediately open it. Instead he taps his fingers against the table. Not a thinking rhythm, but a deliberate *one two one two* rap.

'I've been waiting for more than three years,' he murmurs.

'For what?' *What's he doing?*

'For the girl whose gift is chaos.' *Tap tap. Tap tap.* 'Death is her burden. Wherever she goes, it follows. They say she can either save the world or end it.'

My chest tightens. Each word he says is like a blow, each one more painful than the last.

They say she can either save the world or end it.

Me. He's talking about me. 'They?' I finally manage a word, spoken in a strangled breath.

Daniel eases his eye open. It looks glassy, unfocused. 'I don't know where the voices come from, and I don't particularly give a damn. That's just what they say.'

'Do you see the future? Like Gavin?'

'No,' Daniel says. 'I don't have visions. I just hear whispers – about *you*. First more than three years ago, and then in the cave they started up again.' He studies me closely. 'Whenever I look at you, they don't stop. They just grow louder.'

Death is her burden. Wherever she goes, it follows.

I'm the girl whose gift is chaos.

'When exactly did they start?' I ask him, though I already know.

'Before the fae destroyed everything.' He hesitates before asking, 'I take it you were there that first night.'

I understand what he's really saying. *You were supposed to prevent it.*

No wonder Daniel didn't want me in his city, why he's spoken to me with hostility ever since my arrival. He knew exactly who I was. I'm the girl who let the cities fall. I'm the girl who ended the world.

I'm the girl who will bring death and destruction with me. Always. *Always.*

'I was,' I say. My breath shakes as I exhale. 'So you want me to leave.'

Daniel is quiet, as if he's considering his next words carefully. 'I've treated you unfairly. You didn't have to save my life, and I won't forget what you did for me. I'm in your debt. But I can't put the people I love in danger by letting you stay.'

I don't want to do that, either. The people he loves are the same ones I love. I've already done enough damage to their lives. Lonnrach is looking for me, and he won't stop until he finds me, takes my powers, and kills me.

'That's why you didn't want Catherine listening?'

'No. I didn't want her to hear my premonition about you. She'd tell me it doesn't matter.' He pushes his dark hair back in frustration. 'I had to convince *you* that it does, because you can get her to see reason.'

I think I see where this is going. 'Don't tell me you want me to lie to Catherine.'

'That's not what I'm asking,' he says. 'I'd never lie to her. But she would handle it better if you told her why you have to leave.' Daniel smiles. 'She's stubborn where you're concerned, in case you hadn't noticed.'

I nod, trying to consider what I'll say to her. I already sent her away once because I feared for her life. I'm responsible for Catherine being on that road when the fae attacked, and Daniel was there to save her, not me.

Death is her burden. Wherever she goes it follows.

It'll follow me here. Lonnrach will find me and kill them all. And I may not have the power I need to protect her—

Kiaran's words flash in my mind. *They say a crystal from the palace is still here, hidden somewhere. Full of old magic.*

'You should know,' I say quickly, before I stop myself. I decide to trust him, to risk the little I know. After all, he saved Catherine's life. I still grateful for that. 'They're not just looking for me. The fae want something else, too.'

'Do you know what it is?'

'A crystal that's hidden somewhere on the island. Have you heard anything about it?' He shakes his head and I say, 'I have to find it before the fae do, but Derrick will insist on coming with me. He won't be here to hold the wards if they attack.'

'What are you proposing?' he asks.

'Give Derrick time to strengthen them before we go.' He hesitates and I add, 'A few days. That's all I'm asking.'

'Fine.' He sounds reluctant. 'A few days. And then—'

'And then I'll leave.'

Chapter 26

The next day, I stand at my window watching the snow fall outside in the fake Edinburgh again. Only a few days. I'm not certain where I'll go or find shelter. The pixie city hasn't been much of a home at all, but the illusion of my old bedroom – my old house – makes me regret leaving.

Just for a few hours, I'm tempted to pretend it's real, that I'm back *there* again. That I'm in my old life before the battle, when everything seemed so much simpler.

Derrick flies to my shoulder, startling me with his sudden presence. 'Listen to me,' he says sternly. 'This is *my* home. You're not leaving. Say the word and I'll toss the Cyclops out on his arse.'

I've been waiting for more than three years.

For what?

For the girl whose gift is chaos.

Death follows me; it has followed me since my mother's murder. I am a conductor trying to avoid a bolt of lightning in a thunderstorm. 'You won't,' I say softly. 'His premonition wasn't wrong, Derrick. And I still have to find the crystal from the old kingdom. You know I do.'

'That could take *ages*,' he whines. 'My ancestors buried every-thing. Hell, they buried the trophies of their victims. There are a million skeletons on this island. Lonnrach will have to dig those all up first.'

'And what if Daniel is hearing the whispers again for a reason?'

'*I don't care,*' he snaps. His halo is burning bright red, flickering like flames. 'I finally have my closet back. I have you back. He's ruining *everything.*' A pause. Then: 'Do you think Catherine would be offended if I lopped off one of his ears?'

I transfer him to the palm of my hand, holding him up so I can meet his eyes. 'Is that what this is really about? Losing your closet?'

'Of course.' He blinks up at me, wide-eyed and innocent. He's anything but innocent. 'What else would it be?'

'Kiaran told me, you know. About your family and your home.'

Derrick's glow immediately dims to nothing, and his wings tuck in. I hear the wee hitch of his breath and he looks away. 'Did he.'

Derrick lost his kingdom and everyone he loved, and when I leave he'll be forced to choose between me and the home he just got back. I don't blame him for clinging to the things that have become familiar. Such simple things. His closet, the mountain of dresses. Me. This room. *I've been sleeping in my own version of your closet for the last three years and it never smelled the same.* Even though this room is fake, I had to be here to make it real for him. That's what family does: They bring home with them. Derrick and I have become family.

I stroke my fingers down one wing, then down the other. 'I wish I could hate Kiaran for you,' I tell him. 'As much as you hate the *baobhan sìth* for taking my mother from me.'

'I don't want you to,' he says. And there's such hurt there. No matter how long ago he lost his family, that pain still burns inside him. 'I've had thousands of years to mourn my family. But know this: there's not a day that passes when I don't believe Kiaran is so far beneath you that he should crawl over glass at your feet and be thankful that someone decided he was worthy of kindness.'

'Then what changed your mind?' I ask him seriously. 'About wanting me to kill him.'

Derrick is quiet for the longest time, wings fanning softly. His golden glow is slowly returning. 'I see the way he looks at you.'

I swallow, afraid of his answer. 'And how is that?'

'Like he wishes he was mortal.'

He flaps his wings to glide above my palm. 'Back to sewing, then. Calms the nerves. I'll weave another spell around the wards tonight, but tell that one-eyed fool that when I leave, good luck finding another *sithiche* to do the sewing.' With a huff, he barrels into his closet and shuts the door behind him with a loud thump.

Like he wishes he was mortal.

No, I can't focus on that now. I look out at the snow again, and this time, I've decided. I'm going out there to see the city as I imagine it before I'm exiled to an uncertain future of being hunted by the fae.

I square my shoulders and pull aside the panel next to the window. The button that detaches this part of the wall is there against the wooden paneling. Right where I installed it in my real room – a hidden escape so I could sneak out of the house at night to hunt.

Holding a breath, I press it. A portion of the wall lowers like a drawbridge to the garden, its metal gears clicking as it descends. I shiver at the frigid blast of cold air and the snowflakes and wait as the teak panels along the detached wall flip up into steps.

As I descend into the garden, I close my eyes and imagine the weather slightly warmer, the rain and wind softer. The weather turns precisely as I had envisioned, just chilly enough for me to keep my coat on.

Rain patters against the leafless branches of the trees as I cross the grass to the back gate. It opens and closes with a creak of the hinges, just as it always did. My fingers linger on the metal as I step out into the street. The street lamps along the lonely road are all lit, the wet cobblestones glistening in the light of dusk.

I've never seen the city so quiet, so empty, not even when I went on my late-night hunts. Even then the buildings around me had lights on, servants in the basements gossiping as they completed their chores. Now I walk down the desolate street and there is no sound, nothing but rain and my footfalls. The buildings around me are immaculate white brick and stone, one right after the other – and without a soul to occupy them. Charlotte Square is a barren place of rich buildings left abandoned.

Down on Princes Street, I stare across the dark, grassy park at the remains of the castle perched on its crag. Nothing but the front part is standing; the rest of the stone stronghold is scattered in pieces across the grass below.

I close my eyes and picture the castle precisely how it was in my memory of *before*. The castle was such a prominent structure in the city, towering right in the centre. It was beautiful, its foundation of it created to look like it was carved out of rock.

When I open my eyes again, the castle is whole. Complete. Beautiful once more. I almost cry at the sight of it. *It's not real*, I remind myself. *This is an illusion.*

The landscape senses my mood and I watch the castle walls dissolve as if water had been thrown onto a painting. The whole parts of the building crumble and fade back into ruin.

I blink back tears and walk the streets of my imagined Edinburgh. It's so cold and empty that I begin to regret coming. I could never be one of those people Catherine described, who go behind their doors for one last glimpse of the places they loved before they die. There's too much pain here, too closely entwined with my guilt.

I begin to notice how false it feels, how limited my imagination is. How the farther out from the city centre I walk, the more my memory of the place begins to blur, and so do the buildings.

As I reach Holyrood, the tenements glimmer as if under water, eventually composing themselves into what I *think* they looked like. All I recall are tall structures, but not the features, not the things that made each one unique. Now they begin to mirror each other. A long row of buildings that look *exactly* the same. I try to change them, to test my memory and recall the nights I ran through these streets on a hunt, but can't. The bricks and stone and mortar simply rearrange themselves into more of the same.

I lose the illusion. I let it all go and picture the buildings as they were when I came back from the *Sìth-bhrùth*. The walls collapse into ruined brick and rubble, completely taken over with moss and ivy.

It's a reminder, a message I have to accept. *This is what you've already left behind. There's nothing else.*

I shut my eyes. My fault. All my fault. All I had to do was reactivate the seal and all of this would still be here. It would all be as it was.

When I open my eyes, I'm in the Queen's Park. The grass is the same pale amber it turns every winter. The muddy trail that leads up to Arthur's Seat is just ahead, the ruins of St. Anthony's Chapel beside me. I breathe in the scent of the park, and the smell is exactly the way it was that night: fire and ash and rain.

Around me, the battle is frozen, a perfectly formed picture of my memory. The fae soldiers have me surrounded. Each of them is stopped in action exactly as they were when they tried to break through the shield of light that surrounded me from the seal.

At my feet is the seal, how it looked during the battle. I drop to my knees and press my fingertips to the outer edge, to the parts of the clock-face, to the pieces of the compass – then to the symbols Kiaran had me draw. The gears glow with a tawny sheen, *tick tick ticking* in a pleasant hum.

'Aileana.'

I look over my shoulder to see Gavin there; I hadn't even heard him come down the path. He wears the same clothes he did when he went out riding, mud-covered with faint stains of blood.

I can't help it; my gaze immediately goes to his scars, those new features on a face I have memorized over the years. Now I have to leave him again.

'What do you want, Galloway?'

His attention is on the battle all around me and the ruined city in the distance. I watch as he studies the ruined tenements. He stiffens as he scans the battle and takes in the way each soldier is stuck in a fighting stance to attack me.

The girl whose gift is chaos.

'Why are you out here?' he asks. 'Don't do this to yourself.'

I focus on the seal again. It doesn't seem as beautiful as it once was, perhaps because it's simply a product of my memory, not the uncanny fae invention that was so magnificent that I ached to create it.

'Do what?' I ask flatly.

'Surround yourself with this.' Gavin flings a hand to the view of the city. 'Bloody hell. Your room I can understand, but the entire damn city?'

'I imagined it because it's all I can think about.' I suppress my irritation, my anger. 'How did you even know where to find me?'

'Easy,' Gavin snaps. 'I followed the trails of guilt. Which looked like entire streets of destroyed buildings.'

'You came through my door. You followed me here,' I remind him. 'Why?'

Gavin sits next to me in the cold grass. He's quiet for so long. I watch his chest as he breathes, the slow inhale and exhale there. Finally, he says, 'I needed to explain myself. Why I said those things to you before I rode off.'

I put up a hand. 'You really don't need to. I understand.'

'No, you don't understand,' he says tightly. I see how conflicted he is, as if he's debating telling me. 'I've spent the last three years convincing myself that this was all your fault.' Finally his eyes meet mine. 'I blamed you for it. Every day.'

I go still. The ache in my chest returns. 'Did you?' I speak calmly, so calmly, in a voice that doesn't match how I feel at all.

I've become skilled at making it seem as though emotions don't affect me, that I don't feel any more. But in this place, the weather doesn't lie. I can't pretend well enough for it to remain unaffected by the turmoil inside me. The clouds darken, heavy and black.

Gavin's attention doesn't waver from me. 'You weren't here to deal with the aftermath,' he says. 'You didn't see them slaughter everyone we knew, and you weren't there when we lived in ruined buildings that smelled of death. We used to pack up every morning to move again in the hope that they wouldn't find us. And I blamed you. I blamed you every damn day. We needed you, and *you weren't there.*'

I can't breathe. I'm afraid that if I do, I won't be able to control my tears. My eyes burn with them. The clouds open and it begins to rain, fat droplets that roll off my hair and into my eyes. I don't even feel the cold. I'm empty. 'Gavin—'

'Don't. Let me finish.' The anger seems to extinguish inside him. 'When I saw you outside the city and you hadn't aged a day, I realised … *Christ.*' Gavin's breathing is hoarse, his body trembling from the cold I can't control. 'You're just one person, and I blamed you for not saving the world.'

I watch the raindrops trickle off my fingertips and onto the seal. How can I make him understand? How can I explain to him that Lonnrach took me and I paid for what I did?

Before I realise, my thoughts have changed the landscape again. The hills of the park disappear like a washed canvas and the new place begins to take shape around us. The structure forms into an arched room —

'No,' I whisper, backing away so fast that I collide with a mirror. 'No no *no.*'

I twist and strike at the mirror with my fists hard enough to bruise. I claw with my fingernails. I can't *think*. I'm breathing so fast that I can't get in air.

'Aileana!'

Hands grab me from behind, but I wrench myself away. *'Don't!* Don't come near me.'

This is really going to hurt.

'Aileana.' Gavin's calm voice breaks through my panic. He says my name again, crouching beside me. He whispers it over and over, as if reminding me who I am.

I never heard my name in this place. It was never spoken. First I was *Falconer*, and then I wasn't even that any more. I was Nothing. No one.

Then Gavin's hands are on my arms. I jerk away, but he tries again, so gentle. 'You're all right,' he says, and then I'm letting him put his arms around me. I bury my face in his shoulder so I don't have to look. My body is shaking. 'You're all right.'

It's not all right. What he did to you, it's not all right.

'Just breathe,' he tells me. 'Breathe.'

Gavin holds me while I try to control myself, to calm myself down. I keep my eyes squeezed shut. I press my fingertips to the bite-marks on my neck. My pulse is beneath those scars. I concentrate on the rhythm, on the way each beat reminds me: *you're alive. You're not really there. This is an illusion.*

Your name is Aileana Kameron and you're alive.

When I settle down enough, Gavin pulls back slightly. 'What is this place?' he asks.

'The prison. Where Lonnrach kept me in the *Sìth-bhrùth*.'

I don't need to see Gavin to sense his surprise. I can feel it in his embrace, how still he is. I open my eyes. This time I'm able to look at the place that was once my prison and bury the fear inside of me. The domed ceiling arches so high above us, every inch of space covered in mirrors. The reflection doesn't show Gavin; it shows me sitting on the floor with my nails digging into

Lonnrach's teeth marks as I try to remember. As I *force* myself to remember.

I pull away from Gavin to feel for the twin scars on my own arm. The way the skin is grooved against my fingertips. Eighty-two teeth. Two thousand two hundred and fourteen individual marks.

'The mirrors were there to amplify my memories,' I say, keeping my voice even. 'Lonnrach would come here and he'd steal them from me for information. He'd—' I lift my sleeve. 'He did this to me. He said he needed my blood to see.'

'Aileana—'

'Aithinne said he only kept me here for a couple of months in fae-time,' I continue, 'but it felt longer. I don't remember—' I pause at the memories that threaten to overtake me.

When I speak again, I keep my voice deliberate, almost cold. 'Do you understand why I can't forgive you for the wisps, Galloway? You brought me back *here*. After everything I did to escape, you were the one who made me go through it again.'

Gavin looks stricken. This time, he doesn't reach for me. He doesn't try to touch me. I watch him take in my new scars, the tiny ones interspersed between Lonnrach's. Scars he was responsible for.

'I can't tell you how sorry I am,' he says. 'There are no words. Nothing excuses what I did to you.'

Even though I haven't forgiven him yet, his words calm me. They calm me just enough that the mirrored room disappears around us and we're back in the Queen's Park. The soldiers no longer surround us. Gavin and I are alone with nothing but the seal between us.

'You have to know,' I say. 'I blamed myself too. I believed you were all dead and thought what happened with Lonnrach was my punishment. I've replayed the last moments in the battle a thousand times. I should have been stronger—'

'No,' he interrupts, reaching to squeeze my palm. 'I never told you about my vision. What I saw.'

'What?' I whisper.

'When I finally pieced it all together, I foresaw you attacking Sorcha. She would have won and all this still would have happened. This was always meant to happen. I was just so angry that I couldn't admit to myself that it was never your fault. Not really.'

I don't tell him what I really think: that it feels like the fates use Gavin's Sight to taunt us with visions of future events that we can't prevent. I couldn't stop Scotland from falling to ruin despite his warnings. What good is being able to see the future if you can't change it?

'So here we are,' I say with a bitter laugh.

'Here we are,' Gavin repeats softly. He looks down at our hands. 'Some things can't be prevented. I should have realised that sooner, when I still had the gift.'

That draws my attention. '*Had?*'

'I haven't had a vision since the night you left.'

I make my face go blank, so he can't tell what I was thinking before about his power being more like a *curse*. 'I'm sorry,' I say.

Gavin's smile is quick, forced. 'Liar.' He takes in our surroundings again. This time, without the soldiers there, I notice how his attention lingers on the landscape. 'You never did answer my question about why you came here.'

Because even though it's an illusion, these are still my memories. Because I don't have a home any more. Because the fae took it from me. 'I just wanted to see it,' I tell him. 'Before I leave.'

'Daniel told me.' He pauses. 'He told me about the voices, too.'

Death is her burden. Wherever she goes it follows.

I wish I had never heard Daniel's premonition. I wish I could forget those words.

'I don't want to put the rest of you in danger,' I say.

'What will you do out there?' he asks.

Lonnrach will never stop hunting me. An immortal can afford to be patient; all he has to do is capture me and take me to the *Sìth-bhrùth* again. This time, he'll lock me up and keep me bound. And when he finds whatever it is that he's looking for, he'll come back to finish me off and take my power.

'I don't know,' I tell him. 'If Lonnrach overpowers me again, I'll end up back *there*, Gavin. I can't—'

Now you know precisely how it feels to be that helpless.

I can't be like that again. I won't go back to being the girl Gavin saw curled up on the floor, reliving memory after memory, trying to recall what it was like to be human. To be loved.

This time Lonnrach won't let me escape. 'He'll try and kill me for my power, and I don't even know how to use it against him,' I say. Gavin looks up at me quickly, as if he's struck with an idea. 'What? What is it?'

'You won't like it.'

'In case you haven't noticed,' I say, 'I'm don't have a wealth of options.'

He hesitates. 'Seers wake up with the *taibhsearachd* after dying and coming back, like I did when I was ill. Maybe power works in the same way.'

I consider his words. Derrick told me that when you die, you go beyond the veil. If the gift of Sight runs in your family and you manage to come back from the dead, you return with the ability.

Of course, Derrick told me long ago that only men have the Sight. There wouldn't be any guarantee that I'd come back different.

But if I did, Lonnrach would never be able to bind me again. I'd have the power to prevent him from getting into my mind. He couldn't manipulate me. He couldn't break me. I'd have exactly what I needed to help Aithinne kill him.

It would be worth dying for that.

'What is it like?' I ask him. 'Dying?'

Gavin stiffens. 'I wish I could forget,' he says.

'That bad?' I had hoped death would be more peaceful.

'When you cross the veil, it's not...' He considers a moment. 'It's like a purgatory. Designed to draw you in and force you to move on to wherever finality is.'

'Did you see your father?' I can't help but ask. That would be worth it, too. If I could see my mother one last time.

'No,' he says softly. 'He would have moved on from that place. There's a reason the dead mostly stay dead. When you're on the other side everything fights to keep you there.'

A thought occurs to me. 'What if you have someone who can bring you back?'

Gavin pauses, his eyes searching mine. 'Then it might be less of a risk.'

Chapter 27

After leaving my imagined Edinburgh, I stand in the doorway of the closet and tell Derrick my plan. He sews a coat as I speak, barely giving any indication that he's listening except for the occasional nod. At the end, he's silent.

'Well?' I prompt.

'Let's see...' He taps his chin. 'Fraught with danger. Uncertain chance of success. Personally, I think it's a terrible idea. I've heard death is exceedingly unpleasant.'

I didn't think Derrick would approve, but at least he could have made it clear before I told him the *whole* blasted plan. 'Would you care to elaborate, please?'

'It's unpleasant because you have to *die*, that's why,' he says stitching a pocket onto the coat. He looks at Gavin. 'She didn't get this pish from you, did she? Because I'm still looking for a reason to lop off one of your appendages after what you did to her, and this looks like the perfect excuse.'

'For god's sake,' I mutter.

Gavin backs up with his hands raised. 'Don't blame me. I might have presented the idea, but she's the one who sauntered off with it.'

Derrick narrows his eyes. 'Aileana, is that true?'

'Yes,' I snap. 'Well, not the sauntering. I don't saunter.'

'Does... this mean I get to keep my appendages?' Gavin asks.

'For now,' Derrick says, holding up the needle in a clear threat.

I inspect the pile of fabric he's sitting on and see that it's not just my imagination – it *has* got bigger. Like he's making up for three years of no dressmaking with an entire wardrobe all at once. God, he's *already* made it! He's going to create a closetful of things I can't wear or take with me.

Gavin eyes the pile of clothes. 'So are you planning a ball, or is this just something pixies do for amusement?'

Derrick glares. 'It's something I do to keep myself distracted, you ninny. I'm being forced to abandon my closet because your friend the Cyclops had some damned premonition.' He lands on a dress, wings flicking. 'I don't even know why we're listening to what some unidentified voices have to say, anyway,' he mutters. 'Now I'll have to burn her entire wardrobe before I begin anew someplace else.'

'Derrick, I *told* you about the dresses.'

Generally I try never to get between an obsessive pixie and his clothes-making, but Derrick really might burn them all if he feels offended. He has always been protective of his creations, and I've never had to refuse them before.

Derrick spits out a sewing needle and lifts a sumptuous piece of thick brocade lined with fur. He flies to me with the garment, his wings glittering and glowing gold. 'Fine, no more dresses. Put this new coat on.'

Resigned, I remove my tattered, bloodstained wool coat. 'I need to find Aithinne. Where is she?'

'Don't know. Lift your arm.' I sigh and let him fit the coat around me. It's gorgeous, a form-fitting garment that cinches at my waist and makes me look smaller and more delicate than I actually am. 'Why do you need Aithinne?'

'Because she can heal me and bring me back.'

'Oh, I see you're still entertaining this ridiculous idea.'

I'm quiet as he straightens the wrinkles down the front of the coat. Derrick might know what happened with Lonnrach, but I don't think he's realised how it's affected me. How it's changed me.

'You *know* why,' I whisper. 'You know why I have to do this.'

He stops at my shoulder, suddenly serious. 'I do,' he says quietly. 'That doesn't mean I have to like it or approve of it.'

'Then just accept it.' I try to say it lightly.

Derrick stares at me for so long, I watch emotions flicker across his face before he finally goes back to smoothing wrinkles. 'Fine,' he says reluctantly. 'If we're doing this, it's a hell of a lot more complicated than just having Aithinne mend you. Even if she is able to revive you, that doesn't mean she'll be able to find you on the other side. What use is the body without the mind?'

Gavin considers that. 'It makes sense. I told you: Everything fights to keep you there.'

'Any ideas, then?' I ask Derrick.

'If you insist on going through with your reckless plan,' he says, inching back to inspect the coat, 'you'll need something to direct Aithinne once you go through the veil.'

He's zipping around me so quickly to check his stitching that I give up trying to track him. 'Like what?'

'*Brìgh*, perhaps,' he says. 'Sìthichean used it in the past to trap human essence within the bulb of the plant to feed on later. If we trapped some of yours, Aithinne might be able to use it to track you.' He stops to think, his wings buzzing. 'Then again, maybe it won't work.'

'*Maybe* it won't?'

Derrick shrugs. He starts undoing stitches at my shoulder, then pinning and sewing again. 'I can't be certain. You could just die and not come back at all.'

Helpful. Very helpful. 'Where might we find some?'

'I hear it grows along the river on the other side of the door, but I don't go in there.'

We don't go in there. Never go in there.

As if he reads my mind, Gavin says, 'No. Don't even think about it.'

I suppose it wouldn't be wise to point out the obvious: that Gavin had absolutely no problem asking the fae beyond the door to torture me when I first arrived.

I set my jaw and look away from him. 'We can ask Aithinne to retrieve it, then.'

'I wouldn't have her do that,' Derrick says. 'You risk her energy interfering with yours in the *brigh*. It might obscure your path through the veil.'

'Then we're going to have to go through the door.'

Derrick stops, just finishing up a stitch. 'I wasn't suggesting that, either.'

'Do you have a better plan?'

'Well, no.' He looks over at Gavin, as if to say, *Can you help, please?*

Gavin puts up his hands. 'Don't look at me for ideas. I just got to keep my body parts.'

Derrick glares. 'Fine.' He buttons me up. 'There. Now you don't look quite so horrid.'

I sigh. 'Can you find Aithinne?'

'She's probably behind the door with the others. She leaves a trail down there that smells like snowdrops and rainy mornings.' He looks resigned when he sees the look on my face. 'Very well. Let's go.'

Derrick flutters out of the closet past me and follows Aithinne's scent through the darkened labyrinthine tunnels to the faery door beyond the field of *seilgflùr*. When we reach the door, he runs his fingers over the carvings and sniffs. 'Aye,' he says, 'she's definitely in there. God, this is a terrible plan.'

I step up to the door and press my ear to it, but I hear nothing, not even the lulling music that drew me to it the first time. Now that I'm close, I realise the symbols look like they've been burned into the wood. I breathe in the scent of ashes and grip the door handle.

'Wait,' Gavin says. 'Perhaps Derrick should go in first and see if it's clear.'

Derrick hovers next to me and levels him with a glare. 'Oh, I see. Just throw the pixie to the wolves, eh?' At Gavin's confused expression, he adds, 'It's not safe for me in there, either, you outrageous arsehole. They think I'm a traitor for having Aileana as a companion and for letting humans stay here. Good god, don't you know *anything*?'

'Gentlemen,' I say sharply. I check the blade at my hip and glance at Gavin. 'I'm going in. If you aren't, then step back.'

Derrick immediately flies to my shoulder and sits there. 'I'm going, too. Just in case this silly plan fails.'

Gavin reluctantly steps up beside me. 'I suppose I ought to come with you to make sure you don't start a war.' He looks at me sharply. 'No killing. If you slaughter any of them, you void the treaty. It's the only thing stopping *them* from going after everyone in the city.'

I hate the reminder of the treaty. What Catherine told me still doesn't make this right. It's like housing a lion with the cage door wide open. 'Fine.'

'Promise me.'

Promise me. I can't believe he's asking that. 'Unlike you,' I say tightly, 'I've always kept my word.'

Gavin flinches.

'Ouch,' Derrick breathes. 'You deserved that, Seer.'

A flash of hurt crosses Gavin's face. 'If anything happens, we run,' he says. 'The people in the city who went in never came back out.'

I push down the alarm that rises at his words and nod. Then I square my shoulders and twist the knob.

It's quiet and dark as I enter. Too dark. Too quiet.

'Do you see anything?' I whisper to Derrick. The fae have better sight than I do.

Before he can answer, the lights suddenly turn on. Like a single switch was flipped and everything – every building – is suddenly illuminated from the inside. I take it all in – the glowing metal architecture, the carved marble streets, the gnarled, twisting trees – and I can't help but be in awe of its beauty. It's even more grand than the human city. Every structure has been carefully constructed with symbols and swirls carved into the metal, designs and pictorial representations of trees and flowers.

The buildings are pointed, towering. Each one has arches above the entrances, so much like those I saw on the outside of the prison at the *Sith-bhrùth*.

Beneath the glass dome that spans across the entire city, lights twinkle and swirl. No – not lights. What illuminates the city isn't electricity, but fire. Flickering flames that float beneath hovering glass bulbs all over the city. They rise to the sky, casting shadows on the roads.

The streets themselves are made of what looks like white marble, but I know better. Marble doesn't shine like that. Marble doesn't look like it has trapped gemstones gleaming within.

Gavin swears softly. 'I can't say I expected this.'

'Shh.'

There are still no faeries visible. I take a careful step forward and a noise to my left startles me. When I look, there's nothing there. Gavin's hand suddenly clasps mine. His palm is hot, clammy.

'I don't like this,' Derrick whispers. 'I don't like—'

Before I even blink, the fae are everywhere. *Everywhere.* Crawling down buildings, flying through the streets, slithering across the marble, coming right for me. Hundreds of them. Some with flashing razor teeth and others with wings that look sharp enough to cut steel. Their eyes glow with an uncanny light as they snarl at me, coming closer as a group.

There are fae I've never seen before – of all different kinds.

Running through my mind are Kiaran's lessons for identifying them all. My eyes rove over black-eyed, mud-coloured faeries with grey clothes. Massive felines the size of wolves with two rows of teeth they flash in a snarl. Faeries that slither like shadows across the ground.

'I'm just going to say it,' Gavin murmurs. 'I really regret this decision.' He jumps as a cat-like fae leaps from a building window near us and lands smoothly on its paws. 'Really ... really regretting it.'

I can't help my instinctive response; I unsheath my sword and grip it by my side. 'Don't,' Derrick whispers. 'Remember what Gavin said.'

Damn. I shut my eyes briefly but I don't put the sword away. I might need the threat of a weapon to keep the fae at bay.

'Two lost humans,' one of the shadow creatures says. A brollachan, from the looks of it. It's a creature without form, a shapeless thing.

I watch it slither over to Gavin. He tenses, his fingers curling into fists. 'I like him,' it whispers. It crawls up Gavin's leg. 'Come with me. I can take you.'

Another faery appears and smiles at me with sharp teeth. Water spills from her hair and clothes as her pitch-dark eyes take me in.

Suddenly, she leans forward, her tongue darting out to leave a wet trail across my cheek. I flinch and she grasps my wrist in a hard grip before I can move away. 'This one smells sweet,' she whispers in a voice that makes me shiver.

Derrick bursts up from my shoulder and snarls. 'Back off, you muddy hag.'

The hag in question hisses back. 'Traitor pixie.' The other faeries snarl at the name. They all know who he is. 'I could take your human,' she whispers. 'I'd eat her and leave you her bones.'

I gasp when nails slash through the leg of my trousers, my skin. A faery looks up at me with eyes deep as emeralds and wings like black, curling branches. I don't remember this one from my lessons with Kiaran.

It licks the blood from my leg. 'Falconer,' it hisses.

The fae bare fangs, flashing teeth as they close in. With a quick swing of my sword, I press the blade to the neck of the faery who cut me. 'Do that again, and I'll slice open your throat.'

Gavin tenses beside me. He doesn't realise it's a threat I don't intend to carry out, but the faery doesn't know that either.

'Damnation, Aileana,' Gavin mutters.

'Kill the Falconer,' one of the fae from the crowd hisses.

'Drain her blood,' whispers another. 'Eat them both.'

'Aileana ... ' Derrick says uncertainly.

I back away from the crowd, as much as I'm able, but they're inching closer. They're ready to strike.

'Take Gavin and find Aithinne,' I tell Derrick. 'The others will follow me. I'll run and get the *brìgh*.'

A few are starting to circle Gavin, as if sensing he's easier to take down. I need to distract them. His body wouldn't be able to handle their bites if they got to him, and he can't run as fast as I can.

'The river is just beyond the buildings,' Derrick says in a low voice. 'The flower is blue and has a bit of a glow to it. You can't miss it. Good luck.' He flies to Gavin's shoulder and whispers in his ear.

Ready.

I address the crowd. 'You want my blood?' I raise the sword, slice open my palm, and hold my bloodied, dripping hand aloft. The creatures hiss and their eyes flash in the darkness. 'Try and take it.'

They dive for me in a swarm of teeth and claws. I dodge out of the way, rolling across the slick marble. Then I'm on my feet and running. I bound down a dark close between the buildings, the hoots and hollers of fae loud behind me.

I make the mistake of looking up. The fae are crawling along the buildings on either side of me, claws slicing into metal. A *cat sith* – a massive faery feline – leaps for me, claws out, and slices through my new coat, just barely missing skin.

Derrick is going to *kill* me for ruining his new work.

I hit the ground, spinning into a crouch. My sword is in my hand as I lunge forward. Just when I would have sliced into the creature to kill it I remember. *If you kill one of them, you'll void the treaty.*

Damnation. I slam the hilt of my sword hard into the cat's temple and kick its ribs with the edge of my boot. It hisses and howls at the impact.

I look up to see the other fae coming at me and I squeeze my bloody fist so it drips onto the ground. Two of them stop for it, licking the ground desperately. The others howl, running faster in pursuit.

I round another building and spot a line of dark, twisting trees up ahead. *The river.* I break for it, leaping across the grass. I shove through the branches of the trees; twigs snap with the impact. Water surges over the rocks at the banks of the river, the current strong.

The flower is blue and has a bit of a glow to it. You can't miss it.

The fae are close. I can hear the stomp of their collective feet, the vibration through the soil. *Where is it, where is it?*

I scan the banks and spot patches of delicate, shining flowers just where the water touches. I vault over one of the large river rocks and grasp the plants without stopping. They come out of the ground easily, roots still attached, and I shove them in my coat pocket.

Time to get the hell out of here.

I sprint back in the direction of the door and take off down an empty side street, my boots pounding against the marble sidewalk. I dodge through the twisting trees in a centre square, through a garden of sharp brambles and thorny roses. My clothes and coat catch and I pull and tug myself through. The towers of the city around me seem never-ending, with nowhere to hide.

Just when I think a close is tight and dark enough to conceal me, the flaming lights follow me in at the command of the fae. My blood drips behind me as I run. The fae stop to lick it and fight each other for a taste before they bound after me again.

As I'm rounding a corner, Derrick zips down from the buildings above. 'This way,' he tells me, breathing hard. His wings hum as he flies in front of me. 'Back to the door.'

I'm panting, my legs are burning as I sprint beneath a glass archway of one of the buildings. 'Where are Aithinne and Gavin?'

'Just up ahead.'

Derrick leads me down another street. My muscles strain to keep up with his speed as he dashes across a square I haven't passed through yet. I bloody well hope he knows where he's going.

A growl behind me draws my attention. I dart a glance over my shoulder to see the fae are close, so close they're practically nipping at my heels. I pump my arms, trying to gain speed as I recognise the close that leads to the door. Just up ahead, almost there. I run faster, my chest aching from breathing so hard.

Just before I reach the door, I see Aithinne and Gavin. Aithinne grabs my shoulders so I don't career into her. Sighing at me in a chastising way, she pushes me gently toward Gavin and steps between us and the oncoming horde.

Her eyes are glowing, turning molten silver as they do when she uses her powers. Before I can speak, she reaches her hand out to the fae, palm up. The burst of power that comes from her is strong, coating my tongue and my throat.

A ripple moves through the crowd, freezing all of the fae in place. Just as Sorcha did during the battle. Not one of them moves. 'You all look ridiculous,' Aithinne says with disgust. 'Fighting over humans like animals. It's no wonder they hate us.' She curls her raised hand into a fist and they all gasp as if being choked. Her power makes my stomach clench. 'Maybe I should do them the favour.'

'Aithinne,' Gavin says sharply. 'Don't.'

'We came into their territory,' I say. No matter how vicious the fae are, Catherine warned me to stay away. 'Let them go.'

I may hate the treaty and the fact that the fae can claim any human who wanders into their territory, but this is the world I left behind. This is how Catherine and Gavin and their city survive. I've already done enough damage to their tenuous truce just by coming here and threatening them with a blade.

Aithinne keeps a tight hold on all of them for a moment longer. 'Go back inside,' she tells the fae. 'All of you. The humans are leaving with me.' She releases them and ignores their low growls of protest as she walks us all to the door.

'Bad idea,' Aithinne says, shaking her head as she ushers us out. 'That was such a bad idea. If Derrick hadn't come for me, one of those *sithichean* probably would have brought me your intestines to wear as a necklace. And I don't even like jewelry.'

'But we found you,' Derrick says brightly. 'So, you see, mission accomplished!'

'A bit of a ludicrous accomplishment, but at least you're not dead,' she says. 'Now what was so important?'

I tell Aithinne everything I told Derrick, but I don't say what I'm really thinking. I don't tell her that I want to do this because if I could fight Lonnrach, it would be worth it. I don't tell her that what Lonnrach did to me made wish so often for death that it doesn't scare me any more.

I don't tell her, because she already understands. I can see it in the way she looks at me. She knows. She *knows* precisely why.

We'll make him pay. I'm going to help you.

As if hearing my thoughts, she nods but still seems hesitant. Her gaze narrows in suspicion at Gavin. 'Wait. Is this *your* idea?'

Gavin straightens, his expression shuttering. I've never seen him so guarded before. 'Aye.'

Before I blink, she's so close to Gavin their bodies are practically touching.

'After what you did to Aileana, why should I trust anything you come up with?'

Gavin drops his gaze but says nothing. He doesn't have to. The sudden brush of flower petals on my tongue indicates that Aithinne is using her powers to get inside Gavin's mind. She's reading him with that alien fae expression. His jaw tightens in response.

'You still fear death,' she tells him. 'Your experience through the veil is not one you'd like to repeat, and yet you'd send the Falconer there. This is how you would atone for what you did?' Her mouth twists. 'You demand a high price for your friendship.'

Gavin raises his chin. 'If I could go for her, I would. If I could make it so she would never hurt again, I would.'

'I don't believe you.'

'You're already in my mind,' Gavin says, and I don't miss the anger there. 'See for yourself.'

Aithinne studies him, as if he both interests and disgusts her. The taste of her power thickens in the air, only for a moment. Then she pulls back and scowls at him. 'Ugh! I only wanted the answer. I didn't need to see the rest,' she says. 'You have a foul mind, Seer.'

Gavin smirks. 'I take it you didn't like what you found in there.'

Her expression hardens and she shifts her attention to me, ignoring his question. 'It's difficult to bring back the dead, you realise.'

I reach into my coat pocket and hold up the *brìgh*. 'I took this while we were inside. Derrick says it might help.'

Now that we're on the other side of the door, I can examine the plant properly. It's delicate, with a thin, vinelike stem with sparse petals. The flower on the top is shaped rather like a lilac, only with more pointed petals. In the centre is a small bulb that emits a beautiful blue shine.

Aithinne glances at it. 'Some of your energy in that will help, but it's the price I'm speaking of.'

'Then I'll pay it,' I say quickly.

Derrick pinches me and hisses. 'What the hell is wrong with you? You don't say that without hearing the terms. Haven't I taught you anything?'

'It isn't for her to pay, pixie. It's for me.' Aithinne looks at me then. 'But if you want this, I'll do it.'

'Then you'll need me,' another voice says. I turn to see Kiaran heading down the path between the fields of *seilgflùr*.

He looks hesitant, like he regrets what he's about to say. I realise he heard everything. 'Blood for blood, Aithinne,' he tells his sister. 'If you're willing to do your part, I'll do mine.'

Aithinne's face softens in a way I've never seen before. She seems so young compared to him. 'I never thought I'd hear you offer that again.'

Chapter 28

The following morning, after I change and clean myself up, Kiaran guides us out of the city and through the long tunnel out to the sea. The beach is just below the tall, jagged cliff side. The water laps against the pebbles there in a calm, soothing rhythm.

Though it's only early afternoon, the winter light has already dimmed to near-twilight, casting the sky in hues of light and dark blue. The colour reflects onto the ocean, turning it the startling, vivid colour of sapphires.

As the tide comes in, the rocks grind against each other, as if the sea is groaning with age. Wind bites my cheeks and sprays sand and salt on my lips.

I wear a pale shift that Derrick has made for me; soft and light and warm. Aithinne wove the *brìgh* in my hair, the glowing blue flowers forming a crown around my head. When I die, some of my energy will be absorbed into the buds, a small piece of my life force left behind.

Kiaran leads me across the beach, leaving Derrick, Aithinne, and Gavin at the cave entrance. As soon as the tide hits my bare feet, I gasp at the cold. We walk into the water slowly. Kiaran grasps my hand and I feel his power, warming and soothing.

I offer him a grateful smile. He doesn't smile back.

Wading into the water wearing the shift and the crown of

flowers makes me feel like a sacrifice. I catch the way Kiaran gazes at me – as if he's thinking the same. As if he's about to lose me.

But I have no choice.

Kiaran looks away. Despite his power, the sea water is freezing the farther in I go, so cold that my lungs constrict. I'm growing numb with each step. Snow falls heavily around us as the waves lap around my waist.

Kiaran's hand tightens around mine and his sudden rush of power warms me up again. His heat is an unbelievable thing, a radiating glow that presses into my palm.

'I'm surprised you agreed to this,' I say. I glance back to shore. Aithinne waits there with Gavin, Derrick on his shoulder. Snow gathers around them.

'If there were another way, we wouldn't be here.' We're far enough out and Kiaran stops me. His hands are on my arms, gliding up and down as if to warm me. 'I made you a promise,' he tells me. 'I still intend to keep it.'

'MacKay, I—'

What? I feel like I should tell him something important, in case I don't come back. Something meaningful. Something that tells him I *want us just like this. I want us just like this, and more.*

As if he reads my mind, Kiaran kisses me softly. Then he pulls back and I wish he didn't. 'I'll have to release you at the last second,' he says. 'Or I'll break my vow.'

'Right.' I can't die while he's holding me down or the faery vow will kill him, too. Only, his death will be longer and more agonizing.

'Kam.' His eyes are intense, as if he needs me to understand. 'There's no shame in changing your mind.'

'I know.' *But what if Aithinne can't bring me back?* 'Do you think it'll hurt?'

He grasps me closer and the warmth of his body breaks though the cold. Snow falls from his hair onto his eyelashes, where it melts against his skin. His eyes are so beautiful, reflecting the slate-grey sky, his irises the colour of lavender.

'I don't know,' he says.

I lick the ice off my lips, tasting the salt there. It's so quiet out here, only ocean waves crashing around us. It's these moments when I realise that my time with Kiaran is such a fragile thing. At any moment, my human life could end and he'd still be as unchanging as the sea.

'Not even a half-lie?' I say. 'That's not like you.'

He brushes his fingertips along my cheek and I shut my eyes. 'No half-lies,' he tells me. 'No reassurances, either. Just come back.'

I dart a glance to the others on the beach. Waiting, watching. 'You and Aithinne will take care of everyone if I don't, won't you?' I ask him. 'Promise me. Just one more promise.'

He lowers his hand. The air around us is suddenly so cold that I nearly choke. It snows harder. My every breath is painful. Kiaran's expression has gone from gentle to harsh so quickly. There's the Kadamach in him; it's still there despite everything.

'No,' he says, his eyes burning. 'I won't give you a reason not to fight like hell on the other side.'

'MacKay—'

'Know this.' His terrifying fae voice is back, lulling. The words roll off his tongue and make me shiver. 'If you don't come back, I'll leave them all to Lonnrach's mercy.'

I jerk away, my fingers curling into fists. Damn it, he's ruining my goodbye on purpose. 'You wouldn't.'

Kiaran watches me with that same distant expression, so cold and deliberate. His faery mask. The part of him that I forget about when he strokes my face or whispers to me in his language or makes me promises. The part of him that lurks just beneath the surface, always. And it isn't kind. It isn't gentle. The Kadamach in him is hidden under a guise that is gossamer thin.

'They mean nothing to me.' His voice is soft, melodic.

'Then why fight by my side to save them? You could have let the Seers die yesterday and it wouldn't have mattered.'

'Because it would have mattered to *you*.'

Just like that, my anger is gone. I find myself moving closer to him until our cold, wet clothes mesh together and his lips are close to my own. 'What am I to you, MacKay?' I whisper.

He draws me to him, whispering things that send shivers down my skin. '*Tha mi duilich*,' he breathes against my temple, so low I only just hear it. 'When you come back, I'll show you.'

'Is that a promise, at least?'

'Aye.' I feel his smile, then his lips are on my forehead, so light. So achingly soft. 'Don't forget why you're there,' he tells me. 'What's on the other side won't want you to return. *Turas mhath leat*. Ready?'

I take a breath and nod. Kiaran pushes me under the cold water.

At first, everything is fine. Then my lungs begin to burn. Though I know what I have to do, I can't help but struggle. I buck against Kiaran so I can break to the surface to draw in breath, but he holds me tightly, his body weighing me down. The cold is an impenetrable thing, so heavy on my skin. I open my mouth to breathe, but can't. Soon, my body goes limp.

Kiaran releases me. I realise this is the last moment I have to change my mind – I have just enough strength to go back to the surface. It *hurts*. The pain is spreading through my chest —

No. I have to do this. I stay under the water, feeling my body sink *down down down* until my back is against the pebbles at the bottom of the sea. My last memory is Kiaran pressing his lips against mine.

Chapter 29

I'm in a dark forest. The trees are tall, towering, with spiked branches like blades. I can't see where they end, only the stars above so bright – glowing greens and blues and teals. The sky is a vivid dark blue, so beautiful and like nothing I've ever seen before. I lower my gaze to study a narrow path that extends through the woodland. An arch of trees frames the path at both ends, and either way looks like it leads out of the thick forest.

After a moment's indecision, I choose a direction and run, sprinting across soft and spongy dirt. There is no sound in the forest, not even my footsteps. No animals, no rustling of any kind. I keep running for the arch of trees, my breath coming fast. I run until the sweat beads my brow, until my breath is a roar.

The trees around me seem to grow higher and thicker and darker, but I focus on the path, on the arch. Surely it can't be far. It looks like the end of the path is *right there*, tantalizingly close. I run until I think my lungs will burst, until my chest aches. The trees around me stretch thin, toward the stars.

I have to slow to a jog. My breath heaves. I swallow, but my throat is paper dry. A voice whispers across my mind. Kiaran's. *Just come back.*

When I can't even jog any more, I walk. I focus on Kiaran's name, on what I have to do. I recall his words in the water, before I was so cold that I felt my body die. *What's on the other side won't want you to return.*

Then this path really doesn't lead anywhere. How many foolish souls have taken it, running either way only to get nowhere at all? I have no time to waste.

I break for the trees off the path, walking slowly around the twisted trunks of the forest. Even with careful, deliberate steps, I trip over roots and fallen branches. Soon, I can't see anything. I am enveloped in darkness so thick that no light penetrates.

That's when I hear the screams. People cry out my name, voices I know from my life in Edinburgh. Those who died during the fae attack. They wail, blame me, and curse my name. They are a thousand voices I can't drown out, coming from all directions.

You failed. You let us all die. You failed.

The guilt is a physical weight that presses down on my shoulders, my chest, until my body is heavy with it. The guilt forces me to replay those final moments next to the seal when I hesitated to click the last symbol in place – and that was all it took. One moment – a single second – of hesitation and it was all over.

Death is her burden. Wherever she goes it follows.

Just when I think I can't take any more, I remember Gavin's words. *She would have killed you and all this still would have happened. This was always meant to happen.*

This was always meant to happen. I would never have succeeded. No matter what, I would have always ended up right here. In this forest.

Don't forget why you're there.

I hold onto Kiaran's reminder and scramble through branches. I try to get away from the voices, but they only grow louder. *Your fault.* Their accusations are unrelenting in the darkness. *Your fault your fault your fault my fault* —

I hold back my tears. *Focus.* I drag myself onward, forcing myself into a run. I breathe in air that's suddenly cold – painfully so – as I make my way through the trees. I concentrate my thoughts on the people who are alive and need me to come back. I won't fail them again.

As if sensing my resistance, the voices grow louder, an endless cacophony. Tree branches catch and try to hold me. And I realise that they aren't branches after all – they're hands.

Cold fingers close around my arms, hard enough to bruise. Their touch is so frigid that it burns. I bite back a scream as I struggle to pull myself out of their grip, but they hold tightly, so tightly. My breath is quick as I shove and push my way through the blackness. I have to keep going.

They scream my name. They beg me to help them. They scratch me and make me bleed. More hands seize me, unrelenting, but I shove through.

Suddenly, they're gone. The voices, the frozen hands, the darkness. I am standing in front of a fire in the middle of the woods. I collapse in front of its warmth, my breath coming fast.

Just as quickly, I realise: *This shouldn't be here. This shouldn't —*

'Found you,' a voice whispers from behind me.

I whirl. A figure stands in the trees, a heavy cloak obscuring any features – but I am sure from her frail, tiny body that she's a woman. Her hair is long, white as bone, and fine as spider webs. Its strands catch in the starlight and glitter like quartz. Despite the darkness, her eyes glisten and she watches me the way one might observe an insect in a jar.

Finally, she steps into the firelight, and cold dread fills me. Her features are so difficult to distinguish; one moment she is a young woman, almost childlike, with a fullness to her cheeks and a flush to her skin. The next, she is old, skeletal, and frail. The cloak around her isn't fabric at all, but shadows, thick and dark and curling at the edges.

Every moment the woman's face changes, old, then young, then even younger. She doesn't speak, just studies me with a recondite gaze.

It's her face that makes me back away. I recognise her.

She's the one from my nightmare.

My back presses to the trunk of a tree, and I can't help but look around us, half-expecting to find laughing crows with blood-dripping beaks. 'You were in my dream,' I say. 'Who are you?' I speak with care, with the knowledge that, at any moment, she might attack and I have two options: fight or run.

'You've read the old stories, Aileana Moira Rossalyn Kameron,' she says, stepping farther out of the shadows.. 'You know my names, just as I know all of yours.'

Any surprise I would have had at hearing my forenames – ones I haven't heard in the longest time, that she *shouldn't* know – is eclipsed by the sudden fear at the sight of her staff. My pulse speeds up and I can't take my eyes off it, how the grass beneath the ancient wood withers and frosts over as she draws closer.

No one has seen the Cailleach for thousands of years.

This is her. I know it from the stories. I feel it in my bones.

'You're the Cailleach,' I whisper.

The thin lips of her bony face curl into a smile, one both warm and frightening. 'Aye, *mo nighean.*'

I stay still, unsure. The Cailleach is the oldest faery, the most powerful of them all. Some consider her a goddess, but I know that's merely how ancient humans approached the immortal fae: as deities to be appeased.

She was once the sole queen of the Seelie and Unseelie courts. They say she left the human and faery worlds she created to reside in this realm – the place between life and death.

The Cailleach has so many identities; she could strike joy in people just as easily as she could inspire fear. I read stories as a child that claimed she shaped the mountains and rivers with her hammer and brought winter with her staff. In a warm mood, she would give humans fertile land, a water source, and all the things necessary to live. In a fit of rage, she'd destroy everything and kill everyone in her path.

I shut my eyes briefly. The Cailleach must want me dead. She wouldn't have given me that message in my dream if she didn't. I must have been on the brink of death from the faery venom for her to invade my dreams like that.

'What do you want with me?' I ask. My voice doesn't waver. I refuse to appear weak, even to the Cailleach.

I'm certain she hears the unasked question at the end: *Are you here to destroy me?* The Cailleach has only two purposes: help or destruction, never anything in between.

The temperature around me drops, the way it does when Kiaran becomes angry. Only the Cailleach's power makes it more intense, a choking cold that makes me hunch over and hug myself for warmth. My fingers grow numb and my skin burns. My vision dances with stars and I hear the deafening boom of thunder in the distance.

The Cailleach leans down and grasps my chin, her fingernails biting into my skin. With my hazy vision, I meet her eyes, cold and endlessly black. There is no humanity in that gaze, no compassion.

'I'm here to make sure that this time you don't make it back,' she tells me, in a voice that ices my spine.

After this, you're on borrowed time, Falconer. I'll see you again soon.

She pretended to be my mother. She invaded my mind. The thought of it turns my skin hot with rage. I narrow my gaze and fight against her control. Deliberately, I straighten. I let the cold wash over me. *I won't let you control me.*

I swear she almost smiles. She drops my chin and the temperature rises suddenly. I'm left breathing hard, swaying from dizziness, but I manage to stay standing.

'Why?' I manage between breaths.

'You're a Falconer,' she says simply, moving to stand near the fire. It lights her momentarily steady features, her high cheekbones and heart-shaped mouth. A face that is just as immaculately fae as the rest of them.

I hear the double meaning in her statement: *you slaughtered my own.*

I look around for any way to escape. Running into the forest might lead me back to the voices. Fighting the oldest faery in existence might not be terribly wise —

'Look at me,' she snaps. Her voice is a cold blade down my arms; it draws my attention back to her. 'My daughter, Aithinne, should *never* have created your kind,' she says. 'Your existence has been catastrophic for both humans and the *sìthichean*.' She studies me, her eyes dark and endless. 'Surely you can see that?'

I stare at her, cold to my core. *Should never have created the Falconers.*

Created the Falconers.

I slowly piece together everything I've learned about Aithinne. She fought alongside the Falconers. She was trapped during their battle with the fae. She has the ability to heal. To bring back the dead. The gift of creation, inherited from the Cailleach. Her mother.

Kiaran's mother.

'Falconers are human,' I whisper. 'The fae can't create humans.'

I recall Daniel's words, so matter-of-fact. *You're not human.*

The Cailleach's eyes linger on me. There are a thousand thoughts in the way she regards me, starting with pity and ending with distaste. Because no matter what, humans will always be beneath the fae, both in strength and experience. We don't have a thousand lifetimes that chip away our emotions.

We burn bright, and we burn out. That's what it means to be human.

The shadows of her cloak snake up to reveal her pale fingers, long and gnarled and spotted with age. She leans down and presses her fingertips briefly to the wet soil, the skin of her hand growing more youthful and pearlescent as I watch.

From the ground grows a single vine. Long and thick as a tree branch, it curls around itself over and over until it forms a seat.

The flowers along the vines blossom, the petals a bright, glowing teal.

'Sit.' The Cailleach gestures. 'And I shall show you the truth. Everything you desire.'

I hesitate. The fae don't offer anything freely, not without an exchange. 'What do you want in return?'

I could die in the chill of the Cailleach's smile. I feel the weight of her years like I'm being eaten up by the ground, a force pulling me down into the earth.

'Ah, *mo nighean*. I have already taken from you,' she murmurs. 'I have your life. There is nothing else you could offer me. I could keep you in my forest for an eternity, but instead I offer you truth. This is not something I give freely.'

The version of truth the Cailleach offers is always brutal; I don't want to accept. If what she said earlier is true, then she's drawing out my time here so Aithinne can't find me.

If you don't come back, I'll leave them to Lonnrach's mercy.

If Kiaran is the Cailleach's son, that isn't a threat I should take lightly. I trust him with *my* life, but not the lives of my friends – not Gavin or Catherine or Derrick.

They mean nothing to me.

'And if I refuse?' I ask carefully. *Am I allowed to refuse?* To offend a faery is to invoke her anger, and the wrath of the Cailleach is unparalleled.

The Cailleach's expression is ruthless. 'It's your choice, of course,' she says lightly, but her words don't match her face. 'I may have limited powers in your realm, but I know that every-one you have left is in that pixie kingdom. Surely you want them safe?'

This is what *choice* means to the fae: *deny me and I will kill everyone you love. Deny me and I will make you sorry.*

I have to accept. I'll find a way to trick the Cailleach if I have to, but right now I can't refuse her offer. 'Very well.'

She reaches for me, with a hand that has thinned enough

to show bone. Her face changes again, and it is how I imagine Death – skeletal, with eyes like an endless abyss.

The Cailleach touches the crown of my head and before I can do anything, the *brìgh* that was in my hair falls to the ground. The flowers are withered and dead, the glow within the centre bulb gone entirely.

Her cavernous eyes meet mine. 'It's just you and me, *mo nighean*. My daughter will never find you now.'

I feel the first cold touch of fear, then her fingers brush my face. Her touch is like a blade driving through my skull. I bite my tongue to keep from crying out.

'Open your eyes,' she tells me. '*Look.*'

I do as she commands and I realise we're not in the forest any more, not near the fire. I'm not sitting in a seat made of vines and flowers. We're in a field surrounded by the dead.

Human bodies lie at our feet, scattered across the dark meadow. Most of them are women. Some have their throats slit, and others lie with their backs to the sky as if they had tried to run. Their blood glistens in the moonlight, the scent of death lingering in the air.

Oh god. I double over. I almost cast up everything in my belly. I couldn't take a single step and hit grass. 'What did this?'

The Cailleach betrays no emotion. 'My son.'

Kiaran. Kiaran did this. 'Why?' I can barely speak.

I think of the way Kiaran looks at me when I manage to get through to him, how he looked when he told me he missed me. The way his lips pressed to the scars at my throat —

I killed humans every day. Until I spoke a vow.

He did this. He killed all of these people.

'Most humans can't resist the lure of the Wild Hunt,' the Cailleach explains. 'Every herd needs to be culled, *mo nighean*, even human ones. This is my son's purpose.'

'This isn't a purpose,' I snap. 'It's a pointless slaughter.'

The Cailleach looks disappointed at my response. 'Death *always* serves a purpose.'

She moves among the bodies with the grace of water. She leans down and lightly touches the face of a young woman. Before my eyes, the girl's flesh sinks into her skull. Her bones wither and fade to dust. And from the earth rises a single flower, beautiful and perfect.

'My son is the fire that destroys a forest,' the Cailleach continues. 'My daughter is the rain that makes it green again. This is the course we tread over and over throughout the ages.'

I want to tell the Cailleach that I don't think mass slaughter is part of the natural order. That I would never be willing to stand aside while the fae hunted in my city – the way I did when Sorcha killed my mother – because that's just what they do. Humans don't exist to be killed whenever the fae desire. Exactly what *purpose* does that serve?

I swallow all my anger back and ask, 'Why are you showing me this?'

The Cailleach plucks the flower and crushes it in her fist. It falls like ashes from her fingers. 'This is where it all began. This Hunt, this field, and these deaths. Kadamach declared the war right here.'

The war? 'They're Falconers, then,' I say flatly.

'No,' the Cailleach says. 'The men of their village all had the Sight. The women who died here couldn't resist the song of Kadamach's Hunt.'

That clenches my stomach even more. If these women weren't Falconers, they would have been helpless. They were just scared humans who got in the way of a Wild Hunt, and Kiaran had slaughtered them like they were nothing. They had no way to defend themselves, no power against him. The men – the Seers – who lie in this field must have died trying to save them.

'And I suppose the fae didn't give a damn about them,' I say bitterly.

She turns her gaze to me, and it's hard, unforgiving. 'Plenty of *sithichean* died on this battlefield alongside your humans.'

Good, I almost say but don't. 'And their deaths weren't *pointless,* either, I suppose?' I say, trying to keep my tone even.

'Don't bait me, child. This was necessary to secure the future of our kind. Kadamach played his part to perfection.'

I rake my gaze across the land, over the hundreds upon hundreds of dead women and men, and I can't control my fleeting, awful thoughts. The one that stands out most is the memory of Lonnrach's words: *you should have killed Kadamach when you had the chance.*

Kiaran's past is littered with the dead; his secrets could fill the spaces between galaxies. He lured humans with the same song Lonnrach's soldiers used to kill those in my city: my family, the people I knew my entire life. And just like those soldiers, he left humans scattered across the land like waste.

'I don't understand,' I say. 'What part?'

'To live the same tale through the ages,' she says softly, almost to herself. Then: 'We are all creatures of war, *mo nighean.* Kadamach taught you that, did he not? Battle is in our blood.' The Cailleach turns away, the shadows of her veil crawling like snakes on the ground. 'It's how our civilization rose. It's how we became conquerors.'

Chapter 30

The Cailleach glides through the lines of bodies, each one sinking into the earth as she does. 'Come. We're not finished here.'

In a blink, we're walking down a dirt path between wee stone huts with thatched roofs, the village dark and quiet. Not even a rustle of birds in the trees. Snow falls around us, melting as soon as it touches dirt. The Cailleach moves across the road with the careful, frail walk of a crone, her back hunched, salt-white hair loose around her shoulders. Her skin sinks into her bones again, withered and leathered and old.

Just around the bend is a bonfire. Glowing cinders rise into the sky and snuff out, leaving behind the scent of burning yew. Thirteen women are gathered in a half circle around the dancing flames. Their voices fill the night, some in winged whispers, others in firm voices, all in a language I've never heard before. They wear crudely dyed layered hoods and dresses to protect them from the cold.

I recognise one of the women. *Aithinne.* Her eyes glow silver and gold in the firelight, her hair sleek and black as ink. She looks like a goddess, shining in the moonlight. A falcon perches on her bared shoulder. Not even its formidable claws can puncture her invulnerable fae skin. It seems content to rest there, its wings tucked in, its back straight and proud.

Aithinne raises a hand to silence the harsh voices of the

women around her. That's when I look at their faces, the tears, the anger, their palpable grief. I've never seen a group of people look so helpless. So *hopeless*.

'Who are they?' I ask the Cailleach.

'The first Falconers,' she says. 'They were the sole female survivors of their village. My daughter sang the song that lured them here.'

I stiffen, expecting the worst after what the Cailleach showed me in the field. When the Cailleach promises truth, it always hurts. It lifts the veil from the secrets people keep and strips everything bare until you wish you'd never seen it. You wish you had never accepted.

Aithinne manipulated these women to come here. After what I learned about Kiaran I'm half-expecting her to murder them right in front of me. *Don't make me hate you*, I think. *Please don't make me hate you.*

I study the women, the smudges of dirt on their faces, their clothes splattered and smudged with blood, the tear tracks down their cheeks. They are not warriors, not the hardened Amazons of myth I thought they'd be. Instead, they're scared women who have just lost their families, who have learned first hand how brutal the fae can be.

When Aithinne speaks, it's in another language – and yet I understand the words. The Cailleach's doing.

'I have called you all here to reach an accord,' Aithinne says in a commanding voice I've never heard from her. One woman begins to protest, but Aithinne's power cuts across the bonfire like a stock-whip to shut her up. 'I didn't give you permission to speak.'

I flinch, remembering Lonnrach's voice in my ear, whispered through sharp teeth. *I didn't say you could move.*

This isn't the Aithinne I've come to know, the Aithinne who saved my life. Who offered to take my memories of Lonnrach if it eased my pain. She sounds like *him*, like she doesn't give a damn about humans.

263

More than that, she stands with all the confidence of a warrior, a leader: shoulders thrown back, chin high and proud, those uncanny eyes full of fire. The falcon on her shoulder pulls back its wings and beats them briefly. She is an unrelenting presence, powerful, terrifying, like her mother.

This is the Aithinne who had never been trapped underground for two thousand years of torture.

She's speaking again, circling the fire and watching each woman with that unreadable gaze. 'None of you have need to fear me. I'm not the one who slaughtered your families.' She comes to a stop, her skin shining. She is a magnificent, frightening, and so very inhuman. 'But I can offer you vengeance against the one who did.'

I glance at the Cailleach. Her expression has hardened, eyes sunken into her skeletal face. Whatever Aithinne is about to do is the source of her mother's rage.

My daughter, Aithinne, should never have created the Falconers.

A wave of uncertainty passes through the group. The woman who tried speaking before suddenly finds her voice, hoarse, barely audible. 'This is a trick.'

I expect Aithinne to respond as harshly as she did before. But instead, I see a flicker in her gaze, a weakness in that hardened armour. She grieves, too. 'No tricks. No deceit. I want you to take from him what he stole from you.' Then, a whisper. One I just barely catch: 'What he stole from *me*.'

'What does she mean?' I ask the Cailleach. I don't want to ask, but I need to know. 'What he stole?'

The Cailleach leans on her staff; it freezes the ground all the way to my bare toes. 'She grieves the loss of her subjects. Those my son killed. My daughter was born too soft. Calling on humans to fight on her side in a war ... ' She curls her lip in disgust. 'I would have killed her for it myself if I could. '

Her *subjects*? The pieces start to connect: I fit together stories and everything I know about Kiaran and Aithinne. Everything I learned about the fae.

Two kingdoms of light and dark, each with one monarch, and the faeries of each kingdom served a single purpose: the dark kingdom brought death, and the light kingdom brought creation.

My heartbeat pounds in my ears. The women around the fire are standing, but I can't even focus on what they're saying any more. All I can think about is Kiaran sitting on the rocky beach after the battle with the *mortair*.

Why were you searching for the crystal?

I was Unseelie, Kam. What do you think? I wanted it to kill the Seelie Queen.

'Aithinne is the Seelie Queen,' I whisper. 'Isn't she?' Then I say the words I didn't want to, the part of the story I hope isn't true but I know with everything in me that it is. 'And Kiaran is the Unseelie King.'

'Aye,' the Cailleach says quietly.

I think back to all those times I tried to piece together Kiaran's past and I tried every combination possible – each more awful than the last – but I couldn't imagine this, not this.

My affection for Kiaran has blinded me. Even with the glimpses I saw of Kadamach, I could never truly comprehend the awful things he did because a part of me didn't want to. I didn't want to think of the thousands upon thousands of people he was responsible for slaughtering. Because the Unseelie King wasn't like the other fae. He lived and breathed death. He would burn the world to ash.

You'll always be Kiaran to me.

Kadamach. His name is Kadamach, and he's the Unseelie King.

Now I understand why so many hesitate when the Cailleach offers them the truth. Truth is never as pretty as a lie. It's never as appealing. It's a sword to the gut, the thing that reminds us that some people aren't who we thought they are.

Truth forces us to confront the ugliest parts of the people we love. The monstrous parts.

I drop my gaze. 'I've had enough.'

The Cailleach is unmoved, her face back to its beautiful form. Now that I see it again, I realise how very much she looks like her children. The same dark hair and flawless features and bottomless eyes.

'You accepted my offer,' she says, her staff thumping against the ground. The snow falls around us. A cold wind slices across my neck and I shiver. 'I'm not finished yet.'

'Why do you care if I know the truth?' I say bitterly. 'You want me to stay dead. You're only showing me these memories to keep me here.'

The Cailleach's beautiful face sinks into a skull, only for a blink. She is an ocean of secrets, a faery as old as death itself. And yet … and yet there is something almost vulnerable about how frail she becomes sometimes, how she looks at me.

'That is only half true, *mo nighean*,' she says, her voice trembling as a human's does in their advanced age, in their twilight hours before death. 'I told you: I took from you, too. Since I cannot offer you life, I offer you this. It's all I have left to give.'

'You took—'

We're interrupted by a scream of agony. There's a woman kneeling by the fire, Aithinne's hands pressed to either side of her head. They're both bleeding, Aithinne from her hands, the woman from the cuts on her face. The falcon has gone.

Aithinne's expression is one of complete concentration, her eyes tightly shut. She looked like that when she healed me. *God, how that hurt.* The woman screams again and I'm shocked when light seems to emanate from beneath her skin.

'What's she doing?' I say. The other women look equally anxious, distrustful, but they remain in their places, in their semicircle around the flames.

'This is how you earned your ability to kill my kind,' the

Cailleach says, sounding tired. She leans on the staff as if she can barely stand on her own any more. 'You have my daughter's blood in you, her powers. *My* blood.'

So they're not my powers. The Falconers were created because Aithinne couldn't bear to kill her own brother. We were created for their war.

'Then I'm part Seelie. Not human, after all,' I say bitterly.

'Human enough,' the Cailleach snaps.

I watch Aithinne step away from the woman. Over and over, the future Falconers kneel before her; again and again they give the same agonizing scream. Not one of them declines. Not one of them decides to leave, or shrinks back in fear. This is who they are to become: warriors. Pain is simply the first part of the battle.

I think of Aithinne's words as the last woman stands. *In the end, we are all the stag.*

A single screech sounds from the forest, then a dozen more. I step back sharply as falcons emerge from the trees, their wings fanning the fire. Each bird has black and white stripes that run from the very tips of their wings across their feathered bodies. They dive for the women, each falcon claiming one. Their claws sink into the women's tender skin, drawing blood as they perch on their shoulders, calmed now. The women gasp in pain, but no one screams.

They each have a falcon, connected to them by blood. They've earned their titles. *Seabhagair.* Falconer.

The last falcon flies to Aithinne and resumes its position on her shoulder. But her hands are shaking and her nose is bleeding, dripping over her lips and down the pale column of her neck. She no longer holds herself with the same confidence and power, with that spine-straight-shoulders-back stance. Her skin has lost some of its effervescent luster; not much, but still noticeable.

'It weakened her,' I say softly.

The Cailleach looks at me again and her face is old, wrinkled, her skin pale and dull. Her white hair is no longer shining; it's stringy, thin. 'As the last Falconer, you hold all of the powers she lost this night. When you die it is restored to her. She will be whole again.'

Unless someone steals it first, I realise. *You have something I want*, Lonnrach told me that night of the battle. I have Aithinne's blood inside me. *The Cailleach's* blood – old magic.

If Lonnrach succeeds in finding the crystal and taking my power, he'll use it to kill Kiaran and Aithinne.

Without a monarch, the Sìth-bhrùth will wither. Someone must take her place.

And you think you're worthy.

No, but I will be.

Something must show on my face, because the Cailleach says, 'Now you see why I can't let you live.' She turns away from me, away from the bonfire, and begins down the road again, her frail body so thin beneath the shadows. 'Come, *mo nighean*. I have one last thing to show you.'

Chapter 31

We are in the *Sìth-bhrùth*, at the loch Kiaran once brought me to. Where I first saw Sorcha and tried to kill her. The place looks so different than when I saw it last; lush, fertile. It's still night-time here, the stars above moving in intricate patterns of swirls and streaks of light across the sky. The trees – so high around us – are full of leaves a vivid green; when I saw them last, they had been skeletal, dead. I look closely and see the colours in the bark, the blues and greens and reds like an opalescent gemstone.

A figure flickers at the corner of my eye. Aithinne. She walks across the water, and it's as though she wanders through space, between the expanse of stars. She looks even more human than she did when we left the bonfire. More like the Aithinne I know.

She glances around, as if she's waiting for someone. A meeting? Kiaran once told me that this place was considered neutral ground, the only location where the Seelie and Unseelie could meet without conflict.

When Aithinne reaches the rocks along the banks of the loch, she stares straight ahead, and I realise there's someone in the trees, a shadowed figure.

'You sent for me, Kadamach,' she says softly. I note the hesitancy in her voice, the uncertainty. I wonder how long it's been since they've spoken. 'Let me see you.'

I suck in a sharp breath as Kiaran slips out of the trees, tall and beautiful, dressed all in black. His dark hair is pulled back from his face, his skin immaculate and glowing. His eyes – they're not like his at all.

Not Kiaran. *Kadamach.*

I thought I'd seen glimpses of Kadamach before, when Kiaran's gaze would simply become empty. Brutally so, as if he had buried all those new emotions because things hurt less if you don't feel.

Kadamach isn't like that. His eyes aren't just empty; they're desolate and dark, like a cold bite of winter wind that strips away every ounce of warmth from your body. There's nothing there. *Nothing.*

I almost tell the Cailleach to take us out of there. I don't want to see whatever revelation this is, another awful truth that will eat away at me from the inside. Now I know why Kiaran and Aithinne left their pasts behind, why they keep their secrets. Each one is worse than the last.

I don't have an admirable past, Kam. I never led you to believe I did.

Knowing some of the things Kiaran did isn't the same as seeing it.

That's when I notice Kiaran is carrying: a young woman. He cradles her body against him, her blood splattered dark against the pale skin of his hands. She's bleeding so heavily that it drips onto the rocks at his feet. *Drip drip drip drip.*

Aithinne's attention is on the blood-splattered rocks, on his hands. I note her intake of breath, uneven, shallow. 'You've brought me another gift, then,' she whispers.

I swallow hard, feeling sick.

'I don't share your enthusiasm for slaughter, Kadamach,' Aithinne says. Her hands are in fists; they betray her feelings. How very much she cares. 'You should have had the *sluagh* deliver this one for you like all the others.'

'This isn't like that,' he says. His voice washes over me like a river in winter. I could drown in the cold of it. 'Not this time.'

Kiaran kneels and places the woman on the rocks. Her face is turned toward me, her eyes closed. She's not beautiful in the way that Catherine is. But she's striking; her features are strong and fine. Her hair is long, a blonde so pale it's almost white, and tucked into a long plait that rests across the rocks. The colour of her hair contrasts with her tan skin. Scars dot her cheeks, her chin, her eyebrows. Even in death, she looks like a warrior.

I recognise a hint of emotion in Kiaran's hardened gaze, like the first drops of rain in a vast desert: longing. He strokes a finger across the woman's cheek, leaving behind a blossom of blood there.

God, this is her. *Her.* The Falconer he fell in love with.

I didn't love her nearly enough.

Aithinne looks at him, shock evident in her beautiful features. 'Kadamach?'

He snatches his hand from the woman's face, as if it burns. 'Bring her back,' he says sharply.

I shut my eyes briefly, remembering his words to me. Kiaran had to watch her die, and then had to watch me die. Just like this.

Aithinne blanches. 'No. Don't ask that of me.'

Kiaran stands and his anger is dark, vicious. Shadows crawl from the ground, thick and heavy and hungry. It's become so cold that the flesh of my fingers is red, numb. A thin layer of ice covers the loch. Frost forms along the trunks of the trees around us and along the damp pebbles at my feet.

'You created their kind.' His voice is a savage whisper. 'You sent them to slaughter my subjects because you couldn't do it yourself. I may have started the war between us, Aithinne' – his voice drops to a rumbling growl – 'but *you owe me this.*'

Her head snaps up, eyes blazing. 'I owe you nothing. You're not the only one who lost those under your protection. *You* drew first blood, Kadamach. '

Kiaran looks down at the woman's body, his anger dissipating. 'And how dearly I've paid for it.'

Something softens in Aithinne. As if she hasn't seen this side of him before – or has, but not for a long time.

I can sense the history between them, the years before their war. Were they a family once? Before all of this? Kiaran was willing to be imprisoned for eternity to save Aithinne. They share such a long past. I wonder how it ever healed.

'I've never asked you for anything,' he says quietly. 'Never. Bring her back. Bring your damn Falconer back.'

'I can't,' Aithinne says. 'I'm sorry, I—'

'You need my blood,' he says, sounding so mechanical.

He draws his knife from its sheath and brings the blade down across his palm. I flinch at the same time Aithinne does, watching the blood pool there. Watching how the cold has gone out of his gaze until all that's left is the part of him that I've come to care for. *Kiaran.*

'Take it,' he tells her. 'Take however much you need.'

If you're willing to do your part, I'll do mine.

I never thought I'd hear you offer that again.

His blood. Kiaran offered it for her, and he offered it again to bring me back. This was the moment that separated Kiaran from Kadamach. He was willing to try and save us.

'Kadamach.' Aithinne's commanding voice cuts across the darkness, unyielding. She's not swayed, even though her gaze is full of pity, grief. I can tell she wants to help him. 'Kadamach,' she says again, more gently this time. 'I said I can't.'

'Why?' He speaks in anger, but I can hear the defeat, the breaking of hope.

'Because, *mo bràthair*,' she replies, 'I can't bring back anyone you've killed.'

A breath explodes out of me. He killed her. He *killed* her.

I didn't love her nearly enough.

No wonder he pulled away from me when I told him that

Kadamach was capable of love. A sentimental fool, he called me. Because he had already killed the woman he loved.

'Why?' I don't know if I'm asking myself or the Cailleach. 'Why would he do that?'

'I told you,' the Cailleach said stonily. She watches the scene before us as if she's seen it a thousand times, without an ounce of compassion. As if she doesn't care how much her son grieves, and finds it a bit disappointing that he does at all. 'Kadamach was not made to love. His gift is death.'

Tell me, how much do you need to learn about my past before you understand that there isn't a single part of me that's human?

He may not be human, but as I watch him mourn the woman he lost – the woman he loved – I see that she left him with some small piece of humanity.

I was mistaken before. The first emotion I saw in Kiaran wasn't longing; it was shame.

The truth is we're both running from whatever fate has been decided for us. He is the faery whose gift is death and I am the girl whose gift is chaos.

We go together like fire and black powder.

Wherever she goes, death follows.

I wonder whether the voices Daniel heard were talking about all the people I've lost, or if they were talking about Kiaran. Perhaps he's my curse. Perhaps I'm his weakness. Together we left the world in ruins.

Kiaran runs his fingers over the woman's face again, tracing the scar that bisects her eyebrow. I watch him want her. She made him *feel* and he lost her and I ache for him.

'I couldn't stop myself,' he says. His voice is calm, collected, but I watch the rise and fall of his shoulders, the shuddered breath there. 'I couldn't—'

'Shh. I know.' Aithinne kneels next to him. Their foreheads press together, and for a moment I imagine them when they were young, sitting like that, sharing secrets the way twins do. 'I know.'

'Will you do something for me, Aithinne?' Kiaran says, closing his eyes briefly. 'No one else is capable of transferring power. Take it out of me. Whatever it is that compels me to hunt. I don't want it any more.'

She pulls back. For a moment, I think she will refuse him, but I know she won't. That's not how their story begins.

'I can't take all of it or you'll die,' she says. Kiaran turns away, as if expecting to be disappointed, but she grips his arm. 'But I can take just enough that you can make a choice. Who you kill, and if you don't want to. You won't need the Wild Hunt to survive any more.'

Kiaran nods, and Aithinne stares at him. I can see that she loves him. No matter what he's done, or how brutal their war became, she still loves her brother. 'I have to take away the part of you that holds power here.'

'I know that,' he tells her.

'No. Kadamach—' She grips his hand firmly. I can see how that surprises him, as if she hasn't touched him with affection in the longest time. 'You need to understand. The part of you that's Unseelie will be gone,' she says. 'You won't be able to enter the *Sìth-bhrùth* after this and you'll have to give up your kingdom. One step beyond neutral territory will kill you.'

'So be it,' he says.

A memory flashes of Kiaran and me at this loch, what seems like a million years ago now. We sat on those very rocks, Kiaran gazing with longing across the water. *It's a sacrifice I made, Kam. I can never go back there.* His choice. It was his choice to start over in the human realm.

Then I blink and the Cailleach and I are by the bonfire in the forest again. I am still sitting in the chair of vines and blue blossoms, my skin as cold as frost. The Cailleach releases me, looking older and frailer than ever, the thin bones of her shoulders jutting out beneath her shadow cloak. She leans on her staff and looks into the fire, the flames reflecting in that empty, dark gaze.

'What happened?' I ask. 'When Aithinne took out his powers?'

'My daughter, young fool that she was, didn't realise that when you remove power, you need a vessel to hold it. Someone else has to accept it.'

'Or?'

The Cailleach's thin body shudders. 'It becomes divided, *mo nighean*. You already know this from experience: as each Falconer died, their power spread among the survivors.

'My son's power went into every *sithichean* who resided in the *Sith-bhrùth*. Seelie became Unseelie; those with the power of creation now craved death. They can't survive without killing, just as my son couldn't. When he made that choice, the kingdoms fell. My children destroyed them both.'

I think back to the mirrored room, when I finally broke my silence with Lonnrach and asked him why he hated Kiaran so much.

Your Kiaran is the worst sort of traitor, and his sister is no different. Now it's up to me to fix their mistakes.

Lonnrach was Seelie; Aithinne was his queen, and she sacrificed her throne. So did Kiaran. Now I understand what Lonnrach meant when he referred to their *mistakes*.

Aithinne's words to me in the destroyed Edinburgh flash in my memories. *You're not responsible for something we started.*

Kiaran and Aithinne began it all: the Falconers, the battle that trapped Lonnrach's soldiers underground. They're the reason every fae I ever hunted existed for nothing but the kill. Lonnrach even mentioned the small number of humans the fae lured into the underground were barely enough to keep them all sated – because they needed that human energy to *live*.

There's just one last thing. One final truth I need to hear. 'What did you mean,' I say quietly, 'when you said you took from me, too?'

275

The Cailleach is a sunken shell, thin and cavernous. The grip of her shadow cloak slips to reveal her collarbones. Her ribs are visible beneath the thin skin of her chest.

'You don't really think the *baobhan sìth* could have killed all the descendants of the Falconers, did you?' she says in a dark whisper. 'Not with my son protecting them. His powers are far greater than hers.'

I swear my heart stops. I can't breathe. I stare at the Cailleach's ageing form and the old rage inside me stirs. I suddenly recall Sorcha's words on the snowy cliffs when she froze all those soldiers. That she was risking *her* wrath by warning Kiaran. *Her.*

'You helped her slaughter the Falconers. Didn't you?'

'Aye,' the Cailleach says. 'I used what power I have left in your world to interfere.' I think she's looking at me, but I can't see beyond the hollowed eyes of her skull. 'I helped her take your mother from you.'

In an instant, the rage inside of me surges, unbidden, unrelenting. I had almost forgotten how it felt, how the heat of it sets my skin aflame, how it whispers in my ear and tells me my purpose is vengeance. Retribution.

I rise from the vine seat with the slow, deliberate movements of a killer. There's no fear in the Cailleach's gaze. No remorse. It makes me want to slay her slowly. And without a weapon, I'll do it with my bare hands.

I leap for her, poised to break that thin, skeletal neck. A bolt of lightning strikes the ground in front of me. It cracks the earth with a tremendous clap, and the force of it knocks me off my feet, sends me sprawled on my back. I release a breath through the agonizing tightness of my chest.

'This is the way it has to be,' the Cailleach says, approaching me. 'My daughter must have her powers restored.'

'I don't think so.'

I surge toward her, my fingers closing around the delicate skin at the Cailleach's neck. But she moves fast, smacking her staff into the side of my face. I hit the ground again, clawing into the spongy dirt there. Blood drips from my lips and splatters against the dark ground.

The Cailleach grabs me by the front of my shift, picking me up with little difficulty. Her talon-like nails dig into my skin.

I meet the cold abyss of her gaze and try to hit her, to do *something*, but my arms are pinned at my side, dead weights. The taste of her power is an excruciating thing, all needle-like electricity on my tongue.

'You can't best me,' she says. 'So I'd advise you to simply accept your fate. Wouldn't that be easier?'

I find myself able to move my tongue, my lips. I mutter, 'I'll kill you first.'

The Cailleach sighs and releases me. Though I'm standing, I still can't move to strike her. She looks frail again, so frail. As if she might break. If I were a better woman, I'd pity her for her apparent weakness. But I'm not a better woman. I'd rather take advantage of her delicacy and use it against her.

'I'm dying, *mo nighean*,' she says in that soft, shaky old woman voice.

I hear the slightest tremor of fear there. The fear of an immortal creature, who has been alive since the creation of mountains and the movement of glaciers, who is finally, *finally* facing the uncertainty of her death.

'When I chose to reproduce,' she continues, 'I gave up my immortality. Like my mother, who was the Cailleach before me.' She holds out her hand, the skin gnarled and old again. 'This is the curse of my lineage. I die the same as a human, only more slowly. I must have someone to take my place before I am gone.'

Lonnrach's words about the *Sith-bhrùth* come back to me.

The land was whole, and now it's cracked right down the middle. It's all falling apart.

It's falling apart ... falling apart ...

Without a monarch, the Sìth-bhrùth will wither. Someone must take her place.

The Cailleach – or perhaps the one who came before her – created the worlds, the seas, the landscape. She made them possible. If she dies, they'll go with her. If the *Sìth-bhrùth* is breaking apart, the same might happen to the human realm. She's formed them both with her hammer and staff.

All at once, my blind rage dissipates like smoke. I can think more clearly.

'If I die,' I say, 'and Aithinne's powers are restored, Kiaran's won't be. That can't be undone. The fae will still be corrupted.'

The Cailleach draws up, her face shuttered. Her young self returns: beautiful and formidable and strong – and even more frightening. 'Aye. That's the path your ... *Kiaran* chose. He can't be fixed.'

Fixed. As if he were broken.

'Kadamach was always stronger than Aithinne,' the Cailleach says, backing toward the fire. 'He had proven himself worthy to take my place. Until he fell in love with that *human*.' Her eyes are hard, glinting like steel. 'My daughter might have created the Falconers, but your death undoes that. My son ... for Kadamach to fall in love is unforgivable. *Weak*.' She spits the word as if it's a curse. 'He's not fit to rule.'

'It isn't *weak* to love someone, or to have compassion.'

Do you think me weak because I feel?

No. Never. That's what makes you Kam.

'You're a fool girl,' the Cailleach snaps, folding her frail body closer to the fire. 'This is the way it's always been, the curse my lineage has carried for ages. Two children born to power. Each rules a separate kingdom to prove their worth. The strongest one always begins the war and kills the other. Kadamach failed in his task.'

And kills the other.

Aithinne's voice echoes in my mind from that day in

Edinburgh, her voice all too knowing and sad. *We are all the stag.*

She understands fate. The life of a hunter and the death of its prey. Because she and Kiaran were always destined to be one or the other.

Yet Aithinne let herself love the brother who was supposed to kill her.

'You would let that happen,' I say tightly. 'You would let your children go to war?'

Her teeth flash, razor-sharp. 'Why wouldn't I? *My* mother did.'

My skin goes cold.

The Cailleach's shadow cloak creeps along the ground, curling like snakes around my feet. 'My sister was the Unseelie monarch before Kadamach,' she says. 'I slaughtered her to unite the kingdoms. This is the way it's been through the ages: one Cailleach to replace another.

'My daughter will have to make the same choice I did. After she kills her brother, I'll pass my remaining powers to her and I'll die. She'll take the throne.'

I refuse to believe we can't decide our own fates. That Kiaran is destined to be death and I am destined to be chaos and Aithinne is destined to be queen. We're not pawns. This isn't a game. At what point can we choose?

'She loves him,' I snap. 'Doesn't that mean a damn thing to you? You killed your sister and now you want your daughter to—'

'It doesn't matter,' the Cailleach says. 'She can't let Kadamach live. If she doesn't kill him ...'

'What?'

'She'll watch the world she loves die with me.' Her power around me is suffocating, down my throat like black ink. 'The cost of their choices has already destroyed everyone you love. Soon, it will tear the realms apart. Yours *and* mine.'

Now I know why the stories always had the Seelie and

Unseelie kingdoms at war, why it always began with a Wild Hunt.

War was supposed to bring thousands of years of peace to the fae. But Aithinne's choice to create the Falconers was the first step to counter her fate, and set her against a story that had been repeated for generations before her.

It affected Kiaran's life; he was never supposed to fall in love with a Falconer. And it began a ripple effect across the centuries that eventually led to the destruction of our world.

I think of what Gavin told me in my imagined Edinburgh.

Some things can't be prevented.

'Now you understand why Aithinne must do this,' the Cailleach whispers. 'Which do you think she'll choose?' Frost creeps over the grass beneath the Cailleach's staff. 'To let the realms wither to dust, or to let live the brother who would have slaughtered her?'

'I won't let that happen,' I say. There has to be a different solution. There *has* to be.

'There's nothing you can do,' she says coldly. 'One of them has to die.' Her lip curls. 'It should be Kadamach.'

Desperation gives me the power to break whatever hold she has on me, snapping the strings of power that keep me trapped here. She staggers at the sudden onslaught, her young face slipping back into its crone form.

I run. I hear her shouting as I leap through the dark trees. I keep going until I can't see any more, until I am entirely surrounded by blackness. The voices of the dead call my name again. Their hands grab at me, but I fight, I claw. *Kiaran Kiaran Kiaran Kiaran.* I repeat his name like a prayer, a desperate benediction. *One of them has to die. It should be Kadamach.*

Then I'm in the clearing again. The fire is still burning. The Cailleach stands in front of me, calm and old and surrounded by her shadow cloak. 'You can't run from me, *mo nighean*. Not here.'

I don't care. I try again. I break through the trees. Branches slice through the skin at my shoulders, my neck. They rip my clothing as I shove them out of the way. I'm bleeding all over, but I don't stop. I keep running. I have to get to Kiaran.

I'm back to the fire again, to the damn Cailleach. My knees hit the ground in front of her shadow cloak and I heave in air, the first feelings of hopelessness beginning to overwhelm me. She'll keep me here like this for ever, just as she said she would – unless I make the choice to die.

Her fingers lift my chin. I gaze into her old, wrinkled face with a shuddering breath. 'It would be such an easy thing for you to let it all go, *mo nighean*,' she says. 'No more death, no one you have to be responsible for. You could dance in lavish balls for eternity, if you wanted.'

No. *No.* I don't want balls, or parties, or dresses again. No elevenhours or fourhours or being forced into marriage. Those things all kept me caged, made me a girl too sheltered to understand any real danger until it met her on the street with sharp teeth and claws and ripped her life away.

But the Cailleach is a force drawing me in. She makes me want to shed all my responsibilities and never go back into that living world that made everything so hard, that made each day a struggle.

She leans forward and I'm drawn into that cavernous gaze. 'You could see your mother again,' she whispers.

Kiaran's words are like moth wings across my mind. *Don't forget why you're there. What's on the other side won't want you to return.*

I'm not the girl who lost her mother any more and who can be enticed with promises to see her again. I'm not the girl so blinded by vengeance that my sole purpose is to *hunt kill maim*.

I'm not that girl. I'm *not*.

I'm someone else forged in a mirrored room, like steel melted down and made stronger. I don't need vengeance. I only need myself.

Familiar power rushes through me, hot and brutal. I've felt it before when killing fae, but this time it's stronger, near overwhelming. It's electricity through my veins, beneath my skin until I'm about to burst.

I jerk away from the Cailleach. 'No.'

Then I reach out, palm up, and power explodes out of me. It slams into her. She's lifted off the ground, her body smashing into one of the trees.

I'm on my feet and walking toward her slowly, deliberately. Power grows inside me, hotter as I approach. When the Cailleach looks at me, I see the first flicker of fear in her gaze.

'Tell me how to get out of here,' I say, my voice low.

Her eyes spark. 'Never.'

She raises her staff to ward me off, but I'm too fast. I grab hold of the staff and tear it away. With a sharp cry, she lunges for it, but I'm quicker than her frail old body. I dodge out of her reach.

Without her staff the Cailleach looks even older. Her body is skin stretched over bones, her eyes dull.

I release my power again. The burst hits her so hard that it snaps the tree in half.

Then I hear it: the pounding of boots through the forest to my left. I turn just as Aithinne bursts through the trees, panting hard. She's shaking with exhaustion.

'There you are!'

Her arms are around me and I suddenly forget all about the Cailleach and my powers. *Take me back*, I almost tell her. *Take me with you.*

'Good god, you are a difficult woman to find,' she says. 'The *brìgh* wasn't—'

Her words cut off and her entire body goes rigid. I realise the Cailleach is on her feet. She's staring at Aithinne with her young face, the skin smoothed to perfection. Her expression is unreadable.

'*Màthair*,' Aithinne whispers.

'It's been a long time,' the Cailleach says.

Aithinne rakes her with a look and sways on her feet. *What's wrong with her?* 'Not nearly long enough,' she says. 'I would have preferred another thousand years before seeing your face again. Perhaps two.'

'Daughter—' The Cailleach reaches for her, but Aithinne jerks back, shaking her head.

'So I'm back to *daughter* now, am I? After you wanted Kadamach to kill me.' She laughs bitterly. 'What was it you called me after I made the Falconers? *Masladh bith-bhuan, mo màthair.* Your eternal shame.'

I look at the Cailleach sharply. Before, I only wanted to force her to tell me how to get out of here. Now I'm tempted to smack her with the staff. On principle.

'Aithinne,' I say deliberately, before I do something I may regret. 'Let's go.'

As we turn to leave, the Cailleach calls Aithinne's name. 'If you let the Falconer die, you'll have your powers back. The throne will be *yours.*'

Aithinne sighs and I notice then that she's trembling. 'Oh, *Màthair,*' she says sadly. 'You've never understood, have you? I don't want it. I don't think I ever did.'

Then she gently takes the staff from me. In an instant she has a blade in her hand, slicing down her palm. Her hand is shaking so badly that the cut is jagged. She holds onto my arm and presses her bloodied palm to the intricate carvings of the staff.

'Goodbye, *Màthair.*'

'Aithinne!'

Aithinne lifts the staff and slams it to the ground. The Cailleach cries out while the ice from her staff freezes the ground at our feet. The fire is snuffed out to smoke. Above us, clouds build from nowhere, dark and thick. I hear a distant boom of thunder.

Lightning strikes the staff and Aithinne and I are enveloped in light.

Chapter 32

I gasp and choke. Beach rocks dig into my arms as I twist to cast up the water from my belly. I vomit and cough, my lungs and chest aching. I rest my forehead against the frigid stones as I heave in air, shivering uncontrollably. My shift is soaked and clings to me like ice pressed to my skin.

I sense a presence next to me, but I'm too dizzy. I shake my head once.

'There now. You're back and good as new,' says a shaky voice. It's Aithinne. She looks weak and tired and her nose is bleeding. She smiles her familiar smile, then says, 'Easy.'

Before I can say anything, a high-pitched squeal pierces the air. Derrick barrels into me, all wings and arms and legs tangled in my hair. 'You're alive, you bloody idiot, you're alive!'

Gavin comes to sit next to me, his blond hair plastered to his forehead. He unbuttons his heavy wool coat and wraps it around my shoulders. I accept it gratefully, my fingers so numb I can barely keep it closed.

'Welcome back to the land of the living,' Gavin says. He gestures upward with a familiar half-smile. 'I'm guessing it worked.'

I realise then that there are drops of water suspended in the air all around us. They glisten like millions upon millions of shining diamonds stretching across the beach.

In wonder, I touch one. It undulates as my finger passes

through it, then breaks into a dozen smaller droplets. 'Am I doing this?' I ask Aithinne.

She gives me a weak smile. 'Controlling it takes some work. If you breathe out calmly and picture them slowly lowering—'

I blink and the drops fall to the ground with a heavy splat.

'Or do that instead.' Then she says reassuringly, 'You tried.'

'Sorry.'

Gavin takes a moment to recover, swiping at his wet hair. He holds up a dangling strand of *seilgflùr*. 'This might not be as impressive as suspending water, but I guess you won't be needing it any more.'

Won't be needing it? I touch the base of my throat, expecting the thistle to be where I left it, but it's gone. With a startled gasp, I reach for Derrick, closing my fingers around his body.

'Igh!" Derrick cries, grabbing for strands of my hair. 'Not so tight. I'm a pixie, not a damn flower.'

With a huff, he releases my plait and sits on my palm – and for the first time, I see him without the aid of *seilgflùr*. It's so different, like having a veil lifted from my eyes. His face is the same, his elfin features unchanged, but there's a lovely effervescent glow to him that he never had before – like the way Kiaran looked when we were in the *Sìth-bhrùth* for the first time. Derrick's wings glisten like morning dewdrops. The wee veins inside them look like strands of gold.

Derrick shifts uncomfortably. 'Are you just going to stare at me?' He motions to my clothes. 'Aithinne had a hell of a time bringing you back.'

That's when I look down and see that I'm covered in blood, my shift entirely drenched with it. I hiss in a sharp breath. '*Bloody hell*,' I murmur. 'What happened?'

Derrick flies off and lands on Gavin's shoulder. The silence is an unbearable thing. It's Aithinne who answers. 'After the *brìgh* lost your energy, it took me hours to find you.' Her voice trembles with cold.

Hours? After the Cailleach wilted the flower, she must have been shifting us between memories to make Aithinne's search even more difficult. No wonder she decided on *truth* over any other 'gifts' she could have bestowed.

Aithinne looks so fragile, like she'll break. The blood from her cuts streams down her arms. Her nose is bleeding; so are her hands, her wrists, her arms. Some are thin cuts, some dug to bone.

Blood for blood, Kiaran had said. Was this the sacrifice she had to make to bring me back? Aithinne's dark hair is loose from its chignon, sticking to the ice flaked to her forehead. Even her skin is blue.

'Here,' I say, slipping Gavin's coat from my shoulders to wrap around her. I glance at Gavin, but he's not looking at me. He's watching Aithinne, as if he wants to help but isn't certain how.

Her wounds aren't even closing up, certainly not as quickly as they usually do. Her blood is dripping onto the beach rocks. 'You're not healing.'

Aithinne sways a bit, her skin growing even more paler. 'Part of the sacrifice,' she whispers. 'Can't use powers to heal, and I had to use more blood than I expected.' Her eyes are unfocused. 'You know, I don't think I feel well. I think …'

'Shit,' Gavin murmurs, reaching her before she pitches forward. He scoops her up in his arms. 'Aithinne?' She doesn't respond; her eyes are closed, cheek pressed against his chest. 'I need to get her inside,' he says. The front of his shirt is already soaked through with her blood. 'One of the fae can stitch her up.'

'No.' Aithinne suddenly squirms against him. 'Don't let anyone see me like this.'

'Take her behind your door, Seer,' Derrick says. 'I'll stitch her up myself.' A wee grin crosses his face. 'I'll even be gentle.'

'You'd better be,' Aithinne breathes.

Now that that's settled, I ask, 'Where is Kiaran?'

Gavin and Derrick both look to the water. I follow their gaze across the beach, to the ocean waves tumbling in. Kiaran stands fully clothed, the waves around his knees.

He's staring out to the horizon. Blood trails from his hands in the water behind him. Then he looks over to the beach, and his eyes meet mine. My heart drops. His eyes. *His eyes.* The look in them reminds me so much of Kadamach. The deep, never-ending darkness in them. The hopelessness.

'He went out there when Aithinne couldn't bring you back,' Derrick says.

I'm about to go get him when Aithinne grasps my wrist. Her eyes are still unfocused, but somehow she finds the strength to pull me down until her lips are at my ear. Her message is whispered for me only. 'Today was a reminder that he'll lose you someday.' Her next words are spoken with regret: 'Falconers always die young. Always.'

She loses consciousness and Gavin turns to take her inside.

My gaze meets Kiaran's again and it's like the entire world dissolves away. *I know*, I want to tell him. *I know everything.*

He looks away from me sharply, as if he heard my thoughts. Maybe he did. Before I can stop him, he strides out of the water to the dark entrance of the cave.

Later that evening, I stare at the pile of pieces on my worktable, a collection Derrick has no doubt been amassing during my entire three-year absence. There are broken flintlock pistols and watch fobs and pinions and screws, scraps of metal from various sources.

'They're for you to work on,' Derrick had said, as he fussed over me after stitching up Aithinne. 'Look at all the shiny ones! Those are my favourites.'

I think what happened to me frightened him, though he'd never say so. Aithinne had healed my body right away, but she had spent several hours searching for me through the veil. It seemed like so much longer, as though the Cailleach and I had been drifting in and out of memories for an eternity.

'I need to be alone for a while,' I tell Derrick. 'Just to understand what happened.'

His wings flick together. 'You want me to be quiet?'

I smile and shake my head. '*Alone* alone.' I brush a hand down his wings. 'Can you go and check the wards again?'

I can't help but be worried about the Cailleach. Even though Aithinne told her she didn't want the throne, the Cailleach doesn't strike me as someone who takes no for an answer.

I may have limited powers in your realm, but I know that everyone you have left is in that underground kingdom. Surely you want them safe?

'Fine,' he mutters. 'But you had better tell me everything later.'

He flies from the room in a stream of light. I sigh and look out the window. It's snowing again in the fake ruined Edinburgh. My house is the only one in the square still left standing. From here, I can see the destroyed walls of the castle – the way the vines have overgrown in what was once the gardens on Princes Street.

I consider wishing the room in some other place. Argentina, perhaps. Or the West Indies. Somewhere warm. Somewhere that looks nothing like Scotland, where I can sink my toes into warm sand and forget for a while.

But then I look outside and watch the snow fall onto the pavement that no longer exists and I wish for nothing else.

One of the cogs Derrick was just handling rolls to the floor with a sharp rap that draws me from my reverie. I scoop it up and place it among its metal companions. My eyes rove over the shapes, the way they fit together.

Once I would have been able to piece them together with little trouble at all. It never took any planning or forethought; building came as naturally to me as breathing. Inventing new weapons was like putting together a complex puzzle – an exciting new discovery. At the very least, it staved off my nightmares.

Now I don't even have that small bit of comfort. Today the shapes seem foreign. I can't figure out if they fit together. I don't know what to make, or how to make it.

I pick up a piece and hold part of an old clock-face. *What would I do with you?*

Without meaning to, I feel the power inside me uncoil. It flows through the veins of my arms, down my wrist, and pushes out of my palm, its heat warping the metal. The hands of the clock-face spring up and twist to become petals. The other metal parts curve around it to form a flower stem made of glowing, melted gold.

It's beautiful. I'm in awe. I made that. *I made it.*

A swift knock at the door breaks my concentration and I drop the golden flower to the carpet with a thump.

The bedroom door behind me opens and clicks softly closed. *'Derrick.'* I sigh, turning in my chair, 'I *told* you—'

My breath stops. Kiaran. He's still soaked from the waves and the rain. His clothes drip onto the carpet. Now that I have the Sight, I realise just how much he shines, a tawny sheen to his glistening skin. And his eyes are so luminous, bright. I was wrong to compare the colour to lilac. The flower pales in comparison.

His hand is bound with a torn scrap of linen, blood seeping through the fabric from a cut like Aithinne's that still hasn't healed.

I stare at the crimson stain blossoming through the white material and remember him stroking the dead Falconer's face, leaving a streak of red against her tan skin. I flinch and turn back to the metal pieces, not even seeing them.

What do I say? I don't even know how to begin. 'How's your hand?'

Oh, for god's sake.

Kiaran doesn't answer. His boots thump across the carpet, and suddenly he's close to me, so close that we're almost touching. 'What happened on the other side?' he asks.

When I don't respond, he puts a hand on my cheek and turns me to face him. His eyes are so different than they were in the past. Not *empty*. 'Kam?'

What do I tell him? The truth the Cailleach showed me? Kiaran tried so hard to hide from that part of himself. He changed his name. He sacrificed his throne. He gave up everything, and I wasn't supposed to know about it until he was ready to tell me.

The way he looked down at the other Falconer, the way he touched her ... I wasn't supposed to see that, either. I was an intruder in his most intimate and private memories. Just like Lonnrach was in mine.

I pull away from him and watch the snow fall again in big fluffy flakes that cover the ground and turn trees white. 'I'm sorry,' I say.

'*Kam.*' His voice is hard. 'Tell me.'

Just don't look at him. 'I saw the Cailleach.'

If I weren't listening, I might not have heard his sharp intake of breath. The air between us turns cold. He moves away. 'Then she offered you something. I assume it wasn't life.'

The snow falls harder, harder now. Not even the front steps of the house are visible. 'She offered me truth.'

The silence between us stretches vast; it seems like hours. If I were to look at him again, I know I'd find his expression cold and calculating as he decides what to say next. Kiaran is careful like that.

'I see,' he finally says.

And that's it. He doesn't explain; he doesn't need to. He knows what I saw and what I learned.

'Why did you kill her?' I keep my gaze on the blizzard outside, the intensifying weather, even though I can barely see the ruins of the city through it. 'That's the only thing I don't understand.'

I don't need to explain who I'm speaking of. He knows. I can tell by the way he tenses beside me, by the way he goes so quiet.

'Nothing had ever surprised me like she did,' he says. He

stands by my chair and watches the snow fall. 'I never thought I was capable of feeling anything until I met her. I never thought I could ... *want* anyone. Not the way I desired her.'

But you murdered her, I almost point out. I don't say anything; I keep my gaze on the snow piling high outside, lit gold from the street lamps. 'Not even Sorcha?' I ask tentatively, and then wish I hadn't. It's just a guess, a stupid guess.

Kiaran looks at me sharply but I don't meet his gaze. 'Did she show you that, too?'

I wish I wasn't right. I didn't want to be. Tears prick behind my eyes. 'She didn't have to,' I say. 'I've seen the way Sorcha looks at you.' *The same way I look at you.*

Kiaran's hand curls into a fist. 'Sorcha was my consort,' he says evenly.

My fingers brush the scar that holds the memory of when I first met Sorcha, when I first realised she and Kiaran knew each other. *You're still bound by your vow to me. Feadh gach re. Always and forever, remember?*

'Then your vow—'

'It's an old custom to make a vow to one's consort. So I said the one that bound us together.'

He made you think he cared about you. Kadamach doesn't give a damn about anyone, least of all you.

I wish Kiaran had told me all of this before when we ran through the streets at night and killed monsters together. None of it would have mattered then because Kiaran was my means to an end. He was how I planned to achieve my vengeance. *Teach me everything you know and I'll tear out her heart for what she did to my mother. Tit for tat.*

But now ... now I wish he had no past, that he was a slate wiped clean the moment he saved my life and whispered six words: *We're going to kill them all.* Then it wouldn't hurt so damn much that the faery who murdered my mother was also his consort.

'How did you meet the Falconer, then?' I ask, not wanting to talk about Sorcha any more.

A slight smile plays on his face. 'She tried to kill me.'

Most people would be dismayed by an attempted assassination, but Kiaran seems to regard it as either flirtation or flattery – possibly both. 'And that must have warmed the cockles of your dark Unseelie heart.'

'Of course not,' Kiaran says. 'But after several attempts I began to admire her tenacity.' His face softens. 'That was the first emotion I'd experienced in a thousand years and I wanted to *know* her.'

Something in me stirs, something I haven't felt in a long time. I hardly recognise it at first, it's so foreign to me: I'm *jealous*. I knew about the other Falconer and that Kiaran loved her, but listening to this is like a knife twisting through my gut.

I don't say anything; if I do, I'm not certain I could keep the jealousy out of my voice.

'We met in secret for months. Until one of my subjects brought me a Seer,' he says. 'It was one of my amusements: to tear out their eyes before I killed them, just to see what their last vision was.'

I try not to picture it, and I fail.

'The vision was of me killing *her*.' Kiaran speaks so mechanically, as if he's practised this. He isn't watching the snow fall; he's reliving his memory, the moment of his past that changed everything. 'I thought I could prevent it from coming true if I stopped seeing her.' His jaw clenches and he looks down. 'If I stopped hunting humans.'

He goes quiet, and I wonder if he'll continue. It's suddenly so clear now why he refused to tell me about Gavin's vision before the battle. *You would try so desperately to prevent it, and every conscious decision you made would only help the vision come to pass.*

Kiaran takes a breath. 'Without the Wild Hunt, I started to die. My kingdom began to crumble. When I was at my weakest,

Sorcha brought me a human. She was trying to save my life – *our* lives.' He closes his eyes briefly. 'I couldn't stop myself. And of all the humans Sorcha could have chosen, she made sure it was—'

'Your Falconer,' I finish for him. I'm torn by so many emotions. Sadness. Jealousy. Anger at Sorcha.

And ... and ... *wanting.* How stubborn emotions can be, how complicated and difficult. Despite all the things Kiaran has done – things I've seen – I still care for him. I want him. I want him like he was when he was in those frigid waves with me, whispering encouragements in my ear. I want him the way he was in the ruins of Glasgow, tracing my scars as if he were memorizing them. I want him just like this, laid bare and vulnerable. I *want.*

And I'm starting to wonder if he was ever truly mine to want.

'Catríona,' Kiaran breathes, in a way that makes my heart ache. 'That was her name.'

Her name rolls smoothly across his tongue like water. He says it reverently. He says it like he's repeated it every day of his life. *Catríona Catríona Catríona.*

'It's a beautiful name,' I tell him. I try to keep my tone even.

He's not listening to me. He's still caught in his memory. 'I vowed that I'd never take another human life. So I asked my sister to—' He glances at me. 'But you know the rest.'

'Aye,' I say quietly.

The kingdoms fell anyway, and he and Aithinne were the cause. God, the burdens they carry. Knowing that the choices they made for themselves – the ones that went against the Cailleach's designs for them – were the very things that destroyed everything. And yet the very things that made him Kiaran.

He is so close, I can feel his warmth again. I try to shut out everything the Cailleach showed me, everything I've just heard. I want to forget how he feels about Catríona and the things he sacrificed because she left him with that small piece of humanity. I want him to help me forget it.

Then he touches my shoulder and I shrink back, because I

can't pretend. 'No,' I say softly. 'I'm not her.' I shove the chair away from the table. I put distance between us, drawing nearer to the door, but it's not far enough. 'I won't be your replacement for her.'

He's there in an instant. He grips my arms and turns me roughly. His eyes blaze. They have an uncanny glow, one I didn't perceive before with my human sight. It's mesmerizing. 'Is *that* what you think? That you're her replacement?'

I try to pull away, but he draws me closer. 'What else am I supposed to think? She and I are both Falconers.'

'That doesn't mean anything to me,' Kiaran says. He presses his warm hand to my cheek. 'What you are never mattered. I want you because I never feel more alive than when I'm with you. I want *you*, Kam.'

Then his lips crush against mine and he's kissing me. God help me, but I kiss him back. I press my body to his and —

No. I need to know. 'Do you love me?' I whisper against his lips. 'Like you loved her?'

Kiaran pulls back – and his sharp intake of breath tells me all I need to know. 'Kam.'

I jerk away, trying to ignore the surprise and hurt on his face. He reaches for me but I evade him. 'I can't,' I whisper. 'I can't do this. I need to go.'

I stride out the door.

Chapter 33

I walk through the cavern and onto the dark beach. I need to think things through. I'm surprised to see Aithinne wading in the water, her feet barely touched by the foamy ocean waves as they roll in. She has her trousers rolled up, calves bare. Her coat sways behind her, and her hair is wild and free and long.

The moon casts its light across the surf in a trail that leads right to her, and Aithinne's skin seems to glow in response. Now that I have the Sight, I see she shines, as if her skin were made of opal.

The air is brisk, even more so than it was when I was here before I died. But the chill doesn't bother me; the hum of power beneath my skin spreads warmth through my veins. The wind has died down, leaving everything still. There is nothing but calm swells and the crackle of rocks rolling against each other as they move with the waves.

I pull my coat tighter around me and move to sit on the beach not far from where Aithinne stands in the water, a safe distance from the tide. I don't venture any closer. Getting soaked through once today is quite enough for me.

'I see you were completely serious when you said you loved the water,' I say.

Aithinne doesn't answer for a long time, just tips back her head to the moonlight. Finally, she steps onto the beach, moving gracefully over the pebbles as she comes to sit next to me.

I can't help but notice the number of stitches along her arms. Though finely sewn – apparently Derrick won't do less than perfect stitching under any circumstances – the dark thread contrasts with the pale glow of her skin. So many cuts. Dozens.

'There's something special about the sea, isn't there?' she asks, her voice startling me. 'My kind always believed it could reveal hidden things.' She glances at me. 'Even your deepest fears.'

'Is that so?' I say flatly. I'd rather forget what it was like to drown, what I saw on the other side.

I'm haunted by the voices calling my name, by the feel of their hands grasping my clothes to keep me there.

'If we were feeling particularly brave,' she says, 'we would submerge ourselves into the water and whisper *innis dhomh. Tell me.* The waves would show us our past, our future – secrets that affected our lives. Sometimes they tell us things we wish they hadn't.'

'Aithinne,' I say. 'You're dancing around a question. Just say it.'

'Not a question; an observation. You've had a conflicted look about you since we met through the veil. At first I thought it had to do with my mother trying to murder you, but …'

I stare out at the ocean and try not to think about Kiaran.

Do you love me? Like you loved her?

Kiaran left a mark on me. It's not physical, not like Lonnrach's. It's as if when my memories were emptied, my mind filled with pieces of Kiaran, *feelings* that kept me sane in the mirrored room. He did it without realizing and I let him without realizing. God, how I wish I hadn't.

'Falconer?'

'Why didn't you want the throne?' I ask abruptly.

She shrugs. 'It was all battles, fights, and court. Humans are far more exciting. You have colourful swear words and *cake—*'

'Aithinne. Now you're dancing around an answer.'

She's quiet as she watches the waves come in and out, as if the ocean were breathing. 'I've always known it would come down to Kadamach or me,' she says. 'I couldn't hurt him. I thought I could once, but ... ' Aithinne shrugs. 'So I accepted that I would be the one to die.'

I look at her, and I don't see the Aithinne from the bonfire, the faery who told the first Falconers to seek their vengeance and make her brother pay. Aithinne wasn't hardened by war; she was *humanized* by it. After everything Kiaran did, she still loved him. She never stopped.

I don't say anything. I'm afraid that if I do I'll say the wrong thing or she'll stop speaking. There's so much more I want to know about their past.

Aithinne tips her face to the moon again. 'Kadamach and I were created together, you know. Our minds were once indistinguishable.' Her expression hardens. 'Then we were separated, raised in different kingdoms, and trained to destroy each other. When he killed my subjects on the battlefield, I knew he would come for me next.'

'So you created the Falconers,' I say.

'The Falconers, the *mortair*,' she says softly. 'I built an army to send against him. Only Kadamach and I had the power to kill each other' – her voice turns harsh – 'but I wanted his kingdom devastated for the grief he caused mine.'

'The Cailleach showed me what he did.' I watch the waves go in and out and try not to remember. I can't. 'Where he started the battle. I wish I could forget.'

'I know what you saw,' she says quietly. 'It was the very thing that drove me to create your kind.'

'But you never killed him. Why?' I would have hunted him for what he'd done. I would have savored finding him and murdering him.

'I couldn't do it,' she whispers. 'I didn't hate him enough. I thought I did, but when he asked for my help ... ' She looks at me. 'We had just spent so long at war that we couldn't remember anything else.'

I press my shoulder to hers. She gives me a grateful smile. 'I can feel him *here* again' – she taps her temple – 'and we haven't been connected like that in so long. After everything we've been through, I won't betray him. Not when I've just got him back. I want us to have a thousand more years to make up for all the time we lost.'

'We'll find a way to save the realms without either of you dying,' I tell her. It's the only thing I can say. I can't tell her to choose – I can't *let* her choose. 'I swear it.'

Is she going to cry? I don't believe I've ever made a faery cry before – except Derrick, and that was only while I was reading him *A Christmas Carol* and Scrooge stopped being a bastard; Derrick said he had something in his eye.

'Really?'

'We're friends,' I say firmly. 'You stood up to your maniacal mother—'

'Homicidal,' Aithinne interrupts. 'Why mince words?'

' – to aid me. I'm returning the favour. You'll just have to let me help you. Such a hardship, I realise.'

Aithinne smiles. 'I want you to know, I never regretted creating the Falconers. Whatever power I lost … it made me feel a little more human.'

'It's too bad we all die young,' I say lightly. 'You'll have it all back when I'm gone.'

Aithinne doesn't avert her gaze. Her irises whirl like melted steel. 'Aye. And that is my only regret.' She sighs. 'I still need to rest after today. I'm not feeling at all like my usual self. Will you be all right?'

I nod. 'I just need a few minutes.'

Aithinne leaves me there, her footsteps quiet in the sand as she retreats back into the cave.

*

I stay on the beach and watch the way the waves breathe, how the rocks press and roll against each other with a groan like a ship rocking at sea. Eventually, my power ebbs and fades on its own, leaving my skin cold again. The frigid wind picks up and I'm forced to leave for the warmth of the city.

I make my way to the cave and notice a silhouette at the lip of the cavern. Kiaran. 'Let me guess,' I say, drawing nearer, 'your sister told you where to find me.'

His smile isn't visible in the darkness, but I can hear it when he speaks. 'On the contrary,' he says. 'She told me I looked like I needed fresh air. It wasn't until I saw you that I realised she decided to engage in her second-favourite hobby.'

'Subterfuge?'

'I was going to say meddling, but you're not wrong.'

Kiaran steps forward and I back away from him before I even realise. Just like that, the smile I didn't need to see is gone entirely – I can sense it by the way his body goes still. I wish I could see his expression. It's too damn dark, even with my new vision.

'Kam.'

'Don't.' I put a hand up and walk past him into the cave. The flickering lanterns illuminate the passage back into the city. 'There's really nothing to explain.'

Before I blink, Kiaran is standing right in front of me, blocking me from going further. God, were his eyes always that bright? That beautiful?

'You didn't give me a chance to answer before,' he says. 'If you had, I would have told you there was no comparison.'

Hesitantly, he reaches for me. His fingers trail to my neck, tracing a path to my shoulder. I shut my eyes at the sensation, the way he touches me as if he can't get enough of it.

'Is that all?' I try to keep my voice steady.

Kiaran moves in closer, sliding his hand gently up the back of my neck. 'I never fought by her side. I never faced an army with her and marveled at how exquisite she was in battle. I never tended to her injuries or watched the stars with her or went out of my mind trying to find her.' His forehead presses against mine and I can't think, I can't move, I can't breathe. 'I want you, Kam. And I should have told you that so many times. I should have told you that in the *Sìth-bhrùth.*'

I break into a smile. 'I thought Lonnrach had created you, remember? I wouldn't have believed a word of it.'

Kiaran smiles back. 'I would have found a way to convince you. First by using my language: *Tha gaol agam ort le m' uile chridhe,* Kam.' He breathes the words against my skin. 'Then I would have translated it and said that I lo—'

I press my lips hard against his. 'No declarations. No theatrics.' I rise on my tiptoes and whisper in his ear. 'You made me a promise, MacKay. Show me what I mean to you.'

'Your room. Now.' He sounds almost breathless.

Then he takes my hand, and he's pulling me through the cavern back into the city, past the flickering street lamps and into the dark closes. This late at night the streets are almost empty, just as they were in Edinburgh. My heart slams as I lead him onto my balcony and then into my room. The door closes with a click. No sign of Derrick, thank god.

Kiaran grasps my shirt and kisses me, a hard press of his lips against mine. As if forgetting himself, he murmurs in his language, over and over again. The words cascade off his tongue in a rolling accent that makes me long for more, that makes me *yearn.*

'Tell me what you're saying. Translate.' I press my lips to the underside of his chin, the space above his shoulder. I'll kiss him everywhere.

'You want to know what you mean to me, Kam?' His lips trail down the curve of my neck. 'Every day I wonder when your human life will end, and it scares the hell out of me.' His words are hot on my skin. 'You make me wish I didn't have for ever.'

Falconers always die young. Always. I wish those words weren't true. I wish he were human or that I were fae and we had a thousand lifetimes to do this.

His hands are on either side of my face, the gentlest of touches. '*Aoram dhuit.*'

I will worship thee.

'You said it was a pledge. Do I make it, too?'

'No, Kam.' His eyes lock with mine just before he presses a kiss to the pulse of my throat. Then his lips are at my ear, whispering, 'You let me honor my words.'

I can't hold back any more. Before I realise, I'm grabbing him by the front of his shirt, and my back is to the wall and I'm kissing him and kissing him and kissing him. He laughs with surprise as I reach for the buttons of his shirt – undoing one, two, three – until he impatiently rips it off.

Then his lips are on mine again. On my cheek, my shoulder, lower. Our clothes are tossed aside and I have a brief glimpse of his muscular, gleaming body before he presses me to the wall. Kiaran grips my thighs, lifting me to wrap my legs around his waist.

He keeps his promise. I can't get enough of his lips, his kisses, his hands, his touch, everywhere.

And I finally know what it means to be worshipped.

Chapter 34

Sometime in the night I open my eyes to find Kiaran asleep beside me. We're facing each other, our bare legs tangled together beneath the heavy counterpane. The near-full moon shines bright enough through the window that his features are illuminated, the sheen of his pearlescent skin catching in the light.

In all the time I've known Kiaran, I've never seen him sleep. It softens his features. He looks younger, almost vulnerable. He holds me in a tight embrace, his fingers curled in my hair, and something about the gesture makes me feel safe, comforted.

What draws my gaze are the markings across his shoulders and down his arms. I know from kissing them earlier that they stretch down his torso and across his entire back, beautiful swirled designs upraised along his skin as if cut there by a fine blade. I reach to touch them with my fingertips.

Kiaran's lips curve into a smile. 'Do you like what you see?'

Damn. I flush, my face hot, and snatch my hand back. 'How do you do that? How do you always manage to catch me staring?'

'Mmm.' Kiaran pulls me closer, kissing me softly on my forehead, my cheek, the curve of my neck. Featherlight touches that bring back the memory of his hands, his lips, everywhere. 'I'm an excellent guesser,' he tells me.

'Oh? Then what am I thinking right now?'

'That you like this.' Kiaran's hand slides down to my hip. 'That you want us to stay this way.'

Something about the way he says it makes me go still. 'You think we won't?'

'Kam—'

'Wait.' I press a finger to his lips. 'I've changed my mind. Don't answer that.'

Kiaran looks amused. 'What shall I say, then?'

'Something else. So then I don't have to think about you and me or Lonnrach or wherever that bloody crystal is. What's your favourite colour? Do you have a favourite colour? To how many places can you recite pi?'

'Kam.'

'No. Not that. Let's start over.' I prop my chin in my hands. 'Tell me—' Kiaran's lips brush mine. 'Tell me ...' He kisses me again, harder. What was I going to say? I can't recall. 'You're doing that on purpose.'

'I learned it from you,' Kiaran says. 'Improvization.'

I should have known he'd use that kiss after the wisp attack against me. 'Very clever.'

'You said to start over.' Kiaran trails his lips down my jaw. 'Shall we begin again? I'm Kiaran.' Another kiss. 'You're Kam.' Another. 'Pleased to meet you.'

I laugh. 'Introductions don't generally include kisses, MacKay.'

'This one does.'

'You're making this far too easy for me,' I say. 'First I'm supposed to charm you. Then ensnare you when you least suspect.' In a swift move, I roll on top of him, trapping him beneath me. Our bodies are perfectly lined up, pressed close. I pin his wrists with a triumphant grin. 'Ha! There now. You're mine, Kiaran MacKay.'

The way he looks at me steals my breath. He's gazing up at me like I'm powerful. Like I'm magnificent. I don't think I've ever felt more beautiful.

Then he breaks my hold and he's whispering against my lips. 'I am,' he tells me. 'I'm yours.'

I wake to find Kiaran standing by the window, his back to me. The moon outside frames him in a halo of light. I study the span of his back, the length of his spine, the designs etched into his skin there that must have been burned by fae metal.

I rise from the bed and move to stand behind him. He doesn't say anything as I slide my fingertips up to the skin at his shoulder to explore the pattern there. Some of the swirls are tiny, some larger. It's the most beautiful work of art I've ever seen.

'What does it mean?' I ask him. I follow the lines over and over, feeling how the skin is upraised in tiny, intricate patterns.

'When a *sithiche* makes a vow, their skin is marked with it. It's a reminder we wear for eternity, a penance,' he says. 'That one is my promise to Catríona.'

There's an ache in my chest, a dull throbbing. 'Your penance?'

Kiaran closes his eyes and reaches for my hand, as if he craves the comfort of touch. As if I'm about to disappear. 'Each sign represents a human I've killed.'

I hold my breath, my eyes roving the length of the design. Oh, god. If I tried to count them, I would lose my place. There are so many swirls, so many. I can't help it, I rise onto my tiptoes and slide my hand up the design, from his wrist to the underside of his arm.

Kiaran lets me continue my exploration across the span of his back, over his shoulders, to his other arm. Thousands of swirls. *Thousands.*

I can't even breathe once I reach his other wrist, where the design finally ends. I recall his endless dark and hopeless gaze when I saw him in the past.

Kadamach was not made to love. His gift is death.

Kiaran wears his marks just like I do. They're memories and shame and hurt all at once. If anyone should ever ask me what happens when chaos and death meet, I should tell them that together we bear the scars of our gifts. They're a reminder of what happens when we try to choose our own fate.

'Kam,' he whispers.

And that's it. Only my name, as if he's saying: *Do you understand?*

'You chose a human name,' I say softly. I hadn't even realised it until I said it. 'Kiaran MacKay is a human name.'

'Aye,' he says.

'Why?' I follow the marks up his spine and feel him shiver beneath my touch.

'I wanted something of my own,' he says. 'So I chose my name.'

Kiaran's entire life was planned for him from the moment he was born until his death – a pattern, just like the Cailleach described. It's remarkable how something so small and simple can become so important. Something that says *This is mine. I chose this. I own this.*

A name. Just a name. If I had to start all over, maybe I wouldn't choose to be Lady Aileana Kameron, daughter of the Marquess of Douglas. Or even Falconer, the girl whose gift is chaos. Maybe I'd just be Kam, the girl who endured.

I find a branch of his design that is smaller and more intricate and I touch my fingertips to each swirl. One after the other.

'What made you hunt your own kind?' I ask. 'I've always wondered.'

Kiaran almost turns, but I stop him. I run my hands over his shoulders, over the lives he took. I'm memorizing his marks, just as he did mine. It's my turn.

'I saw the part of me I tried to destroy in them.' The words rolling off his tongue, his accent thicker with emotion. 'So I killed them all.'

I go still. *Isn't that what I did?* The fae I killed were all substitutes for Sorcha. Whenever I looked at them – without fail – I saw *her*. Each time I killed one of them, in my mind I was killing Sorcha and avenging my mother's death.

I lean my forehead against his back. I feel the puckered skin against mine and wonder who they all were.

His gift is death.

Wherever she goes, death follows.

'Don't you ever feel cursed?' I whisper against his scars. *I do.*

'Every day,' he says.

Kiaran turns to face me and I can't help it – I press a kiss to his collarbone, my fingers trailing where the marks end just there. 'Let me see your vow to Sorcha,' I say. Because that's all I can say. *Show me. We can compare our curses. You already know all about mine.*

He takes my hand and presses it to his chest. The design across his pectoral is different from the others. It's all harsh lines and jagged, thorny branches that split off in a web that begins right over his heart.

This one isn't beautiful. This is a vow of obligation, tradition, not made out of love. I hate the way Sorcha has marked his body. I hate that he wears a promise to her simply because it was *expected*.

'Now I understand,' I whisper.

'What?'

I meet his eyes. 'What you said to me in Glasgow, when I accused you of wanting me to hide my scars. I look at this and I hate her even more.'

He threads his fingers through mine. 'It's my reminder, too.'

'Of your vow to her?'

'No, Kam,' he says. He looks at my own scars, just at my shoulder. One, two, three bites. Fifteen memories. 'My entire existence was planned before my birth. This mark represents the path I could have taken. It's my reminder that I'd rather die on my own terms than live an eternity on someone else's.'

Chapter 35

*T*onight is Hogmanay, the last celebration before the New Year. It'll soon be 1848, and despite spending all that time imprisoned, I still feel like it *should* be the final weeks of 1844. All that time I missed, I can hardly believe it's gone.

I force the thoughts from my mind and stand before the bedroom mirror in a gown Derrick made for me. Its deep, dark crimson makes my freckled skin look smoother. Sleeves cover the scars on my arms and the scooped neckline shows off the slope of my shoulders. The waist cinches in to an extreme curve before belling out in full skirts adorned with white lace.

Beneath the layers of petticoats and skirts, I wear boots and trousers out of habit. Despite that, I look about as trussed up as one of those bloody Christmas trees in the middle of Charlotte Square. Now I remember precisely why I detest these damn things.

'I can't breathe,' I tell Derrick.

'I made you a dress that can be torn away in case of emergencies and flipped into a coat, and you're complaining about being able to breathe? How ungrateful!' He flies up to my shoulder and wrinkles his nose. 'Ugh! *Uuuuugh!* And you smell like the *daoine sith.* He's left his scent all over you like piss on a tree.'

'Derrick!'

He flies off my shoulder like he's been chased by the hounds of hell, settling on my dirty coat instead. I imagine it smells a great deal like mud, sweat, and *me*.

'Now I can't even sit on your shoulder,' he whines. 'He's *ruined* it. I can't *believe* you after everything the Cailleach told you.'

I glare at him and inspect the dress again. He's even sewn hidden pockets in it for my weapons. I slip Aithinne's sword in its specially made pocket, where it hangs heavily against my thigh – but you wouldn't know it was there just by looking at me. Good god, Derrick is brilliant, my breathing complaint aside.

'You said you didn't want me to hate him,' I point out.

Derrick sulks, his wings fanning. 'That was *before* he ruined your perfectly good shoulder seat with his vile smell.'

'Very well.' I wave him away from the coat and pick it up to drape the fabric over my shoulders for a moment. I try not to cringe at how it smells. What on earth did I rub up against on that beach? 'There. Now I stink of sea creatures. Happy?'

Derrick flies up and sniffs me. He still doesn't look terribly pleased even as he settles beneath my hair. 'It'll do. I suppose.'

I sigh. 'Are you going to weave more power around the wards? We probably ought to leave tomorrow.'

'Aye. I might have to do it a few more times before then to make sure it'll hold.' He flutters toward the door, then pauses with a grin. 'Want to come with me?' At my expression, he says, 'You died, you were brought back, and you aren't the least bit curious to see what other gifts came with the Sight?'

'Of course I am.'

After that metal flower I created, I want to test the limits of my power. I want to see what I can do to Lonnrach when I see him again.

I peer at myself in the mirror, expecting to look just a wee bit different. Perhaps more faelike. I do, after all, have the blood of the Seelie queen in me. Alas, I'm the same freckled ginger I was yesterday and not even a hint more shiny.

'I don't feel any different,' I say.

'Of course not,' Derrick says. 'You were already born with power, you silly human. It just needed to be woken up.' He flies to the door. 'Well?'

'I promised Gavin I'd be down a half hour ago.' I lean toward him and whisper. 'Come get me in fifteen minutes just in case I need to be saved.'

'From whom?' Derrick flicks his wings. 'Don't tell me you're already fighting with Kiaran after you and he had—'

'For god's sake.' I glare at him. 'Not *Kiaran*. Daniel. Or possibly Catherine. I still haven't told her we're leaving yet.'

Derrick sputters a laugh. 'You haven't …? Oh, I can't *wait* to see that.'

I glare at him. 'Fifteen minutes.'

'Thirty. I plan to eat everything on the food tables.'

'You can eat them in ten. I'll give you twenty-five, just in case you need to go outside and vomit it all up.'

He looks satisfied with that. 'Deal.'

I nod once and step out of my room. I'm immediately engulfed in the aroma of pine and mince pies and fire and the spices from mulled wine. I'm struck by memories of home, celebrations in the Assembly Rooms, the ballrooms illuminated by firelight. At the time, I thought them so mundane, so dull and exhausting. I never stopped to enjoy the scent, the heat of the flames, the glittering ballroom.

Lanterns float around the buildings, illuminating some of the darkest wynds between the tall tenements. And whatever shadowed closes the lanterns miss, lights strung from window to window more than make up for it. The city is a glowing place, vibrant and beautiful and bright. An orchestra plays in the centre square, fiddlers playing a tune I remember from my stays in the country. People are dancing around the bonfire in the middle, a happy jig with clapping and laughter and skirts swishing. They all look so happy, so joyful, as if nothing terrible happened beyond these walls or in their pasts. I admire them for it.

Derrick flies past me with a shout of glee. 'If you'll excuse me, I believe I see some mince pies that need to be in my mouth posthaste.' With a wink, he swoops down and attacks the pie table with vigor.

I shake my head with a smile and lean against the railing. I hum the tune played for the reel below, swaying with the music. If I close my eyes, I can pretend I'm at the Assembly Rooms back in Edinburgh, listening to the dancers clap and laugh and chatter. The fiddles play on, the music jaunty.

It makes me wish I didn't have to leave. My time here may not have been ideal, but listening to this – hearing people laugh and dance and play instruments – I missed this. When I was imprisoned, I thought I would never see another human again. I didn't hear music. There was no joy or voices, except those in my memories.

If I leave tomorrow, I don't know when I'll have this again.

'Do you intend to go down or just watch?' a voice says.

I whirl to find Gavin behind me on the balcony, holding two steaming mugs. He's dressed just as I remember him – the perfect gentleman. Black trousers and a silk waistcoat, his dark blue cravat perfectly knotted, his overcoat immaculately pressed. I recognise those clothes. He wore them the night of the battle, when he was supposed to escort me to the Assembly Rooms to announce our engagement. Even his hair has been tamed, pressed down formally. All in contrast to his scars, imperfections on an otherwise immaculate, gentlemanly appearance.

It's Gavin's scars that serve as my reminder that he's not the man he once was. Neither of us are the same.

'Would I be welcome if I did?'

Gavin hands me one of the mugs. The scent of mulled wine fills my senses, the heady spices of it, the sweetness. God, I love that scent. Mother used to call for mulled wine in the library during winter. We would drink it next to the fire and play chess or solve puzzles as it rained outside. Those were comfortable days, safe days. My mother used to sip her wine and declare it *perfect* every time.

'Of course you are,' Gavin says, his voice interrupting my memory. 'Just because you're leaving doesn't mean you're unwanted.'

'Daniel's premonition scared him,' I say. 'I don't blame him for not wanting me here.'

'Aye,' he says softly. 'But that doesn't mean I don't wish you would stay.'

'Maybe after I kill Lonnrach. But before that ... I wouldn't risk it.' I rest my arms on the balcony, looking down at where Catherine dances with her husband. 'I still don't know how I'm going to tell Catherine.'

'It's easy. You just say the words.'

Daniel vacates his spot in the quadrille to twirl Catherine in a move that is completely out of step. She laughs.

'Easy?' I laugh bitterly. 'What about when she learns I have fae blood in me?'

'Aithinne told me everything while Derrick stitched her up. About the kingdoms. About you. Do you know my first thought?'

'What?' I'm afraid of what he'll say.

Gavin shrugs, a quick smile passing across his face. 'That it made a hell of a lot of sense.'

I smack him on the arm. 'You cad. You scared me on purpose.'

His smile vanishes. 'Aileana. It's just another thing that makes you who you are. Like your eye colour or hair colour or the freckles on your nose.' His eyes meet mine. 'Do you think it somehow makes you less of her friend? Less worthy?' His voice drops lower. 'Less human?'

I look away. I can't help but think of Kiaran's words last night. *Every day I wonder when your human life will end and it scares the hell out of me.* I may have faery blood in my veins, but one day he'll lose me.

'No,' I whisper. 'I've never felt more human.' Because *Falconers always die young. Always.* And I've already cheated death once. So has Gavin. 'You never told me what you saw through the veil.'

Gavin stiffens. I see the reflections of the floating lanterns in his eyes, so bright and beautiful. The fiddle music below slows to a waltz, a song that makes my heart ache. *Cuachag nan Craobh.* 'The Cuckoo in the Grove.' I haven't heard it in years, not since I was a child.

'No,' he says softly. 'I didn't.'

'It's all right.' I watch the people below, how they spin and spin and spin in the waltz. Their laugher doesn't fit my sudden somber mood. 'You don't have to.'

I wonder if, given the choice, I'd keep what the Cailleach showed me a secret. Maybe I'd keep all those memories about Kiaran buried deep in the cavernous part of my heart, where my grief is stored. I wouldn't have to remember his murders, his *gifts*.

I could kiss Kiaran and he could touch me and whisper words to me and I could pretend that Kadamach was a separate person altogether; a doppelganger, a devil. I wouldn't have to acknowledge that part of him is still there, and the only difference is that Kiaran lost his powers, chose a human name, and had thousands of years to bear the mark of each life he took.

Gavin and I are both quiet now. He watches the dancing below and sips his mulled wine. The tension in his body is clear in how tightly he grips the handle of the mug.

'Did you ever hear the story of Thomas the Rhymer?' he asks suddenly.

I shake my head. I remember the name, but I never read the story. I stopped reading the human faery stories after my mother died. They were the stories that taught me that iron would protect me. That all I had to do was cross running water and I'd be safe. That if I stuck to the city, the faeries would never find me. There is truth, and there are the lies humans tell themselves to feel safe from the fae. And those lies nearly killed me.

'Sir Thomas claimed the queen of the fae took him into the *Sith-bhrùth* for a time. When he returned, he had the gift of prophecy.' Gavin sounds bitter, as if he's memorized the story and hated it more each time he read it. 'He foretold of war and death in poetry.' He looks at me then, his eyes haunted. 'I read it when I came back with the Sight. I wondered whether Thomas got the whole thing wrong. If he thought he'd gone to the fae realm, but he'd actually died instead.'

Gavin stops, and when it doesn't seem like he'll continue, I lean forward. 'What?'

I wish I could take that memory from him. I wish I could take all the bad ones and lock them away in the same place I keep mine.

He gulps his wine. 'True Thomas was a lying bastard. If he saw a fraction of the things I saw through the veil, he wouldn't have written poems. He would have wished he'd stayed dead.'

Do you wish you had stayed dead, too? I almost ask him the question, but then think better of it.

Gavin stares down at the dancers. 'I saw them, you know,' he continues raggedly. 'All the people I never saved from the fae. I watched them die, their corpses weighing me down until I couldn't breathe. I had to dig my way out of them.'

I hesitate, then take his hand. It's an utterly familiar gesture, one I'm not certain I should make. Then his fingers tighten around mine, and I feel calluses that weren't there before my time in the *Sith-bhrùth*. His smooth gentleman's hands have become rough, hardworking survivor's hands. 'I didn't tell Aithinne everything,' I say. 'I left out the way they all screamed for me. Everyone in Edinburgh who died.' I touch Gavin's face then, his scars. 'You are far braver than I. You saw it happen. I wish I could have spared you that.'

It's as if Gavin doesn't hear my words. That haunted look never leaves his face. 'You speak of bravery,' he says. 'I've never felt brave.'

I smile. 'You don't need to feel it for it to be true.'

I finish off my mulled wine. The drink flushes my cheeks, reminding me of the days when I didn't fight faeries and was just a girl in white dresses.

I could be that girl again, just for a few hours. Just for tonight. 'So, are you going to ask me to dance?'

A ghost of a smile plays on his lips. 'I've quite forgotten my manners, haven't I?' He puts out his hand, palm up. 'May I have the pleasure?'

'Always,' I tell him.

The balcony lowers us to the city below, and Gavin escorts me to the centre square. No one stops to look at me and stare. No one makes me feel unwanted or uncomfortable. There is no tension among the dancers, no craned necks or whispered words about my mother's death. I have no past here, no reputation to uphold. No title to honor.

Gavin and I begin the steps of the schottische and I am struck by memories of the two of us as children dancing around his drawing room. I am the girl in white dresses again. I laugh and I whirl and we weave in and around couples. The heady taste of the mulled wine has gone to my head and the lights are dizzying. This isn't like the schottische I'm used to, so formal. This is a country dance, a joyous dance, with fiddles and clapping and laughter.

'I haven't seen you laugh like that,' Gavin says as the dance ends. 'Not since we were children.'

I smile at him. 'I could say the same for you.'

He takes my hand, bows, and presses a quick kiss there, and it says everything. Forgiveness, remorse, regret. Hope.

Someone behind us clears his throat. I turn to see Daniel standing there, unsure. His clothes aren't anywhere near as fine as Gavin's, but he's still well dressed, handsome. I suspect the fae had something to do with all the fine clothes here tonight.

'Lady Aileana, might I speak to you?' He glances at Gavin. 'You don't mind, do you?'

I stare at Daniel in surprise, but it's Gavin who speaks first. 'Of course not, old chap.' He smacks him on the shoulder. 'I'll just have to find another partner, then, won't I?'

Daniel offers an elbow to escort me. I take it hesitantly. He leads me to a quiet corner of the square, next to the steaming mugs of mulled wine, and he hands me one. I sip it, waiting for him to speak, but he doesn't. As if now he doesn't know what to say.

'I'm sorry for the way I've behaved while you were here,' Daniel finally tells me. 'I wanted you to know that.'

'Did Catherine put you up to this?'

Daniel peers over at his wife. Gavin cuts between her and a partner and dances his sister around the other couples. 'I haven't told her yet.' He notices my face. 'I see you haven't either.'

'Frankly, I've been avoiding it,' I say. 'I doubt she'll be happy with either of us.' Especially me. The last time I left Catherine to keep her safe, she nearly died. 'I was going to tell her tomorrow, just before I leave.'

I try to think of the places I'll go. I have no home. I have to leave everyone I care about to keep them safe again. Isn't that the life of a Falconer, anyway? It doesn't matter how well I fight or how strong I am; my mere existence will always put the people I love at risk.

After a moment, Daniel clears his throat and says, 'She'll want you to stay, you know.'

I stare at Catherine in her long dress, laughing as she dances with Gavin. Despite everything she's been through, she's still the same. Her heart hasn't hardened and she isn't broken, and she's never once given up faith on me. Not ever. We may not be linked by a mother or a father, but Catherine is my sister and always has been. We are stronger than blood.

'You and I both know the truth, don't we, Mr. Reid?' I say. 'We must do everything we can to survive and sacrifice for those we love. Sometimes there's little place for sentiment at all.'

Daniel takes a sip of his drink and I notice it's not mulled wine; it's whisky. Fine choice. 'I never thought I'd see the day when an Edinburgh debutante said that.' He takes a long, hard look at me. 'I'd have bet on pulling gold out of my arse first.'

I smile. 'What do you think they teach us in etiquette lessons?'

'How to ensnare a husband, I assume,' he drawls in that rough accent of his.

'Wrong,' I say. 'In that world, we survived by marrying. In this one, we learn to adapt. An Edinburgh debutante is taught self-preservation from childhood. It's all we know.'

It's the first time I've ever seen Daniel look quite so taken aback. 'Then we have something in common, don't we?'

I recall what he said about his father, his first death. 'Aye. I just hope you realise how very lucky you are. She's an extraordinary woman who believes you worthy.'

Daniel is staring at his wife. 'She is,' he says. 'And, believe me, I know.'

As if she hears him, Catherine glances at Daniel, and I see how much she loves him. How her eyes light up and her lips curve into a smile at the sight of him.

I look down at my wine and take a sip. 'I never got the chance to thank you.'

He frowns. 'For what?'

'For saving her life,' I say. 'I was the reason she was in that carriage. If I hadn't—'

'They come swift as the night,' he interrupts. 'They descend like shadows. You could have locked her in a vault, and they still would have found her. Do you know the truest burden of having the Sight?' He looks at Catherine, watches her dance. 'It's knowing how fast they kill. That if you save one person, you've failed to save one hundred more. It's knowing that I happened to be on that road when her carriage was being attacked, instead of some other road, with another carriage. One where those other people didn't survive. It's living with that every night. You know a thing or two about that, don't you?'

'Aye,' I whisper. 'I do. I—'

A hush comes over the crowd. The entire city goes completely silent around us. The fiddlers have stopped playing, and everyone has stopped dancing. I hear a few hushed whispers, and look to the source of their attention.

My breath catches. It's Kiaran and Aithinne, looking every bit like fae royalty. Aithinne wears a delicate lilac dress that falls like a waterfall over her long legs. No petticoats, no corset. Just a beautiful, form-hugging dress that glitters as though it's been dotted with stars. Her long dark hair is loose and gleaming, down to her waist.

And Kiaran ... I've seen him dressed like a gentleman before, but never like this. Not in evening wear, with dark trousers and waistcoat and a perfectly tied cravat. Then his eyes meet mine. I've never seen such blatant *wanting* before. Like he'll consume me. I could drown in that gaze.

Now he's walking through the silent crowd toward me, and suddenly he's there, and my hand is in his. His lips are at my ear. 'Dance with me.'

And then we're dancing, and nothing else matters. His hand is pressed to my lower back, our bodies close as we spin. It's as if we're alone. No one else matters. No music, or whispering, nothing. It's Kiaran and me, and this is our first dance. And it's as graceful and smooth as when we go into battle together. We fit together, my body against his, his cheek pressed to mine as we spin.

'You never told me you could dance,' I say.

I feel his soft smile. 'Isn't this what we did every night?' He whispers against my skin. 'We always fought like this. Like we were waltzing.'

That's when I open my eyes and I see the sea of people around us, staring. I don't know how long we've been dancing without music. It could have been minutes. It could have been hours. It doesn't matter.

'Everyone's staring,' I whisper.

'Of course they are.'

Kiaran's eyes meet mine. Now that I have the Sight, I see just how vivid they are. I see the years there. The pain, the exaltation, even the flashes of Kadamach. But it doesn't matter, because he looks at me and he sees me, and he's Kiaran and I'm Kam. 'They're wondering why I came tonight,' he says. 'Why I chose you.' His lips brush my cheek. 'Why I'm kissing you.'

'Why *did* you choose me?' It's all I can do to keep my wits about me when he's kissing me like this. Because when Kiaran kisses, he does it with the whole of himself.

He whirls me around with so much grace it's as if he isn't even trying. 'Because you challenge me,' he tells me. And then we're not dancing any more. We're standing pressed together, our hands entwined. 'I chose you because you're my equal.'

Then we're kissing right there in front of everyone. And nothing else seems to matter. Certainly not etiquette, or what anyone else thinks. It's only his lips on mine, the pressure gentle. It's only us. And I can't stop —

Which is when Derrick arrives out of thin air and careens into my shoulder in a mess of wings and limbs. '*Hullooooo!* Don't mind me, I'm just interrupting your brazen cuddle to steal the lady for a few minutes.'

Oh, damnation, not now. I'm really regretting not giving Derrick that extra five minutes. 'Derrick,' I say through clenched teeth. I step back from Kiaran and try to control the pixie's wriggling body in my hair. 'Not—'

'My god.' Derrick collapses on my shoulder. 'I am full of pie. I can barely even move my wings. I—' He squints over at Kiaran and smiles in delight. 'Oh, hulloooooo, villainous wastrel!'

Kiaran is clearly not impressed. 'You've a bit of pastry on your jacket.'

Derrick swipes at the morsel, snatches it, and eats it. 'Was just saving a wee snack for later.' He giggles.

For god's sake.

I look pleadingly at Kiaran. 'Just … save that thought. Don't go anywhere.' *I'd like to resume the kissing.* 'I'll be right back—'

'Kiaraaaaaaaaaan.' Derrick giggles. 'Or would you prefer I keep *villainous wastrel*? I never asked.'

Kiaran arches an eyebrow. 'I suppose that depends. Would you prefer *pain in my arse*?'

Derrick bursts into laughter. 'Arse! Aileana. He said *arse*.'

'Hell,' I mutter. 'Will you excuse me for a moment?'

I don't wait for Kiaran's response. I take Derrick with me to the lift and don't say anything until I reach the fourth floor. 'Let me just say, if *someone* gave you honey, I'll—'

'No, no, no,' Derrick says, gliding off my shoulder. He now looks suspiciously lucid. 'You said to save you after twenty-five minutes. So I did.'

'I said to save me if I was around Daniel and in obvious distress.' *Not when I'm kissing someone in obvious delight.*

'Firstly, *I* was the one in distress watching you kiss Kiaran because *ughhhh*.' Derrick wags a finger at me. 'And secondly, you never said anything about distress, you said—'

'Forget what I said.' I narrow my eyes. 'Are you telling me that down there was all an act?'

He grins. 'I would have been *perfect* in the theater, wouldn't you say?'

'Good heavens,' I murmur. At least I don't have to deal with a drunk pixie. 'Let's just check the wards, all right?'

I follow Derrick onto the balcony and press the lever that sends us up. As we rise above the city, music echoes all the way to the top of the structure. A cloudless moon shines down on the festivities, adding its light to the floating lanterns. It all looks like something out of a dream.

The balcony takes us higher and higher, past the lanterns and closer to the moonlight. All the way at the top are shelves carved into the rock beside the balcony. There are no doors up here, no people, nothing but black crystals placed deliberately along the shelves, one right after the other. They vary in size – some are as small as my palm, and others the length of my arm.

I freeze when I see them, immediately thinking of Kiaran's words. *They say a crystal from the palace is still here, hidden somewhere.*

A crystal. Just one. I ask warily, 'Crystals?'

'Of course, you ninny,' Derrick says, fluttering across the upper balcony. 'Crystals are the best for directing powers. Everyone knows that.'

I sigh with relief and open the balcony gate to follow him. My dress rustles against the rock as I edge toward Derrick, who is hovering in front of the crystals. Though the ledge is lined by a railing, I'm high enough up that the view makes my stomach clench.

Derrick presses his hands to a particularly large crystal. 'These connect to the *neimhead*,' he says with a soft smile. 'The city is built right on top of it.'

'Catherine told me about that,' I say. 'What do you use it for?'

'Here.' Derrick ushers me closer.

He grasps one of my fingers and presses it against the surface of the crystal.

Inside the rock, a light brightens. The pressure of my finger makes the surface ripple like water. I feel an electric current from my hand all the way to the tips of my toes, so full of energy that I shiver. It's not an unpleasant feeling, but it's warm, powerful.

'You feel that?' At my nod he says, 'That's the *neimhead*.'

'You never told me anything about these,' I say, pressing my fingers harder against the stone. It's as though the crystal connects to something inside of me. Energy rushes through my veins, beneath my skin.

'Most have been destroyed by human development,' Derrick

says. 'This kingdom sits atop one of the most powerful *neimheads* in existence. It's why we never needed to be part of the kingdoms to thrive separately.' He smiles proudly. 'Didn't need those bastards.'

The energy from the crystal is actually making me feel light-headed. No wonder the fae built the old kingdom out of them, if they're that powerful. 'What does it do, then?'

Derrick flies to sit on the pointed edge of the crystal. As soon as he touches it, the glow inside grows, like light beneath water. 'It's the source of power that drives the entire city. I've heard it can be used for a lot of things, but right now we're using it to amplify our power to keep the wards up.' He grins slyly. 'Why don't you try?'

I pull away, startled. '*Me?*'

'No, the *other* redhead wearing a dress big enough to hide a herd of cattle.' He reaches for my hand and grasps a finger to pull it back, but I resist. 'Come on. This is not the time to be a coward. Don't you want to see what you're capable of?'

'Well, of course I do—'

'Then try.' Derrick offers me an encouraging smile. 'You just breathe it out like air. It's not difficult.' He waves a hand at me. 'Now close your eyes.'

I arch a brow and sigh. 'Really?'

He glares. 'If you don't close your eyes I'll change that dress so quickly you'll look like a furry citrus fruit before you can even call me a bastard.'

I scowl, but do as he asks. His wings buzz like a hummingbird's and his feet are on my wrist as he presses my fingertips against the crystal.

I feel it again, the power inside me, like smooth water across my palm. I'm surrounded by the scent of the sea – salt and sand and wind above the city – as the touch of water becomes a current that flows over my skin, through my veins. As it heats around me, the air thickens and each breath becomes more and more difficult. A painful ache spreads through my chest.

Derrick is breathing hard, too. 'You feel that?' At my nod, he says. 'Good. That's your power.'

The pain blossoms, becoming more acute. At first I try to push through it, but then it lances through my body, quick and agonizing. I bite back a cry. 'It hurts.'

'You have a lot of it,' he says shortly. 'Now push it into the crystal, you silly thing, before you faint.'

Breathe it out, he'd said.

I do it slowly. With each breath, I nudge the power down my arm and into my hand. I press my palm into the hard surface of the crystal. It responds, becoming a soothing current again – like waves quelling fire. With every breath, the pain begins to ebb until finally, *finally*, it's gone completely. And I feel like I've just run across the entire blasted countryside.

I open my eyes and Derrick is staring at the crystals with a growing smile on his face. 'You did it,' he says with a whoop. 'Look at that!'

The crystals are shining, and when I look deep inside one of them, it's as though there are stars turning in there. Whole galaxies I created. The entire line of crystals is aflame with light that brightens the top of the structure like beacons.

When I look at them, I don't feel joy, or elation, or relief. The response was too too strong to ignore. I feel like I've gone three rounds with a redcap and almost lost. Something's wrong.

Kiaran's words replay over and over in my mind. *There are stories of the first sithichean kingdom.*

A place of immense power, created by old magic that doesn't exist any more . . .

A place of immense power. Like the strongest *neimhead* in existence. 'Derrick,' I whisper, dread filling me. 'What's the *neimhead*?'

Derrick looks confused. 'I told you, it—'

'No.' My tone is sharp. 'What does it look like? What's it made out of?'

'I don't know! It's been there since before I was born—' I go still. Derrick's eyes grow wide as if he suddenly realises why I'm asking. 'Are you thinking what I think you're thinking?'

I'm already moving before he can say another word, running across the balcony to the elevator. My heart is slamming against my chest, fear making my skin hot. We have to get out of here. We have to get everyone out of here *now*.

Derrick zooms next to me. 'I should have known,' he says. 'I bloody well should have known.'

'Don't dwell on it now.' I shove the lever to send the elevator down. 'Go warn Kiaran and the others. Hurry!'

He zooms down to the crowd below. Not a second after he leaves, the blaring warning sirens blast all around me, the sharp howl piercing my ears. In the city below, I hear people already beginning to disperse.

They're already here. It's too late.

The balcony stops and I yank open the gate. '*Kiaran!*' I see him pushing through the crowd, calling my name. When he reaches me I'm trying to speak through my rushed breath, 'It's the *neimhead*. That's what Lonnrach wants. They're—'

A sudden pain lances through my skull and makes me stagger. I cry out and sink to my knees.

'Kam?'

Falconer, Lonnrach's voice echoes through my mind, making me go cold. *Found you.*

Run, I try to scream it, but the word lodges in my throat. Lonnrach's influence hasn't left; he has me weighted down, my tongue immobile. I feel for my powers, breathing just like Derrick told me to. Lonnrach's hold tightens and it hurts like his bite.

The siren suddenly cuts and a loud boom shakes the city, like a clap of thunder from the top of the beehive. Everyone goes quiet. I follow their gaze – it's all I can do, all Lonnrach will let me do.

And at the top of the structure, a crack forms, a fissure in the rock. *Oh god.* Another boom, a snap, and the fissure expands. The power of the crystals – Derrick's and my power keeping the other fae out – is being warped, tested. The fae above strike it again.

I cry out in pain. Kiaran grips my arms, but I can barely hear what he's saying through the agony. I can feel my powers straining to break Lonnrach's influence and keep the wards up at the same time.

Lonnrach's voice enters my mind again. I swear I hear his smile. *You won't be able to hold it for long. Give up now.*

The other fae slam against the wards again. My body shakes with the effort. I'm dimly aware of blood streaming from my nose and people jostling around me to escape. Kiaran is yelling something, but I can't hear it over the rushing heat of power inside me that I can barely hold any more.

Again.

And I feel the first droplets of water on my face. Frigid, just like the sea.

'*Run!*' Someone screams, and I realise it's me.

In one last, desperate effort, I push my powers out of me like I did with the crystal to sever the influence Lonnrach has over me. Only then do I realise my mistake – my hold over the wards buckles. I strain to steady my power and hold the fae out, but I'm too distracted by the chaos all around me. All at once everyone at the ball flees for the back of the cave, jostling and shoving each other.

My control snaps, and the top of the rock structure caves in. A wall of seawater comes down.

Chapter 36

I grasp Kiaran's hand and we race across the city square to escape the wall of water. The sea is closing in. Waves crash around us, the frigid water rushing around my ankles. The bottom of my dress soaks through, the fabric heavy.

'Kam!' Kiaran brings us to a halt once we're far enough from the cascade. Still, I can barely hear him over the chaos, the falling debris. 'We have to get the humans out *now!*'

People are screaming, their cries drowned out as they're sucked under the powerful waterfall. Without hesitation, Kiaran brings us to a halt and reaches out with his palm. The burst of power that comes from him is enough to sicken me.

Then it's as if time stops. The wall of water slows to a standstill, everything quiet above us. People splash and shove their way through the water to escape, some shouting orders and encouragement.

'Can you keep hold?' I ask Kiaran.

He looks like he can barely manage his answer: 'For now.'

I use the lull to yank at my dress, tearing the top layer the way Derrick showed me. Then I quickly discard the petticoats, flinging them into the flooded street. The remaining fabric fits like a long coat over my trousers, hanging all the way down to my boots. If we're going to have to fight, I want to be ready.

Kiaran's face is a mask of intense concentration, his eyes

glowing that uncanny vibrant lilac. 'They're fighting me,' he says. 'I won't be able to prevent them all from coming through.'

I nod and race through the water to Gavin and Daniel, who are helping Catherine in her heavy, waterlogged dress. People have stopped to stare at Kiaran, at the frozen wall of water. 'Go!' I urge them.

Daniel looks up at me as I approach, then glances at the people rushing out of the cave. 'The tunnel leads to the underground river in one of the deeper caves. It opens to the sea. The fae built us a ship there for emergencies.'

'Take it,' I say. 'Don't stop for anything. We'll hold them off.'

Then I hear it, the distant rumbles I've been dreading. The *mortair*. They're coming, pounding through the surf overhead. A massive piece of rock falls from the top of the cave and slams into the water a few feet away.

Oh, *hell*. They're breaking the top of the structure so they can fit inside.

'*Kam!*' Kiaran's warning shout echoes through the cave. 'They're starting to slip through!'

A buzzing draws my attention and Derrick flies from the upper balcony. 'Aileana,' he pants, flying to my shoulder. 'Lonnrach's destroyed the crystals. I can't reinforce the wards—'

'I know,' I say, gritting my teeth. 'I couldn't hold them.' I can't look at Derrick's face, not when I know his home is being destroyed again because of me. 'Help the others get to safety.'

'But—'

A cracking above us makes me jump. Another massive chunk of the upper rock dislodges and slams into one of the tenements, sending a wall crashing to the ground. Then water explodes around me, splashing high. I can't *see* —

The water settles, and a giant cat-like metal creature rises to its full height. It's sleek and shining silver, dripping with water as it towers over the tenements across the square.

'*Run!*' I shout again.

The cat-like *mortair* barrels toward us. Its sleek metal body cuts through the water like a blade, sending crashing waves around the city. Its interior gears turn and twist to drive its shining limbs forward at a breakneck speed. The others will never outrun that thing. They won't make it to the ship unless I do something.

I draw the sword from its sheath in my dress-turned-coat and rush forward to meet the *mortair*. Aithinne appears alongside me, as if from nowhere. Wearing trousers and a short black jacket, no less.

'Hullo!' She grins. 'I didn't miss anything fun, did I?'

'Where on earth have you been?'

'I had to make sure the other fae got out safely with the humans. Now if you'll excuse me' – Aithinne winks – 'this one's mine.' She holds up a sword I haven't seen before, golden and gleaming. 'I've a new weapon to test.'

Before I can protest, she takes a running leap forward to land on the *mortair*'s body. As sleek and quick as a predator, she leverages herself onto its back and hacks off its head in one single swipe of her new blade.

I pause to admire how efficiently she kills. *Job bloody well done.*

My admiration is short-lived as another *mortair* leaps through the ceiling above, and another, and another. I can't keep up with them. Waves splash high and drench me in frigid seawater. I can barely stay on my feet through the deluge; the spray is so overwhelming that I can't see the metal creatures through it.

Once the onslaught stops, I barely have a moment to recover before I'm sprinting between the massive feet of two *mortair*. I arc my sword to cut them down at the ankles. The blade slices through them easily; the scent of scorched metal overwhelms my senses.

Metal groans above me as the *mortair* fall, their limbs thrashing in the water. I shield myself to block the water, the salt searing my eyes. Too late I notice a *mortair* raising a paw right at me. The light of its weapon whirls fast in its palm.

Damnation! I dive for the water, rolling hard across the wet cobblestone street.

BOOM. The tenements above me shatter and fall. Rock slams into the ground around me. Someone grabs my arm from behind. *Kiaran.* He shields my body with his as a wall of the building breaks over his back.

He lifts it off with an irritated groan. 'I *hate* these damn things.'

'Just hold back the sea and as many fae as you can. Aithinne and I will do the rest.'

He gives me a look. '*Just hold back the sea,* she says.' With a shake of his head, he takes his position again, deep in concentration.

I rejoin Aithinne in fighting the *mortair.* She and I go after them, one by one, in explosions that rain dirt and rock all around us.

Kiaran uses his powers to protect us – but the *mortair* keep coming. There are at least a dozen, towering over the city's tenements. Their large bodies take up so much space inside the central part of the cavern that I can barely see the buildings around us.

My sight is filled with metal limbs and whirring gears. It's suffocating. Between the water and the *mortair,* the space becomes so confined – the scent of burning metal so overwhelming – that I can barely stand it.

My power unfurls inside me, strong and hot through my veins. It makes me move faster. It keeps me focused. My body is a weapon, graceful and smooth. I whirl in the water like a dancer, like a faery, cutting and slicing just as fast as Aithinne. Together we take them all down.

Then I look up and see one of the *mortair* heading straight for Kiaran and I don't even think. I leap in front of him, a sudden memory of the Cailleach's voice flashing through my mind: *You have my daughter's blood in you, her powers. My blood.*

Time to test my powers further.

I watch the cat-like *mortair* come at me, its razor-sharp metal teeth bared and its claws. I put my hands out and my power stretches inside of me. *Stop.* That's all I think. *Stop.* And I am awash with the burning sensation of fire through my veins.

When I open my eyes, I am surrounded by light. It's golden and so luminous that it scorches my eyes. It's so different from when I shared Kiaran's powers. It's not a force outside of me, not something that feels out of my control or like it doesn't belong.

This is me; this is what I'm meant for. It is power in my veins and light in my blood and the beautiful sensation of freeing it. It's *mine.*

I stop the creature in its tracks. The burning tang of metal singes my nostrils as I breathe deep, remembering Derrick's words. *You just breathe it out like air.*

My gaze meets the creature's, and I see a hint of a sentient being there, the pain I'm causing it, and I don't care. I push more of that light. It pours out of me, pulsating, strengthening, and I give it only one command: *burn.*

The air between us heats, it magnifies and glimmers like a mirage. The creature glows red and melts like metal thrown into a fire. Just as I did with the metal flower I created with the clock, I warp its limbs. I force them to twist around each other.

I make the water rise, tugging at the droplets with my mind until the *mortair* is covered in water to cool the hot metal. I release a burst, a single pulse from that place deep in my blood, a push of power that shatters the metal like glass.

The creature collapses into the still water like ash. Nothing is left but a single claw the size of my palm. It floats toward me and I grasp it in my fist. A memento. A treasure. A sign of victory.

Then, all at once, all that power snaps back inside me. I have a painful sense of being filled, of stuffing all that light into my veins again, until I'm dizzy and my vision blurs. When it fades, I sway on my feet.

Someone catches me around the waist with a whoop.

Aithinne. 'You did it!' She looks proud, so proud of me. 'You were magnificent.'

I melted the *mortair*, using my powers just like a fae. Not a human.

Human enough, the Cailleach's voice whispers in my mind as I open my fist and stare at the single metal claw. It has punctured my palm and drawn blood. *Human enough*.

Kiaran shouts my name and I look up just as more *mortair* leap through the top of the structure and land on the other side of the square. And not just *mortair*, but other fae, too. Redcaps and *cù sìth* and *daoine sìth*, all pushing against Kiaran's power. Oh god, I can't fight that many.

'Time to run,' I tell Aithinne. And I'm on my feet, splashing through the water. 'Kiaran, let go!'

A wall of water comes crashing down. We all run, the massive wave pouring through the city at immense speed behind us. Aithinne leads the way through the streets as we try to stay ahead of the current.

Water rushes around our legs, slowing our movements, but we keep going, keep running. I hear the clicking and pounding of mechanical limbs behind me and know the creatures are after us, pursuing through the water.

My clothes stick to my skin, limiting my movements and making running harder. My body is freezing, my limbs cold and tired, but sheer will keeps me going.

Aithinne leads us through a tunnel, down another narrow passage with light at the end. In a single burst of power, she collapses the portion of the cave behind us. The current of water stalls, but it's leaking through the rock; soon it will give way.

Keep running, I think. *Keep going*.

That's when I see Daniel, Catherine, and Gavin still in the tunnel, Derrick buzzing frantically around them. 'They're hurt,' Derrick says, reaching me. 'The water came in through the other exit.' I barely have time to take in the gash on Catherine's forehead, the way Gavin's leg is bleeding.

Catherine flounders and Kiaran snatches her up in his arms.

'Through the other passageway!' Daniel shouts.

Behind us, water explodes into the tunnel, bursting the rock dam apart.

If we slow even a little, it'll drown us all. We're not going to make it. I think of the light, of the powers unleashed with my first death, and I make a decision.

I stop to confront the wall of water.

'Kam, don't!' I hear Kiaran shout behind me.

I glance at him, then at Catherine in his arms. 'Save her like you saved me.'

And I turn to face the water, the mechanical creatures running with it, and whisper, 'And let me give you more time.'

I unleash my power again. All the light I have inside of me becomes a force that hits the wall of water and the mechanical creatures with such force that I slide backward on my feet. I try to push again, but I don't have the strength this time. Not enough.

Human enough, I think. *Too human.* I try to focus on holding back the water and the faeries behind it. I grow lightheaded; the pain of using that much power builds and builds until I cry out. I collapse onto my knees, and the first streams of water break through and rush around me.

I look back to make sure my friends are almost to the end of the tunnel. Almost there. Almost. I only have to hold it a little longer.

The water is rushing around my shield of light, faster and faster. Blackness seeps in at the outer edges of my vision and is starting to close around me in shadowy tendrils. *Just a little longer.*

Then I sense another presence there. Aithinne. Standing right next to me through it all. She grasps my hand, and through my fading sight, her uncanny eyes meet mine.

'I don't want you to die young,' she whispers. 'Will you let me show you?'

I nod, the only movement I can manage.

Her power rushes through me, a torrent that fills me up and makes my veins burn with white-hot fire, like I'm being ripped apart. And all I can hear is the Cailleach's voice in my head, whispering *human enough human enough human enough*.

'You're resisting,' Aithinne says. 'Let all your power go.'

I feel my body sway with exhaustion. My human body. My body that was never meant to hold fae power or wield it like this. For a human, my body is strong. For a human, my body is exceptional. But it isn't enough to hold Aithinne's power. It is a shell of mortality. An exhausted thing of skin and bone.

I sway forward. Aithinne's hand tightens around my palm. 'Just breathe. Let everything go,' she whispers. 'You're doing this. You can finish it.'

And I do. I let the light funnel out of me and I feel like it breaks my bones apart. Like my skin is burning. Like I am detached and without shape or form. The mechanical creatures howl, burn red, and disintegrate to ash.

And the darkness finally closes around me.

Chapter 37

I catch the scent of a fire, hear the crackle of wood, and feel the heat of the flames. I press my fingers to the ground – the barest of movements that I can make – and realise I'm lying on a thick blanket of wool that is soft against my fingertips.

All I recall is stumbling out of the cave with Aithinne. The others helping us through the forest as my vision spun and spun and spun. I don't remember collapsing once we found somewhere to rest for the night. I don't even remember closing my eyes.

My entire body hurts. My eyes are so tired and heavy that I have difficulty opening them. And when I do, I see trees towering above me. They are snow-tipped, with skeletal branches that creak and groan. Snow falls on my eyelashes, my cheeks, cooling the heat there.

A rustle comes from somewhere close by, but I can't turn my head. Catherine's face is suddenly in my field of vision, her brow creased with worry. 'Oh, thank goodness. I was worried you'd … well. Well, you know.' She glances over her shoulder. 'She's awake.'

Suddenly, a giant ball of light comes hurtling at me. And there's Derrick, at my neck, his wee hands pressed to my skin.

He curls there, warm wings against me. 'You intend to be a martyr, don't you? That's the only thing that explains you *staying in the cave with the giant wall of water*, you bloody insane human.' He's tangling himself in my hair, wings flicking my ear. 'Let me just say: you're lucky you're like a damn cat with nine lives, or you'd be seafood. Welcome back!'

I swallow. My throat is dry, painfully dry. 'What happened after we made it out of the cave?' My words come out as a croak, a barely understandable wheeze. 'I don't remember much.'

'Not a lot. You destroyed nearly all of the fae in that tunnel, so we escaped through the forest while the others regrouped. You and Aithinne barely made it here and now you both look like hell.' He shrugs.

I manage to turn my head – an excruciating movement – to see Aithinne beside me, still asleep. She's been bundled up even more than I have, her slight form lost in a sea of blankets. Her skin is pallid. Her eyelashes are kissed with snow and her lips are blue.

I don't want you to die young.

Aithinne has helped me so many times now. She could have let me die, and she'd have all her strength back, all of her powers as the Seelie Queen. She'd be that faery at the bonfire, tall and proud and terrifyingly beautiful, able to silence someone with the flick of her wrist. She could have let that wall of water come at me, stepped back and taken her role as monarch again. But she didn't. She didn't let me die.

Whatever power I lost … it made me feel a little more human.

Ignoring my aching muscles, I reach under the wool to grasp her hand. Even under the warmth of fur, her fingers are icy to the touch, limp in mine. And when I press my skin to hers, I feel her power there as surely as I feel my own. Blood to blood. Like to like. As though we are extensions of each other.

Derrick's wings are flicking painfully hard against my sensitive skin. 'I don't understand how they found us with the wards up.'

'Lonnrach would have destroyed the whole island until he found it,' I say. 'It was only a matter of time.'

I wonder if the Cailleach helped. I didn't think she'd have the power to extend her influence through the veil again, not if my mother was the last Falconer she helped kill. But maybe she tried one last time.

I look at Catherine. 'I'm so sorry. About everything.'

She looks at me sharply. 'It's not your fault.'

I almost tell her that Lonnrach only knew the city was on Skye because he pulled it out of my memories. I was naive enough to believe the wards would keep everyone safe. They were never safe, not really. Not while Lonnrach still lives.

Catherine looks at the fire again, her eyes narrowed with anger. 'The truth is, they've merely been biding their time until the day they find us and kill us all.'

My eyes grow heavy again, and I close them briefly, then ask, 'The others? What about them?'

Catherine shivers and covers herself with her own blanket, wrapping it closely around her. She's wearing her underthings; her ballgown must have been soaked and torn from the run. My own trousers and shirt appear to be dry now; thank goodness for small favours.

'Daniel, Gavin and … and … Kiaran –' she says his name as if she's saying it for the first time, as though it's a word that doesn't fit in her mouth '– went to scout the area. To make sure it was safe. The fae spread out not too long ago.'

I remember Lonnrach's words in my mind, the malice of it, the joy. *Found you.* I shake my head. 'What about the city? Everyone else?'

'Some took the ship and left with our fae allies. Didn't wait.' She stares off into the distance. 'That was always our plan from the very first. If we were ever attacked by the fae again, we'd take the tunnels, board the ship, and get out to sea. Even the fae can't open a portal on open water to attack them.'

Derrick's wings flick against my cheeks. 'That's because they don't need to. I just hope your humans don't run into any sea-dwelling *sithichean*. Private creatures, like pixies. Not a part of the kingdoms. Loathsome things. They smell, have poor manners, and eat people.'

Catherine stares at him blandly. 'My, you certainly know how to reassure a lady, don't you?'

'Oh, I know *precisely* how to reassure a lady.'

Catherine narrows her eyes at him, then focuses her attention back to me. 'We were the only ones left behind, so I think almost everyone made it out.' Her expression grows distant, sad. 'I only saw a few of the older ones. I don't know that they ... ' She swallows hard. I notice then that her eyes are wet. 'I suppose we'll just have to find someplace else, won't we?'

She says it so lightly, as if she's trying not to care. But I see the truth she is trying to hide. No home again. We are all orphans, all wanderers. Seeking a home until we are plucked off one by one, or killed together.

We all go quiet. Because, really, what does one say after loss? Catherine has been through this so many times before – finding somewhere, staying there for a short while, only to have it be destroyed. And people die every time.

I reach out to Catherine, a movement that feels like being pricked by thousands upon thousands of tiny needles. My hand lies on the blankets, palm up. An offering. An apology. A request for forgiveness. She slips her hand in mine and squeezes tight. My sister not by blood but by bond. Aren't those the best kind of sisters, anyway?

'I'm sorry, Derrick,' I whisper. 'You lost your home, too.'

Derrick curls into the space between my neck and shoulder where the thick wool and the heat of my skin meet. His wings are like silk against me. 'Lost it before,' he murmurs, in a voice I can barely hear. 'I've lived without it for thousands of years. I'm sure I can trudge on.'

He tries for nonchalance, but I can hear the wistfulness in his voice. All of his things were there. His closet. The tapestries he wove of his victories. His former life now lost to the enemy. 'Too many sad memories there, anyway.'

'And happy ones,' I point out, thinking of his tapestries.

'You know perfectly well how tainted those can become,' he says quietly.

There's nothing I can say to that. He's not wrong. 'Where are we?' I ask.

'Leitir Fura,' Catherine says. 'Or, at least, somewhere near it. Father used to keep a journal of his travels up here, and I often read them. The ashwood didn't use to extend this far before the fae came.'

Before the fae came. I look at the scars on her wrist, how they snake up her arm in dozens of half-moons and long scratches. *Before,* when Catherine didn't have to do whatever it took to survive.

'We'll have to move again soon,' Derrick says. 'I can hide us for now, but if we stay in one place too long they'll find us.'

Catherine nods, her eyes on the fire. 'Of course.' I hear the slight catch in her voice. She sounds unsettled, unfocused. 'Catherine?'

She doesn't look at me. 'It was silly of me, wasn't it?' Her voice is carefully controlled, but I hear the hurt beneath it. The longing. The sadness. 'To hope that we'd finally—' She blinks and looks down at our clasped hands. 'They destroy everything, don't they?'

Her eyes meet mine, and I see the fire there. I recognise it as surely as if I were looking into a mirror.

'I *hate* them,' she whispers fiercely, tears finally falling onto her cheeks. I wrap my arms around her and she sobs into my shoulder, her tears burning against my skin. 'I hate them so much.'

I hold her. I don't know how long she cries. It could be minutes. It could be hours. I hold her, and let her rage. And I whisper to her the whole time. Two simple words: 'I know.'

Chapter 38

*M*y sleep is filled with fitful dreams plagued by the Cailleach's skeletal face, her withering skin. In my dreams, she whispers in my ear, a constant message. *Now you know why I can't let you live. Now you know why I can't let you live.*

In my dream, Sorcha is there, too. In the background, behind the Cailleach. Always there, always watching, always waiting. Until the part when the Cailleach fades, and Sorcha stands alone in front of me, speaking in her language, words that are thick and throaty and lyrical.

Then something seizes my chest, a pain lancing through me that makes me stagger. And Sorcha laughs and laughs.

I wake with a start, gasping for breath. I'm sweating under the wool blankets, my breathing ragged, my heartbeat unsteady.

'Bad dream?'

I turn, and Sorcha is there, standing between the trees. She wears a long coat of what looks like silk, lined with fur that goes all the way up to the collar and frames her pale face. She stands out against the snow, her lips a plump red, her eyes so green that they scarcely look real. Sorcha has never looked more beautiful, nor more dangerous.

Crimson suits you best, says her voice from my memories. I shove that memory away, burying it deep down inside of me, where I hide the parts of myself that leave me the most vulnerable.

She watches me with glittering eyes filled with malice, with murder – and I'm alone with her. The fire has gone out; only empty blankets around the ashes indicate the others were here at all.

My hand slides along my hip for my sword, but it's gone. I shut my eyes briefly. *Damnation.*

Sorcha smiles and pulls the sword from behind her back. 'Looking for this?' She tests the edge of the blade with her finger. 'It's a lovely one, isn't it? Aithinne always did exceptional work. Of course, you'll no longer be needing it.'

She pulls back and tosses it into the trees, her fae strength sending it flying deep into the forest. Her self-satisfied smirk makes me want to slit her throat.

'If you hurt my friends, I'll—'

'You'll do what? Kill me?' she says with a laugh. 'I sent each one off on their very own hunt. I wonder how many will make it out alive. Between us, I'm betting against the blonde human girl.'

With a snarl, I shove out of my blankets and throw myself at her – but my body is still too slow from using my powers. Sorcha has me by the throat before I can even blink. With a sharp-toothed grin she shoves me into a tree.

'Now that wasn't nice, was it?' Sorcha watches me closely. 'Look at you. A little less human than the last time I saw you.' Her fingers tighten around my neck and I try not to gag. 'That's how Lonnrach found the city, you know. A human using the powers of the Seelie Queen without the skill to conceal it.' She clicks her tongue. 'You were like a beacon in a storm, little Falconer. Not even that pixie's shield worked to block that amount of power.'

Human enough, the Cailleach's voice whispers from my memories. Derrick must have thought he was hiding me when I connected to the *neimhead*, never realizing that some of my energy must have leaked out. *A beacon in a storm.* Damnation.

I shove against her, but she's too blasted strong. 'At least you gave up that *I'm just here to help* pretense, because any more of that nonsense and I was going to run you through with something sharp.'

'Oh, but you're wrong,' Sorcha whispers. The *baobhan sith's* breath is on my neck, and if she wanted, she could drain me of blood in less than a minute. 'I can't tell lies, Falconer. I *was* helping. Just not *you*.'

What if I told you I was on your side, Kadamach? That I wanted you to win against my brother? 'Kiaran,' I say softly. 'This was all for him.'

'It's *always* been for him,' she says. 'Unlike Kadamach, I don't abandon my friends.' She draws a sharp fingernail down the length of my throat. 'You see, If I allowed Lonnrach to capture you again, he would have put you in a place where no one could get to you until he found that crystal, not even me. I couldn't risk him performing the ritual alone, not when the life of myself *and* my consort is at stake.'

Hand to my throat or not, I almost gag when she calls Kiaran her consort. It takes all my training to keep my expression even.

'Yet you were helping the Cailleach.' When she just blinks at me, I say, 'For god's sake. You don't strike me as being *that* simpleminded. She wants Kiaran dead every bit as much as Lonnrach does.'

'Ah, the Cailleach.' Sorcha laughs. 'To think I once eagerly joined her little crusade to end the Falconer line. But then I met you – the *last* one.' Her fingernail moves back up to my cheek where it almost breaks the skin. 'I intended to kill you, but Lonnrach mentioned he had thought of a way to steal your power and take the thrones for himself.

'Then I realised how *I* could use you. The Cailleach ceased to matter.' She flashes her teeth in a frightening smile. 'As for Lonnrach, all I had to do was assure him I'd capture *you* while he focused on finding exactly what I needed. My brother is so oblivious. He'd would make a terrible monarch.'

Her voice isn't as affecting as the last time I saw her, not as beautiful or lulling. My awakened powers must give me the ability to hear beyond the influence of her voice. I feel her in my mind, as if she's seeking to test that. Small, probing tendrils of her power snake across my consciousness.

Sorcha pushes against my mind and I push back. She looks like she loves that.

I grit my teeth against the sudden pain of her fingernail digging into my neck, drawing blood. 'And how do you intend to use me?'

'Sorcha wants your powers for herself.' I turn to see Kiaran in the trees, blood splattered across the front of his shirt, blade dripping. He's breathing hard, as if he just slaughtered a small army. 'Don't you? Your brother was looking for the *neimhead* to generate enough energy for a power transference, and you've been waiting for him to find it.' He grips his sword hard. 'Neither of you will take the Cailleach's place. I'll kill you first, even if it means I'll die with you.'

Sorcha smiles. 'Such a low opinion you have of me, Kadamach. When this is over, you'll thank me.'

'Let Kam go, Sorcha,' Kiaran says in a tone he gets before he stabs things. He might stab Sorcha, even if he can't kill her.

'*Kam.*' Sorcha spits the word out as if it's foul. 'Is that what you call her?' Her nails dig deeper into the tender skin at my neck and I bite my tongue to keep from crying out. Blood blossoms in my mouth and I taste its tang. 'Your latest little Falconer pet. It seems this is a lesson I must teach you twice, Kadamach.'

Sorcha pulls me in a rough embrace, and before I can blink, she whisks me away with the speed of a storm.

We are over the cliffs by the sea, so close to where the city once was. Sorcha's arms are tight around me and then we're falling, falling, falling.

She lands us on one of the sea cliffs in the snow, where the waves slam the rocks and spray water into my face. There are fae here, *cù sìth* and redcaps and smaller *mortair*, mechanical creatures with wings and sharp beaks that peck at the ground.

They are digging in the deep ravine that was once a part of the city, the redcaps smashing rocks with their hammers and leaving it to the hounds and metal creatures to dig the rest of the way.

A massive wall of seawater is suspended to one side of them, hovering in the air as if it could fall at any moment. The fae must have cleared away all the buildings in the city – or perhaps most of it was destroyed when the underwater caves were breached. Now they're using their powers to keep the sea at bay as they search for the crystal.

I remember Tavish watching them when they breached the perimeter shortly after my arrival. *They're digging.* I thought – we all thought – they were searching for me. But this is what Lonnrach was after; he wanted the *neimhead*. And I helped lead him right to it.

Lonnrach oversees the digging with a satisfied smile. His salt-white hair blows in the breeze as the sun sets behind him. He looks beautiful, every inch the Seelie faery he once was.

Then it comes, a flash of memory, before I can even think to stop it. Lonnrach's second and third rows of razor-sharp teeth descending.

I freeze. *No. No no no.* I won't go back to this. I won't be his prisoner again. I won't let him take little pieces of me again. I won't let him take the fight out of me.

Sorcha tries to drag me away from the cliffs and I buck hard against her. She briefly loses her grip and I slam the heel of my hand into her face.

'You disgusting little—'

I wrap my fingers around her wrist. *Melt.* I breathe out my power just like I was taught. I command it. I feel it roar in response. *Melt.* I want her to die like the *mortair*. I want to see her disintegrate to ash. I want —

Sorcha's fingernails suddenly dig into my hair. She pulls me up against her. Her nose is bleeding, stark against her pale skin.

Her lips curve into a smile. 'That tickled.' She pulls me closer. 'As long as I'm bonded to Kadamach, you can't kill me with your powers. You don't have the strength.'

She drags me by my hair across the grass. I try to fight her again – I kick and slam a fist into her gut, but she tightens her hold around my neck, fingernails digging in, drawing blood. She shoves her power into me, and the pain is so acute that I cry out.

Lonnrach turns at my scream. 'My lost prisoner.' He glances at his sister. 'Took you long enough.'

I hate his voice. I hate the way it makes me feel like I'm right back in the mirrored room at his mercy. I'm on my knees again, unable to fight back. Already I'm starting to tremble, just as I always did whenever he drew near.

'I had three humans, two former monarchs, and an exceedingly angry pixie to deal with.' Sorcha ticks off her fingers. 'Could you do better?'

Lonnrach's gaze flickers to the hold Sorcha has on my hair. 'I never had to drag her anywhere.' He flashes his teeth at me then, as if to say, *Remember these?* 'Everyone has a breaking point, even Falconers.'

'You must not have broken her completely,' Sorcha says, 'since she escaped.'

Lonnrach narrows his eyes, then continues to watch the fae dig with the sort of concentration and impatience I wouldn't expect from an immortal – but he's been waiting for this moment.

Sorcha's lips curve into a smile as she leans down, and I catch a glimpse of her smooth fangs. 'Watch, Falconer.'

I follow her gaze and see that the fae below have increased their speed. They're tossing aside the muddy rubble, their hands and claws shoveling so fast they're a blur. They're uncovering something. They burrow farther, down and down and down, around an object – a dark pointed rock in the soil.

I catch my breath. It's the crystal.

I hadn't expected it to be so big. It's a magnificent object that is like no gem I've ever seen. Even the most polished of diamonds would never match it in beauty. It gleams like the sea at midnight, even from this distance, with an unearthly internal fire. Thousands upon thousands of flames inside it flicker, glitter, and swirl around each other. They create a light that burns like a beacon.

'It's beautiful.' It isn't until I hear the words that I realise I've spoken aloud.

Sorcha's eyes are ferocious, the anticipation making her fangs elongate until a single drop of blood emerges and snakes its way down her lower lip. She licks it up. 'After all those stories,' she murmurs, 'we *found* it.'

She's so entranced by the crystal that her hold on my throat slackens and eventually she draws her hand away. She doesn't even look at me. Perhaps she thinks I can't escape, or perhaps she's simply too enthralled. Lonnrach is, too. The crystal is immense, now at least as tall as any of the tenements in Edinburgh, and the fae still haven't reached the base.

Sorcha looks at me, still wearing that smug smile. 'And it was under the pixie kingdom this entire time.'

My mind flashes to the tapestries of Derrick, the battles and blood and death depicted across the walls.

One giant tapestry was older than the others. Derrick wasn't in it. It showed the pixies gathered in battle. A looming figure in the background that I'd thought was a castle. Not a castle after all; it was the giant crystal. The fae were protecting it. And if they hid it, they must have had good reason.

I inch away from Sorcha, backing out of her line of sight as the spectacle below holds her attention. My hand slides to the weapon compartment in the coat Derrick made for me. I had hoped for a small blade, but there's nothing. *Confound it.*

I glance between Lonnrach and Sorcha. They each have a sword, and Sorcha's is hidden under her billowing long coat.

But Lonnrach's is *right there*, within arm's reach.

One step back. Two. Slowly, slowly. The two faeries don't even notice. The deafening sounds of rock and metal grinding as the fae uncover the crystal muffles any crunch my boots make in the grass. I wait until the metal of a *mortair*'s beak grinds against the rock, and I snatch Lonnrach's sword from the sheath.

He lunges for me with a shout, but my sword hand is quick. I slash him across the torso. Blood blossoms along his crisp white shirt as he drops to his knees. I almost move in for a killing blow, but I stop myself.

He's not mine to kill.

'Falconer.'

Sorcha grabs my coat, but I slam my boot into her thigh. Her grip loosens and I race toward the digging fae, my feet slipping down into the crevasse, my ankle painfully taking my weight. I don't stop, not even when I hear Sorcha's warning shout from above.

The other fae turn to me, their uncanny eyes glowing, and they attack.

My power rushes inside of me in response. It is a brutal force that takes me over, ignites me. My stolen sword becomes an extension of me, burning with flame. I slice through the first redcap that comes at me with a hammer swinging, no effort at all.

The mechanical creatures are on their feet, and one leaps into the air right for me. I slash. Light bursts from my sword and tears through the metal so easily.

Then I hear a shout from above. Aithinne. 'Destroy the crystal!'

Destroy it?

More fae attack before I can respond. I slice my sword through the air, plunging into another fae. Everything happens in a blur of movement. With my powers awakened, I am quicker, agile, strong. I'm suddenly aware of Kiaran and Aithinne fighting fae with me.

Their swords slash, their powers scorch through stone. I watch rock strip away and the earth crack open from the force of their blows. A violent storm surges above our heads, created by the fae to fight back. Water breaks from the suspended sea wall in a violent swell that knocks me off my feet.

The crystal. I have to get to the crystal. I whirl and slice through another fae. My movements are quick as I break for it again, my boots pounding across the uneven earth as I dodge attacks.

But before I can reach it, Sorcha is there, her sword out in a quick arc that nearly guts me. I dodge and parry. But she is agile, much faster than I am. I slash once, slicing her cheek open. Her fingers touch the injury and she looks surprised.

'Something to remember me by,' I tell her.

She flashes her teeth, licking the blood away, and leaps for me. I whirl, my movements defensive.

With every stroke of my sword, I remind myself that although I may not be able to kill Sorcha with my powers, this sword was forged with fae metal. Her body isn't invulnerable the way Kiaran's is. If I manage a killing blow, Kiaran will die with her through their bond.

I do the only thing I can do: I defend myself against her assault, my sword clanging against hers, releasing sparks of power. I slam it into her to shove her away.

Then I can feel her in my mind. A forceful presence, pressing her way inside of me. 'You may have power, Falconer, but I know all the ways to break you.'

Sorcha shows me the girl I once was, the bloody girl by her mother's body. She tries to bring it out of my heart.

She doesn't understand.

I'm not a creature of vengeance any more. I'm not just the girl whose gift is chaos. I died and came back. I'm the girl who endured.

I knock her off her feet. I slash my sword, almost moving in for a killing blow at her abdomen—

Killing her kills Kiaran.

The blade changes trajectory at the last second, catching her at the shoulder. I hiss in frustration and she smiles. 'Can't kill me, can you, Falconer? You're not ready to lose Kadamach.'

'Stop talking!'

I launch myself at her, but she's on her feet before I can blink, dodging my attack. She's quick. She moves as swift as a feline hunter, twisting away from me as I strike.

She slams into my mind, digging, digging, digging. Not showing me the girl this time, but trying to turn me into her. I stagger back, crying out against the pounding pain at my temples.

While I'm distracted, she knocks the sword out of my hand and slices her blade across my cheek. The wound stings, and I feel blood drip down my neck, a mirror of the injury I gave her.

'Something to remember *me* by,' she whispers. She glances at where Kiaran is fighting the *mortair*. 'I hoped he'd come for you.'

I freeze. 'What?'

'Bait,' she murmurs. 'Part of the plan.'

Bait. I look over at Kiaran, fighting his way through fae. His power singeing the earth black. *Bait.* She knew they'd come. I open my mouth to scream at him to leave. 'Kia—'

Sorcha's fist smashes across my face. I stumble, spitting blood onto the muddy ground. Before I can recover, she grabs me by the arm and throws me. I roll through dirt and smack right into the base of the crystal.

'Kam!'

Sorcha doesn't stop. As if they understand, the other fae rush Kiaran and Aithinne and surround them. Dozens of fae hold them back as Sorcha pulls me up by the neck. She slams me against the crystal.

'I've been waiting for this,' she hisses. 'The last Falconer inherits enough of Aithinne's powers that I can amplify them through the *neimhead*. Enough to overpower her.'

I glare up at her, licking blood from my lips. 'So you can steal my powers to kill Aithinne?' I say bitterly.

'No, you silly girl. Your powers will revert back to their rightful owner.' Her fingernails dig into my skin, hard enough to bruise. 'You see, it was Aithinne who bound the part of Kadamach that made him the Unseelie King. I need her power to reverse it.' Her lips curve into that nightmarish smile. 'She made a mistake, putting her powers in human bodies. Bodies that I *can* kill, right down to the last one. And with the crystal's help you'll have just enough of her power to help me unbind it. This ends with you.'

Then she drives her blade through my chest and into the crystal behind me.

Something breaks inside of me. The fae stop fighting as Kiaran sinks to the ground with a scream that cuts to my very soul. Shadows rise from the ground, enveloping him in dark tendrils. He hunches over, his fingers digging into the dirt. The fae around him suddenly keel over, too, dropping to their knees as his power is ripped out of them. Even Sorcha is writhing in agony.

My vision hazes, but I can see how Kiaran's body trembles, how his shoulders shake. The soil breaks, an awful crack of the earth around his palm. The shadows come thicker, darker, until I can't see him any more. He has no shape; he's become enveloped.

'No,' Aithinne whispers, rushing to me. Her eyes are wet as she looks helplessly down at the sword. 'Falconer. I can't heal this.' Her voice breaks.

I can't speak. I feel lightheaded, dizzy, as though I'm floating. I fight to keep living. But I can't. I feel myself leaving my body, the same way I did when Kiaran put me into the sea. Floating ... floating.

The shadows clear, and Kiaran looks up. As I take my last breath, I meet his dark, hungry gaze, and I know he isn't Kiaran any more. He's the Unseelie King.

Chapter 39

I am standing on the top of a cliff at sunset. Far, far below me, waves crash against the rock in a soothing rhythm. The spray is cool against my skin; it smells crisp, of salt mixed with the scent of heather on the air.

Trees stretch along the top of the cliffs on either side of me. The colours are like autumn in Scotland, red and orange hued, only much more vivid. It's as though the entire coastline is aflame.

Where am I?

The thought is fleeting, replaced by calm. It's so still and serene here. At the horizon, the deep turquoise seawater meets the blazing sky. As the sun dips lower, the firelike clouds only grow more intense. The astonishing hues like deep slashes of paint. I close my eyes briefly against the lovely warmth of it.

I sense another presence behind me, a sudden familiar sensation of cold fingertips down my spine. Not menacing like last time; not a threat. A reminder.

She is here.

I don't turn as she moves to stand beside me on the cliff. Out of the corner of my eye I notice her face doesn't change this time. It remains skeletal, her skin weathered and old. Her cloak of shadows wraps deep and dark around her.

Suddenly I remember everything. Sorcha driving the sword

through me and into the crystal. Pain lances through the centre of my chest where the blade sliced through bone. I press my hand there. I let the ache settle until I can think clearly.

Kiaran. His dark, hungry gaze as his bound powers surged back inside of him. Now he'll need the Wild Hunt to survive again.

Don't you ever feel cursed?

Every day.

He's back in the human realm bearing the weight of his curse and I'm ... I'm ...

Falconer. I can't heal this.

Tears prick the back of my eyes. 'You're not just visiting me in a dream again, are you?'

'No, *mo nighean.*'

I laugh bitterly. 'I suppose you got your wish then, didn't you? I'm really dead this time. Aithinne has her powers back. Did you come to gloat?'

'I came to make you an offer,' the Cailleach says softly. She sounds so weak, her voice shaking.

'Then I refuse,' I tell her. 'Make all the threats you want. I don't want your truth.'

This time I meet her ancient, skeletal gaze. I'm surprised by the sadness there, the unease. The Cailleach has lived for thousands of lifetimes. She created the land. She formed the realms. And she's fading just like I am. Like a human.

In the end, we are all the stag.

'It isn't truth I offer, *mo nighean.* Not this time.'

I'm almost afraid to ask. 'Then what?'

'I created your world and mine,' she says. 'When I die, the realms will fracture. It's already begun in the *Sith-bhrùth.* You've seen this.'

'Aye.'

'My children have refused my powers,' she says quietly. 'I must have a vessel to pass them on to. I'm offering them to you.'

I look at her sharply. I'd be shocked if I weren't so suspicious. The fae don't offer anything without a price. The Cailleach threatened to kill my family last time. She tried to kill *me*. 'Why would you do that?' *Why should I trust you?*

Now she looks bitter. 'You are my only blood.'

'I see. You're dying and I'm your last chance at passing on your legacy.'

'I am selfish, *mo nighean*,' she says tightly. 'So are you. You wish to return to your human friends, and I'm offering you another chance at life. Do you know how rare it is for a human to come back from the dead twice?'

The Cailleach tried to kill me once before. I can't trust her that easily. 'What's the price?'

When she looks away, I almost laugh again. Of course there's a price. There's always a consequence when the natural order is disrupted. I know that better than anyone. Not even the Cailleach herself can change it.

'I can bring you back to life,' she tells me, 'but eventually my powers will kill you.'

'So I'll be dead either way. Why would I take that offer?'

Her lips tighten to a thin line. I notice how her shoulders tremble, as if she's barely managing to stay standing. 'Ask my daughter about *leabhar cuimhne*. The book of remembrance. If you find it, you can remove the curse. This is my final gift to them.' Her gaze drops to the ocean below.

'The curse?' I ask.

'My daughter will explain,' she gasps. 'Accept the offer, child.'

I would be foolish to believe her and yet ... god help me, I'm tempted. 'And if I don't?'

'Our realms will be destroyed.' I can barely hear her. Each word is spoken in a soft breath, as if it pains her. The Cailleach suddenly looks much weaker. She's fading fast. 'The book was lost when the old kingdom fell. You have to find it,' she whispers, her voice fading. 'The worthy can find the door.'

Worthy? 'Wait. Where's the door? What door?'

But she's withering, her skin flicking away from the bones of her face. Her eyes are sinking in. She's dying, her body decaying and shrinking like a corpse.

'Accept,' the Cailleach breathes. Her face contorts in pain. 'You must accept now.'

I barely have time to think. She's turning to dust before my eyes. I have no choice; there's no time for any more questions.

'Very well,' I whisper. 'I accept.'

In a burst of strength, her skeletal hand grabs mine. Excruciating pain sends me to my knees. Her powers rip through me, imprints into my bones, and marks itself in my veins. I'm screaming. My body feels like it's breaking in half, every piece being reforged by the strength of her power.

The Cailleach's voice is in my ear. 'I'm scared, *mo nighean.*'

Her withered body embraces mine. I hold her as her power breaks me. I hold her as her skin disintegrates and her body decays. I hold her even as her bones turn to dust.

Then she's gone and I open my eyes.

And I'm alive.

Glossary

Aileana Kameron's Notes and Observations of the Fae

[*Re-created at will in the Pixie Kingdom, and added to with annotations and addendums. Certain notes have been excluded, including those made by a certain pixie in residence ...*]

As I have come to learn, the stories of the fae from my childhood are the result of several thousand years of diluted oral history. [*Dear younger self: Let's not forget half-truths, omissions, and made-up rubbish.*]

What remains of the fae world now is but a shadow of its former magnificence. The Seelie and Unseelie – two warring kingdoms of light and dark fae – had once conquered whole continents. Humanity was driven practically extinct from what the fae called the Wild Hunt, a systematic attempt to capture and kill the strongest humans, especially those with the Sight [*According to the Cailleach, the Unseelie King requires the Wild Hunt to survive. Without it, he and his subjects grow weaker and eventually die. I will add, but choose to ignore, her statement about the culling being necessary to the natural order of things. She is, after all, a murderous harridan with questionable judgement.*] It was the never-ending war between the two kingdoms that nearly collapsed them, and the final war with the Falconers that finally

~~destroyed them both~~. *[Oh, what simpler days these were when I wrote this note, and now I hardly know where to begin …*

The Unseelie King and the Seelie Queen ended their war, breaking the fate that had been planned for them since their birth. They couldn't have known that decision would have catastrophic consequences that led to the destruction of both kingdoms.]

After everything Kiaran has taught me, I've come to realize that only one truth has endured across time: ~~Never trust the fae~~. *[Too late.]*

Aileana Kameron, 1844. *[Revised in – I can't believe I'm writing this – December 1847]*

Baobhan Sìth

[Sorcha:] ~~Solitary fae (Possibly belonged to a kingdom in her past)~~ *[Nonsolitary faery. The Unseelie King's former consort.]* She is related to the *daoine sìth*, yet distinct because of her strong telepathic abilities. She is magnetic, with long dark hair and the most vivid green eyes I've ever seen. Her smile is both haunting and terrifying, a thing of nightmares. Her power tastes heavy, as if blood is being forced down my throat. Aside from slaughtering the Falconers, she murdered any other *baobhan sìth* born so that her abilities could remain unmatched. *[Except for her brother, Lonnrach.]*

Strengths: She is highly intelligent and cunning, her ability to kill aided by mental powers that can deceive a person into meeting her on a dark road of her choosing where she drains her victims of blood. *[~~One distinct note about Lonnrach is his ability to extract~~*

~~*Lonnrach's expertise is that he*~~

I'm not ready to write about this yet.]

Kill amount: ~~20 36 87 103 Too many to tally off the map any more.~~ *[Disregard. The map, like my misguided quest for vengeance, is no longer my primary objective.]*

354

Weaknesses: ~~No known weaknesses. I will find one.~~ [*Sorcha: Kiaran. I don't know how I'll use this information.*]

[*Lonnrach: I still can't.*]

Brollachan

Usually a solitary faery, though the one I encountered in the pixie city lived with other fae under forced circumstances. A *brollachan* is a faery without shape or form, a shadow figure with glowing red eyes. This creature steals energy by inhabiting a human host and slowly depleting his or her life force. To any other human, this would look like a sudden illness.

Strengths: Their shadow form makes them harder to kill.

Weaknesses: Exposure to light.

Cat sìth

A solitary faery, though forced to live with the fae in the pixie city. This is a catlike creature. Like its counterpart the *cù* sìth (faery hound), the *cat* sìth comes in a size that is unnaturally large for a common pet or even a wildcat, though unlike the *cù* sìth, this faery is not Unseelie and prefers to hunt on its own.

Strengths: Speed, size, agility.

Weaknesses: Not terribly intelligent creatures. Ruled by instinct rather than intellect.

The Cailleach

Nonsolitary faery. The Cailleach is the queen of the fae and the oldest among their kind. Her power was so great that she was once considered a goddess. Legends claim she shaped the hills, mountains, and lochs of Scotland with her hammer and staff, and that she created both the human and faery realms. The position and power of the Cailleach is passed down through lineage. Two fae children are born to rule separate kingdoms of light and dark (Seelie and Unseelie) and raised to view each other as competitor to their throne. The strongest of the two starts the war, kills the other, and takes the place of the former Cailleach. If this process is interrupted or altered, the realms begin to fracture and crumble. I have seen proof of this in the *Sìth-bhrùth*, though this degradation hasn't extended to the human realm. Yet.

Strengths: At the Cailleach's full power, there would be no stopping her. She can command the elements, she has skills of mental influence that make Sorcha's look weak in comparison, and she is adept in battle.

Weaknesses: She's not at full power. Her decision to have offspring is causing her to age and die slowly the way a human would. She must pass on her powers to one of her children before she dies. This has only made her more eager to murder me.

Daoine Sìth

Nonsolitary fae, both Seelie and Unseelie (light and dark fae). They are unearthly beautiful, a warrior race ~~known for wreaking destruction and for how they once drove humans to near-extinction (what Kiaran calls the Wild Hunt)~~ *[See opening].* The *daoine sìth* once ruled not only the faery realm (*Sìth-bhrùth*), but had once managed to conquer nearly every continent on earth. ~~Kiaran claims there was once a distinction between Seelie and Unseelie rule, but over time, both courts became equally power-obsessed and ruthless.~~ *[The Seelie Queen and the Unseelie King were raised in separate kingdoms knowing they would one day have to kill each other. Only one of them can replace the Cailleach.]*

Of course, Kiaran is being vague on strengths and weaknesses – but I have managed to garner that their powers include the ability to command the elements.

Weaknesses: ? *[The Unseelie depend on human energy to stay alive. When the Unseelie King was stripped of his power and it became absorbed by the fae in both kingdoms, this weakness extended to those previously Seelie.]*

Kiaran's power, at least, tastes earthy – sweet, floral, something wild. Which is indescribably lovely when he's being pleasant, and nauseating when he's not. *[Still quite true]*

Each uisge

Solitary fae. A water horse that is related to the kelpie, but more dangerous and aggressive. It lures humans to a water source using the power of its unearthly beauty, appearing primarily in the form of a horse, but has also been known to take the form of a handsome man. This was the first fae I ever fought and I spectacularly failed to kill it. I learned my lesson here: Iron doesn't work against the fae.

Strengths: In water, their fur becomes an adhesive that is impossible to escape, which aids them in drowning their victims. I doubt I would have lived through my own attack had Kiaran not intervened, and I still have the scars to show for it.

Weaknesses: Their power is diminished on land. However, they circumvent this by remaining near water at all times.

Mara

In *Gàidhlig*, they are referred to as *droch-spiorad*. Nonsolitary fae, though they have chosen not to belong to either court. They live in packs within the dark forests of the *Sìth-bhrùth*. From what I could see of them, they are hulking creatures with pitch-black fur and glowing eyes.

Strengths: They can see better in the dark than I can.

Weaknesses: With a bright enough light, they all scatter.

Mortair

Nonsolitary, though their status is a bit complicated because they were created by the Seelie Queen. They are building-sized mechanical fae made of near-unbreakable material that is constructed in armourlike plates across their entire bodies. The inner core (heart) of a *mortair* glows and powers the entire machine, including the weapon in the centre of its palms. Aithinne created them to be sentient, though not terribly intelligent. Their primary purpose is to seek and destroy.

Strengths: They are *massive* and strong. And since they aren't intelligent, they can't be reasoned with. If you interfere with their programmed mission, they will strive to kill you. Lesson learned.

Weaknesses: Aithinne's sword is the only thing that can pierce their armour. Second lesson learned.

Pixies

In *Gàidhlig*, they are referred to as *aibhse*.

Small, winged-fae, mostly nonsolitary. Pixies, like other smaller fae, are only distantly related to the larger types of *sithichean*. They once had their own realm, lands, and kingdom that was separately ruled somewhere on Skye, ~~but mass-migrated to Cornwall sometime before the Falconer battle with the daoine sith~~ *[the survivors left for Cornwall after Kiaran destroyed their city and nearly slaughtered everyone in it.]* Pixies' power shines in a halo around them, the colour of which can change depending on the pixie's mood. Can feed off of human energy, as do most other fae, but largely choose not to. Power tastes of gingerbread. Apparently cannot help but mend clothes and steal shiny objects. *[They are keepers of ancient relics precious to the fae, which they buried all over Skye.]*

Strengths: Extremely fast flyers; adept with small, sharp weaponry.

Weaknesses: Honey, torn ballgowns *[and closets]*

Will-o'-the-wisp

In *Gàidhlig* they are referred to as *Teine sionnachain*.

Nonsolitary, though they do not belong to either of the courts. The will-o'-the-wisp is smaller than a pixie and distinctly more otherworldly in appearance, with black eyes overly large for their faces, pointed ears, and dark, onyx-like skin. Before the

Wild Hunt, they shunned civilized contact, preferring to live in forest caves far from Scottish cities. They are a feral species and I still have to remind myself not to kill them on sight after they attacked me. What vicious, awful creatures.

Strengths: Their numbers. They live together in the thousands and attack in a swarm.

Weaknesses: Individually, they're incredibly fragile. Unlike pixies, they cannot survive on their own.

Personal note: Don't kill them, even if you want to. Not here.

Acknowledgements

It's only right that I begin here by thanking my oldest friend and critique partner Tess Sharpe, to whom I dedicated this book. She and I have been sharing our writing for so long that with each manuscript I work on, it becomes more and more apparent that she's shaped and influenced my writing (and my life) in such a profound way. I don't think I would have become the author I am today without her unwavering support and kindness and honesty. Tess, I'm so glad to have known you all these years. This one's for you. I hope you like all those 'Tess scenes'!

I continue to be grateful to my agent, Russell Galen. He knows exactly the words to say to cheer me up, and has never, ever doubted me and my work even when I can't help but doubt myself. Receiving his emails never fails to brighten my day. And to Heather Baror for sending these books to editors around the world. I love seeing the support for this series grow internationally, and that wouldn't have been possible without her.

To Gillian, my incredible editor at Gollancz in the UK. The Vanishing Throne was a bear of a book for me, and she always remained patient and confident that we would get it right. Her insightful suggestions made this book into something I'm incredibly proud to have written. And to Ginee, my editor in the US at Chronicle, whose keen eye for detail brings out the best in my writing. Thank you both.

To the team at both Gollancz and Chronicle, I couldn't be more grateful to you for supporting this series. You've all been so wonderful and enthusiastic and I feel blessed to have you.

I can't end these acknowledgments without thanking my family. Especially my mom and dad, who helped me get through writing this and my PhD dissertation at the same time. It was the most difficult and stressful time in my life, and every phone call was my lifeline.

To my husband: I don't care if you don't believe in souls; you're my soul mate, Mr. May. Always and forever. Come give me a hug when you read this.